'A skilful, witty mash-up, playing with tropes of romantic fiction (yes, that popular genre writer turns up in the village and is not so bad after all) and crime fiction (closed community, dark secrets) ... really entertaining' Aly Monroe

'Shades of *Fargo* and *Twin Peaks* – and there's no higher praise than that' Rod Reynolds

'So satisfying ... a truly great read' Lilja Sigurðardóttir

'Delightfully dark' Antti Tuomainen

'A fantastic debut ... Darkly funny, tense and a lot of poking fun at crime writing' Tariq Ashkanani

'A hugely enjoyable read with thrills (and laughs) as Hannah sticks her nose in where it's not welcome. Great fun!' Michael J. Malone

'So atmospheric' *Crime Monthly*

'Compelling' *Foreword Reviews*

'This reminded me somewhat of the more recent, meta efforts of the great Anthony Horowitz ... the character is writing herself into the investigation as he's taken to doing ... delivered with the most immediate of present tenses' The Bookbag

'If you like a classic mystery with characters who will get your dander up just as quickly as they entertain, that is packed with tension, surprises and an atmospheric setting, then this is highly recommended' Jen Med's Book Reviews

'I had a brilliant time with *Thirty Days of Darkness*. It is just such an entertaining and compelling read. I had no idea what was going on or who could be the culprit, but I had fun trying to figure it out. I would definitely recommend it to fans of Nordic crime fiction with a twist' From Belgium with Booklove

'Fascinating ... funny and touching, this is a real thriller ... a remarkable dive into the secrets of a family and a small town, and a very original way to explore the mysteries of literary creation' *Le Soir*

'The most original thriller of the year: realistic, suspenseful and romantic to the very last page' *Politiken*

WHAT THE READERS ARE SAYING

★ ★ ★ ★ ★

'Deliciously dark'

'Hannah is brilliantly drawn'

'Fluctuates between tension and hilarity'

'Up there with the best Nordic Noir'

'Wit, excellent writing, great characters and a fantastic plot'

'Blends grit and pitch-black humour to perfection'

'Fantastically atmospheric'

'Delightful, laugh-out-loud funny ... utterly captivating'

'Full of suspense, intrigue and horror'

'Atmospheric and surprising'

'Packed with tension'

'I hope we get to meet Hannah again. Just wonderful'

'Darkly tense and funny'

'Exceptional writing and brilliant characters'

'Beautifully dark and atmospheric'

'Hannah is a great character'

'A marvellous read, full of tension and surprises ... impressive'

THIRTY DAYS
OF DARKNESS

ABOUT THE AUTHOR

Jenny Lund Madsen is one of Denmark's most acclaimed script-writers (including the international hits *Rita* and *Follow the Money*, and the current box-office success *The Land of Short Sentences*) and is known as an advocate for better representation for sexual and ethnic minorities in Danish TV and film. She made her debut as a playwright with the critically acclaimed *Audition* (Aarhus Teater), and her debut literary thriller, *Thirty Days of Darkness,* first in an addictive new series, won the Harald Mogensen Prize for Best Danish Crime Novel of the year and was shortlisted for the coveted Glass Key Award. She lives in Denmark with her young family. Follow Jenny on Twitter and Instagram: @JennyLundMadsen; and Facebook: facebook.com/jenny.lund.madsen.

ABOUT THE TRANSLATOR

Megan Turney is a literary and commercial translator and editor, working between Norwegian, Danish and English. She was the recipient of the National Centre for Writing's 2019 Emerging Translator Mentorship, and holds an MA(Hons) in Scandinavian Studies and English Literature from the University of Edinburgh and an MA in Translation and Interpreting Studies from the University of Manchester. She has previously translated *Smoke Screen* and *Unhinged* by Jørn Lier Horst and Thomas Enger for Orenda Books. You can find a list of her other translations and work at www.meganeturney.com.

THIRTY DAYS OF DARKNESS

JENNY LUND MADSEN

Translated by Megan Turney

**ORENDA
BOOKS**

Orenda Books
16 Carson Road
West Dulwich
London SE21 8HU
www.orendabooks.co.uk

First published in Danish as *Tredive dages mørke* by Grønningen 1, 2020
First published in the United Kingdom by Orenda Books, 2023
Copyright © Jenny Lund Madsen, 2020
English translation copyright © Megan Turney, 2023

A catalogue record for this book is available from the British Library.

Hardback ISBN 978-1-914585-61-6
B-format paperback ISBN 978-1-914585-62-3
eISBN 978-1-914585-63-0

Typeset in Garamond by typesetter.org.uk

Printed and bound by CPI Group (UK) Ltd, Croydon CR0 4YY

For sales and distribution, please contact *info@orendabooks.co.uk* or visit
www.orendabooks.co.uk.

For Trin

THIRTY DAYS
OF DARKNESS

PROLOGUE

His heart was in his mouth. Why should it end here, like this? He wanted to scream, to tear himself apart, to hit someone. Kick them in the head until their life ebbed away. It didn't matter if it were *him*, as long as it was someone who deserved it. In that moment, it felt like the whole world deserved to die.

He picked up his pace. The field was sodden and muddy as always. He loathed it here. It was dark and cold and dank. All the fucking time. He turned and started walking towards the water – he wasn't sure why. He could hear the waves now. The closer he got to them, the stronger the urge to hurl himself into the sea and leave everything behind. He wanted to get away from this place. Hated this town and everyone in it. He was freezing. He'd been so upset he'd left without his coat. He considered turning back, but that would mean losing face. And losing was the last thing he wanted to do. He wanted to win, to beat them all. To leave, conquer life and return – show them what he had made of himself. He couldn't wait any longer – there was too much he wanted to do. Fuck them. He was almost down at the shoreline now, could taste the waves on his lips. He licked around his mouth, felt as if he were capable of anything. He could end his own life, end someone else's – it didn't matter whose. He was worth something – *he* had the power, he could do anything he wanted. He stopped, tore his jumper off and stood there, acutely aware of the November chill clawing at his bare skin. It was painful – and soon it would be fatal. Again, he contemplated throwing himself into the waves. Ending it all. But instead, he dropped down on his knees and, voice breaking, gasping for air, he started sobbing, screaming. Didn't care that he was now sitting on the damp, clammy grass. Although it was quite mild for the season, the cold still permeated his body, spreading through him, into his heart. It was all so unfair! The fact that everyone else could just sit at home, in their warm living rooms, no problems, lives that hadn't just been destroyed, while he was here, outside in the middle of nowhere like some animal. He let go entirely and wept, and then he felt the self-pity begin to set in. There was only one thing he truly wanted in that moment: to be held. He knew who would hold him – who would always be there for him, even though he had just rejected her. This thought alone gave him solace, and his crying subsided. But the cold still shook his entire being. He just wanted to return to her, have a hug and a cup of tea.

But something caught his eye: car headlights, in the distance. Heading his way. He recognised those lights, even from here. No one else in town drove a car with those blinding white lights. Shit. This was the last thing he needed. He sure as hell didn't want to end up talking to that idiot. He stood up and tugged his jumper back over his head. Wanting to get home now – to live, not die. But as he began to make his way back, he heard a voice call out behind him, shouting his name. Had he heard that right? He was about to turn round, but before he could, he felt it. The blow. As if the sky had fallen down on top of him. He collapsed to the ground and only just managed to register the wet grass beneath him and the blood streaming through his hair. He could just about sense someone grabbing hold of his legs and dragging him down onto the beach. He tried to move, but couldn't. Lost consciousness entirely. No longer aware that the person had hauled him all the way out to the exact spot where he had longed to lose himself just a short while earlier. Out into the ice-cold, pitch-black, perilous ocean.

1

A hand intertwines with another atop the shared armrest. They lean back simultaneously. He turns to look at her a millisecond before she turns to him. He is scared of flying but tries to hide it; she isn't but pretends she is. They make love with their eyes, falling for each other all over again as they soar into the sky.

```
Her: I camped out on a mountain.
Him: I went skiing.
Her: I took your breath away.
Him: I danced in Brussels.
The plane ascends. His slightly sweaty hand…
```

Ach! What now? How the hell do you plot out the early stages of two people falling in love? How are you meant to portray those emotions without sounding like a knock-off version of Goethe, or worse: a way-too good Barbara Cartland? Regardless: too trite. Holding her finger firmly on the delete button, she erases the entire paragraph and washes away the feeling of inadequacy with an entire, large glass of red wine. Then another – it takes more than just the one glass to expunge the feeling of mediocrity. Hannah Krause-Bendix has never received a bad review. Not once has anyone had a single negative thing to say in any of the reviews of her four novels. A literary superstar, twice nominated for the Nordic Council Literature Prize. Didn't win, but that doesn't matter; anyway, she doesn't believe that the hallmark of good literature is how many awards it's won. She's actually refused the numerous other prizes she's won over the years. No – Hannah sees herself as a forty-five-year-old living embodiment of integrity and will *always* maintain that it is beneath her to seek commercial success. Her editor may very well be the only person alive who knows that this is actually a lie. Dialogue, from the top:

```
Him: There are streets in Copenhagen that only
exist in my dreams.
Her: But does that make them any less real?
```

Delete. Again. Hannah has never tried her hand at the falling-in-love trope in her books before, and thus far, it feels as if the whole venture is more likely to end up as a one-night stand than some happy ending. Restless, she steps away from the desk: German design, mahogany, strong enough to bear her (usually) ingenious words. Recently though, there hasn't actually been anything to bear – the words just won't come. And today's the same, apparently. She paces around her penthouse apartment, all sixty-seven square metres of it, so it doesn't take long. She stops at the window, opens it and releases a plume of smoke over the city's rooftops. It's a beautiful day. Copenhagen looks good in the autumn sun, as do its people, who seem to insist on wearing short-sleeved tops even though it's already November. As if bare skin can be convinced it's still summer. She envies them, sometimes, the people down there, with their carefree faces and soya lattes in disposable cups, pushing their offspring around in prams, waving as they pass each other. Copenhageners really do have a knack of looking so happy on Sundays. For a brief moment, she considers whether she should go to today's event after all. Bastian will be fawning over her for months if she does. That is an appealing thought, at least: a grateful, compliant editor for a while. How refreshing. She stubs out the cigarette and straightens up. No, she isn't about to spend her afternoon at some tedious-as-hell book fair, signing copies for a mob of people incapable of distinguishing between books and literature. And anyway, her absence isn't exactly going to disappoint a whole bus-load of screaming fans. Hannah's readership is as small as it is elite – despite her literary recognition, she is still an author only by the grace of arts council funding. She writes the kind of literature in which an old man takes a sip of coffee, then stops to think for about forty pages, before taking another sip. By that point, it's not only the coffee that's gone cold. So have most of her readers.

Hannah walks into the kitchen and tries to visualise the purpose behind this action. Nothing. She invents a hunger that's not really there, given the fact she only had breakfast an hour ago. Has it really only been an hour? The digital clock flashes at her from the oven. The sight makes her cringe. Not eleven o'clock yet and she's already on her third glass of wine and fifth cigarette. That will have to stop. From now on, no more alcohol before midday. A vow she's made to herself time and time again, and one she will undoubtedly break. Christ, what a cliché of an author she is. She opens a few cupboards, closes them again. Same ritual with the fridge: open, close. But the hunger won't be lured into being – there's nothing she wants. Why has inspiration been so hard to find lately?

Correction: it's not the inspiration that's hard to find. There's plenty of that. It's more the ability to process it: getting it down into written form. A feeling, a sharp reflection or a meaningful word don't lay the groundwork for a good story anymore. The rest simply won't come. Or rather, what does come is so bad that it ends up fluctuating between perfection, the pretentious and the trivial. She can't quite seem to touch that nerve – the nerve that made her previous works positively tremble. Her talent lies in portraying people. She has this intuitive knack of describing a character in such a way that her reader doesn't simply feel as if she knows that human being, but that she *is* that human being. Hannah is an observer. When people compete for the limelight at dinner parties, she doesn't draw attention to herself by being loud and obnoxious, or by making dramatic gestures. She prefers to keep herself to herself – offering only a fleeting smile at the occasional droll passage of conversation – and to observe. And that's when she notices those whose eyes wander, whose words, empty of any meaning, reveal a certain distance, or a desperate attempt to hide something. But what, exactly? A mental imbalance? Boredom? Or, perhaps, something far too beautiful and pure to reveal to the outside world? Hints and suggestions such as these are what Hannah likes to ponder on – likes to use to compose her extraordinary narratives, offering her readers some special worldly wisdom. But Hannah's started to doubt whether she or her writing actually make her readers any the wiser. Make herself any wiser, even. It's all just endless trains of thought put down on paper. That's why she decided to try her hand at a romance, to get herself back on track. Or maybe to dig her teeth into something new.

But it's particularly tricky to plot out a love story when you've never had a relationship last beyond the first milestone – and it's even trickier when you don't actually believe in plots. She glances out of the kitchen window, over the courtyard, where a group of children seem to be playing a game. If collecting rainwater from a large barrel and watering the flowers can be considered a game. Their broad smiles and happy squeals suggest it's a fun one. Hannah sighs and contemplates what it must be like to live such a light and happy life. She shakes off the thought, deciding that she can't just mope around the apartment, feeling sorry for herself. If she's honest with herself, a lot of her problems are of her own making, especially when it comes to her love life. It's not that Hannah's incapable of love. She falls in love quite often, actually. It's just that it never lasts particularly long. On the whole, she has little patience for others, so when it comes to relationships, she's disappointed before anything's even started. Disappointed might be the wrong word. Bored is probably more precise. Although that may be because she spends all her time probing around inside the minds of her characters, so she always feels like she's about ten steps ahead of everyone else. She misses that feeling of being surprised by someone she can't quite figure out. She's starting to doubt whether she'll ever get to feel that again.

Bastian doesn't doubt her though. Never has. Although he does have hideously bad judgement. If it weren't for the fact that he's her best (gah, fine – only) friend, biggest fan and steadfast editor, she would've shaken him off years ago, mainly because of his commercial pandering. What is odd though, and she's often thought about this, is why exactly he puts up with her. Hannah is Bastian's only real author. The other 'authors' he represents churn out cookbooks, thrillers, popular fiction – all the shite people buy because it's harmless and easily digestible. Books that have answers, good people and bad people, problems that can be solved. In Hannah's books, there are no answers. There aren't even questions. Her writing forces her readers to think for themselves. Immerse themselves. Feel. But the reality is, there are few who can these days. Hannah sighs, all the way out to her fingertips. She knows only too well that if one of them should be giving the other the slip, it's not her – Bastian should've ditched her years ago. She's difficult, and she doesn't sell. So the fact that he's insisted on keeping her on at the publishing house for the last fourteen years must be down to one of three things: prestige, philanthropy, or terrible judgement. And whenever she spends any time reflecting on it, she always ends up coming to the same conclusion – that it's the last reason that's the most likely. She should do something to pay him back, she thinks in a split second of rationality. And in that split second she has called Bastian and informed him that she will, in fact, be attending the book fair that day. Nothing but garbage seems to be coming out of her pen anyway. Bastian is pleased.

2

Once outside the Bella Center, Hannah stops to light a cigarette, thoroughly regretting coming. As she fills her lungs with the courage to confront the book-fair attendees, she watches the throng of people pass through the grimy glass revolving door, the rotating mechanism and hand-power funnelling grey-haired Jutlanders and children in and out of the book world. These are the people she's going to have to talk to. Christ alive, kill me slowly.

'Sorry, but could you possibly take that cigarette a bit further away from the entrance?'

Hannah turns and finds herself looking straight into the hair of a woman who, in another age, would have made an excellent milkmaid. But, in this life, she appears to be a teacher, with her dyed hair having clearly grown about four centimetres since she last visited her small-town salon. Hannah lowers her gaze, looks directly into the woman's affronted eyes. The teacher sends a concerned glance back at the unruly group of children standing behind her.

'The smoking area is over there.' The woman points towards a smoking shelter so far away that Hannah can barely see it.

Hannah smiles demonstratively. 'Right, I'll go all the way to Sweden for a smoke, shall I?'

'Think of the children. They might be encouraged to start smoking if they see others doing it. Or they might get cancer.'

'From seeing me smoke?'

'From breathing your smoke.'

Wearied, Hannah looks at the milkmaid teacher, then down at the children, who are all gaping up at her as if she were Darth Vader. She bends down so she's face to face with the first in line: a snotty little boy with red cheeks. Offers him the cigarette.

'Fancy finishing this off for me?'

The boy shakes his head, terrified. Hannah straightens up, looks at the teacher again.

'See – I'm not encouraging anyone to do shit.'

Hannah stubs out the cigarette, turns and enters book-fair hell, just about catching the sound of the woman yelling at her to pick up the remains of her cigarette and put it in the bin.

Bookseller booths line the walls of the labyrinth, through which all sorts of people – from reading groups of grey-haired, white-wine women, to young couples dragging their bored kids around with them – seem to be meandering aimlessly. Some on the lookout for their next big reading experience, others wandering around in the hope of catching a glimpse of their favourite author – most of them probably there simply to avoid the boredom of home. Draping a scarf over her head, Hannah manages to avoid encounters with any colleagues, readers or journalists as she battles her way forward. But soon she breaks out in a cold sweat, and gasping for air, she feels the agoraphobia reach its peak as she finally arrives at the booth, where she finds her books have been set out on their own little table. So this will be where she'll be spending the afternoon, sat here signing her books. Bastian isn't even here, as he promised he would. She notes, regretfully, that no dent appears to have been made into her stock of copies, and she doesn't think that'll be changing anytime soon. Behind them is a tired-looking intern from the publishing house – alone. Hannah removes the scarf and the intern looks up with no trace of recognition.

'There's a special offer on those books today: two for one. An author we can't seem to sell much of, but they're really good. They won the Nordic Council Literature Prize twice.'

Hannah feels the fatigue settle into the pit of her stomach. 'The author has never won the Nordic Council Literature Prize.'

'They have – Hannah Krause-Bendix. She's really one of the best authors we have here in Denmark, it's just that not many people know of her. But she's actually my favourite author.'

Hannah feels a sudden urge to pull out the revolver she fortunately does not have tucked away in her bag. Sarcasm and humiliation are her only weapons.

'So she's your favourite author, is she? Which of her novels would you recommend?'

The intern hesitates, fearful of being caught out in a lie.

'*I Come in Silence* is epic.'

'Epic?'

'Yes, I mean, it's a bit weird, but that's her style. It's super deep.'

'Deep?'

'Yeah, I mean, it's difficult to explain, because—'

'Because you've never read it?' Hannah interrupts.

The intern blinks a few times, her gaze clouded over with uncertainty, but doesn't manage to summon up any rebuke. Hannah gets there faster.

'You shouldn't be at a book fair trying to sell books that you claim to have read when you clearly know less about literature than an illiterate—'

'An illiterate what?'

Bastian pops up behind Hannah, all six foot of him looming over her. He looks expectantly at Hannah, and then, taking his eyes off her face, he moves his gaze in an equally inquisitive line to the intern, who – now shrinking behind the counter – looks close to tears.

'An illiterate moron.'

Hannah seethes at her failure to come up with a more refined insult, yet at the same time notes, with even more irritation, that the intern seems neither horrified nor ashamed enough to pull off a full-blown breakdown. Instead, the young girl straightens up, presumably in the belief that her boss – the tall, kind Bastian – will, with great fanfare, escort the strange assailant out of the building.

'Claudia here is new, she's studying comparative literature.'

Probably still convinced that Bastian will grab Hannah's arm and lead her away, Claudia pushes her shoulders even further back, and turns to him.

'I was just trying to tell this customer here about Hannah Krause-Bendix, but she totally had a go at me instead.'

Ah, a woman playing the victim. How boring.

Claudia the intern eyes Bastian: why wasn't he escorting her away yet? Hannah's actually starting to enjoy the conflict. If she's lucky, Bastian might even fire Claudia. If only the torture could be drawn out a little, for Hannah's sake. People who lecture others about things they have absolutely no knowledge of should die slow and painful deaths. On the other hand, she'd also like to hurry up and get started on what she actually came here for, and this discussion won't lead to many books being signed.

'I don't know if you usually just read Facebook updates or fashion blogs or whatever, but you clearly don't read novels. If you did, then you'd know that *I'm* Hannah Krause-Bendix. I'm the one who wrote these books you're standing there trying to peddle as if they were pickles.'

Claudia gasps.

'Hannah, she's new.' An attempt by Bastian to take the edge off Claudia's humiliation.

'I couldn't have known it was you, especially when you look so different from your photo ... I mean, you look so much older in person.'

Claudia fumbles around with Hannah's books, trying to rearrange them. As if that's going to help. Hannah swallows a snappy comeback and, instead, takes off her jacket and chucks it behind the table.

'Why don't you go buy yourself a nice hot, organic soya latte while I sit here and sign my epic novels for the next hour?'

Claudia glances at Bastian. Like a school child asking whether they have permission to go to the toilet.

'You can take a break.'

Claudia slinks away from the desk and disappears into the crowd. Gone, too, is her straight back and proud chest.

'Good to see you in all your staff-intimidating glory.' Bastian drums his index finger on the table.

'Was it really so difficult to find an assistant who has read at least one of my books?'

Bastian grimaces. Hannah sighs – of course. If Hannah doesn't find a new audience for her books, and fast, the next step in her career will be to drive all her unsold copies to the nearest landfill.

'You should know, I'm only doing this out of the kindness of my heart.'

'Can you at least smile at people?'

'Devilishly or sexily?'

'In a friendly way, please. I know you have it in you.'

Bastian smiles, opens his suit-clad arms wide – why does an editor have to dress like a businessman? Hannah remembers the time when soft velvet and wool were core staples of Bastian's uniform, but that was before the economic boom of the noughties. And before he became an editor. Suits of various cuts and colours have been his garb of choice since starting at the publishing house. Hannah is convinced it's deliberate – to signal his transition from a literature-loving student to a permanent member of the literati. From wanting to work with books because you love books, to working with books because you love money. A transition Hannah has never experienced herself. But, in the privacy of her own thoughts, she is glad that Bastian has. She looks down at the table laden with her own works, feels a pang of gratefulness for Bastian's commercial transformation, because if it weren't for him, her books wouldn't be at the book fair at all. Even if she does still miss the woolly, velvet man she met for the first time in the late nineties, at a reading of Inger Christensen's *Butterfly Valley: A Requiem*.

'Is this on?'

Hannah looks up. A microphone crackles. The same microphone currently amplifying the sound of a thin, female voice. The voice matches the body, which is somehow even thinner: Natasja Sommer. On a stage. Also on the stage: two chairs, a little coffee table placed between them and two glasses of water. The uneducated culture journalist taps lightly on the microphone – a hollow, drumming sound. Yes, it's on. Behind her, on the wall, a poster. Hannah's heart skips a beat: it's a photo of Jørn Jensen, the world's worst crime writer, the primary object of Hannah's loathing. And it looks like he's about to be interviewed by Natasja Sommer. Right now. On that very stage. Hannah takes a deep breath. She should never have come to the book fair.

3

Smile, smile, success, success. Hannah flips through the book-fair catalogue and eyes her colleagues' portraits and photographed book covers, popping up as small, grating reminders of how long it's been since she released any new work herself. She slams it shut and looks up, over the booth – which is easy as there's nobody there – to the area just in front of the stage directly opposite her, which is packed full of people. From her lonely outpost, she gazes over at the waiting audience and feels an acute urge to crawl inside a teeny, tiny cell deep within her own body, the smallest one she can find. Why exactly does she hate Jørn so much? It's not because he sells. Or because people read him. Or love him. She's not that primitive; she doesn't really acknowledge the success of writers of his calibre. She looks down at her nails, flexes her fingers, as if they contain some unknown mystery. Which they do, in a way. They translate her thoughts into words, bring her soul into the world, materialise it. That's it. That's what Jørn's books lack: soul. They don't contain the deepest, most original thoughts that only an individual can bring forth. His are simply reprints of other people's thoughts, churning them out like some mechanical book factory. Yes, his books may be exciting, they may have a moral to their story. But those qualities are cheap, easy, because they're based on a formula. Where's the originality, the heart, that which separates the author from any other person who's taken a writing course and has a decent sense of suspense dramaturgy? And the language. Why doesn't he make an effort with the language?

A round of applause erupts from the crowd as Jørn steps on stage. He kisses Natasja Sommer on the cheek and looks out at his fans, a broad smile on his face. He tries to look humble, but fails – it's hard to hide such a giant ego. Someone in the audience wolf-whistles, as if he's a rock star. Ah, Denmark, you cultural wasteland; please do encourage talentless people as much as you can! Hannah stares, eyes fixed on Jørn, like an owl about to extend its claw and capture a mouse. But her claws remain on the counter, they even retract a little – Jørn is unassailable. Natasja Sommer commences the interview with a flirty tone, and Jørn starts talking, self-assured, well rehearsed, his words like fuel on Hannah's burning skin.

'I'd like to be able to write a book in about eighteen minutes and then move on to the next.'

Fire!

'Writing is a craft, a job like any other. That's why it's important to have a strict work ethic: to sit down for a certain amount of time and write, and don't stop until you've written the number of pages you set out to. And it's just as important that you eat well and exercise too, to stay sharp, mentally.'

Flames!

'I see it as a duty that I never bore the reader, to always try and reach as many readers as possible. After all, there's a huge industry dedicated to this kind of book, so you could even say that I see myself as a bit of an entrepreneur, creating jobs for others: at the publisher, the printers, in the shops.'

Inferno!

Hannah can't stand listening to any more statements about literature as a function of the market economy and desperately fumbles around for her phone, finds it and calls Bastian. Straight to voicemail. Shit. She considers slipping out, but as the thought comes to her, two teenage girls approach the booth. She watches them as they look over the books, picking them up at random. She tries to shut out Jørn's voice, to no avail.

'How would you describe the relationship between what we might call the heavier, more literary genre, and the popular book culture, which you yourself belong to?'

Hannah's ears prick up at Natasja Sommer's question. Jørn nods slowly, maybe to show his understanding of the question, maybe to underline that the answer is complicated. He radiates authority – media-trained authority.

'I see it like this: it's a good thing that there are bestselling authors like me, who help make it possible for others to get published. From this point of view, popular fiction can be seen as a necessity, as it means that those who don't really sell can still publish their books.'

Burn me alive!

So my existence is courtesy of you, is it? she thinks. Because you write your stupid books, I get to publish mine? Because you're not ambitious with the way you use language, I get to be with mine? The claws slowly unfold. The two teenage girls come over to Hannah, one of whom dumps a book on the counter.

'Can you gift wrap that for me?'

Hannah's gaze moves from the book up to the girl, whose box-dyed hair is far too black for her already-pale skin, making it shine and only calling further attention to the transition from child to adult. She also has no eyebrows. Hannah has no time for people with no eyebrows; she thinks they lack character. Could she not at least draw some on? But it isn't the girl's appearance that makes Hannah recoil in disdain. Rather, it's the book she has placed before her: *The Woman Who Whispered for Help*. By Jørn Jensen. Hannah picks it up as if it were a pair of homeless man's lost pants, and turns it over. On the back, a picture of Jørn in some rugged outdoor situation, leaning against a tree, arms crossed, staring directly into the camera, as if he were trying to psychoanalyse the lens. Above the photo: nothing but words of praise from the critics against a starry sky. Mainly reviews from obscure blogger sites that Hannah's never heard of. She lifts her gaze from the photo to the man himself.

'I don't expect to be a successful writer for the rest of my life – you've got to know when your time's up. Stop while you're ahead.'

Jørn looks directly at Hannah as he says this. Only momentarily, but long enough that it can't have been random. She thinks she notices a hint of mockery in his smile, perhaps as a little payback for all those times she's turned her back on him at various events. Years' worth of accumulated irritation charges through Hannah and takes control of her hand. She raises it, and before she knows what she's doing, she's thrown *The Woman Who Whispered for Help* directly at Jørn. It's probably all his years in the Danish army that make his reaction to incoming flying books so sharp, as he almost miraculously jerks his head quickly to the side, managing to avoid, by mere millimetres, being smacked square in the forehead with his own best-seller. The book makes contact with a stand behind him, displaying a photo of the book cover. It overturns, topples off the stage and crashes to the ground.

The entire festival turns to look at Hannah. The eyebrowless teenager points at her.

'It was her, she threw it.'

Natasja Sommer's hand is now covering her mouth in shock, clearly unable to handle anything not written down in advance on her neat little interview cards. Jørn, on the other hand, maintains his composure. He stands, to get a better view over the crowd, and steps to the edge of the stage. His eyes meet Hannah's – she does nothing to evade his gaze.

'Well, well, well. There's clearly one person here who isn't excited about my new book.'

The crowd laughs. Hannah reaches boiling point.

'I haven't read it, but I imagine it's just a reprint of one of your other books, only with a new title. Or rather, a kind of new title – as far as I remember, wasn't your previous release titled *The Woman Who Sighed after Sex*. I read that in a day.'

'So you've read it. How flattered I am.'

Jørn smiles smugly at the audience, who laugh and smile up at him in return. Now the initial shock has subsided, the audience have rapidly adapted to this new form of entertainment – here we have lines drawn, a clear, mutual aversion between two renowned writers, a literary feud. Far more entertaining than just one man talking into a microphone on stage.

Natasja Sommer has regained her poise, holds her breath. The newspaper photographers snap away. Hannah blinks, has an out-of-body experience for a brief moment: this is all happening right now, and it's almost as if an invisible syringe injects her with something containing equal parts panic and aggression. She represses the former, and adrenaline gives her courage.

'There's no need to be flattered, it was a truly awful reading experience. I've held writing courses for children in the fourth grade who are more eloquent.'

Hannah's stab is made with malice. The corner of Jørn's mouth twitches – attacks on one's abilities hurt the most. Especially for a man who's sold millions of books, as well as the film rights to an English-speaking country.

'Well, we can't all write little, intellectual novellas for the elite.'

Hannah is prepared for that exact argument. She's heard it before.

'In principle, we could. But it's not an either/or discussion. They're not mutually exclusive, and this isn't because I hate crime fiction either. I only hate badly written crime fiction, which people wrongly believe is good; the work, for example, that you write.'

Jovial Jørn has left the building. Now it's pure self-defence.

'You may think my books are bad, but I'd argue that there are many people who would disagree with you. Such as my millions of readers.'

People clap at this, but Hannah takes no notice of them, after all, the audience is mainly Jørn's fans. She finds peace in the knowledge that, in both national and international literary circles, she's the queen of high-brow. Even if those circles are rather small.

'The tastes of the majority are rarely a marker of quality.'

Hannah hears the words come out of her mouth, hears that they are more vicious and personal than she had intended. In fact, Jørn isn't the problem, it's everything he stands for that is. And, of course, the fact that he's up on that stage, teaching people about literature like that. No! He does deserve it. He *is* the problem.

A camera from one of the TV stations has found its way over to them – who would have thought that authors were capable of creating this much drama outside of their books? Hannah notices them and wonders what the hell she's gotten herself caught up in. But she can't walk away now, nor can she bring herself to stop – not unlike a car skidding down an ice road: the only way to avoid disaster is to continue onward, heading in the same direction at the same speed, and hope that you come out the other end alive. Jørn follows the same strategy.

'To be honest, I think it's rather conceited to stand there and claim that you have better taste than all of the people who read my books.'

No. He can't be allowed to reduce this to a question of morality.

Good taste, bad taste, that's not what this is about.

Hannah reaches over to an unnecessarily tall stack of Jørn's books and holds up a copy.

'This is mediocrity with page numbers. Poor taste is fair enough, but mediocrity that knows it's mediocre and doesn't strive to be anything more than that, or to be a little bit different – that's the real threat to our society. This book represents all those who don't bother to put in even the smallest amount of effort, those content to just sit on the cliché shelf. And make money out of it. Any idiot can write a book like this in a month.'

Jørn pauses. He and the audience hold their breath.

'Okay then. If any idiot can do it, that must mean that you can too?'

Hannah stays silent. She can sense where this is going. A turn she hadn't anticipated.

'Of course she can!'

Hannah swivels round and catches sight of Bastian, towering over the crowd – has he been there the whole time? And what the hell is he thinking, interrupting with that?

'I, for one, think that's an excellent challenge. Writing a crime novel in one month? I think there are many of us here who'll be looking forward to reading that book.' Jørn has managed to gain control of the conversation again with a smile, the impudence now resting just below the surface.

Nodding and clapping from the audience. Cameras flashing, people chatting. Is this a media stunt or a genuine conflict ending in an actual competition? Either way, the entertainment value has ramped up a notch. This moment may be one for the history books.

All eyes turn again to Hannah, who in turn looks from Jørn to Bastian. In the space between the two men she sees that any control she had over the situation is sliding out of her hands. There's only one way forward.

'Sure, in one month, I'll have written a work of crime fiction better than anything you've ever published.'

Hannah has surprised the crowd – and herself, even. She turns on the spot and marches away from Jørn, the audience, the media. Bastian quickly overtakes the horde of followers. The pledge hangs in the air behind her.

4

Hannah only just has time to light a cigarette before Bastian finds her in her backroom hide-out. Judging by the silence, he's managed to shake off the last few stalkers.

'That was the best marketing trick I've ever seen. The book's already sold in the hundreds of thousands before it's even been published!'

Hannah looks up at Bastian. 'Bullshit!' She stubs out the cigarette without even taking a second drag.

Bastian takes in a deep breath. Knows her too well. 'You mean you're not going to write it?'

'I can't. Crime? I write introspective prose. I can't even plot out a simple romance novel properly.'

'But just think – what if you could?'

'Yes, and? Then there'd just be one more god-awful crime novel in the world.'

'Not awful. You don't do awful.'

'Your flattery is driven purely by the profit you think you'll get.'

Bastian rests a hand on Hannah's shoulder.

'You'll write a good, different kind of crime. In a month. It'll sell well, you'll have proved your point to Jørn and the rest of the book world – you'll have sparked a debate. And then you can return to your novels, which have now aroused widespread, popular interest. Everything you publish will be discussed far and wide – read far and wide. People will suddenly start reading your earlier works. *I Come in Silence* will have to be reprinted. You'll make your mark on Denmark's literary history.'

Hannah can see it unfolding before her. Slowly starts to look at it all in a new light.

'Maybe I *could* write a good crime novel, but not in a month. And that's the essence of this whole thing – the fact that bad crime fiction is bad *because* they're produced at such speed, and are superficial in both language and content. That, I could probably achieve in a month.'

'The quality isn't as important, so long as the book's done. It's not the content, but the truth behind the statement: any idiot can write a crime novel in a month. It puts the genre into perspective.'

'But is it right to use all that paper to print such a bad text? It wouldn't be worth sacrificing the rainforest for.'

'In a hundred years, your novels will be mandatory reading material in all Danish schools.'

Hannah mulls it over.

'I've got writer's block.'

Bastian scrutinises her.

'You need some new inspiration, new surroundings.'

'I've just been to Berlin. And I wrote four pages in fourteen days.'

'No, you need something different. Nature, silence. You need to go to Iceland.'

Hannah stares at him.

'Why Iceland?'

'I know someone up there, a friend of the family. A woman you can stay with – she's got this huge house in some rural town. You can get away from everything here, have the time and peace to write. And in a month, you'll come back with a crime novel.'

'And what if I don't?'

'Then at least you'd have made an honest attempt.'

Bastian moves his attention to his phone, while Hannah thinks over this situation she's got herself into. She has a feeling that she's suddenly come to a decisive point in her life. This could be quite the opportunity. Or perhaps her biggest mistake. Bastian looks up from his phone.

'Go home and pack your bags, you're on a flight to Reykjavik in four hours.'

5

The baggage carousel kicks into motion, alerting those awaiting their suitcases with a mechanical click, promising an imminent reunion between them and their luggage. People swarm around the mouth of the belt as it spits out each bag at an unpredictable pace. Hannah waits in solitary dignity away from the epicentre – why don't people realise the belt carries the luggage *all the way round*, and that it may, therefore, be beneficial to spread out a bit? For God's sake, that's what it's bloody designed for. With her arms folded across her chest, she observes the other passengers: what exactly does that achieve? What are they afraid of? That someone else is going to run off with their copy-and-paste suitcases full of their dirty laundry?

They have travelled through the morning together, flown alongside the retreating darkness, and an hour back in time. An almost poetic, collective experience, in a way. One of those rare circumstances that makes Hannah feel like part of a group: All of us together, high above the Earth, and if we were to fall out of the sky, we would die together. Hannah finds the idea of a collective death mollifying. But here they all are, her fellow passengers, alive and safe, hovering around the conveyor belt like hyenas surrounding a dead animal. The sense of community dissipates entirely as they fight for their luggage.

She drags her black suitcase toward the exit, its one broken wheel screeching behind her as it tries to pull off to the right. She should've replaced the suitcase many trips ago. Hannah looks around, tries to get an impression of Iceland thus far – the airport doesn't seem all that different to Denmark's. Or from any other airport anywhere else, for that matter: stone, metal, glass. All neatly arranged. Perhaps that's why all arrival gates look the same; so you can't tell what country you're in. Maybe it's meant to give the impression of a smooth transition: a few hours ago, you were in another country, far away, and now you're here, yet it looks the same. A kind of deception; the human brain couldn't keep up with the change without it. Or maybe it's because most travellers are xenophobic. Hannah notices, however, that the neutrality here at Keflavík, Iceland's national airport, is offset by a few ultra-nationalist symbols in the duty-free shop: flags of Iceland, souvenirs, chocolates shaped like famous Icelandic buildings and postcards with turf cabins and waterfalls. Icelandic vodka, Icelandic sweets. Who, hand on their heart, actually has use for a cap with horns bearing the Icelandic flag? Hannah peers in as she walks by: American tourists. She feels something icy run down her side from her right armpit. Cold sweat. She can't get out of the floodgates of Keflavík airport fast enough – with one last hard tug, she forces her suitcase back on track and hopes that her host for the month, Ella, is waiting on the other side of those doors, as Bastian has promised.

Outside the arrivals hall, Hannah regrets, for the third time, taking on this project. She's done two rounds of the car park with her dying suitcase in tow and smoked two slow cigarettes in front of the entrance – their meeting point. But no Ella. Hannah shuffles back, further under the roof, and looks up at the sky. Various shades of grey and about to rain. And she's not convinced that the air is anywhere near as fresh as she was promised. Where is Ella? Hannah has a sudden, nerve-racking thought: what if there is no Ella? What if there is no writing retreat set up for her – it was all just a ruse to lure her up here, so Bastian could finally get rid of her? No, he wouldn't do that. Ella's probably just had a heart attack and died on her way here. She is an older woman, after all. Oh, fuck. What if she is lying lifeless in a ditch? With frozen fingers, she fumbles around with her lighter and inhales the smoke of another cigarette deep into her lungs, holds it there a moment and exhales. She contemplates a curious, colourful sculpture made of steel and glass across the car park. The artwork tilts to the side a bit, unfinished at the top, as if it's trying to stretch up to heaven, but chooses not to at the last minute. It's not too late to turn around. Icelandair runs a shuttle service, maybe she can hop on the same flight she arrived on? Maybe she'd even get the same seat.

Hannah suddenly catches sight of an approaching Jeep, one that looks like it may be combing the car park for lost Danish authors. Through the filthy windscreen, Hannah believes she recognises the woman Bastian fleetingly showed her a photo of. Hannah raises her arm, waves it around a good while to get the woman's attention – and eventually gets it. Watches as a smile breaks out on the woman's face, the Jeep changes direction and pulls over. Out steps Ella, agile and surprisingly complex in her physical appearance: tan, reddish hair, gold jewellery, lipstick, yet wearing a grey fleece and clogs. Tucked under her arm: an old sheet of cardboard with *Velkomin Hannah* written on it in red marker. The sign is held up with an outstretched arm. The woman smiles with all her sixty-something years and points to herself:

'Ella.'

Hannah shakes her hand. She's aware that Danish is semi-compulsory at school here, but also knows well enough that it's a myth that all Icelanders speak and understand it. And, not wanting to appear like a dumb imperialist, she has planned to spend the next month speaking English.

'Hello, I'm Hannah. Thank you for letting me stay at your house.'

Ella comes out with a stream of something in Icelandic, gesturing with her arms, and starts to heave Hannah's suitcase, which is almost as big as she is, into the car. Hannah quickly interprets the situation:

Ella can't speak Danish or English! In her mind's eye, she aggressively shakes Bastian for not having disclosed this important piece of information. Intentionally, she's sure. Had Hannah known that to be the case, she'd never have left Denmark. But she's here now. Hannah grabs the other end of the suitcase, moments before it is about to overpower the woman.

'I'll take it.'

The car is a Jeep Cherokee, and going by the ratty seats and radio complete with cassette player, it hasn't been new for many years. *Tik-ke-dee-tak, clunk; tik-ke-dee-tak, clunk.* The engine plays its own melody, sounding most like a farewell song. Hannah glances, a look of concern on her face, at Ella, who – now driving them out of the airport – seems completely unaware of the engine's imminent failure. Or maybe she's just used to it. Hannah sighs – if there's a fatal road-traffic accident in store for them, then it's the driver rather than the car who'll be responsible. Her eyes jump from the embroidered sofa cushion Ella seems to be sat on, lifting her up just high enough to see over the wheel, to the pair of thick glasses balancing on the tip of her nose. The nose itself so far forward that Ella's breath seems to dance on the windshield – settling on the glass and then disappearing. Settling, disappearing. Hannah wonders whether it's common practice in Iceland to perform mandatory health checks before you're allowed to renew your driving licence. But, then again, Ella's probably not old enough for that. As they overtake a Mercedes and narrowly avoid an oncoming bus, Hannah starts to doubt whether Ella even has a driving licence. One hundred and ten kilometres an hour. On a country road. Come to think of it, maybe dying wouldn't be that bad. It'd mean she wouldn't have to write the book.

The engine definitely sounds as if it's on the verge of collapse now. Hannah points with her entire body toward the car heater, hoping that she's signalling towards the engine. And then demonstratively covers her ears. Ella nods in a 'yes I know' kind of way. Says something in Icelandic.

Switches the radio on and then turns it up for Phil Collins' 'Another Day in Paradise'. She bops along happily, side to side, hands moving with the music, the steering wheel and car following after. The car ploughs forward, now zigzagging across the road. The sounds coming from the engine add to the dissonance. Wonderful. If there's one person Hannah hates more than Jørn Jensen, it's Phil Collins. She refuses to let him be the soundtrack to her death. She fishes out her phone, makes a call, and Bastian answers immediately. A hello would be superfluous.

'I need you to book me a return flight.'

'Did Ella not come and get you?'

'No, she did. But she's driven us into a ditch, we're both sat here in the mangled car. I can't feel my legs.'

'I can tell that Iceland's already ignited your imagination. Ella's great, isn't she?'

'Why didn't you tell me that she can't speak English? Or that she drives like a lunatic and loves Phil Collins?'

'Ach, come on. Phil Collins is good.'

'Please. This was all a terrible decision, I don't know whether I was having a stroke or what. But what I do know is that there's a flight back to Copenhagen tomorrow morning. And I'll be on it.'

'What about your novel?'

'It's not a *novel*. It's crime.'

'Will it write itself?'

'Hopefully. I'm genuinely sorry, but I can't do this. I want to go home.'

Hannah can hear Bastian release a sigh somewhere in Denmark.

'I'll see what I can do.'

'Thanks.'

Hannah hangs up, leans back. Defeated. Mumbles to herself:

'Jesus fucking Christ, what a ball ache.'

Ella slams on the brakes. Turns down the radio. They sit there on the side of the road.

'What is it?'

Hannah sits up, looks around, unsure of what she's looking for. Senses a change of mood.

Ella stares ahead. Eventually leans over Hannah, opens the glove compartment, finds a scrap of paper and a ballpoint pen. Then writes, with all her concentration. For an entire minute. As if the words must be extracted from somewhere deep within her. She holds the paper up in front of Hannah, who reads … something that appears to be a combination of broken Danish with Icelandic and English influences.

You use masse swearing og foul language.

Hannah reads it again. As if she doesn't recognise the words in front of her. Looks up at Ella. Not without a significant knot clenching in her stomach.

'You can speak Danish?'

Ella writes again. The words seem to come out a little easier this time.

Jeg understand. Kan write a bit.

The knot in her stomach tightens. She stays silent for longer than just a dramatic pause.

'I actually have more beautiful words in me.'

Ella writes.

Use them.

Hannah stares at her. Notices Ella's eyes for the first time. Bright green. How could she have managed not to notice such startlingly green eyes? Hannah nods.

Ella puts the car back into gear and her foot down on the accelerator. Hannah turns to look out of the window, at the nature surrounding them, that she also hadn't noticed until now. The car devours the road, they drive in silence. *Tik-ke-dee-tak, clunk; tik-ke-dee-tak, clunk*. Almost silence.

Six hours, Hannah had read that it takes to drive to the little fishing town of Húsafjörður, where she'll be a resident for the next month. She could have actually taken a flight – the town seems to have a local airport that facilitates domestic travel to and from the capital, Reykjavík – but Ella insisted on picking her up in Keflavík. Hannah wonders whether Ella had a long enough break before the drive back, but she doesn't dare ask. She glances at her out of the corner of her eye – Ella doesn't seem tired. Hannah leans back in her seat, settling in for the several hours she'll be spending on the somewhat hard car seat, driving further and further away from the city, deeper into the Icelandic wilderness. They've already passed through the flat, lava-made moon-like landscape of the west, and are now sailing toward the more lush landscapes of the south-east. Even though the brownish-yellow colours of autumn dominate the vast plains, there are still traces of green here and there, and Hannah finds herself surprised at just how green Iceland is, even now, as winter looms. But the mountains do not defy the season: with ease, they lift the snow towards the sky, and Hannah stares at them with the kind of fascination that only someone from a completely flat country can have. As a writer, she should really have some sort of inherent symbiosis with nature, it should inspire her to dig out and use sublime words. But in reality, nature frightens her, both the thought of capturing it in writing, and quite literally, which is why she's always turned inward in her writing. Not because people are easier to describe than nature, but because it feels more authentic.

Even though it's only been a few hours since she landed, twilight is already descending around them. Hannah remembers having read something about the sparse daylight the country experiences at this time of year, but she doesn't feel fully prepared for the impending thirty days of darkness. She takes a deep breath in, and with it, feels like she's drawing in the landscape around her too. Has a vague feeling of how nature here becomes even more beautiful at dusk.

Neither of them speak. Ella concentrates on driving, listening to the radio, which is now broadcasting the voice of a man speaking Icelandic. Hannah picks up a few words every so often, fragments of what he's saying, but gives up on trying to understand the context. She doesn't take the initiative to talk to Ella either – has never been able to muster enough polite, superficial niceties to keep a conversation going, free of awkward silences. Small talk. How do people do it? Instead, she thinks of what she's read. About Iceland. And Húsafjörður. The population of the fishing town comes to about twelve hundred of the three hundred and sixty thousand people who live in Iceland. Geothermal energy makes up most of the country's energy, including its heating and its electricity – in other words, it's a very sustainable country. The people of Húsafjörður once lived off fishing alone, but its tourism industry has now overtaken it as a source of income.

To Hannah, Iceland has always seemed to be inhabited by people with a kind of light grandeur – whether that's because of the country's volcanoes, its waterfalls or the sagas, she's not sure. She was once invited to a private viewing of the work of an Icelandic artist who made miniature lithographs, and she turned out to be the only Dane present. She spent the entire afternoon at a party where the only language used was Icelandic, even though everyone was practically fluent in both English and Danish. It wasn't hostile, the party – there were smiles and nods, acknowledging her presence, and in her silence, rare for Hannah, she had felt social for once. If she had observed her silence from the outside that evening, she would've leapt at the opportunity to fabricate an exciting story about who this woman was. But as she stood there, sipping her glass of red wine, observing, listening, without understanding anything being said, she could sense the pride in the room. Not like the Danish, Lilliputian pride, always begging to prove itself. But a self-assured confidence, an inherent, radiating pride. The fact that exact level of confidence had led to Iceland's over-optimistic fiscal policies and investments of the early 2000s, which had in turn threatened to plunge the volcanic island into poverty was, of course, a downside.

Húsafjörður flashes at them as they fly past the road sign. In the dark, it is difficult to discern the little settlement, but Hannah can just about make out how the scattered houses separate the land from the sea, and as they approach, she notes that the town looks as if it were built during the economic boom of the 1960s, with the less-

than charming concrete architecture that entails. Not exactly the
idyllic writer's retreat she'd had in mind – although she doesn't
really know what she actually had in mind. A wooden cabin with a
turf roof, like the postcards in the airport? They overtake a teenager
riding a bike without any lights, and drive past a closed petrol
station. Everything seems to exude 'countryside'. Her telephone
rings. It's Bastian.

'Now what?'

'There are no more seats on tomorrow morning's flight, but
there's space on the SAS flight at eight pm that stops in Oslo. It's
not been easy finding you a last-minute ticket, so this trip will be
coming out of your profits.'

'What profits?'

'Pack it in. Are you taking the ticket or what?'

Hannah hesitates.

The car guides them up to a house located a fair way away from
all the others. A house that seems to have an entire area of the town
to itself. Ella turns off the engine, and Hannah stares at the building,
currently shrouded in darkness and silence. Built of wood, and
clearly surpassing the age of its owner, Hannah guesses that the two-
storey house must be far too large for just one person. A half-moon
hangs in the sky above the house, and around it, Hannah can just
about detect a whole array of constellations. It dawns on her just
how many years it's been since she last saw the stars. In the city, it's
easy to forget they're there.

The sound of someone clearing their throat on the other end of
the line. Bastian.

'I'm waiting, credit card and fingers ready. Am I confirming the
reservation, yes or no?' Bastian's voice now impatient.

Hannah takes another look up at the house, at all of the
possibilities she hasn't yet considered. Another moment passes. She
breathes in, feels calmer than she has in a long time.

'No. Don't book. You'll have your novel in a month.'

She opens the car door and steps out.

6

Ella opens the door without using a key. At first, Hannah presumes she left it unlocked as a result of the forgetfulness that comes with old age. The ease with which she is invited inside, however, suggests that Ella chose not to lock the door – and that you don't need to lock your doors in Húsafjörður. In what Hannah would describe as one sweeping motion, Ella carelessly chucks her fleece onto the chest of drawers by the front door and makes her way through the narrow hallway into what must be the living room. Hannah struggles to haul her suitcase inside, and removes her shoes and coat, placing the former neatly on the hallway floor and hanging the latter on a peg, as if a space has always been reserved for it there. She inhales the smell of a lived-in home – and somehow finds it inexplicably reassuring. She walks along the thick, carpeted floors, heading deeper into the house, the wheels of the suitcase leaving deep tracks in her wake.

'Þetta er mitt heimili.'

Ella flings her arms open wide. Hannah looks around. The structure of the house is exposed, with load-bearing wooden pillars from floor to ceiling, reinforced by transverse beams. The panelled walls are painted blue, the ceiling white. Hannah imagines there must be a beautiful wooden floor hiding beneath the thick, wall-to-wall carpet, which Ella is clearly very fond of – Hannah wonders whether it's an aesthetic choice, or a cold-feet-related one. She digs her toes into the long, yellow-brown wool and concludes that the latter is most likely. The room – a combined kitchen, living room and sewing-machine centre – is large, and probably quite bright in the daylight with its four tall sash windows. Not particularly energy efficient, and they aren't exactly doing a great job of keeping the November chill out. Hannah shivers and spots a radiator, the dial turned up as high as its settings allow. And remembers that the country's abundance of thermal energy makes it almost free to keep Icelandic living rooms warm. Ella lights the small fireplace anyway, fiddling about with the fire tongs, sparks flying everywhere, none of which seem to bother her. Slowly, the heat from the flames begins to spread through the room, and Hannah feels her body loosen up by a micrometre. It is then that she starts noticing the room's details. A rocking chair so old it doesn't look like it was made this century – or last. Antique tools of wood and metal hanging on the wall as décor. And then something that looks like a collector's treasure trove: a display case full of elephant figurines made of porcelain, glass, wood – a collection consisting of every art style imaginable, from the abstract to the naturalistic to the caricature. Hannah steps closer to the display case; the contents look like a lifetime's work. One figure in particular catches her eye – a particularly realistic-looking bull elephant, beautifully carved from a type of wood she doesn't recognise. The elephant's trunk hangs down and brushes the ground, its back right leg bent beneath it, as if it were resting. There's something sad about it.

'Minn uppáhalds.'

Hannah starts, turns to see Ella standing right behind her. She looks, uncomprehendingly, at her host. Ella picks up a newspaper and pen from the coffee table. She writes:

Min favourite. I bought it in Indien.

Hannah looks at her again, surprised.

'You've been to India?'

Ella writes again: I have been to many places. Love elefanter. They kan carry a whole family.

Hannah looks around the room again, suddenly noticing something. The absence of photos.

'Do you not have children?'

Ella shakes her head, writes something: Sadly.

Ella doesn't look all that sad about it though – instead, she gestures for Hannah to stay put for a moment while she disappears. She comes back into the room with a portrait of a teenage boy. Hannah takes it in her hands, looks at it with sincere curiosity – normally she hates looking at other people's family photos, but there's something inexplicably intriguing about this boy. It's not his appearance, though. It's not that he's unattractive – with his light-blond hair, dark eyebrows and those characteristically high Icelandic cheekbones, he's good-looking enough, but nothing exceptional. No, what makes this boy so special is the way he holds himself, doesn't shy away from the camera, but exudes a captivating confidence. And his gaze. He has the same green eyes as Ella, piercing, engaging.

Ella points at him: *'Frændi.'*

'Friend?'

Another shake of the head. Ella stops and thinks, as if there's a word in Danish but she can't quite grasp it. Again, she gets the newspaper and writes along the edge.

Nephew. Thor.

Hannah nods, understanding now.

'Does he live here too? In town, I mean.'

Another nod, followed by more writing.

Min whole family live her.

'That's nice.'

Ella shrugs, which Hannah has difficulty interpreting. But really, she understands well enough: if she were told she had to live in a small, remote town with her entire family, she'd have thrown herself off the tallest building in Copenhagen long ago. Her parents are nice enough at a distance, but she'd rather her sister lived further away than just Ringsted. They get together for the obligatory holiday celebrations, important events, but all other contact stopped years ago, after a mutual, unspoken agreement. Not for any particular reason, it's just that the kind of differences between them can't be overcome simply by being related. Hannah knows it's a taboo thought, but sometimes she fantasises about a life where her sister, her sister's husband, their two children and her dad didn't exist. Then she could be completely free to be herself, without having to think about them, sitting in their prim and proper detached houses in suburban hell, interpreting her every move. She knows how they talk about her, how they say she's lost. Her niece passed on that choice of wording without knowing what it meant. She also knows that none of them have ever read a single one of her books. And her sister's kids are ugly as well. That's the kind of thing you can't say out loud, but she's been close to implying it many times. Once without even having been drunk.

'Is my room upstairs?' Hannah points to the staircase.

Ella looks disappointed, and conjures up a box of chocolates and a bag of ground coffee, from a drawer and a cupboard, respectively, holding them up demonstratively. Hannah shakes her head as if to say, *No, thank you* – she's tired, and although Ella seems nice enough company, she doesn't have the capacity for anything else today. And anyway, shouldn't you wait for your guest to settle in before you offer them coffee and chocolate? She's also not tempted by the prospect of a long conversation with Ella, who would have to write down everything she wanted to say on the crumpled edges of the newspaper. It's hard enough getting to know another human being when you share the same language, let alone trying to do so without words. An impossible task. Hannah also happens to have a few bottles of red wine in her suitcase, and has, several times since arriving, fantasised about opening one of them.

Ella looks at her expectantly, the coffee and chocolate still in her hands.

'No, thank you, I'm unbelievably tired, and it would be nice to unpack before bed. So I'm ready to get started on the writing tomorrow.'

Hannah surprises herself with the addition of the last sentence – she doesn't need to give her host an explanation, nor lie about her work ethic. Yet, for some reason she feels as if she owes Ella something. But Ella shrugs, puts the coffee and chocolate back where she found them and leads Hannah upstairs. Like the rest of the house, the first floor is solidly built, and also smells a little like an old ship.

Hanging on the wall above the bed of the small attic room is a crucifix. Hannah looks at it, thinking the impaled Jesus looks particularly miserable. To his right, a portrait of the Virgin Mary, chaste and praying, that looks like a souvenir you'd bring back from some Catholic country.

Hannah nods towards her new roommates. 'Are you religious?'

Ella lets out a laugh so short and surprisingly cold that Hannah has to keep from flinching. Ella grabs the notebook that Hannah just placed on the night stand. She goes to stop her, but too late – Ella has already flipped through it, found a blank page and is scribbling down a sentence. She holds it up:

Måske I would be religiøs if there was en religion that recognise women. But impaled, naked men hjelp me sleep more sound at night.

Perhaps she has more in common with Ella than she first thought. Hannah smiles and points to the image on the wall.

'And the Virgin Mary?'

Ella smiles, as if she also thinks it a bit silly, and jots down another sentence:

Thor brought them hjem for mig from Spania. Thinks I am devout Christian.

'And you can't bring yourself to tell him that you're not?'

Ella nods. And then turns abruptly as if a thought has just hit her, opens a wardrobe, picks out two towels and places them neatly on the freshly made bed.

'Thank you.'

Hannah shifts her weight from one foot to the other, her mind on the unopened bottle of wine in her suitcase. Now Ella really has to go.

'Well, I'm getting pretty tired now. Thank you for coming to get me today.'

Ella doesn't leave, and instead opens the drawer of the night stand, with Hannah growing ever more impatient behind her. What now? Ella pulls out a book, a hardback, and places it in Hannah's hand.

'*Hrafnkels saga Freysgoða.*'

Hannah looks down at the book, surprised. The cover is ocean blue, the Danish title written in gold underneath a medieval illustration of a man on a rearing horse. *Hrafnkels saga*. She turns it, feels the book in her hand. Ella writes something in the notebook again:

You write bøker about murder. De Icelandic sagas are about murder, revenge og honour. Best stories in the world. Use dem.

Hannah stares down at Ella's handwriting, feels her irritation rise a little more. Typical. An old woman trying to fob her books off on someone else, and one of the Icelandic sagas at that. As if Hannah can't come up with anything herself. As if Ella knows better than she does. And what was Ella thinking, writing in her notebook? Hannah's most cherished possession, her confidant, her friend ... Hannah snatches the notebook out of Ella's wrinkled hands, and demonstratively holds the ocean-blue saga up in front of her. Summons the most tolerant smile she can muster.

'Thank you so much for the inspiration. I'll use this for some light bed-time reading.'

Ella takes the hint and steps back towards the hallway. Glances again at the notebook, very much aware that her communication device has been taken away. Then she smiles the international 'let me know if you need anything' smile. Hannah forces a smile in response as Ella turns and leaves, but she doesn't need anything at all. Least of all tips on how to write. Over her many years as an author, she's come to learn that everyone has a good idea for a book, and that many will attempt to make their ideas a reality through her. But she's no typing monkey, spending her days writing up other people's thoughts. She finds her own inspiration. Hannah closes the door firmly behind Ella and lies down on the bed, her longing for sleep suddenly overpowering her longing for wine.

But her lack of sleep has unsettled her, so she stares out of the window and into the darkness from the aggravatingly soft bed – can already feel the back pain setting in. She reaches up and grabs the crucifix, shoving it into the drawer of the night stand, but for reasons unknown to her, she leaves the portrait of the Virgin Mary where it is. Maybe because it's nice to be looked at? She turns, sinking deeper into the mattress. What should the novel be about? She left for Iceland without a single idea, had hoped that something would come to her once she got here. But here she is, in Iceland, in the house, and still not a single spark of inspiration.

Something about a murder. And someone who solves it. So simple.

She turns again. Ach, she's lying on the softest of soft beds and can't think of a damn thing. Which is especially difficult when all her brain wants to think about is that bottle of red wine she wants to liberate from its cork, and the throbbing pain in her lower back, reminding her that death can also be painful. She listens: a disconcerting nothingness. The silence nips at her body.

At 2:34am, she gives in, gets out of bed, flips open the suitcase, fishes out the corkscrew, grabs the bottle and opens it. She downs a mouthful straight from the bottle and sits at the desk. From there, she scans the room. The sloping walls over the bed, the night stand beside the bed, and the desk in front of the window. There's also a cupboard, an extra chair and a chest of drawers. That's it. Hannah likes it, the room. Likes the idea of herself in it. Writing. She lets her hand glide over the desk, looks out of the window. This is where she will write her crime novel. Here, where the night is dark blue.

7

Hannah awakes to the sound of bacon sizzling downstairs and the smell of a new day. She stretches reluctantly, and as she swings her legs over the edge of the bed a little too quickly, and her feet touch the floor on her first morning in Iceland, she feels the blood drain from her head. She clutches onto the bed frame for a moment as she waits for the brain fog to ease off and to regain her balance. Once she can see clearly again, her eyes meet the bottle of wine she

opened last night, now on the desk, empty. She takes the bottle,
wraps it in a towel and puts it back in her suitcase, pushing it down
to the bottom. She camouflages the lump with a pile of clothes.
Looks down at what she's just done. She doesn't usually hide the
evidence of her alcoholism. She hears Ella whistling.

'Good morning.'

The stairs creak under Hannah's just-washed body – the illusion
of morning freshness already disappearing, she fears, by the time
she has reached the kitchen. The sight of Ella's happy hospitality
and the large breakfast table instantly silences her inner cynic.
Should she have been more accommodating to her host last night?

'That smells incredible, what are you making?'

She accompanies her question with a curious look at all the food.
There are so many dishes, there's barely room for them on the
kitchen counter. Hannah speculates whether a welcome committee
is on its way – there seems to be enough food to feed the entire
town. A red-wine headache stabs at her temple at the thought. Ella
grabs a spatula and flips over an omelette, smiles as she slides a piece
of paper towards Hannah with her other hand. The menu. Hannah
looks at it.

'Allt það besta.'

If Ella had been hurt by Hannah's rejection the night before, she's
clearly forgotten about it now. Or hides it well. She's exuberant –
perhaps bad company is better than no company?

'Are there other people coming? There's enough food to serve a
midsized refugee camp.'

Ella shakes her head, scribbles something down on the menu:

Du are den only refugee here.

And the only one who's going to have to fight their way through
all the fish balls, *skyr* and open sandwiches, Hannah thinks as she
reads through the list of food on offer, wondering how inappropriate it would be to say that she doesn't have an appetite in the
morning. Very.

'Can I help?'

Ella gestures for her to take a seat at the table, and Hannah obeys. The freshly brewed coffee is poured into a mug, the omelette transferred to a plate and a basket of flatbread pushed towards her. Hannah helps herself, has enough decorum to try a bit of everything, but after three mouthfuls, chokes on a fish ball. It gets stuck in her throat – somewhat like Jørn's debut novel, and she feels as if she wants to vomit. She forces herself to swallow and tries to smile. Looks around for something to help shift the ball, knowing full well nothing will. The light glares in through the windows.

'Bragðast þetta vel?'

Hannah has a good enough ear for language to understand that Ella asked how the food is, and she nods and smiles. And, luckily, manages to force the mouthful down.

'Lovely.'

But the ball transforms into a living, wriggling fish in her stomach, and starts to flop around. Hannah swallows again, trying to hold back the convulsion she can feel rising from within, but in vain: just as she stands up to run to the toilet, she vomits over the table. The contents of her stomach look like someone's emptied an entire bottle of red wine – with clumps in it. Ella leans back instinctively, looks more fascinated than horrified. As if she thinks it quite an achievement, actually, to have managed to hit both the *skyr* and flatbread in one go.

She breaks out into a wide smile, and Hannah tries to smile too, but can't. Pale, she reaches for a napkin with a Christmas motif.

'I am so, so sorry.'

She struggles to regain her composure. Feels as if she still has a school of semi-chewed fish wiggling around inside her, swimming toward the nearest exit. Her stomach turns, but it's empty. She's forced to steady herself with both hands against the edge of the table. Christ, how embarrassing.

'I'm really sorry about this.'

When did she start repeating herself?

Ella reaches for a glass of water, and wafts her arm about in a dismissive, 'don't worry about it' kind of way. The gesture doesn't help ease Hannah's shame. Ella begins to clear up, seemingly with no hard feelings, as if the throwing-up stage of the breakfast was all part of the plan, and now it's time for the next item on the agenda. The fresh food coated in red-wine vomit is scraped into the bin. Hannah rises, starts gathering up plates to help. Ella stops her with an authoritative hand. Shakes her head. Opens a cupboard at lightning-fast speed and pulls out a bag of oats. Passes them to Hannah, who accepts them gratefully.

'Do you have milk?'

Hannah leaves the house with no specific goal, just an abstract plan to take a better look at the town and the rather feeble hope of finding some inspiration. Trying to shake off the morning's vomit faux pas, she follows the path towards the more built-up area in the centre, picking up the pace a bit as she's pummelled by the wind, which forces her to tighten her scarf and button up her jacket. The clouds creep in from the sea, their colour suggesting that rain is on its way. She increases her pace again. She can see the mountains to the north now, in the daylight. They look as if they're holding hands, almost like they're forming a protective chain around the town. Or a fence too tall to climb.

After about half a mile, she finds herself in what she believes to be the centre of town, where a closed convenience store and a ditto clothes shop appear to be the only retailers on the high street. She looks around: no human activity to report, not even a single sound. A flock of seagulls monitor the area from the sky – has she come to a ghost town?

'*Kysstu mig!*'

A ragged man with a huge, unwieldly beard grabs her arm. Hannah recoils in horror. Looks at him and instinctively identifies him as the town idiot, which there's bound to be in a place like this. His grip on her arm isn't strong, and she squirms free. Tries to reason with him in English.

'I'm sorry, I don't understand.'

'*Kysstu mig.* Give me a kiss!'

His lips pucker up under the filthy beard, his eyes boring into hers expectantly. Hannah almost has the urge to kiss him – she can't explain why, maybe just to surprise him. And herself. But the man smells of rotten herring, and rebelliousness does have a limit.

'Maybe another day.'

'Do you have any money?'

Ah, of course, after love comes money. Hannah pulls a crumpled bank note out of her pocket and extends it towards his grimy, out-stretched hand. She drops it onto his palm with a question:

'Is there a café round here?'

The beard grins. 'You're asking the right man. I know everything about this town, I see everything that goes on here. But I don't see a lot of fancy little cafés around, do you?'

Hannah smiles, has to hand it to him: a town idiot with sarcasm as flawless as his English. Maybe he's not such an idiot after all.

'Okay, no café. Where do people go to … meet up?'

'Home. The beach. Or Bragginn.'

'Bragginn?'

'The only bar in town.'

'Is it far?'

'I can show you. I was going to use this there myself.'

Hannah's donated bank note wafts about in the wind, held up by a dirty hand. Fine by her, she didn't have any higher ambitions for it anyway – being used at a bar is as good as anything else he might spend it on. One alcoholic cannot judge another. The rags turn and head off in the other direction, and Hannah follows, and wonders if she'll ever be so lonely that she starts begging strangers on the street for a kiss.

8

The familiar smell of a stuffy tavern emanates from Bragginn before they've even opened the door. Hannah follows her new friend inside and looks around the murky dive bar, a little disappointed – brown on brown, and other than the bar itself, there are just two tables, decked out with worn-out wax cloths, vases containing fake flowers and a few ashtrays. White plastic chairs are placed at the tables. Sat around one of the tables are a few locals – weather-beaten men who may have been fishermen, once upon a time, but who now look like they've given up. A larger variant of the same 'potential former fisherman turned miserable old man' sits at the slot machine. A woman in her early fifties stands at the bar with a dog at her feet, talking animatedly to the bartender – judging by her tone, the subject is clearly a very emotional one for her. The barman listens wearily, as if he's heard the same story a thousand times before, which he likely has. Everything looks like a piece from a typical dive-bar jigsaw puzzle. But one person doesn't fit. A dark-haired man sat at the bar, probably around the same age as Hannah, of an appearance most would deem attractive, or, rather, too groomed and well-functioning to be hanging out in a place like this on a Wednesday morning. Reading a book too ... and Hannah also clocks the glass of Coca-Cola in front of him. The town idiot leaves her side and heads to the bar, converting the money Hannah gave him, plus a little of his own, into a pint of beer. Pint in hand, and having already forgotten that Hannah is there, he makes his way over to the group of jaded old men around the wax table cloth. Hannah struggles up onto one of the high barstools next to the reading, Coca-Cola-drinking man. He looks up from his book, addresses her in English.

'Tourist?'

Hannah nods.

'Danish?'

'Yes. Is it that obvious?'

'Just a lucky guess. I'd say you could have passed as Icelandic, actually.'

'Why?'

'Hard to say ... Maybe it's the hair. Or the hardness of your gaze.'

Hannah stares at him, probably with some of the alleged hardness in her eyes. She hates being analysed by men she's just met – 'You're the type that this and that.' As if they can figure you out. But there's something about the Coca-Cola drinker that seems different, not as irritating. He waves the bartender over, who looks relieved to have an excuse to get away from the talkative dog owner. Hannah glances at her new conversation partner's cola, suppressing her morning wine craving.

'Sparkling water, thanks.'

Hannah gets her bottle of mineral water, pays and pours it into a glass. The man beside her watches as she does so, curious.

'We don't get many tourists at this time of year. And of all the places in the world, why holiday here?'

Hannah hesitates, not wanting to disclose her project. Doesn't need any more locals approaching her with their good ideas. Or maybe she does, actually. And she has no reason to lie.

'I'm here to write a book.'

'Okay. So you're an author?'

Hannah senses a genuine enthusiasm and straightens her back a little. She nods.

'What kind of books do you write?'

The Coca-Cola drinker closes his own book, giving Hannah his full attention. She takes a sip of the carbonated water, not feeling quite ready to label herself as a crime writer just yet. But, on the other hand, she can't bring herself to explain the reasons why she's shifted from introspective prose to writing crime fiction. She chooses the shortest possible explanation.

'I usually write novellas, but I'm currently experimenting with crime.'

The man stares at her, quizzically. 'You're experimenting with crime? Well, in that case, I should probably arrest you.'

It's Hannah's turn to look quizzically at him.

'I'm a policeman. Viktor.'

Viktor extends the hand of the law to Hannah, and she shakes it.

'Hannah.'

She nods at his jeans and cotton shirt.

'Are you undercover?'

Viktor laughs into his cola.

'It'd be particularly difficult to go undercover in a town where everyone knows who you are. I'm just not working right now.'

Viktor glances at his wristwatch. It's not automatic, he genuinely looks like he's lost track of the time.

'If you're going to commit a crime and want to get away with it, I'd do it in the next thirty-two minutes.'

'Are you the only officer here?'

Viktor nods. Hannah can't quite work out if it's a nod laden with responsibility or pride; maybe a touch of both.

'Do you not investigate crimes committed outside working hours?' Hannah sees her chance to find some criminological inspiration.

Viktor smiles. 'I try to keep up with everything that happens round here, of course, but to be perfectly honest, there's not that much to keep up with. A couple of the local teenagers stole a crate of beer from someone's garage yesterday, and every now and then I'll catch a car with a broken headlight. But that's about it really.'

Right. So the local environment won't provide much inspiration for the book. Hannah wrings her hands and looks longingly at the shelf of hard spirits. Senses Viktor watching her, turns back to him and points to the book.

'What are you reading?'

Viktor flips over the cover so that it's facing Hannah. She reads it, tries to pronounce the Icelandic.

'*Ljóð 1980–1995*. Einar Már Guðmundsson.'

'She won the Nordic Council Literature Prize in 1995.'

Hannah suppresses the childish urge to drop into the conversation something about her own name and the Nordic Council Literature Prize.

'I know him. I was particularly inspired by *Frankensteins kup* when I first started writing.'

Confused, Viktor flips the book over in his hand. 'Oh, right. I'm not familiar with that one. Maybe it's got a different name in Icelandic?'

'Most certainly. I feel like everything's called something else entirely in Icelandic.'

Viktor smiles, takes another sip of his Coke. 'Well, regardless, you must be a great writer if you're inspired by that man. I'll have to read one of your books someday.'

Hannah struggles to work out whether the statement is an attempt to compliment her, or whether it's praise for Einar Már. In her head, she calls it fifty-fifty. She tries to remember when she last got even fifty percent of a compliment from a man. And can't.

'I don't know if you'll like what I write. It's short prose, some call it poetry.'

'Interesting.'

Hannah scrutinises him. 'Tell me, what kind of police officer enjoys reading poetry?'

'What kind of a poet experiments with crime?'

Viktor holds her gaze. She holds his.

'I think that a police officer reading poetry before he goes on shift longs for something more.'

Viktor's gaze doesn't waver. 'And what do you think he longs for?'

Hannah shrugs. 'I don't know. For something new to happen.'

Viktor smiles, shakes his head. He takes a quick look at his watch again, picks up the book. 'What I really want is more peace and quiet.'

Hannah's hope that Viktor could be the key to unlocking a good plot for the book reawakens. 'So your job's not all that peaceful after all...?'

Viktor smiles. 'What I need is some peace from my two kids at home. My wife looks after them, and two others, so I need to get out of the house for a bit, otherwise I'm filled with the urge to arrest all four of them. And there's something not quite right about putting toddlers in jail.'

Viktor slides down from the bar stool. Smooth. He extends his hand. Formal.

'It was a pleasure to meet you. If you happen to come across a murder or the like, you know who to call.'

He smiles. Hannah finds it difficult to imagine him dealing with a crime more serious than the theft of a fishing boat. She nods.

'And I mean it: I'd really like to read your books sometime.'

'It was nice meeting you.'

Hannah watches as Viktor disappears out the door, and once she's made sure he's not coming back, she turns to the barman and utters the cathartic words:

'Whisky and coke.'

The sky has closed in, the darkness now settling around the town, lurking over the mountains. Half drunk, Hannah finds herself outside again, the gale now ushering her back through the streets. She heads home, feeling even less inspired than when she left. She tried to coax some stories out of the beer-drinking locals at the bar, who did actually turn out to be world-weary ex-fishermen, and who unfortunately didn't know enough English to say anything other than 'cheers'. Hannah looks towards the mountains, feels a stubborn optimism. It won't come from the outside, it has to come from herself. And she has it in her, she knows she does. Get home, open a bottle of wine, sit in front of the computer. Write something. She picks up the pace, stomps back up the dark country road.

Only halfway there physically, but already there in her mind, she notices a group of boys – young men would be more accurate – out of the corner of her eye.

They looked about seventeen, give or take a year. Faces flushed and wearing far too few clothes in the ice-cold November wind, running around on turf that looks more like a regular field than a football pitch. It's elevated from the former to the latter only thanks to the two goals they've set up at either end and one giant floodlight, enabling them to see the ball even when the darkness rolls in. Hannah doesn't remember seeing a football pitch on her way into town. Surrounded by the plains, the mountains and the endless, dark-grey sky, the boys look significantly smaller than they actually are. She stops and watches them, fascinated – playing in nature's stadium, concentrating, shouting, intense. Completely engrossed in the match. Until the ball is kicked far past the goal, way off-course, and it rolls to a stop close to Hannah. One of the boys sprints after it. The others look on, one shouts something in Icelandic. The wind swallows his words, but Hannah can sense it was about her. They don't look like they're used to spectators. Two of them laugh. The boy who ran after the ball approaches. Hannah takes a few quick steps towards the ball, gets there before him and sends it his way with a light kick. He stops. Looks at her, smiles.

'Thanks.'

They stand there for a moment, looking at each other, as if they both want to say something more but can't think what. The boy smiles again, takes the ball and punts it back over to his friends and the game. Hannah realises that she knows those piercing, engaging eyes. Ella's nephew, Thor. She walks away from the football match with the feeling that perhaps things do actually happen in Húsafjörður after all. And in that moment, the heavens open. Hannah tries to dart up the road between downpours, but gives up. She practically sails down the last stretch of the gloomy lane. When she eventually reaches the house, Ella is waiting for her in the open doorway, a towel in one hand and a cup of coffee in the other.

9

Hannah has spent the entire night writing, the result of which is half a page of attempted plot. Plenty of words, but nothing about a murder. She's slept for half an hour, called Bastian three times with no success, drank one and a half bottles of wine, been close a number of times to giving up entirely, but still returned to the keyboard each time. She sat in the same position for too long, silently watching the sun rise and feeling her confidence in her success leave her body with each minute that passed. When she eventually drags herself downstairs the next morning, it's with a packed suitcase and the bitter recognition that she cannot write a crime novel. She has already started writing her speech in her head; the thought of Jørn's expression when he hears that she gave up makes her palms sweaty. But there's nothing else that can be done; with hubris, comes one's nemesis. Maybe she doesn't have to go back to Denmark – she could go somewhere else entirely, disappear, start a new life on a little plot of land somewhere, where her failed projects can't find her.

In the kitchen, she finds Ella, sat at the dining table, hunched over, sobbing. Bewildered, Hannah stops in her tracks.

She edges closer to Ella, like a boat quietly drifting into the dock. Gently, she sits down beside the broken woman, unsure of the situation. She's never been a 'hand-on-shoulder, what's-wrong' type of person.

'Has something happened?'

Ella cries even louder. Hannah attempts the soothing hand-on-shoulder method.

'What is it?'

Ella's body shakes, her wrinkled hands covering her tearful face. Hannah didn't think that people of Ella's age were capable of showing their emotions so expressively – don't you reach a certain point in your life where having a breakdown is a thing of the past?

Perhaps not. Hannah has a feeling that something awful must've happened, and that now would not be the time to announce her departure. Ella looks in no fit state to drive anyone to the airport. Hannah asks for the third time:

'What are you upset about?'

This time, Ella looks up. *'Thor er dáinn.'*

Hannah looks questioningly at Ella, who grabs a piece of paper from across the table – it looks like some kind of official letter, but she seems indifferent to its contents. She flips it over and writes on the back:

Thor is dead.

The surprise forces Hannah ten centimetres back into the chair. Thor? But she had looked into those youthful, lively eyes not twenty hours ago. And now he's stopped breathing, his heart has stopped beating, his legs have kicked the ball across the pitch for the last time? That can't be right. Ella must have misunderstood something that someone said to her.

'Who told you?'

'Vigdis,' comes out of Ella's mouth, accompanied with a sniffle. Hannah doesn't follow.

'Who is Vigdis?'

Ella doesn't respond, is instead overwhelmed with a convulsive new round of sobbing, as if she has just been delivered the terrible news for the first time. Or is it more a recognition of what the dead boy means to her that has caused these fresh tears? If he is dead, that is. Hannah's still doubtful. What could he possibly have died of? And can you even be so alive one day, and so dead the next? She tries to find some meaning in all this.

'Ella, I am so sorry to hear about that. How did he die? What do you know?' She is acutely aware of her own hand as it moves up and down Ella's back in a stroking motion. A gesture of sympathy, or an attempt to persuade her to communicate? Ella heaves, the crying subsiding for a moment, and under the palm of her hand, Hannah feels that Ella composes herself a little. A handkerchief, one made of typical, old-fashioned fabric, is pulled out of a sleeve, and Ella wipes her nose. Picks up the pen again.

Min søster Vigdis call, hun said Thor died in the night. Accident.

Tears stream down Ella's cheeks.

'Ég skil þetta ekki! Ég skil þetta bara ekki!'

Hannah is still confused.

'So, Vigdis is your sister, Thor's mother?'

Ella nods.

'And you're absolutely sure that you haven't misunderstood? That maybe he *has* been in an accident, but is in hospital or something like that?'

Ella stares at her. Long. Gravely. And then writes:

Death is not something you misunderstand. I no it is sånn even if I have not seen him. I kan feel it.

'Feel it?'

Ella writes:

Strong six sense.

Hannah takes a deep breath. She was almost ready to be convinced of Thor's death, but could it be just something Ella feels? Did she receive the phone call in a dream, and the dream has extended into her reality? Hannah has never had great faith in a sixth, seventh or eighth sense. She needs hard facts. She stands, goes over to Ella's landline.

'What's Vigdis's number?'

Ella looks up at her. The crying has stopped, but it's left her face sopping wet, like a riverbank after the tide. She shakes her head, is on her feet surprisingly quick, and in the next moment is beside Hannah and the phone is now in her hand instead. Hannah barely has time to acknowledge her agile movement. Ella, now almost angry, hurriedly flips to the back of the address book.

You do not believe me, but det er true. Thor IS dead. Accident at harbour. The world er EVIL.

Something about Ella's handwriting finally convinces Hannah. Maybe the capital letters. Hannah gulps. It's hard to avoid using the same, old cliched phrases when trying to express sympathy.

'I am so sorry, Ella. Is there anything I can do?'

Ella shakes her head, but in the same motion, changes it to a nod. Again, using the address book as a mode of communication, she almost writes over the top of an entry under the name Bjargey.

The memorial ceremoni this aften. Vill you kome?

Ella looks at her imploringly, as if she would find a little comfort in Hannah's presence.

Hannah nods. 'Of course. If you don't think it would be too intrusive having a stranger at such an event?'

Ella stares at her for a moment. And writes:

You liv in mitt house, you are not stranger.

Something stirs in Hannah. She's not sure what.

'Shall I make us a cup of coffee?'

Without waiting for an answer, Hannah heads over to the filter machine and catches a glimpse of her packed suitcase out in the hallway. The journey-home fiasco would have to be postponed.

10

The house radiates death. Hannah has noticed that when someone dies, an air of mystery suddenly develops around them, resulting in a bizarre desperation among those left behind to learn more about the deceased person. And this seems true of both the people closest to them, and those who never even met the person when they were alive. And if they happened to die an untimely death, maybe as a result of a crime, this fascination only grows. We want to know everything about the circumstances surrounding their death and the hours leading up to it: what was the last thing you thought about, the last thing you ate? Did you enjoy your final bath? What were your plans for the next day? And the all-important question: did you know, before that fateful moment, that death was awaiting you? But it's not just the factual circumstances around the transition from life to death that pique one's curiosity about the recently deceased; Hannah has always felt that there's another reason why we show such interest in the dead, namely because of the insight they must have gained. She has fantasised about shaking the deceased awake again, to gain some of that wisdom: You know something about life that we don't, she would say. You know what it's like to be dead. How is it? Does it hurt? Is there anything on the other side? With what final thought does one part with this world? When you think back, were you able to do what you wanted to, find the answers you were looking for, feel like you were alive? At the end of the day, it's not the dead we're interested in. It's ourselves. The death of another forces the bereaved to reflect on their own lives. Through death, we can put everything into perspective, look at the details of one's own life anew. And ponder in what way death may eventually come for *us*.

Like a respectful bodyguard, Hannah escorts Ella into the massive house – the kind you see on those programmes about prestigious, neo-Nordic, architect-designed properties. Grand, open-plan rooms with immense windows looking out onto the landscape, so the mountains almost seem as if they're a part of the living room. Interior design features that suggest a taste for high quality, with expensive designer furniture providing further testimony. A home almost too modern and beautiful to be found in such a remote town. How much money did they spend on all this? The tasteful luxury is, however, disrupted by the monumental grief currently filling the room. Hannah looks around, taking in the tense, tear-stained faces, and finds herself infected by the heavy atmosphere. Before she takes another step inside, a bed in the centre of the room catches her eye. All attention is drawn towards it. Thor's body lies in state. Dead. Hannah feels a lump form in her throat. Why is he here? Is it normal to be present for one's own memorial ceremony? Hannah doesn't do well around dead bodies. She's only ever seen a corpse once before, on the tracks outside Dybbølsbro train station. Two police officers had tried to shield it from view, but hadn't been able to cover it

entirely. She was curious. She caught a glimpse of it as she cycled past
– the body rigid, sprawled across the rails, wrapped in plastic, with
just the head sticking out, uncovered. She shouldn't have looked. Life
went on, as if it couldn't do anything but continue. On the way down
the stairs to the platform, trying to keep her balance while carrying
her bike, she passed some young guy heading the other way,
boombox on his shoulder blasting out music, wearing a pair of
shorts, a cap and a grey sweatshirt, walking with a bounce in his step,
dancing, full of life. She'd wanted to grab hold of him and scream,
Stop! There's a dead person on the tracks over there! But she didn't.
That was her experience – she was the one who saw the body down
there, in the midst of the summer's most violent thunderstorm, not
the boy with the boombox. For him, life couldn't be more alive. And
why would she want to rob him of that? She had taken one last look
over at the bridge above the station, where a car was parked – a green
car that the now cold and rigid person must have driven to the bridge
before he jumped. And all she could think was: *In his moment of
death, I'd been standing in the supermarket, struggling to decide
between buying the red or the white wine.*

'Ella!'

A woman hurls herself at Ella with a smothering and desperate
hug, as if she were trying to unload all her grief onto her. Ella wraps
her arms around the woman and accepts it. The embrace seems to
last for an eternity. Hannah watches the two women in silence as
they hold on tightly to each other, triggering a sequence of emotions
in herself: first sympathy, then self-conscious discomfort, and finally
the less complicated irritation. How long can you leave a guest
standing at an event like this without introducing them? Hannah
shifts her weight from one foot to the other and clears her throat.
Ella hears it and pulls away from the embrace, finally presenting
Hannah to the woman: Vigdis. Ella's sister, Thor's mother, Hannah
understands.

'My condolences. I am incredibly sorry for your loss.'

Hannah studies Vigdis. She must be a good few years younger than Ella, although she also looks like she has aged significantly overnight. Vigdis nods, and, understandably, doesn't seem to have the energy to engage any further with a stranger. Rapid Icelandic sentences tumble out of her anguished mouth. Ella responds, comforting and supportive, suppressing her own feelings to take the weight off her sister's. Hannah looks around the room. The saddened faces turn to each other for short conversations. She can hear grief, surprise and confusion in the incomprehensible Icelandic words. In an attempt to avoid looking directly at Thor's mattress shrine, her eyes explore every corner of the room, as even though something in her longs to look at the macabre sight of the dead young man, it feels inappropriate to stare. Perhaps she's also scanning the room in an attempt to find a hidden nook to escape into – she feels out of place here, like the invading foreigner she essentially is. She notices a man sitting in a corner, as if made of stone, his expressionless face staring at the dead boy. Stoicism, or a rare form of self-punishment? Hannah watches as guests walk past and offer their condolences to the stone man, who doesn't respond. He must be Thor's father, Ægir. Hannah feels the discomfort burrowing further into her skin – she shouldn't have come. She regrets having doubted Ella about Thor's death. Feels guilty in a way. Is it because she wanted a death for her crime novel and was given one? She shakes away the thought. It's not even certain that a crime has been committed. Most likely not. Hannah pulls herself together, has to clench her teeth and stay there for Ella, override her aversion to being involved in other people's intimate moments. But, Christ alive, she could do with a drink. Or at least a coffee. Her sleepless night has just hit her like a hard ball in the back of the neck. She takes a deep breath and eyes a door to something that looks like a kitchen. Walks towards it.

She steps inside and starts – Viktor. Standing with his back to her, about to pour a cup of coffee. Is he here as a friend of the family or as a detective? Betting on the latter, Hannah takes her chance.

'So crimes do happen in Húsafjörður after all?'

Viktor turns – calmly, almost as if he was expecting her to be right behind him. He passes her the coffee he's just poured.

'I thought you'd be here.'

This surprises Hannah. 'Why?'

'Because Ella is not the type of person who would leave her guest home alone on a day like this.'

Surprise, again.

'How do you know that I'm staying with Ella?'

'I am the supreme authority here in town. I know everything.'

Viktor pours himself a new cup of coffee, turns and leans back against the kitchen counter. Scrutinises Hannah, coffee in hand. Hannah takes a sip from her cup. It tastes bitter.

'So you know how Thor died then?'

Viktor, who has been holding Hannah's gaze, now lowers it, shakes his head and takes a sip of his coffee too, all in one movement.

'Was it a crime?' Now it is Hannah who scrutinises Viktor.

'Sorry, but I can't comment on the case.'

'So there is a case?'

Viktor sighs. 'That's not what I said.'

'But are you here as the police or a friend of the family?'

'Sorry, but I really can't say anything else.'

'You've not said anything.'

Viktor smiles. Disarmed. He straightens up as if to head back into the living room. Hannah tries one last time – she can't ask questions once they're back among the grieving.

'Why is he here? The body, I mean.'

Viktor hesitates, as if he wants to share something with her but knows he shouldn't. Want wins over duty.

'It was Ægir, the father's idea. He insisted. I don't like it though. We need to do an autopsy.'

Hannah raises her eyebrows. 'An autopsy.'

'Purely routine when someone drowns.' Viktor's tone reveals

nothing. 'The coroner's coming from Reykjavík, should be here in about an hour, so we'll take the body then.'

'So Thor drowned?'

Viktor nods. 'His father found him this morning, down by the water. Pulled him out himself.'

'How did it happen?'

Viktor sighs and drains the rest of his coffee in one gulp. 'That's a bit of a mystery.'

Viktor puts the cup on the counter. Hannah has a thousand more questions to ask him, but he's already disappeared into the living room. She looks down at the coffee – thick and brown, like slurry. She empties it into the sink.

She returns to the living room, but no Viktor. Damn. Forces herself to go over to the body. At a distance he just looks like a young man, asleep and weirdly exhibited among his family and friends. Close up, however, it is obvious he's dead. Slightly swollen, most likely from having spent so long in sea water. Hannah's unease surprises her, but she forces herself to look at him. His hair is pasted unnaturally to his forehead, and behind his right ear, a piece of seaweed, like a hairpin of death. But what's that? Hannah leans in, reaches for the strip of seaweed, and realises it's covering something. Blood. She feels around behind his ear – there, a little bump.

'Hvernig dirfistu að snerta son minn?'

Hannah quickly retracts her hand, turns and finds herself inches from Ægir's face. The stone man has risen from his plinth. Hannah is suddenly, embarrassingly aware of her inappropriate behaviour, standing there, groping a corpse!

'I'm sorry.'

The stone man stares at her, his eyes disconcertingly empty. Hannah wonders whether he is thinking about hitting her. She instinctively ducks down slightly at the thought. But the stone man seems to be locked into a new position now, like a zombie who's forgotten his mission. Hannah trips backward away from the body, away from the grief and the emptiness.

11

The road is almost flooded – another downpour. Hannah slips and slides back to town, happy to have escaped the odd home chapel, where she has left Ella, promising to meet after the viewing. She stops and shudders, struggling to shake off the feeling of disquiet. She looks in the direction of Ella's house, hesitates for a moment. Continues to walk into town.

Hannah has to knock twice before the door opens. Viktor looks down at her, surprised.

'Did you follow me?'

'I have a reputation back in Denmark for being a bit of a stalker.'

Viktor raises an eyebrow. 'Not to be rude or anything, but I'm busy.'

Hannah tries to peek over his shoulder – the police station doesn't seem to be a public building, but rather, his private home with a sign on the door. The floor is drowning in children's toys. Viktor follows her gaze and makes himself wider in the doorway, trying to hide the mess.

'Come on, my office is this way.'

'In your bedroom or the children's room?'

No trace of a smile, just a slight lowering of his shoulders and a hand gesture that suggests they should head outside. As Viktor closes the door, Hannah glimpses the silhouette of a woman in the kitchen. Viktor's wife? Outside, the plainclothes policeman leads her round the side of the building to another door – a little office with its own entrance. The police station.

Hannah looks around the room, decoding: it resembles a sad real-estate agency from a crappy American film – desk made of undefined, inexpensive black wood dropped smack, bang in the middle of the room, with a dusty old PC, jumbled stacks of paper and a mouse pad with a photo of two children. Probably Viktor's. Behind the table, a fake leather chair balances on four small wheels in front of a packed bookcase, red binders poking out from the shelves. On the wall: a map of the local area and an almost empty bulletin board. All in all, a perfectly average, boring room.

'What a cosy little office.' Hannah sticks her hands into her jacket pockets, trying to look as nonchalant as possible.

'What can I do for you?'

Straight to the point – okay, okay. Viktor stands in front of her, arms crossed.

'I just thought of something, about Thor. Did he get hit on the head before or after he died?'

His eyebrow raises again. Aha! So Viktor hasn't noticed the bump.

The eyebrow settles back into its usual place. 'As I said, I can't comment on the case.'

'Maybe he hit his head when he fell into the water?'

Viktor shifts his weight from one foot to the other, uncomfortable. Hannah can tell he wants to ask how she knows, but doesn't want to expose his own ignorance. She helps him out of the dilemma.

'Behind his right ear there's a bloody wound and a bump. Maybe he hit his head on a rock when he fell in, or hit a piece of wood or a boat, or something, after, when he was floating around unconscious in the water?'

Hannah pauses. Looks at Viktor intently. He is now biting his lip. A perfectly nice man – but a good policeman? A few seconds of silence elapses – counted out by their calm breaths – before she takes the floor again.

'Or maybe someone hit Thor over the head from behind, and that's how he ended up falling into the water and drowning...'

Viktor changes position again, but still doesn't comment on her theory.

Hannah is insistent. 'What do you think?'

Viktor folds his arms even tighter across his chest, as if he's his own straitjacket. 'I think you should stop playing private detective and let me do my job.'

'But are you doing your job when you've let the body of a possible murder victim lie on show for the whole town to see? The whole town, including his killer – if there is one – who could manipulate the corpse and remove any evidence?'

Hannah has managed to get herself up to speed pretty quickly, and is happy that watching an episode or two of some slow, British detective series every now and then has come in use. Sweat starts to form on Viktor's forehead. It would seem that this is a highly unusual case for him, and if there's some protocol to follow, he's already broken it.

'As I said, I'm waiting for the coroner. He'll be here any moment.'

'Why aren't you waiting for him with Thor's family?'

Her question seems to puncture his professional pride. He wipes his brow.

'I don't want to cause them any more stress. You have to go now.'

Viktor loosens the straitjacket and gestures to the door. The sweat on his brow has now formed small droplets.

Hannah doesn't move. 'Listen, I'm not trying to criticise your work. I just want to help. Maybe, if we share our thoughts we could help each other, and find out what happened together?'

Viktor snorts – she's not sure whether it's with uncertainty or arrogance.

Whichever it is, he tries to cover it up with a fake smile. 'Sorry, but just because you noticed a wound on Thor's body doesn't mean I have to share anything else with you. In fact, I would advise you to stay out of this. No, "advise" is the wrong word – I *order* you to stay out of it. Go back to your writing and let me do my job.' Viktor opens the door and nods towards the outside.

Hannah's not ready to let go yet. 'You said that it was Ægir who pulled him out of the water?'

Viktor sighs, tired. 'No comment.'

'But isn't that weird? I mean, for a father to find their own son after they've drowned ... Was he out looking for him?'

Viktor stays silent. But his eyebrow rises and falls again. Ah, so

Viktor hasn't asked Ægir what actually happened when he found his son.

'It's only been six hours. His parents are still in shock. You saw them yourself.'

Six hours. Hannah is still a criminological novice, but to her, six hours sounds like an eternity – the possible culprit could erase or conceal their tracks several times over. If a crime even took place, that is. She tries again.

'But you must have spoken to them? Mapped out how Thor spent his last hours?'

Viktor sighs again, but looks like he may be on the verge of saying something. Maybe feels the need to demonstrate that he's not entirely incompetent.

Hannah encourages him. 'You must suspect that something untoward took place, seeing as you referred to Thor's death as "the case"? And you weren't in the house just to show your respect and check in on the parents. You were there to do what any good policeman would do in such a situation: talk to the family and friends to try and get an overview of the circumstances around the death.'

'No one said anything useful.'

Aha! Viktor can be buttered up with compliments.

Hannah lays it on thick now: 'You're sharp. You've found something out that I haven't.'

Bingo. Viktor hesitates, closes the door and faces her, a new look of confidentiality in his eyes.

'Thor can't swim. The entire town knows it. He's scared of the water and will never become a fisherman – something that was a great disappointment to his father.'

'Is his father a fisherman?'

Viktor nods. 'Thor never even goes near the water. Which is quite the problem when you live by the sea and have to earn from it, as we do.'

'But he did last night...?'

Viktor nods again. 'He was drunk, had a row with his friend Jonni and left his house to go home. Jonni was the last person to see him alive.'

Hannah mulls it over.

'And how is Jonni taking it? I mean, he must be crushed...'

Viktor hesitates, obviously thinking through whether he should say any more. Then he meets Hannah's gaze with his blue-grey, northern-light eyes.

'Jonni hasn't been seen since last night.'

And then, a knock on the door.

A woman sticks her head round the door. She doesn't even register Hannah, just addresses Viktor directly.

'*Læknirinn er kominn.*'

Viktor nods.

With her hand still resting on the door handle, the woman looks at Hannah with elevator eyes – as if only just noticing she is there. What must she see – a bedraggled, alcoholic author, a competitor for her husband's affections, a stranger? Hannah returns the woman's gaze. It seems the woman sees something else entirely. But what?

'My wife, Margrét.'

Margrét extends her hand towards her – straight, almost militant; and Hannah takes it – soft yet firm at the same time. Like the muzzle of a new-born calf.

'Hannah.'

Margrét gives Hannah's hand a little squeeze – sisterly recognition, or a warning? She studies Margrét. Viktor's a lucky man. You would hardly find her on the cover of a fashion magazine, she is too unpolished and angular for that. Fortunately, Hannah loathes the prevailing cutesy-pretty-cheeky-sweet female ideal, by which skinny women with breasts far too large and make-up far too heavy are lauded for their carb-free buns and fashion sense, both before and after childbirth. Margrét is different. Dark hair braided like thick rope down her back, high cheekbones framing her intense brown eyes, matching Hannah's in their persistence. Margrét is tall, but still a few centimetres shorter than Hannah. Her body looks strong, as if it were formed by flowing lava.

Viktor looks at Hannah. 'Sorry, I've got to go. And so do you.' He once again makes a gesture signalling that the meeting is over, but Hannah doesn't want to miss the opportunity to meet the coroner performing Thor's autopsy. She is prepared to compromise, using her own ingenuity.

'Could I just use your toilet real quick? I really, really need to go.'

Shit! Hannah looks around the small, cream-coloured bathroom, at the Disney-character-themed coat hooks from which child-sized towels hang, and the red plastic stool pushed halfway under the sink. She leans against the windowsill. Damn it. This wasn't the plan. She was shown into the toilet before she could wangle an introduction to the coroner. He and Viktor got straight into a car and drove back up to Thor's house. Hannah thinks through her options. She needs to make sure she's a step ahead of the investigation, get hold of knowledge that Viktor doesn't yet have. Make him dependent on her. She leaves the toilet without using it, just turns the water on and off and unlocks the door. She finds Margrét in the kitchen amidst the chaos left by the children's lunch. She's sitting at the dining table, smoking – blowing the smoke out of the window, a wooden train track in pieces, scattered across the floor.

'I know I shouldn't smoke. Give the children lung cancer and whatever. But it's my only luxury.'

Margrét exhales, filling the air outside with a plume of smoke. Hannah observes her: not exactly an Icelandic Mary Poppins. More like a character from a French New Wave film; not Goddard though. More weighed down by the hardships of everyday life. Truffaut perhaps. Yes. She could easily be a heroine in a Truffaut film. *The Woman Next Door*.

'May I?' Hannah points at the pack.

Margrét nods, somewhat surprised, but smiles, as if there were happiness to be found in sinning in company.

Hannah lights the cigarette, leans towards the window.

'So, what made you want to become a full-time babysitter?'

'Why not?'

Hannah is taken aback by the prompt response. Sure. Why not? So simple. Why not indeed?

'It was either that or work at the bar.'

'I'd probably have preferred to work at the bar.'

'Are you an alcoholic by any chance?'

Margrét looks at Hannah directly – no irony, no attempt to create any comedic distance. Hannah is filled with the sudden and unfamiliar urge to be honest, both with the stranger, and with herself.

'Yep. Sure am.'

'Does it make you happier?'

Hannah mulls it over.

'For a while.'

Margrét nods. As if she understands it well and there is nothing odd or shameful about it. Then turns back to the window, looks out as if searching for something specific. Seemingly without success.

'It's a shame – about Thor.'

Hannah takes a deep breath in, sharpens all her senses. 'Did you know him well?'

Margrét shrugs in a way that could be interpreted as yes and no. She stubs out her cigarette and closes the window. Hannah has a feeling that there's something she's not saying.

She observes Margrét, who has now begun to clear away the lunch mess, putting the dishes in the dishwasher.

'I've got to clean up before the kids wake up from their naps.'

Hannah stubs out her own cigarette.

'Sorry, I won't take up any more of your time. I do just want to ask you one thing before I go: do you know where Jonni lives?'

The volcanic woman turns to her.

'Don't stick your nose too deep into all this. This town has secrets that are best left alone.'

Hannah could die of curiosity.

'What does that mean?'

Margrét rinses off one of the plates in the sink, scrapes off some of the dried food.

'I really need to get this done.'

'Okay. Jonni's address, though – do you have it?'

Margrét continues scraping away at the sink.

'I'm telling you: if you stick your nose in too deep, it'll get cut off.'

Hannah stays put.

'I'm sure it'll grow back. Please: where does Jonni live?'

12

Hannah trudges back out onto the country road. How bizarre. Margrét's welcoming familiarity, so quickly replaced by that closed-off dismissal. And those secrets and warnings. What is it Margrét isn't saying?

Hannah managed to get Jonni's address, at least, which turns out to be just a few hundred metres down the road from Viktor and Margrét's police-station home. She looks up, sees Vatnajökull glistening in the distance, Iceland's largest glacier and the local tourist attraction. Hannah has no intention of seeing it up close, she doesn't like the snow, least of all the kind of compacted snow that never melts. On top of which, snow has been taken hostage by the Christmas industry, as if it's some magical powder that when sprinkled over everything will make everyone sappy and tolerant and will engender world peace. But that's an illusion. The world doesn't suddenly become a better place just because there's a white Christmas. Real snow is either dirty or deadly. It's a good thing the ice caps are melting, because we'll be rid of it altogether. Ach, not really, of course she doesn't believe that. She just can't be arsed trekking all that way to see an infernal glacier. It's literally just compacted snow. Compacted false idylls. There are meant to be numerous volcanoes under the glacier as well. What would happen if one of them erupted and melted the whole damn glacier? Would Iceland be submerged?

The sound of her phone ringing pulls Hannah out of her thoughts. After fumbling about for it in her pockets, she picks up.

'Hannah here.'

'Good to hear your voice. Are you okay?' Bastian sounds concerned.

'Why wouldn't I be?'

'I got your email. About you wanting to come home. I've had a busy day so I've only just seen it. Are you at the airport?'

Oh. Right. The email she'd sent Bastian about her crime-writing ineptitude and her plans to travel home.

'I'm still here, decided to stay. There's been a murder.'

'What did you say? A murder?'

Bastian is quiet for a moment.

'You didn't do it, did you?'

Hannah smiles. Doesn't blame him for thinking it, to be fair.

'Yes. I've butchered Ella with her bread knife as she slept, and I've just been arrested.'

A sigh of relief from Bastian.

'Seriously. Who died and how? And are you sure it's a good idea for you to stay up there if there's a murderer on the loose?'

'The victim was a young man – Thor, Ella's nephew. Unbelievably tragic. He drowned.'

'Drowned? But the police think it's a murder?' Bastian sounds as sceptical as he does curious.

'Well, not the police, exactly. The local policeman here, Viktor – he suspects that a crime was committed, and I know it was.'

'Oh, you're the new Inspector Morse, are you?'

'I see myself more as a Jessica Fletcher.'

Silence.

'From that 1980s crime drama, what's it called ... *Hun så et mord*. You know, *She Saw a Murder*.'

'Aha – you saw the murder then?'

'No, wait, it's *Murder, She Wrote*. Anyway, it's not about actually seeing the murder. It's about seeing everything else around it that points towards the real culprit.'

Hannah can sense Bastian smiling.

'I must say, it's a bit of a surprise to find you've suddenly taken on the role of rogue detective. But it can't be bad for the book, I suppose.'

Bastian pauses for dramatic effect.

'Because you'll be using it for inspiration, right?'

Hannah thinks about it.

'To be honest, I don't really know what I'm using it for just now. First and foremost, I want to help find out what happened. For Ella's sake.'

'That sounds almost compassionate of you.'

'Maybe that's exactly what it is.'

Hannah surprises herself. Openly compassionate. In reality, she's just extremely curious.

'At the end of the day, my motive for getting involved is irrelevant. If nothing else, I've never been closer to thinking in terms of "plot" in my life. Which must mean something good for this bloody novel.'

'So it lives then?'

'It's alive and well. Or rather, it's been given another chance at life.'

'Hannah, promise me you'll be careful. I mean it: you mustn't get too deep into something you can't control. You can't put yourself in danger.'

'My entire career is based on being torn apart by people. How could my life be in any more danger than it already is?'

Bastian sighs. 'Fine. But you still have to prepare yourself for the press. I'll try and keep them at bay here, but be aware that it could all go downhill if anyone finds out that you're snooping about up there, investigating a murder when you're meant to be on your crime-writing holiday.'

'Holiday?'

Hannah isn't given the chance to rebuke him as the connection breaks off. She drops her phone in her pocket and gazes over at Vatnajökull again. The glacier looks as if it has crept a little further down the mountain.

The doorbell chimes briefly before the door is promptly opened by a woman in a traditional Icelandic jumper, with deep, dark circles under her eyes.

'Good morning, I'm Hannah, I'm currently staying with Ella, and I just wanted to ... erm...'

The woman stares at her. Expectantly. No attempt made to help mitigate the awkward moment.

'I just wanted to deliver a letter to Jonni. From Ella. She wanted to write him a few comforting words she thought might help, and to invite him up for a cup of tea as well. To talk about what happened.'

Hannah passes the woman the letter, tries to keep her hand from shaking. She looks down at it, and Hannah hopes to Christ that she doesn't open it and read it. Then she would see that the letter is not, in fact, from Ella, but from Hannah, and that it is not, in fact, an invitation for tea and chat and to grieve together, but a request to meet and talk with her, Hannah, about Jonni's friendship with Thor. The woman continues to stare down at the letter, a look of scepticism on her face now.

'Ella has a phone. She could just call if she wanted to talk to Jonni.'

The woman closes the door, but Hannah just about manages to shove the tip of her boot in the gap between it and the frame.

'I know Jonni is missing. So Ella couldn't just call him, right?'

The door opens ever so slightly.

'How do you know that Jonni is missing?' The woman looks at Hannah anew, more critically now.

'I've just been to Thor's house. To the memorial ceremony.'

Fear clouds the woman's face. 'So does everyone know?'

She is clearly afraid of her son becoming the town's prime suspect, people thinking that he had something to do with Thor's death. A justified concern. Hannah shakes her head in the hope of reassuring the woman.

'I spoke to Viktor, the policeman. He mentioned it. I don't think anyone else knows that Jonni has disappeared.'

Hannah doesn't actually know that's the case, but she hopes the statement wins the woman over a little. Just enough for her to pass the letter on to Jonni. If he comes home. The strategy works. After thinking it through for a moment, the jumper-clad woman reaches through the gap in the door and takes the letter, thankfully without opening it.

'I'll give it to him when he comes back.'

The woman's calm conviction catches Hannah off guard.

'When...? Does he go missing often?'

The woman doesn't answer, but Hannah can see by her expression that he does.

'Where does he normally go, and what does he do?'

'I have to go now.'

The woman closes the door in Hannah's face without so much as a goodbye.

13

Hungry. Hannah checks the time. 14:48. She still hasn't had anything to eat yet, and with everything that's happened, it feels like it's been days since she did. On top of that, she's also unsure about how to proceed with her investigation, but feels that she should probably examine the place where Thor's body was found, even though she has no idea where exactly that is. And it's already getting dark. One thing she is sure of, however, is where she might find both food and more information: Bragginn.

Almost as if she were at home, she climbs comfortably up onto the barstool. A handful of resigned ex-fishermen occupy a corner of the bar, but Hannah can't quite tell whether they are the same ones who were here last time. How embarrassing that she doesn't seem to see individuals when she looks at them, but rather a mass of human sadness. She searches the bar in the hope of seeing the town idiot/admirer who escorted her here the day before, but neither he nor the woman with the dog are present. She recognises the bartender immediately, however. He looks like an inveterate heavy-metal fan or a serial killer … Or maybe a bit of both. Around forty-something, but could very well be ten years younger – alcohol and an unhealthy lifestyle have a curious way of both adding and subtracting the years. Maybe he's somewhere in the middle. The shoulder-length black hair looks like it's been scraped back with a comb and is oily like the back of a sticker, but from wax, not for lack of soap and water. Over an Iron Maiden T-shirt, a leather vest fights valiantly to stay fastened over the bulging beer belly.

'Sparkling water or whisky and coke?'

The heavy-metal man clearly recognises her too, and remembers that she's both on and off the wagon, depending on whether or not the police are present. Hannah longs for a stiff drink, but having had no breakfast, it feels extra sinful. She grabs the menu, which looks like it hasn't been updated since the late eighties, neither in terms of the physical menu itself nor the food on offer. Hannah orders a meal that balances alcoholism with sobriety, and the well-known with the exotically local.

'Can I get a whisky and coffee, and the toast with smoked goat's cheese, thanks.'

The bartender nods, slides the whisky and coffee promptly and professionally across the bar and disappears through a swinging door into the back, reappearing a few minutes later, a plate of cheese on toast in hand. The metal man must be the chef as well as the bartender. Hannah peers down at the food, which looks surprisingly appealing, and is even garnished with a slice of red pepper. She attacks the plate with great appetite.

'It's quite the tragedy about that young guy. Thor, right?' She tries to sound as if she's not overly invested and swallows the last bite of goat's cheese.

The bartender nods. 'Awful. He was a good guy.'

'Did you know him?'

The leather vest shrugs. 'I knew who he was. But he wasn't part of the group that hangs out here, if that's what you mean.'

'Did he not drink?'

'I think all of the teenagers drink from time to time. I mean, there's not that much else for them to do around here. He just never came in at the weekend, with the others.'

'But it seems like he was pretty popular, no? I saw him last night, playing football.'

'Yeah, he was ... As I said, I didn't really know him that well, I just heard that he was different.'

'Different how?'

The vest moves up and down again in another uninterested shrug. Hannah senses that she won't find out much else by pursuing this path.

'Do you know where they found him?' Hannah tries to make the question sound casual.

'Down by the water. South of the harbour.'

'South?'

Hannah tries to visualise the layout of the town, going off the little she has seen and remembers.

'Is that near where all the fishing boats are?'

The slicked-back hair shakes. 'No, it's not near anything, really. A particularly odd place to be found, if you ask me.'

Hannah, again, tries to not look too intrigued by the statement. She picks up a crust and takes a bite.

'What do you mean by that?'

The bartender throws his hands out, as if to abdicate any and all responsibility. 'Just odd, is all. I mean, what was he doing there? There's nothing down there but muddy fields.'

'He could have drifted there, maybe? Perhaps from the harbour?'

'I don't think so. He'd have somehow had to have drifted all the way out of the navigation lock, a complicated route right behind the sea entrance, so there's practically no current there. And, there's also plenty of boat traffic going in and out that way as well, so it's unlikely that no one would've seen him.'

Hannah nods.

'I hear that his father was the one who found him. Do you know if he was out looking for him or something?'

'He must've been. What else would he have been doing out there in the wasteland?'

Hannah nods. Good question. The bartender turns to greet someone else – the woman with the dog. They chat, Hannah catches a few words – Thor is mentioned. His death has the entire town talking. Hannah takes a sip of her coffee, feels the warmth and the alcohol spreading through her body, and feels light, light, light. Wants to give herself fully to that feeling, wants to drink another ten cups of the same magic potion, no longer wants to have to think. There are far too many unanswered questions. Impossible to put all the pieces together. And it's not even her job, anyway. Her job is to write a crime novel, and here she is, nosing around, wasting away the hours trying to track down a potential murderer. Who maybe only exists in her head – or is it just a hope she's clinging on to? It would give the tragedy meaning. Thor was playing football just last night. And after that he probably went to hang out with a few friends, had a few beers. On the way back home, he fell in the water. His father grew worried when he didn't come home, so went out looking for him. Jonni heard of his best friend's death and disappeared, as he often does. Would probably come back before nightfall. And that wound behind Thor's ear, that must've happened when he fell into the water. Hannah sighs, takes another mouthful. She should go back home and write something, apply her imagination to what could have happened, rather than trying to figure out what did happen and end up disappointed by life's randomness. No, it would be better to make up a murder with words before she finds out there hasn't even been one. She pulls out her wallet and finds the exact amount. Leaves it on the counter and slides off the barstool, but stops mid-movement. What was that he said, about Thor being different? Different how? And just as the thought comes to her, the door is thrown open and a young fisherman comes barrelling inside, his jacket flying behind him, his eyes wide open.

'Jonni er inni hjá Þór. Hann er með haglabyssu!'

The room freezes. Hannah turns to the bartender, confused.

'What's going on?'

'Jonni is at Thor's house, and he has a shotgun!'

14

Hannah has never seen a leather vest move so fast before. And being the most sober of the bar's patrons, she is the only one with enough wherewithal to hop into the leather vest's car, which is parked right outside. The seatbelt sits loose and unfastened over her right shoulder, and she instead uses both hands to hold on to the door handle as the bartender ploughs through the town as if they're in an action film. They reach the house in a matter of minutes and the leather vest bolts out of the car while Hannah struggles with the lock – fucking hell, it won't open! She crawls clumsily over the driver's seat, tumbles out of the car and catches up with her driver at the door. Where he rings the goddamn doorbell. Hannah gapes at him, speechless.

'It's a bit rude to just barge in.'

'It's an emergency!'

Hannah's heart pounds both upward and outward, her whole body shaking, everything tense. She grabs hold of the door handle, looks at her companion, receives a short, approving nod, and opens the door. Holds her breath as it swings open. She hears a young man shouting, an older man answer, women crying. Quickly, the unlikely rescue duo tiptoe through to the living room, where a lanky young man in jeans and a T-shirt is standing barefoot, pointing a shotgun directly at Thor's father's forehead. Viktor and the coroner look like they're trying to negotiate with the young man, to mediate. Thor's mother is sitting with her face buried in her hands. Ella stands just in front of her, using her own body as a shield and keeping a watchful eye on the situation. The guests still there from the viewing whimper softly.

'Jonni, slepptu byssunni!'

Hannah looks at her companion surprised, unaware that he was capable of summoning such authority in his voice. But then again, he must be used to shouting at drunk people and breaking up fights, maybe even has experience averting potentially dangerous situations. The room turns to face the leather vest and Hannah, who wishes she could become invisible. The leather vest seems to thrive on the attention, however, even though the shotgun is now pointing at him. The young man, who Hannah assumes is Jonni, has a startlingly determined look in his eye.

'Slepptu byssunnni. Þetta endar ekki vel.'

'Það er honum að kenna að Þór er dáinn.'

Hannah looks from the bartender – a lock of his hair has come loose and is resting on his forehead – to Jonni, as she tries to interpret their exchange of words, or at least the meaning behind them. The intensity in the young man's face remains unchanged, and again he turns and aims the gun at Ægir. Purely to point at him, or to threaten him? Hannah's entire body is as tense as a pig awaiting slaughter, and she starts to feel a little dizzy, realising then that she has been holding her breath. She takes a slow, deep breath in, and releases it. Silently. Makes eye contact with Viktor, who looks at a complete loss – this is probably his first time handling a hostage situation. If you could even call it that. She thinks she can see a sense of relief on Viktor's face as he watches the barman take control and, with great self-confidence, step towards Jonni and reach out to him. As if Jonni were drunk and he was helping get him home to bed. He doesn't say a word – it seems as if words are unnecessary. He rests a large, soft, man hand on Jonni's arm, and the entire room holds its breath, with Vigdis taking a cautious peek through her fingers. Jonni lowers his arm slightly, so the shotgun is aimed at the stone man's stomach. The bystanders' relief is on a hair trigger, waiting to be released, but Jonni doesn't lower the gun any further, instead he continues to look deep into Ægir's eyes.

'Það varst þú sem drapst hann.'

He then pulls the trigger, and the shotgun goes off in one big, booming, tiny, almost inaudible click. It's not loaded. Vigdis screams. Jonni finally throws the gun to the floor and sinks to his knees like a man who had been sentenced to death but was liberated mere moments before being led to the gallows. The leather vest kneels down and puts an arm around Jonni, who stares expressionless at Thor's body. Does he even see it?

Viktor puts the young man in handcuffs, and the guests slowly return to themselves. Including Hannah, who steps sideways towards Ella, still with an eye on the scene, not daring to turn her back to it just yet.

'Are you okay?'

Hannah watches out of the corner of her eye as Viktor leads Jonni out of the room, the bartender following behind, as if it is his job to monitor the arrest. Hannah now turns to face Ella, who is still holding on to Vigdis, as if she's protecting a child from an incoming bomb. Vigdis gently wriggles free from Ella's caring arms, walks over to the stone man and holds him. Squeezes him so tight, he might crumble into pieces. Ella watches them. There's a look in her eye that is neither care nor relief, something more like dark contemplation. A longing for a partner to protect her with their love?

'Are you okay?'

Hannah repeats the question. Ella shakes her head, as if trying to reset the world. And then she nods.

15

The coffee is piping hot and charcoal black. Hannah pours them each a cup while Ella finds some biscuits from the cupboard. They sit at the kitchen table, having both been silent the entire drive home, as if there were no words to describe what just happened. They left not long after Jonni's arrest, only staying to help clear away the coffee cups and plates, the other mourning guests having disappeared like smoke from cannon fire. No one wanted to take up any more of the grieving parents' time, or, what was probably more accurate: they all wanted to get home quickly to gossip about what they'd just seen.

With stolen beer crates and souped-up mopeds constituting the town's worst crimes, today must've blown all previous records for drama out of the water, and must, Hannah imagines, have turned the town upside down. What you thought it once was, is no more. Hannah would quite like to pay Viktor another quick visit, to assist in Jonni's questioning, but she doesn't know what reason she could give for just turning up there again. And has the coroner been able to examine Thor's body? Probably not, given he was still lying there in the middle of the room – the coroner had probably promised to wait until the viewing was over before conducting the autopsy. But then, of course, they were interrupted by Jonni and the shotgun.

'What did he say to Ægir?' Hannah looks questioningly at Ella, who stares back, as if she doesn't understand.

Hannah elaborates. 'Jonni. Why was he so angry at Thor's father?'

Ella shrugs. Takes a sip of coffee.

'I might have this completely wrong, but was he accusing him of being responsible for Thor's death?'

Ella hesitates, then grabs a pen and paper:

He is in shokk over the loss. Som we all are.

'But no one else turned up with a hunting gun. Do you think Jonni knows something?'

Again Ella shrugs. Looks as if she isn't all that interested in theorising about a possible crime, motive or suspect. Understandable, in a way. Hannah, however, can't help but poke at her host a little bit more.

'Do Jonni and Ægir not have a good relationship?'

Ella looks directly at Hannah. Smiles an indefinable smile. Writes again:

That is putting it milde.

'What do you mean?'

But Ella stands up, wraps a blanket around her old shoulders. Jots down another message:

I need to lie down. Death take a brutale toll on old bones.

Hannah tries one last time.

'Is it because Jonni was a bad influence on Thor? I mean, encouraged him to drink, liked guns, was a bit temperamental...?'

Ella scribbles down one quick, final message:

Someting like that.

Then she disappears upstairs, heavy steps on a heavy day. Hannah picks up the paper covered in the old woman's handwriting. *Someting like that.* What did she mean?

The Island of Death
Chapter 1

Hannah lights a cigarette and opens a window, the hinges of which resist but give way with a bit of pressure from her thumb. She leans back in her chair, exhales. Outside, the daylight is already fading.

Ach, Christ. She can't call her novel *The Island of Death*. How rudimentary. But what do you call a crime novel? Hmm. Something about murder, death, or with the word 'woman'. Or a singular noun like *The Crime*, or *The Bridge*, or *The Prosecutor*. No, that's more for titles of films or TV series. She needs something that will ensure people know it's crime. Especially as her name isn't exactly associated with thrillers. A short, catchy title would probably work, something that grabs people's attention. Okay. *The Island of Death* can be the working title. Fuck it, it's going to be a load of garbage anyway. She leaves the cigarette in the ashtray, it'll put itself out. Stretches her neck from one shoulder to the other, cracks her knuckles. Here it comes, the world's biggest, best, fastest-written crime novel. A mind-numbingly boring crime novel, but here it is.

```
The grass was greener than normal for November. Tore
laced his football boots with a fresh determination,
as if doing so for the last time. This is how he'd
always tied them, it was just in his nature;
meticulous, a perfectionist, not only with his laces,
but with life in general. What he didn't know was
that this would actually be the last time he ever
tied his laces, and that the imminent football match
with his friends would be the last thing he ever did
in his eighteen-year-long life. By the morning, he
would be dead.
```

Hannah looks up. Okay, okay, not bad. A start, at least. She can allow herself some licence with Thor's personality because, strictly speaking, she didn't actually know him. Although she probably should. She jots down in her notebook: *Who is Thor?* And moves back to the keyboard. The novel has an introduction. Perhaps her venture is not as insurmountable as she'd thought.

For three rigid hours, she writes without once taking her eyes off the screen. When she does eventually look away, the ashtray is full of cigarette stubs, the dark has driven away all the remaining daylight, and the cold stands like a pillar in the open window. Hannah adds one final full stop, releases her breath as if she has just run a marathon, and feels a sense of surprise; she's been on top form. She scrolls through the document, seven pages in total. Hannah smiles, satisfied. She then closes the laptop, does the same for the window and moves her aching, author's body.

Downstairs, the house rests in dark silence. Hannah turns on the light, then the coffee machine. Absent-mindedly flips through a few old magazines as she waits for the coffee to brew. What's the next step? She's made a start on the book, but she needs to know more about the crime itself. That's how she is referring to Thor's death, as the crime – perhaps wishful thinking, but criminal wrongdoing can't be ruled out just yet, especially given the mysterious circumstances. Thor, who was afraid of water, and yet who still went down to the water's edge that night after he'd been drinking ... why? His father, who found him, and who somehow knew beforehand that his son could be found dead in the water. Why did Jonni accuse him of having something to do Thor's death? Even more importantly: did Jonni know that the gun he fired at Ægir wasn't loaded? Will he be charged with attempted murder? And finally: what would Thor's autopsy reveal?

Hannah shakes her head, grabs the freshly made pot of coffee and pours herself a cup. Feels the heat of the cup warm her hands. She takes a sip. There are simply far too many unanswered questions. The only thing that makes even the slightest bit of sense is that Ægir clearly didn't like his son spending time with someone who was capable of turning up to a memorial ceremony with a shotgun. Hannah shudders at the thought of what might have happened had it been loaded. If he had shot Ægir, would he have stopped there? Or would he have shot all the guests too? Including herself? Hannah sits for a while, drinks her coffee, and then suddenly remembers something. The crime scene! How could she forget? The drama with Jonni had made her completely forget about the goddamn crime scene. And now it's dark out, too late to go investigate. Or is it? Hannah glances up at the clock, a little after 20:00. She bites her lip. It is dark outside, but it's not technically night-time yet. She grabs her jacket, leaves the coffee on the table and forgets to switch off the light behind her.

16

Okay, technically it is night – now that it's dark. Hannah shivers and shoves a probing foot into the wet grass. She regrets her mission – the darkness is absolute, and not only is it impossible to explore the area for clues (whatever they may be), she is, admittedly, also scared. A little bit, anyway. She had hoped that there would be at least some sort of light source out here, maybe from a street lamp or the glare from a window in town. Instead, and with significant regret, she has to make do with the useless little beam of light from the torch on her phone. Hannah feels like an idiot in every conceivable way. Makes the decision to turn around and go back to Ella's comfortable sitting room, when she suddenly feels a hand on her shoulder. A scream escapes her, and in an awkward movement, she jerks away from said hand, steps into a puddle hidden beneath the grass, twists her foot and falls onto the sodden field. She shakily points the light from her phone at the figure above her – if she is to die now, she wants to at least get a good glimpse of her killer. The homeless, kiss-deprived man smiles down at her, as if they have just bumped into each other in the toilets at Bragginn.

'It may look like it's a nice, soft place to lie down, but grass is actually one of the worst places to take a nap.'

He extends his hand to her. Hannah hesitates for a moment, then realises that if she has anything to be afraid of in this town, it is probably not this ragged man, who seems genuinely happy to see her. She takes his hand and gets up.

'Thanks.'

She brushes herself off, as if that might help dry her now soaked-through clothes.

'It was here that Thor's father pulled him out of the water.'

The rags point toward the shore. Hannah turns her pathetic phone torch in the same direction, but, of course, can see nothing other than the darkness. She can hear the waves crashing into the land, the sound of the large rocks bearing the brunt of them.

'Did he die in the water or on land?'

She turns the light back to the rags, who shrugs. No, of course not. How could he know? But he does seem to know something.

'How do you know where he was found?'

'I saw Ægir pull him out of the water. Helped him, in fact.'

Hannah stares at him, surprised and confused.

'Is that so? And ... why exactly were you here?'

The rags pause. Hannah can sense a secret fighting its way out of the neglected body. He looks out over the sea.

'I sometimes come here to ... you know ... sleep, after a few beers. Mostly in the summer, of course. I've built a small shack down by the water. I like sleeping in there, waking up to the sight and sound of the waves. It makes me feel like ... I own the whole world.'

He smiles, almost apologetically. Hannah understands him – homeless, yet has a house on the beach. Perhaps you don't need any more than that, even if the house is just a pile of boards to protect you from the wind and weather.

'But it's November. Why were you here last night?'

'I came here early in the morning. It had got late, I'd been at the Bragginn, and yes ... I couldn't find the keys to my apartment.'

He smiles again, this time a little shameful. So he does have a home. Of course, it'll be the case that Húsafjörður has some form of social security.

'And so you saw Ægir pulling Thor out of the water?'

Hannah's heart is hammering against her chest. She feels like she's hit some sort of artery in the investigation. An eyewitness! The apparently not entirely homeless man nods, while continuing to stare out into the darkness, towards where last night's dramatic events unfolded. Is everything clear in his alcohol-ridden memory? Perhaps whatever he knows needs to be coaxed out. Hannah fumbles around in her inner jacket pocket, pulls out a pack of cigarettes. Offers one to the rags. A hand with uncut fingernails grabs the cigarette poking out of the pack.

'Thanks.'

'Don't mention it. What's your name, by the way?'

'Gísli.'

Hannah lights the cigarette for him.

'Hannah.'

They take simultaneous drags of their cigarettes. The darkness devours the smoke.

'Did you see him go into the water after him? Ægir, I mean.'

'No. I just saw him struggling to get the body back on land, and I ran down there to help. I didn't know what was going on, and I only realised that he was dead when we got him onto the shore. But that he was – it was obvious.'

'Right. So what happened then?'

Hannah forces herself not to seem too eager. In the dark, she senses Gísli shrug.

'I called Viktor from Ægir's phone. He wasn't in any fit state to do it himself.'

Gísli goes quiet. As if he was now, for the first time, thinking over the incident, analysing it.

'It was as if he was paralysed. Probably in a state of shock.'

Hannah nods. It'd make sense. That was the Ægir she saw at the viewing. A lost father in a mourning trance.

'Did he say anything?'

'No. Now that I think about it, he was strangely quiet. No words, no crying, nothing.'

'How long did it take before Viktor arrived?'

'Not sure ... It was weird, like, as if we'd transcended time, or time just disappeared. Could've been ten minutes, could've been forty-five. I don't know.'

'Did you go with them, after? Did Viktor question you?'

Pause.

'No. I helped get Thor's body into Ægir's car, and then I watched them drive away.'

Hannah takes one last drag of the cigarette, flicks it into the darkness, watches as the embers withdraw inward and disappear. She shivers, looks up. The sky surprises her every night. The darkness rests on a strip of orange. A thought comes to her.

'Why did you come back?'

Gísli sucks the remaining life out of the cigarette and extinguishes the butt between his thumb and forefinger. Takes a deep breath in.

'Supplies.'

'Supplies?'

Gísli swings an arm into motion and starts to walk off. Hannah takes it as an order to follow.

The little wooden shed creaks with Gísli's weight as he half lies down and searches around behind something Hannah presumes is a mattress. She looks out to sea, can almost taste it from here. After a bit of rummaging about, Gísli sticks his head out.

Hannah squints, tries to focus on him in the darkness.

'It's gone!'

'What's gone?'

'My bottle. I had an entire bottle of vodka.'

What an anti-climax. Was that it? A bottle of vodka?

'This guy who lives up by the glacier makes it. It's not bad. I had an entire bottle.'

Ragged Gísli starts rooting about again in the little shack, and Hannah turns away, irritated. She's out here trying to solve a crime, while he's down there, on the floor, searching for his homemade booze. She leaves, can hear Gísli babbling away to himself in the background – she should probably have at least said goodbye. But she's tired and wet and, to be honest, could do with a little drink of something or other herself. Even if that did happen to be homebrew vodka. Hannah mulls Gísli's story over. Why hasn't Viktor said anything about him? Why hasn't he questioned him? Poor police work, probably. Incompetence is the trait Hannah hates most in people. That, and ignorance. Or are they the same thing?

There is another small ditch to negotiate a little further up the road. Hannah turns the torch on her phone back on, not wanting to get up close and personal with the wet grass again. She carefully puts one foot in front of the other beneath the blue-white light, and stops. The beam caught something. Can it be? She bends down. A strange, almost perverse happiness spreads through her body. Can't help but smile to herself. She pulls off her scarf and carefully wraps it around the empty, broken vodka bottle. On the base: unmistakeable traces of blood.

17

'Viktor's not here.'

Margrét holds the door ajar. Gazes at Hannah – irritated, or curious? The scarf-swaddled bottle, or – who knows? the scarf-swaddled murder weapon – is almost ready to explode in Hannah's hand.

'Can I wait inside?'

'I don't know when he'll be back.'

Hannah studies Margrét. Her tone doesn't sound as dismissive as the words coming out of her mouth. Behind her, the house glows in the silence – are the children already asleep? Hannah has no idea how early children are meant to go to bed.

'I think I've found the murder weapon.'

Hannah holds it up. Margrét looks at the object suspiciously.

'Did Thor trip on a scarf?'

Okay, morbid sarcasm may be a given when you're married to a policeman. Hannah pulls back the scarf slightly to reveal the base of the broken bottle. The volcanic woman lets her gaze move from the object in her hand, up Hannah's arm and to her eyes. A sign of understanding? She pulls the door towards her, and it opens inward. Hannah steps into the hall, relieved. Lays the bottle down gently on the living-room table and sits on the brown leather sofa. Viktor's choice? Hardly a woman's.

'Soft, right? Ugly, but practical. Convenient because you can just wipe the dirt off with a cloth. An advantage with children in the house.'

Margrét walks over with two glasses of red wine and passes one to Hannah, who takes it as if the glass were filled with gold. She tries not to drink it too greedily. Watches the policeman's wife, who lowers herself onto the other end of the sofa, takes a sip from her glass. Hannah lets her hand glide over the brown leather. From the outside, they must look like two lost souls on an oversized lifeboat. Margrét conjures a pack of cigarettes from a small box on the coffee table, offers Hannah one and lights them. She also lights two mammoth candles. Hannah closes her eyes, swills the wine around her mouth, feels comfortable in a way she rarely does. When she opens her eyes again, she notices Margrét sitting and watching her. As if she doesn't quite know what she's let into her home.

'Where did you find it?' Margrét nods at the alleged murder weapon.

'Down by the shore. I also met a homeless, or kind of homeless, guy – Gísli. I think it's his bottle.'

'Do you think he did it?'

Margrét leans forward, taps loose ash into a homemade ashtray. Hannah watches her hand – slender, her movements graceful and confident. Why does she notice that?

'No. He doesn't have a motive. He's just some poor soul who's lost his vodka.'

'Gísli has lost more than that.'

Smoke billows out of the volcanic woman's mouth.

'What do you mean?'

Hannah leans forward, stubs out the cigarette. She senses the other woman's gaze on her again, making her feel self-conscious.

'He was once a professor at Stanford. Mathematics.'

'What happened?'

Margrét shrugs. 'Whatever happens when we think we have everything under control. Something destroys it for us, or we destroy it ourselves.'

'I would've never guessed.'

Hannah stares straight ahead. Feels as if she is being watched again but doesn't dare look at Margrét. Why? Something stirs in her. The wine? She turns back to Margrét, holds her ardent gaze. Is that the trace of a smile? Or an insane twitch of her mouth? Whatever's about to happen, Hannah has no control over it. Is unsure if it's anything good. She reaches for the glass, grabs it and cools her mouth with a large gulp.

'We're all hiding something.' Margrét drains her own glass, stands up.

Hannah watches her as she disappears into the kitchen. Returning a second later with the bottle of wine. Tops them both up and looks inquisitively at Hannah.

'What are you hiding?' Hannah looks up at Margrét, who remains standing.

'Too much. You?'

Hannah shrugs. 'Don't know. Maybe an inner crime-fiction writer. Maybe something worse.'

Margrét seems to hesitate. But sits back down anyway. Hannah realises that she is now sitting a few centimetres closer than she was before. She follows the other woman's hands with her eyes as she fiddles with the pack of cigarettes but doesn't take one out. Hannah's heart starts beating faster. Lava is spreading through her body, pumping from her heart. She moves her hand, slowly approaching the cigarettes in Margrét's hands.

'May I?'

She notices Margrét watching her hands too as she reaches for the pack. Their fingers brush against each other. Something explodes within Hannah. She holds her breath, doesn't dare meet Margrét's gaze. She does it again. Brushes against her fingers with her own. Regrets it. Margrét is sitting completely, utterly still. Hannah can't stop, can't help but do it again. She now strokes the hand holding the cigarette packet. The hand lets go. Takes hold of hers. Slides her fingers between her own. Their hands intertwined. Hannah's heart stops. She dies. That touch. The whole world exists in that touch. The volcanic woman turns her body towards Hannah, fixes her gaze on her and leans forward. Their lips meet, both with their eyes open. Wide open. As if trying to read the other. Until Hannah closes her eyes and pulls Margrét on top of her, sliding beneath her in one movement as she lies back on the brown sofa. Hannah's heart is slamming against her chest. Margrét pulls Hanna's shirt off – it's cold, the room is cold, the air is cold, but the lava flows through her veins. She lets a hand slide underneath Margrét's blouse, feels her breast, and a sigh escapes the woman on top of her. Hannah thrusts herself against Margrét's body, eating from her mouth, can feel the weight of desire pushing her deeper into the sofa. Hannah greedily kisses Margrét's hard, malleable lips as she tries to unfasten her jeans. There is no room between their bodies, so Hannah gives up and instead strokes her hand over Margrét's stomach ... as the light from Viktor's car drifts across the ceiling, illuminating them momentarily, forcing them both to freeze. Hannah listens as the car pulls onto the driveway and comes to a stop outside the house.

'Shit!'

Margrét jumps up, straightens herself out while simultaneously darting into the hallway. Hannah snatches up her top and bra and hurtles into the bathroom. What a fucking ridiculous cliché.

She slams the door shut behind her, and exhales, forces herself to calm down as she puts her clothes back on. Looks at herself in the mirror. What the hell was that? Hannah feels a sudden surge of anger. Not at herself, and not at Margrét. But at Viktor, for interrupting them. She wants to storm out there and kiss Margrét again. Take her home with her, to Ella's house, lock themselves away in her attic bedroom and never come out. Her heart is pounding. She smiles to herself. Fuck. She may have just ruined her own investigation. Her entire project. Maybe she will have to go home after all, and never return. Okay, stop being so bloody dramatic.

Hannah takes a cautious step out from the toilet.

'Did he find anything?'

Viktor looks over at her, surprised. It suddenly occurs to Hannah that last time he saw her in his home, she had urgently needed the toilet then too. Fuck it. He can believe she has a dodgy stomach all he wants, as long as he doesn't suspect the worst.

'The coroner. Did he find anything unusual on Thor's body?'

Hannah keeps her focus locked onto Viktor, who is fumbling around for some papers in a briefcase. He turns his back to her. Margrét has disappeared.

'Margrét said' – Oh, God, what did Margrét tell him? – 'that you found something you wanted to show me?'

Ah, sweet relief! Hannah walks over to the coffee table, resolutely picks up the bottle and walks back over to Viktor. He turns. Frowns. Still with the papers in one hand.

'A broken bottle?'

'Not just any bottle.'

Viktor studies the scarf-swaddled object in Hannah's hand.

'A broken vodka bottle…?'

Hannah sighs, why play this tedious game? He can fucking see what it is.

'It's the bloody murder weapon. Look, there's blood on it!'

Hannah holds the bottle up to Viktor's eyeline, right in his face, almost menacingly.

He takes it from her, somewhat stubbornly, still wrapped in the scarf.

'This isn't the murder weapon.'

Hannah looks at him expectantly. He hesitates. As if he's

deciding whether he wants to elaborate on his argument, thereby convincing Hannah of it and shaking her off, or to keep the information to himself (as he probably should), which would then keep alive both her bottle theory and her self-appointed role as investigator. Hannah chooses to be annoying. If he rejects her bottle theory, he'll have to explain why.

'So, Thor didn't die from a blow to the head then?' Hannah nods at the bottle still in Viktor's hand.

Viktor rubs his forehead – it must be hard for a rural policeman to find themselves leading a murder investigation. Like a boy on school patrol alone at a road-traffic accident. Hannah is about to push him further, when Margrét comes back into the room. The corner of Hannah's mouth instinctively curls upward, so she averts her gaze ... Christ, is she blushing? Margrét leans against the doorframe, arms folded across her chest. Hannah wants to walk over there and pry them apart, wrap them around herself instead. Okay, this could all go very wrong very quickly.

'Listen, I've not come over here to bother you. I just wanted to give you the bottle, but if you're *that* sure that it has nothing to do with the case, then I'm sorry.'

Viktor sighs. Rubs his forehead again. Hannah and Margrét share a fleeting moment of eye contact. Palpitation. With his free hand, Viktor fishes a transparent bag from the briefcase and carefully lowers the bottle into it.

'Sorry. It's been a long day, and it may be that this bottle has something to do with it. Thank you for bringing it over.'

'But something else killed him then?'

Hannah glances over at Margrét, and this time it is Margrét who lowers her gaze. Does she want Hannah to leave? But she needs to know more. This might be the last time she has an excuse to come waltzing over here to coerce some information out of Viktor. Hannah realises it is disappointment that she's feeling. Both at the fact that the bottle isn't probably as important as she thought it was, and that she probably won't have the opportunity to drop by out of the blue again. She remains standing in the same spot. Rewords her question.

'Thor died as a result of something else?'

Viktor's forehead rubbing has now moved down to his neck. If he wants her to leave, he can just say so.

'He drowned, but...'

'But...?'

Come on, just come out with it. Hannah stares intently at Viktor. Glances over at Margrét in the doorway. Suddenly cannot stand the thought that Viktor is allowed to sleep with this volcanic woman, her volcanic woman. To kiss Margrét goodnight and pull her body into his. The situation makes Hannah baulk.

'He was hit on the head, pushed into the water, and then because he was unconscious, he drowned?' Hannah guesses, trying to lure the information out of him. Come on – confirm it.

Viktor shakes his head, hesitates and then gives up.

'It is probably the case that he was hit on the back of his head, but not with a bottle. Something else, something metal ... And ... the marks on his shoulder would indicate that someone held his head underwater.'

So it is a murder. First-degree murder. Hannah tries to conceal her excitement. Impossible. Tries to recall the crime dramas she's watched – what does the detective usually ask next?

'What does that tell you about the murderer then? Have you found any fingerprints, DNA?'

She hopes she sounds as if she knows what she's talking about.

'We won't get an answer from the DNA samples for a few days. But we'll test the bottle as well. Perhaps it can provide us with some new information. Or confirm what we think happened.'

'And what *do* you think? Do you have a suspect?'

Hannah suddenly realises that she's standing on her tiptoes. Without meaning to, she has also taken a step closer to both Viktor and Margrét, and is now standing almost directly between them.

If she just reaches out ever so slightly, she could touch Margrét.

'I've already said too much. You have to keep all of this between us.'

Viktor delivers the sentence with a gesture, pointing to the door. Hannah takes a step towards the hallway.

'I promise that everything said and done in this house this evening will stay between us.'

Briefly looks into Margrét's eyes as she passes her in the doorway. And then Viktor's. He looks perplexed. She leaves the police station, the day-care centre and her new lover's home with a brief farewell and an emotionally confused state of mind.

18

Hannah enters the sleeping house as silently as the creaky floorboards and her own heavy footsteps allow. Restless, she paces around the dark living room, with the strange urge to wake Ella. The need to talk to someone. Or to be alone. She sits, struggling to figure out her own mood. Ends up grabbing a bottle of wine from her room. Throws a log onto the fire and sits before the flames, armed with a glass of red wine and a stinging sensation. Fuck. She forgot to ask Viktor about Jonni. Where is he now? Wonders whether there's some form of prison cell at the home-cum-police-station? Surely not. But what do they do with their criminals here? What do you even do with a young man who's threatened his deceased (murdered!) friend's father with a shotgun? Has he been taken to Reykjavik? Sent home to his parents? Hannah downs half the glass of wine and disappears into the flames. Tomorrow, she must try to track down Jonni. Find out what part he has in this play. Not the protagonist, is Hannah's first instinct. But that doesn't apply to Ægir. Why did he happen to be in the right place at the right time, to pull his son out of the water? And what about Gísli? Are there any other secrets hiding behind those rags? And why was there a broken vodka bottle with fresh blood on it at the scene of the crime, if it's not the murder weapon? She empties the glass in one big gulp. Pours another. The last glass. Absolute last. Of course – it's obvious: No one hit Thor with the bottle – it was Thor who hit the murderer with it in self-defence! Hannah smiles at her own little triumph. If Thor did hit his killer with the weapon, that means the person would have a corresponding wound. She just needs to find whoever has a wound that matches being hit with a bottle of vodka, and then she has the murderer. But has Viktor figured that out too? Viktor. The smile slides off her face. Has Margrét said anything to him? Okay. Calm down. What would Margrét even say? *Oh, by the way, I made out with that author a little bit earlier, the one you think is annoying as hell. It probably would've turned into more than just a kiss had you not come home and interrupted us.* Hannah shakes her head. No. It's unlikely that Margrét would say anything. Unless she's the type of person who would exploit such a situation to provoke a marital conflict, thus helping her escape a loveless relationship or ... Or the opposite. The little non-affair could be used to ignite a new fire in their otherwise extinct marital bed. The third measure of wine finds its way into the glass, and Hannah can't decide what's worse: destroying a marriage or saving it. Brings the wine to her lips, sips, swallows – the warmth spreading throughout her body. It occurs to Hannah that she knows absolutely nothing about Margrét. They've only met twice. Just relax. Relax. Rela... But she has to know more. Because Margrét makes her feel ... Hannah stops that train of thought. What is it exactly that Margrét makes her feel? Something. More than she's felt in years. A joyful sensation erupts from her stomach. She silently raises a glass to herself. How silly. The flames erupt and spit out a few sparks. A little volcano. Hannah finishes off the bottle as she watches the fire devour itself and turn into embers.

They pulled him out of the water at dawn. The local police officer, Villads Axelson, and the town's

greasy-haired bartender. Some of the local fishermen
had crowded round, silently observing as they brought
the saltwater-drenched body ashore. The doctor was
already there. They gently laid the boy on the
ground, where the doctor leaned over him. But there
was no doubt. The fishermen had never seen a more
dead victim of the sea. One of the group, old Axel -
hardened by half a century of seeing the bodies of
fellow drowned fishermen - looked, distraught, down
at the frozen earth, after seeing that Tore was still
wearing one of his football boots.

Hannah looks over the top of the screen, up into the star-strewn
sky. This night writing isn't so bad. A good crime novel might even
come out of it. She counts up the pages. Twenty. How long should
one be, actually? At least two hundred and fifty pages, if it's to be
taken seriously. But she can do that. Hannah almost feels a little
euphoric, grabs the phone and starts to write a message to Bastian,
but stops herself. What does she have to report? That because of
the murder, things are going super well for her, that she's pretty
much stealing from reality in a ratio of one to one, and isn't even
bothering to change the names all that much. Oh, and she also now
has a crush on the local policeman's wife. A potentially complicating
factor in her continued cooperation with Viktor in regard to solving
the murder and uncovering all the necessary information – or
rather, inspiration – for the book. Okay, 'cooperation' may be
pushing it. But it kind of is. No. She should wait to share her
optimism when she has more reason to have any. Hannah returns
to the keyboard, feeling surprisingly wide awake, and wanting to
take advantage of the momentum to get a few more pages under
her belt. She can't know when she might feel this way again.

Knock, knock! Hannah awakens. Slowly. *Knock, knock!* Her eyes fly
open. Curses as she hauls herself out of bed. How long has she been

asleep? Can't have been more than a few hours. The red-wine
headache presses down on her like a lead hat, and begrudgingly, she
opens the door to Ella, who is standing there holding a tray laden
with cheese rolls, coffee and a glass of juice. Ella smiles, as if she has
completely forgotten that her nephew was just recently murdered
and that the murderer is still on the loose. A kind of survival
strategy? Hannah's guilty conscience begins to creep in again – she
should be the one waiting on Ella, looking after the old woman as
she grieves. On the other hand, it does seem like Ella enjoys having
someone to do things for.

'Ég gæti ímyndað mér að þú værir svöng.'

The tray is pushed towards Hannah, who takes it.

'Thank you. I was up late writing last night. Haven't slept much.'

Ella points at the clock radio beside the bed. Hannah turns to
look. 14:31. Fuck. What a teenager she is. To think that she's almost
slept the entire day away. Hannah cringes apologetically, as if self-
control is beyond her ability. Which it may be. She walks over to
the desk with the tray and moves her laptop aside. Ella stands there
for a bit, as if Hannah is a vampire and must invite her inside. Not
that odd given how hostile Hannah acted the last time she was up
here. Hannah gestures, invites Ella to sit on the unmade bed.

She takes a sip of the coffee, leans back against the desk.

'How are you doing?'

Ella shrugs. The fresh smile disappears. She points to the loose
pieces of paper on the desk, nods at them as if to ask for permission.

'Yes, of course.' Hannah passes Ella a pen.

She writes:

I going to se Vigdis nå. Hjelp plan funeral ceremoni.

Hannah nods. 'When will it be, do you know yet?'

Ella writes again.

Next Saturday. Police finish with him first.

'I thought they had done the autopsy?'

Ella shakes her head.

Not done.

'And what about Jonni ... Do you know what they've done with him?'

Jail.

So there is some kind of jail here? Hannah mulls it over. It can't possibly be in Viktor and Margrét's house, can it? Where else would it be? In a small cave by the sea? Was Jonni there last night, under arrest, in the same building that Hannah and Margrét ... An absurd thought. And disappointing. If that had been the case, Hannah could have seen him. Questioned him. She doubts she'll get another chance.

'Is the jail part of the police station?'

Hannah tidies some of the papers, shuffling them together into a pile, trying to give the question an aura of nonchalance. Watches Ella, who tilts her head to the side slightly. Hesitates. And nods. But there was something in that tilt of the head. A scepticism, an unease? Hannah makes a mental note to bring her interest in the murder case down a notch, at least when she's with Ella. She doesn't want to reveal her inspiration for the novel. Talking of inspiration: Ella points to the copy of *Hrafnkels saga*, which is exactly where Hannah put it down that first night, untouched, on the night stand. Looks inquisitively at Hannah.

'I've not had time to read it yet, unfortunately. With everything that's happened...'

Ella nods.

'But it would be good to have a distraction, actually. Get my mind off everything. I think I'll read a bit today. Maybe take it down to Bragginn with me.'

Ella nods, satisfied. Hannah has no idea why reading the damn saga would make her happy. But it gives her an excuse to snoop around town a bit. She must return to the police station and talk to Jonni.

19

Book in her pocket, the early-afternoon darkness beginning to draw in over the mountains, removing all colour from the earth and infecting Hannah's lungs. It seems as if the last remaining shades of green have been sucked out of the landscape over the past few days, as if Thor's death has erased all colour from the town and the surrounding landscape. But the wind is something death cannot expel. Hannah draws her arms tight into her body and tugs her hat down a little further, but the ice-cold wind still penetrates her jacket. She feels groggy and disorientated by the eternal darkness, which drains the days of life before they've even begun. She picks up her pace.

When she reaches Bragginn, she takes a brief glance in through the windows: the usual fishermen, the woman with the dog, the oily-haired leather vest behind the bar. None of them notice her as she quickly walks past and continues further on, into town.

This time she doesn't knock on the door. Even at a distance, she can tell that Margrét's home, from the sound of the children. Shouldn't they have been picked up by their parents by now? Or perhaps those are the sounds of the household's own children. Hannah suddenly realises that she hasn't actually met Viktor and Margrét's children. In a way, she hasn't fully comprehended the fact that they *have* children. It doesn't make her any less interested in Margrét though, as she's always quite liked competing for someone's affection. Despite the fact she rarely wins and has never competed against children before. Fuck, did she have blood or cynicism running through her veins? Competing with children for their mother's attention! Hannah pulls the hat even more tightly over her ears, instinctively shrugging her shoulders. Well, the kids will just have to bring their A game, won't they.

It seems Hannah has been offered an unexpected helping hand, in the form of the darkness. The grass is wet as she crawls on her stomach towards the house from the back garden. The water soaked through her clothes the moment she lowered herself onto the sodden grass, but this time, the droplets don't intimidate her. Imagine being so dumb as to have a window in the cell. It's a little one, but big enough for Hannah to knock on and have a quick chat with Jonni. Even the criminals here have a nice view. She army-crawls her way purposefully towards the small extension at the back of the building, where she has calculated the cell must be, presumably added behind Viktor's office. Why didn't she see the door when she was in there? She scans the room in her memory but doesn't remember a door. But it *must* be there. Because she doesn't remember the little window either, hence the conclusion that there has to be another room on the other side. Hannah is now at the house, and from her crawling position, she throws a glance over her shoulder. Behind her, the lawn takes on the appearance of an infinity pool, as if it were flowing into the sea. Behind that, silhouettes of the mountains, in various shades of grey. Something creaks, no – rattles. Hannah flinches. Looks up. The window directly above her opens. Margrét's hands and mouth poke over the ledge. In the corner of her mouth, a cigarette, which she lights. Hannah pushes herself right up against the wall, and the ashes cascade down onto her. Shit! She cannot be discovered like this. Or has Margrét already seen her creeping towards the house like a fool – and is this some sort of game, a way for Margrét to tell Hannah that she knows she's there? Ash falls onto Hannah's shoulder. Hannah watches it. What should she do? Wait? Continue? Jump up and reveal herself? No, that would be too stupid. Whatever she said, she would still look like a psychopathic stalker. The best thing she can do is wait and hope that the window opening is just a coincidence, and that she can continue on her mission very soon. Hannah waits. Breathes in and out slowly through her nose. An eternity passes by. Finally, a glowing cigarette butt falls to the ground next to her. She has to flinch sharply to the side to avoid it falling in her hair. The window closes, Hannah breathes out, presumes she hasn't been seen. She crawls further along the wall as the embers behind her burn out.

She grabs hold of the windowsill, hauls herself up and peeks in through the little window like some sort of farcical burglar. Presses her face fully against the pane of glass, cupping her eyes with her hands to see inside. But it's dark behind the window, and she can't see shit. Gently, just with the tips of her nails, she taps on the pane. Feels like the slight tapping echoes around the mountains. Nothing. She looks around. Tries with her knuckles. Still nothing. Hannah curses inwardly, but just as she moves to slide down into her crawling-back-to-the-road-position, a little lamp comes on inside. Hannah's heart starts beating at double speed. There, on a small couch, sits a young, thin, pale man with massive, black-bin-bag circles under his eyes: Jonni. He looks over at the small window but doesn't seem to register Hannah. Can he not see her? She knocks again. Waves, tries to lure him over to the window. But he just continues to stare in her direction, his expression empty, as if nothing in the world could be worth his attention. And certainly not a middle-aged Danish author standing there, making a fool of herself. She briefly wonders whether she should actually be afraid, but as hateful and frightening as the young man looked with the gun in his hand, he seems small and innocent now. And there's a wall and window between them.

'Jonni. Can we talk?' Hannah whispers, trying to project it, but doubts he can even hear her. Probably can't. What was she thinking? Of course the small window can't be opened. And she can't stand here and shout in at him either. She contemplates her options. Finds her notebook and tears out a page. Writes. In English, to play it safe. Holds the note against the windowpane:

I want to help you. Find out what happened to your friend.

Okay, that might be pushing it. How can Hannah possibly help Jonni? And how can she be sure that it wasn't him who killed Thor? She tries to get a proper look at him. Does he have any open wounds, any injuries that look like they could have been caused by a vodka bottle? Nothing obvious. But he's sitting with his back to the wall. And he could of course have a wound on his back or on the other side of his body. The young man doesn't react to the note. Hannah flips the page over, writes again.

I know you didn't do it.

She holds the note up for a bit longer than she did before. This time, it seems as if Jonni notices. Is now looking directly at the window, but seems unsure. Then stands up and walks towards her.

'What are you doing here?'

Hannah cowers, spins round. Behind her: Margrét. Standing next to Viktor. Shit.

20

Hannah doesn't stop running until she reaches the doors to Bragginn. Ahh, fucking hell! How embarrassing can you get? First to be caught in the act and then to have so little backbone that you run off without saying a word. What an idiot. What must they think of her? She desperately inhales lungfuls of air, her pulse refusing to slow, wipes imaginary sweat from her forehead and looks around. No one followed her. Of course. There aren't many places to run to in Húsafjörður – if they wanted to find her, they could. Easily. Behind the window: the same old fishermen, stagnating with eyes half glazed over. Hannah pushes open the door, walks in and orders a double whisky while trying to gain control of her shaking hands. She downs the glass in one go, orders another. Bartender Slick Hair pours her another without judgement, and after a brief nod – as if to say *thanks for helping out last time when we intervened in a hostage situation together* – turns to the woman with the dog. Whisky number two is permitted a little more time on the bar, after a first small sip. Hannah stares down into the glass. Okay. What are her options? Go back and apologise, explain herself? No. The situation was obvious; there's nothing to explain. She would just lose face again. Forget it all and go home? No, she can't give up now. Pretend like nothing happened? And what would that achieve? She wouldn't be able to see Margrét again without having to explain herself in one way or another. She's effectively cut herself off from working alongside Viktor, so it doesn't seem like there's much to lose on that side of things. New plan: ignore the embarrassing incident until it catches up with her.

Hannah pulls her jacket off and orders a coke to accompany her whisky. She has to stay sharp. How can she get access to Jonni now? How long will he be detained for, and what happens after that? If anything does even happen after that. She wants to smack herself. Her only chance to talk with the main suspect and she's gone and messed it all up. Christ, come on now. No more self-loathing, it doesn't achieve anything. The wound. She needs to find the vodka-bottle-inflicted wound. Hannah peers around. No one seems to have any large bandages or anything that would suggest that they've been assaulted with a broken bottle. The dog woman is wearing a hat, but the way she sits there, stretching herself out over the bar, the leather vest just behind it, she doesn't look like she would be able to attack a man with anything but her sexuality. She's monopolising the bartender, which is annoying as Hannah needs both a fresh drink and an in-depth interview on the topic of Ægir. Her intuition tells her that she isn't going to find out much by talking to the drunken, Icelandic-speaking fishermen. She sighs and pulls the saga out of her pocket – might as well pass the time by getting a bit of an insight into the national soul of the Icelandic people.

Hrafnkels saga. A lot of men's names, who they were the fathers and sons of, and the names of a hell of a lot of places Hannah's never heard of. She blinks a few times, should've brought her reading glasses with her. Makes an effort to keep track of the family trees and locations as the story slowly starts to take shape. There's this big-shot farmer, Hrafnkel. Rules over this region of Iceland, does whatever he wants, doesn't answer to anyone unless he feels like it. Which he rarely does. Hrafknel has a stallion, Freyfaxi, who he loves more than anything on Earth, and he vows that no one other than himself may ride him – whoever does, he will kill. Okay, a clear enough set-up. Hannah flips through. Imagines it'll just be a matter of someone turning up and riding the horse. There we go. It doesn't take long before a poor shepherd appears and, even though there are many other horses to choose from, climbs onto the stallion. Reading, reading. Hrafnkel's angry, rides off, finds the shepherd and kills him with his axe. And yes, he's sorry to have to do it, but an oath is an oath, and if you make a promise to yourself, you have to fulfil it.

'Another?'

Hannah looks up into the face of the leather vest, who has finally been liberated from the dog woman, who has presumably returned home. Hannah watches gratefully as the bartender's hand pours. She takes a sip and surprises herself: she is genuinely more interested in returning to the story of Hrafnkel Freysgoði – won't he face the consequences of having murdered another man? – than she is in questioning the bartender about Thor's relationship with his father. But books, of course, are so wonderfully patient.

'Did you know him well – Jonni? It seemed you two had a special connection.'

The bartender places both hands flat on the counter, and shrugs.

'I know all the kids in town. But Jonni may actually be the one I know the least about. Him and Thor.'

'Why is that?'

Hannah edges forward slightly on her stool.

'The others all come down here, hang out, drink a bit round the back, if they're not old enough to come inside, you know. But never those two ... I always thought they were decent young men. Never getting into fights or anything like that.'

The response baffles Hannah. If they were so much more virtuous than the others, why has one ended up dead and the other in jail? It doesn't really match the image she has of Jonni either.

'So... Jonni, then.' She tries to tread lightly. 'Why did he threaten Ægir?'

The leather-vest-clad bartender shrugs again. No, sure. How could he know that?

'Do you think that Jonni suspects Ægir, for some reason, of being responsible for Thor's death?'

A slight change of expression that could mean either yes or no. Hannah digs a bit deeper.

'Do you think Ægir may have had something to do with his son's death?'

The face behind the bar does a quick scan of the room. No curious eavesdroppers within eavesdropping range. He leans closer to Hannah, lowers his voice.

'Ægir is responsible for a lot of things in this town. Everyone knows that. But Thor's death?' The leather vest throws his hands out. The single button over his stomach fights to stay in place. 'Never. He loved him too much. His only child, as I'm sure you're already aware.'

A thought comes to Hannah, something she hasn't yet considered, but which now suddenly feels of utmost importance.

'Vigdis – how old is she? I mean, she must be quite a bit younger than Ella, what with having such a young son...'

The bartender shrugs. 'Only a few years younger, I think.'

'But Thor was only seventeen, she must have had him very late? What, in her forties? And Ægir ... He must be at least ten years older than Vigdis, no?'

The ponytail flicks upward as he nods.

'I think they'd actually given up. It was imperative for Ægir that he had a son, but they couldn't. When she did eventually get pregnant, there were rumours all over town that it was a miracle.'

They both fall silent. Stare thoughtfully into space.

'Which is also why it's such a huge tragedy that they've lost him.'

Hannah tries to digest all the new information, and something the leather vest has said returns to her. She searches for the right tone, one that doesn't sound like she's conducting an interrogation.

'What is Ægir responsible for then?'

Again, the eyes behind the bar search the room. No one nearby. But then the woman with the dog suddenly comes back in – she's forgotten her scarf, which for some reason requires both Hannah's and the bartender's help. Hannah feels the anger rising. What a remarkable ability this woman has for consuming people's time, space and attention! Hannah studies the woman in more detail: light hair beneath the hat, and a tipsy, grey gaze. She seems to be more drunk now, and the desire to flirt has disappeared. The bartender is no longer a potential sexual partner, but the person who needs to track down her scarf. The dog starts to bark – as impatient as its owner. It's Hannah who finds the scarf, which had fallen underneath the barstool. Without even a thank-you, the woman disappears outside, into what has now become night, and when Hannah turns back to the bar, her conversation partner is busy selling beers to a couple of the fishermen, who look like they've had enough beers for the rest of their lives. They chat, and the leather vest nods in Hannah's direction. Waves her over. Her curiosity piqued, she walks over to stand beside the fishermen. She is half a head taller than both of them.

'You wanted to know what Ægir is responsible for? These two can tell you.'

One of the fishermen makes a fist with his hand and says a hell of a lot very quickly in Icelandic. Hannah identifies a few profanities in the stream of words, and his tone says the rest: Ægir screwed them over. Hannah turns to the bartender.

'What is it exactly that he did to them?'

'He bought all of their fishing quotas. Or, rather, stole them.'

Hannah frowns, confused. 'How?'

'With money, power and a giant trawler. The smaller boats couldn't compete. His was so much bigger, so what they would catch in a week, he caught in a day. And he sold that at a lower price too, so everyone else went bankrupt. He bought their quotas and hired them to work for him, but for far less than had they would make when self-employed.'

The angry fisherman shakes his fist in the air again, accompanied by something Hannah interprets as additional expletives and curses.

'But not these two, they refused to work for him. So now they've got no work, and one of them ended up losing his family.'

Hannah nods. So in other words, Ægir is not just a stone man, but a callous businessman and local despot. Whose son has just been killed. Like the shepherd in the saga, who was killed by Hrafnkel for riding his horse. But whose horse did Thor ride? That is, if he even did anything that would give someone a motive to kill him. Hannah would have to talk to Ægir. But first, she needs to go home and finish reading this saga.

21

Taking hold of the door handle, Hannah can already sense it. That someone is waiting for her. She has the urge to turn around – but doesn't want to have to deal with a confrontation, especially not with Viktor, who she suspects is hiding behind the coffee aroma on the other side of the door. She holds her breath and listens. The sound of Ella's voice fills the house like a low frequency, preventing the guest from speaking and revealing themselves; but they don't need to: Viktor's coat is hanging on the hook. Hannah closes her eyes – okay, this conversation was inevitable. May as well take place sooner rather than later. She announces her arrival with a hard slam of the door and summons up enough self-confidence to carry her into the living room. But she feels all the air leave her body when the guest turns around. Sitting in the chair opposite Ella is not Viktor, but Margrét. Hannah tries to get a grip on the emotions running wild within her and look composed, but she has to lean against the edge of the table to stop herself from dying on the spot. Ella gestures towards Margrét as if to indicate that she is Hannah's guest too. Good God, what has she told Ella? Not much, hopefully – preferably nothing. Hannah tries to sound calm:

'Hi. It's nice to see you again.'

Ugh God, you idiot. But what else can you say when you're so un-fucking-believably cringeworthy? Margrét watches her, giving away nothing.

'Maybe we can talk about what happened?'

Hannah gulps, her mouth suddenly and completely dry. Okay. Margrét must've filled Ella in on something or other, seeing as she doesn't seem to be making an effort to hide anything. Something has happened. And it feels as if all Hannah's layers are being peeled away – she strokes her arms as if trying to keep them in place. Her embarrassment becomes muddled with an intense desire to see Margrét naked.

'Shall we talk upstairs?'

Hannah feels like a schoolgirl who has finally managed to lure her friend home and now doesn't know how to turn the fantasy in her head – of the two of them in her room – into reality. After closing the door behind them, she walks over to the window, grabs a cigarette from the pack she carelessly chucked onto the desk earlier, lights it, opens the window and sits on the desk with the hand holding the cigarette out of the window. Margrét remains standing beside the bed.

'I convinced Viktor that it would be best that I spoke to you, after we got so...' the corner of Margrét's mouth twitches almost imperceptibly, as if any continuation of that sentence would cause great embarrassment '...friendly.'

Hannah nods. Bloody hell, is she blushing? She looks out into the night, watches as her smoke dances away.

She can't bring herself to look at Margrét when she asks: 'How much does Viktor know?'

'Everything. I mean, we both saw you trying to talk to Jonni.'

Okay, so we're playing that game are we? Where we pretend nothing's happened. Hannah, however, feels a little disappointed, had thought that Margrét would at least acknowledge the moment they shared – if she doesn't, then how could it ever be repeated? Hannah needs to hear Margrét's thoughts on the matter. If she has any.

'And the other thing. Yesterday evening ... Have you told him about that?'

Margrét stares intently at Hannah, who thinks she can see something burning in the other woman's eyes. She shakes her head. And Hannah feels the relief spread through her body.

'And Ella...?'

Again, another dismissive shake of the head, and the relief spreads all the way to Hannah's fingertips. Good, some secrets are best kept secret.

'Was he angry that I tried to talk to Jonni?'

'What is it you want to get out of that boy exactly?'

Margrét scrutinises her. Is it really that difficult to understand? The cigarette burns out. Hannah stubs it into the ashtray and closes the window.

'The truth, of course. About where he was that night. What happened.'

'But you don't think he killed Thor...'

Not a question but an observation, reinforced by Hannah's silly little note, which Margrét now pulls out of her pocket, and which Hannah realises she must've dropped when she was caught red-handed and sprinted away like the utter fool she is.

'Correct. But I do think he knows who did.'

Hannah stops herself from elaborating. Can she trust Margrét? She concludes that there must at least be a fifty-percent chance that she can, and maybe even a little more, given that she hasn't told anyone about their little romp on the sofa.

'I think it was Ægir.'

A laugh escapes Margrét. Hannah can't figure out whether it's because her theory is outrageously ludicrous, or whether it's a derisive 'well we all know that' laugh.

'Is that so far-fetched?'

Hannah observes Margrét, who is now sitting on the bed. She wants to push her down onto it.

'You think Ægir killed his own son? He loved him more than anything.'

'So you're saying it's impossible?'

Margrét shrugs. 'I'm not the detective here.'

'Neither am I.'

'You're acting like one.'

But presumably not a particularly good one, Hannah thinks, when the only thing she can come up with is the half-arsed theory that whoever looks the most guilty must be responsible. Hannah watches as Margrét furrows her brow.

'But then again, Ægir does have a motive.'

Hannah jumps down from the desk.

'What? What do you mean he has a motive?'

Margrét leans back on the bed.

'I'm not one to reveal other people's secrets. Ask Jonni.'

Hannah is even more confused. What the fuck does that mean? And what does it mean that Margrét has now moved further up the bed and is lying down? Hannah takes a step closer. There is only half a metre between them. She holds Margrét's gaze, her heart gallops. She leans forward to kiss the volcanic woman, does so with her entire being, and when the kiss is reciprocated, she falls into an abyss from which she never wants to emerge.

22

It is impossible to say how much time has passed when Ella cautiously knocks on the door. Hannah must have fallen asleep, as she opens her eyes to an empty bed but can't remember Margrét leaving. A sadness washes over her – a feeling of having lost something that she could have held on to, if only she had been more attentive. A few dark hairs on the pillow and a scent that is not her own hits Hannah with a pang of wistful longing. Flashes of memory come to her, of naked skin against naked skin – they aren't fragments of a dream, but a full-blown affair with another human being, who she wants to share a bed with again as they plan their future together. She swings her legs from under the duvet, knowing full well that she doesn't have the romantic inclination to believe her own fantasy. Instead of chasing happiness, she should probably work on shaking off this feeling of melancholy.

Dinner consists of fish and potato, and is consumed in silence. Hannah chews slowly, occasionally glancing at Ella, who for once seems to be enjoying the peace and quiet. Or is she just unsure how to broach a conversation about all that has happened in the last few days? Death, murder and violent threats are an awful lot for someone to process, young or old. And then, of course, that awkward little situation earlier today. Does she know what happened between her and Margrét? Hannah doubts that Margrét said anything when she snuck out, but maybe all women have a kind of sixth sense when it comes to infidelity, especially when it takes place under their own roof.

Hannah suddenly remembers that Ella was meant to go to Vigdis's house, to plan Thor's funeral.

'Did you get all the planning done for the funeral?'

Ella half nods, half shakes her head.

'Will it be held in the church?'

A nod.

'And after that? Will there be a wake or anything?'

Another nod. Hannah notices that Ella has stopped eating. An absolute silence presses in on them, an inexplicable force, demanding its own space in the room. They sit there, acknowledging the silence, giving themselves to it. The wind picks up outside, rattles the windowpane. The fireplace crackles – if it hadn't been for their inner unrest, it would've been quite cosy and harmonious, sitting there in the living room together.

'Ahh!'

Ella's outburst startles Hannah, tearing her from her reverie. The scream is replaced by a primal howl that forces Ella off the chair and onto the floor, hunched over, helpless, the tears streaming down her face, hands, lap. Hannah doesn't hesitate this time, and moves closer to her host in order to wrap her arms around her. She quickly joins Ella on the floor, taking her weight and her grief. They sit like that for a while. Ella crying. Hannah not thinking at all, just being there, completely still. She stares into the flames until the final sniffle escapes Ella, who seems to have aged from the pain. When Hannah, whose thighs are now stiff, helps Ella onto her feet, it is as if their relationship has been reset. They do not speak of what just happened. Ella heads to the bathroom, and when she comes back, she puts the coffee on to brew. Hannah clears the table and washes up, almost as if they are an old married couple – there is something comforting about the thought.

Wrapped in blankets, they drink their coffee, each on her own sofa. Between them, an inherent understanding that doesn't require words. After a short while, Ella leans over the coffee table for her address book, finds a blank page and writes:

Vill you kome to funeral?

Hannah nods. Of course. The way things have developed, it seems the most likely occasion for a breakthrough in the case. Unless, of course, it's solved by then, but she doubts that. She will approach Ægir tomorrow, if she can find a way to do so that doesn't cause too many problems. On the subject of problems, she will have to try to keep her distance from Margrét from now on. No more complicating things, no more detours that could compromise the investigation. As she makes this decision, she is hit with a sudden annoyance – she does not have Margrét's phone number. She glances over at Ella's little address book, now lying open on the table between them.

When she finally returns to her room, it is a little after 2:00am. They must have eaten dinner around midnight, but the many dark

hours are gradually resetting Hannah's circadian rhythms. The
darkness does seep into everything after all. She feels too tired to
write, but knows she must maintain some kind of cadence if she is
to continue to have faith in the crime-writing project's success.
Sleepily, Hannah sits down at the keyboard, a little glass from her
last bottle of red wine by her side. She drinks frugally, and continues
where she last left off.

```
They all know who the murderer is, but no one will
tell her. She questioned the family, friends,
neighbours, but it was as if the murder had closed
in on itself and disappeared, no one wanted to
challenge the status quo, no one wanted anything to
do with
```

Wait! The saga. Hrafnkel, who no one dared challenge, who killed
the shepherd with his axe because the shepherd had ridden his
horse. Hannah grabs the book. How did the shepherd's father find
vengeance for his son's death? She reads hungrily. Learns that with
the help of other powerful farmers, the shepherd's father managed
to drag Hrafnkel to trial and force him to surrender his farm and
all his power, and with further assistance from those same powerful
farmers, the father was able to execute another sentencing of his
own: Hrafnkel and his people were driven off the farm altogether,
and the father then took over. He had the opportunity to do the
same to Hrafnkel as Hrafnkel did to his son, and once and for all
liberate the realm from his tyranny, but the father showed him
mercy, and let Hrafnkel and his people go. This, of course, backfires
when Hrafnkel regains his power and authority and returns, forcing
the father to kneel before him as he takes back his farm. Depressing
reading.

What is the moral? That you can't fight the rich and powerful,
and that – regardless of how brutal they are, how detested by the
people – they will always win? That you have to get rid of evil tyranny

completely, otherwise it will always return and take back its power? Hannah mulls it over. Why did Ella give her this saga specifically? And how can she replicate its plot without it being too obvious? Is there a bizarre connection between the saga and Thor's death?

Suddenly – the sound of a gunshot. Not somewhere in the distance, but in the living room. And another, and one more! The sound of glass shattering, and one last gunshot. Hannah throws herself, terror-stricken, under the table. What the hell was that? After the fourth shot, she hears the sound of a car accelerating from the driveway. She rushes to her feet and just manages to glimpse a set of bright tail-lights disappearing into the darkness. With shaking hands, Hannah wrenches open the door and hurtles down the staircase.

'Ella! Ella!'

The curtains billow in and out of the smashed window, the flames in the fireplace have erupted and spread to the carpet. Hannah runs over and stamps out the growing fire, while trying to get an overview of the damage. Where the hell is Ella? She concludes that there is no one dead or dying in the living room, so she hurls herself into her host's bedroom. Ella is lying in bed, but Hannah can't see whether she is dead or alive.

'Ella?'

Hannah walks towards the bed with heavy, reluctant steps, and with a cautious, outstretched arm, she tries to summon up an ounce of courage. Her shin collides with the edge of the bed, and she notices that Ella's face is completely white. Hannah extends a nervous arm, racking her brains for where you're meant to check for a pulse.

'Argh!'

Ella reaches out to her. Fuck me, she's still alive. Hannah screams in both fear and relief. The scream is contagious, and the two women scream into the dead of night, until they run out of breath. Hannah has never felt so thankful before. Now she's shaking.

'What the hell was that?'

Hannah tries to compose herself. Ella shakes her head fervently, curses in Icelandic.

'They've gone. I saw them drive away.'

Ella jumps out of bed, as if the near-death experience has made her ten years younger. She hasn't been shot then. Good. Hannah follows her into the living room, where they turn the light on and inspect the damage. Opposite the one smashed window, the glass cabinet with Ella's elephant figures has also shattered, and there are several small bullet holes in the sofa.

'A shotgun?'

Ella nods distractedly, taking the young bull elephant from the ruins of the cabinet and turning it over in her hands. It is unharmed. Hannah shudders. The missing windowpane invites the cold November air into the house.

'Do you have anything we can cover that with? And are you able to call the police?'

Ella looks up at her, as if Danish is suddenly completely incomprehensible. Hannah repeats herself.

'The police. Viktor?'

Hannah picks up the phone and hands it to Ella, who understands and puts the elephant back in its place. She dials the number for the police station. For a split second, Hannah wonders: what if it's Margrét who is jolted awake from her dreams and picks up the phone? Inappropriate. She shoves the thought away and walks out to the woodshed that Ella has pointed to, on the hunt for something to keep the Icelandic gales out of the house.

The little cobwebbed light bulb can't quite illuminate the entire shed. Hannah notices the adrenaline in her body for the first time since hearing the gunshots; it has made her unusually energetic. It's as if her lizard brain has taken over and is in survival mode, while her consciousness has gone into hibernation – the chasm between the instinctive need to do something and the inability to understand what has just happened has driven her into a surreal out-of-body-experience. This is how it must feel to be at war. Hannah shivers again. The wind weaves its way between the wide cracks in the walls of the shed – she has to get back inside. Manages to find a few boards and nails, but no hammer.

Back in the house, Ella has ended the conversation with (presumably) Viktor and is now pottering around, picking up shards of glass and dropping them into a bucket. It suddenly hits Hannah that they're acting as if the danger has definitely gone – should they be more scared? Maybe it's because they don't yet understand what happened, or what it means. But she did watch the car disappear herself, and whoever it was seemed to act as though they had completed their mission: to scare the residents of the house out of their senses.

Hannah lets her gaze wander over to Ella's antique tool collection on the wall. She thought she had seen a hammer there, but there isn't one now, just an empty hook where it probably should've been. Instead, she takes a pickaxe down from the wall, feels the weight of the old iron and beautifully carved wood in her hand. Notices the old initials engraved into it: TJ. If only all decor was this functional. With the base of the pickaxe, Hannah hammers the nails into the boards and covers up the window. She is still working on the project when Viktor comes racing up to the house in his police car, about ten minutes later. Hannah chooses to ignore what happened the last time they saw each other in the hope that, despite everything, a shooting-at-the-house episode is more serious than her crawling-through-his-garden episode.

'Stop!'

Viktor comes rushing in, as if the gunfire were still ongoing, and he was yelling at the culprit. But it's Hannah he is yelling at – running towards her, gesticulating.

'What?'

Hannah freezes. Holding up the final nail in one hand and the pickaxe in the other.

'You shouldn't have covered it up. Now it'll be almost impossible for me to find out what happened.'

'I can tell you exactly what happened. Some psychopath drove by and fired a gun into the house, as if we were fucking clay pigeons on posts.'

The snide tone only makes the situation worse, and Hannah doesn't know whether it's Viktor's hopeless police logic, her own embarrassment, or the fact that he is married to Margrét that is making her act with such civil disobedience. Viktor looks like he wants to hit her. Hannah demonstratively climbs down from the chair, as if proud of her carpentry, which she genuinely is. There are, however, one or two nails that haven't been properly knocked into place, and are thus only half attached to the surface underneath. But it's doing the job. Ella walks over to Viktor and speaks to him in Icelandic, likely providing him with a brief summary of the incident. It irritates Hannah that she can't be sure whether it's her version of the night's drama that gets relayed first.

After their witness testimony and one endless photography session later, Hannah lights a cigarette outside as she watches Viktor drive away, having provided a completely unnecessary instruction to lock the door at night. He found three shell casings out on the driveway that seem to have been released from a shotgun. Which almost everyone in town has. Ella manages to convince him that they don't need any type of protection. She would sit there herself, with her *own* shotgun, and hope that the wrongdoers come back. Then she'd *shoot them in the nuts*, as she wrote on a scrap of paper, when Hannah looked questioningly at her. Hannah doesn't fancy staying up, waiting to be taken out by the drive-by shooter on his return, or by stray bullets from Ella's gun. And she feels like she might just die of exhaustion, so after saying goodnight to the new guard dog, Ella, she crawls back into bed.

23

Waking up is hard when you haven't slept. After a few restless hours under the duvet, Hannah ventures, groggily, into the living room, where the cold has settled in like a guest who won't leave. The fireplace is lit, and Ella sits on the bullet-riddled sofa with a blanket wrapped around her, the daylight making the destruction appear forty percent worse than it did last night.

'We should get that window fixed.'

Hannah shivers and grabs a patchwork quilt.

'Is there a glazier in town?'

Ella looks at her questioningly, her nose blue. Hannah points towards the wooden structure, which she can see for herself won't last long. One of the boards has already started to come loose. She swings the patchwork quilt around her.

'Someone who can fix windows?'

'*Einmitt já.*' Ella nods.

'We'll have to get them to come today.' Hannah takes a seat on the rocking chair, feels overwhelmed by a sense of urgency. The figures from the glass cabinet are arranged neatly on the little coffee table. The cabinet, now at a weird angle, looks like it's been moved by about half a metre.

'You haven't tried moving that glass cabinet out yourself, have you? That's dangerous!'

Ella shrugs, and Hannah understands that she must just want to erase all evidence of the night's assault. She stands, finds a few old newspapers and begins to wrap them around the potentially fatal shards of glass protruding from the cabinet's sides. Then the two women, together, manage to haul the cabinet out of the house and into the back garden, where Ella stares at it bitterly for a moment, before turning around and walking back inside with the look of someone who never wants to see that cabinet again. They hoover up one more time to ensure they pick up the last few fragments of glass, and Ella puts a mat down in front of the fireplace where the

flames burnt a hole through the carpet. The window repairman –
who as far as Hannah can tell is a carpenter who also works with
glass – is free to come that same day. Ella will stay at home and wait
for him.

'Do you have any idea who it was?'

The steam rises from the coffee. Mugs in hand, sitting on the
sofas again. A blanket is now draped over the bullet holes, and apart
from the inescapable planks covering the windows and the lack of
glass cabinet, the living room almost looks like itself again. Ella's
ice-green eyes are fixed on something outside of time and space. She
looks like someone confident in what she is saying, without actually
saying a thing.

'Was it someone you know? Do you know what their motive
could've been?'

Hannah is aware that she probably sounds like an echo of Viktor
or some crappy American police drama (maybe both), but her
curiosity makes her interview technique rather uninventive. Tell me
now! Hannah looks intently at Ella, and thinks that she must look
as if she's trying to hypnotise the answer out of the woman. But
neither the questioning nor the hypnosis seems to work – Ella
remains silent.

Hannah makes another attempt.

'Ella, do you have any enemies?'

Her icy gaze pierces through Hannah, who understands that
whoever Ella's enemies are, their names will remain a secret. Right,
okay then. She had to try at least. And it has come as a surprise to
Hannah that Ella does in fact have unfinished business with
someone. If not affability itself, the old woman has always seemed
as if she's swallowed a happy pill. But not today. Hannah can't figure
out whether Ella is afraid, angry or just pensive. Maybe a
combination of all three.

'Would it be okay if I went for a little walk, or are you ... Will
you be alright at home alone?'

Ella smiles a little smile. Nods as she writes a little note on a piece of paper: *I not afraid of being alene*. Hannah nods back, drains her cup and leaves the old woman on her bullet-ridden sofa.

The rain has helped erase all traces of the gun-happy maniac. Hannah can see no sign of any tyre tracks out front. Come to think of it, did Viktor take any photos outside last night? A rare moment of gratitude for the local police officer is added to Hannah's cocktail of emotions, as she just now realises how tactful it was of him not to mention her embarrassing attempt-to-talk-to-Jonni stunt. And she does actually quite like him, the policeman. It's not his fault that his job requires him to keep to himself the answers Hannah wants, and it is also not his fault that he happens to be married to the woman who Hannah has ... Yes, what exactly? Anyway. She must remember to treat Viktor with more respect and kindness.

On the walk up to Ægir's house, it occurs to Hannah that maybe she should, perhaps, be a bit more worried for her safety. Someone tried to shoot her last night, and here she is, walking around in broad daylight like a living, breathing target. She forces herself to calm down and repeats to herself her theory that it was probably just a warning. If someone had really wanted to kill them, they could easily have snuck into Ella's unlocked house and murdered them both in their sleep. Hannah is convinced that Ella knows who shot at them. She also has a strong suspicion of who that person was, and she intends to confront them with this very theory.

It is Vigdis who opens the door. She looks smaller than she did yesterday. Can grief make people shrink by several centimetres overnight? Hannah apologises for disturbing her and explains that Ella sent her up here to ask if there's anything she can help with. Vigdis stares at her, perplexed. Fuck. Fair enough though. What a pathetic excuse. She clears her throat.

'Okay, to be honest, Ella hasn't sent me. In fact, she has no idea that I'm here. And I know you don't need anything else on your plate right now, but I just wanted to let you know that someone fired at Ella's house last night. With a shotgun.'

Vigdis's hand flies to her mouth. Hannah tries not to think about how angry Ella would be if she knew that Hannah was standing here, bothering this poor, grieving mother with reports of a shooting at Ella's house. And judging from Vigdis's reaction, Ella doesn't seem to have called and told her anything. This seems to be an advantage for Hannah, in terms of her cover story at least, but a disadvantage when she allows herself to think about how furious Ella will be when she finds out.

'I just thought you would want to know. Especially as Ella doesn't seem to have that many people close to her.'

Admittedly a little trite, drawing the pathos card, but Hannah doesn't have any other jokers in her hand. Vigdis thanks her, is pleased she told her. She asks if Ella is okay, to which Hannah confirms that yes, she is, and then asks Vigdis if she and Ægir would mind not mentioning the fact that Hannah was the one who told them? They could both just say that they heard it from someone in town. Vigdis nods.

'If it's not too much trouble either, I wondered if I could perhaps have a chat with Ægir, just to see if he has any ideas on ways we could make the house a bit more secure?'

Vigdis hesitates, then opens the door a little wider for Hannah, who is relieved, but also a little irritated at how a woman's appeal for a man's help always seems to be credible.

The stone man is sitting in front of the large panoramic windows, staring out at the mountains. His gaze turns to Vigdis as she announces Hannah's presence in Icelandic. Hannah is somewhat surprised that there seems to be no form of recognition in Ægir's eyes. She could understand if he didn't remember her from Thor's viewing, but she would expect her name to generate some sort of reaction, given he drove past the house in the middle of last night and fired a gun at her. Vigdis excuses herself, to Hannah's relief. But once she has disappeared, Hannah is overwhelmed by an unexpected discomfort. The mission suddenly seems a lot less simple than she had first assumed. She shuffles uneasily in the chair Vigdis gestured for her to sit in. Something about Ægir's gaze makes her particularly awkward. The formerly blank expression has been replaced by something else beneath those deep forehead wrinkles. It's difficult to define, but whatever it is, it brings out a nervousness in Hannah. Or perhaps fear. She tries to stick to her plan and hopes that he won't use the language barrier as an excuse to get out of the situation ... And that her voice doesn't tremble too much.

'I know it was you.'

Ægir stares at her like a calm psychopath. Hannah feels like she's being analysed, examined.

'Last night. I saw the back of your car.'

Hannah's bluffing – strictly speaking, she can't know for sure whether the tail-lights she saw actually belong to Ægir's car, given he doesn't own the only four-wheel drive in town. But she just knows. She *knows*.

'I don't know what you're talking about.'

The stone face doesn't reveal a thing, but at least shows her the courtesy of answering in English. Hannah notices Ægir's hands – large and rough, the veins snaking up his muscular forearms like wires, the grey hair still enviably thick. He hasn't just been, but still is, an attractive man. She lowers her gaze, doesn't want to reveal her fascination. She knows he's lying. Furthermore, she can decode Icelandic well enough to understand that Vigdis summarised Hannah's report of the events of the night before, when she introduced her. He knows exactly what she's talking about, so why this denial, this game?

'You should know – I can't be scared so easily.'

He raises an eyebrow. Rests his fisherman's hands, which almost look like large leather gloves, on his lap – one on top of the other.

'You surely don't have the audacity to come here and accuse me of being responsible? My son has just been killed, and I don't have the time or energy to listen to some crazy Danish woman who is running around, pointing the finger at me for some sort of assassination attempt.'

Hannah can tell that Ægir feels as if he has the upper hand, but she holds her ground. She has him right where she wants him.

'It's not my accusation that annoys you. It's the subject. You know that I've been asking around about your son's death and that the questions have something to do with you. So I'm going to ask you directly: why were you there that night, at the place where Thor drowned?'

'Aaargh!'

Ægir explodes. Springs to his feet and overturns the table and his coffee. His giant body stretches up, almost to the ceiling. He towers over Hannah with his clenched leather fists. Hannah doesn't even try to make any placatory excuses, just launches herself out of the house as if it were on fire. Fuck. That is the second time in twenty-four hours that she has found herself running, mortified, from a failed interrogation. Shit, shit, shit!

Hannah runs down the road, tripping over her own feet, galvanised by adrenaline and embarrassment.

She feverishly lights a cigarette. It glows in the darkness that has already started settling over the town. Wasn't it just morning? Hannah exhales a cloud of smoke, curses inwardly. Apart from the humiliation of being driven out of the house by the wrath of a grieving father, she also has the strong impression that she could not have chosen a worse strategy to coax information out of Ægir. She smacks herself on the forehead, knowing that she has also just revealed to Ægir that 1) she is investigating his son's death, and 2) believes him to be the prime suspect. But if it wasn't Ægir who had wanted to scare her off, who the hell fired that gun at her yesterday? She'll have to refine her technique if she wants to get any closer to solving this mystery. Unless it's already too late. This time, she's going to have to share her blunder with Ella. Or is she? Can she prevent Ella hearing that she's antagonised the stone man? Possibly.

If Ægir feels at all guilty, he may not even say anything. But of course there's Vigdis, Ella's own sister, who will probably mention the incident. Unless Hannah could persuade her not to? She has to go back to the house.

Once in front of the door, she hesitates. What if Ægir opens it? The sneak-around-the-back strategy has proved to be useless, but could she perhaps wait for Ægir to leave the house? Then again, why would he? Resigned, Hannah turns on the spot, has half made peace with the fact that she will have to repent to Ella, when the door suddenly opens. It's Vigdis, who places a shushing finger over her lips and then steps out and gently closes the door behind her.

She whispers, 'I'm sorry that he blew up at you like that. He does that sometimes.'

Hannah stares rather astonished at the guilt-ridden woman before her. Imagine losing your son and then having to run around seeing to the fall-out from your husband's anger. In this case, it was probably a legitimate outbreak of rage, but Vigdis doesn't seem to be aware of that. Good. So they don't talk, and Ægir has a habit of arguing over nothing. That's as much as Hannah can assume from the situation, and even though it makes her feel guilty, it does work to her advantage. It's easy to be forgiving when you're the one in the wrong.

'It's fine. It's my own fault anyway. I mentioned Thor, and I shouldn't have done. I just wanted to offer my condolences.'

Okay, the whole saintly excuse may be a bit transparent. But it lands. Vigdis takes her hands in her own.

'I know it's a lot to ask of you, but could we possibly forget about this little incident?'

There's nothing in the world Hannah wants more than that. She nods, consenting, but still finds it all a little bizarre. Vigdis must have her own reasons for the secrecy, and Hannah thinks she might understand.

'They don't get on all that well, do they – Ella and Ægir?'

Vigdis hesitates a moment, then shakes her head.

'I don't know why, but they've always been that way. Ella doesn't care for him and ... yes, things like this don't make it any easier.'

Hannah nods understandingly. She puts her hand on top of Vigdis's now and is surprised when Vigdis pulls her in for a confidential hug.

'Promise me that you'll take good care of her.'

'Of course.'

Hannah doesn't say anything about the fact that Ella seems perfectly capable of taking care of herself. Now she just has to ask one last, difficult question of her own. Hannah pulls away from the hug.

'Do you ... Would it be best if I don't come to the funeral?'

Vigdis looks at her, confused.

'Because of this? No! You should be there. As long as you're living with my sister, you're part of the family. And, um, not to cause offence, but Ægir will be so focused on some of the other guests that he probably won't even notice that you're there.'

Hannah nods but doesn't understand. Ægir's not all that well liked, sure, but that there are people who would come to his son's funeral who he needs to 'focus on' sounds a little mysterious. Hannah leaves the house of mourning feeling unsettled and with even more questions.

24

Isn't it the case that a simple murder is no longer enough to make a good crime novel these days? Shouldn't there by at least four to five distractions along the way, diverting the reader's attention? And then some kind of shift between the various viewpoints and timeframes in the text, tricking the reader into thinking that it's more exciting than it actually is. That's what Hannah must try to achieve, anyhow. Fifty pages into the book is probably the right point at which to introduce a whole new murder and start to merge the characters' different perspectives, so the readers don't get bored. Hannah sits at her writing spot in front of the window and feels somewhat encouraged. Sure, she didn't manage to cajole any admissions out of Ægir, but his reaction only confirmed her suspicions: he's hiding something. And at the funeral, she plans to find out what that is.

Only one person was hit with a stronger grief than Tore's parents: Esther. She had been his girlfriend for the last three years, and they had only ever had eyes for each other. Childhood friends, they had kissed for the first time on a school trip up to the glacier, had taken each other's virginity on an old fishing boat, the seagulls as witnesses. Esther sat with a cold cup of tea in front of her. Felt empty, as if she didn't care if she lived or died. She could not find the energy to continue living, nor to die. All she could think about was revenge. She knew who the murderer was. In her head, she planned out how she would break in through the bedroom window, the one she knew was always open while he slept. She would slink in like a cat, move noiselessly towards the bed, and then make her presence known before plunging the knife into his chest. She wanted him to look her in the eyes and know what was happening to him, know that she could not accept his murder of her beloved. And that she would get away with it, she knew this for a fact. She had already devised the perfect alibi.

Hannah looks up, pleased. Who knew writing a crime novel could actually be fun? That's because it's not proper literature, so there's no pressure. In fact, she's never felt so at liberty with her artistic expression, has never before written so many words in such a short amount of time. She feels even more satisfied at the thought that she's proving her own theory right, that any old idiot can write a crime novel in a month. She feels a sudden desire to call Bastian. It takes two attempts before he picks up.

'Don't think that just because I'm in Iceland, you can get rid of me entirely.'

'Hannah, how good it is to hear from you. I was just in the middle of a lunch meeting. How's it going?'

'A lunch meeting with who? It's going really well. I've written fifty-five pages. And I'm just now starting to introduce more perspectives, so I'm well on the way to becoming the new queen of Nordic Noir.'

'You're fifty-five pages in without merging the perspectives? You should have at least introduced all of the points of view within the first twenty.'

'Says who? Is that a rule? And who are you having lunch with?'

'I mean, it's not a rule per se. But it is the done thing.'

'The *done* thing? What's up with you? I call you with good news, that I'm making good progress with novel, and you criticise me from all the way over there and refuse to tell me who you're eating lunch with.'

Silence on the other end. An unease takes hold of Hannah.

'Hello? Are you there?'

Now she's really starting to feel anxious. Bastian never hides anything from her.

'Has the write-a-crime-novel-in-a-month project been dropped without you telling me, or what?'

Nervous laughter on the other end of the line. 'No, no, of course not. Christ.'

Hannah can hear the sound of a door opening, street traffic, and Bastian lighting a cigarette. He's stepped outside – away from whom?

'I can't be dealing with this. Tell me who you're sneaking about eating lunch with right now or I'll go out and find a crevasse in the glacier to fall down.'

Bastian hesitates, the sound of sirens in the distance. It's funny. Hannah's only been in Iceland for a few days, but she has already forgotten the daily routine of Copenhagen's emergency vehicles, a sound so commonplace that the sirens stopped interrupting her concentration years ago. Up here, she hasn't heard a single siren, even though crimes seem to occur more often than it rains. Could it be a woman Bastian is lunching with?

'Are you on a date or something, is that it?'

'No. I'm just getting a drink with...'

'With whom?'

Another pause. A long sigh, presumably accompanied by the stubbing out of his cigarette.

'Jørn Jensen.'

'Sorry, what did you just say?'

Hannah's ears are ringing, but there's no interference on the line.

'I know it sounds strange, but he's actually quite a nice guy.'

'A nice guy?'

Hannah's mouth has gone completely dry.

'Yeah ... so ... we got to talking after the book fair, and then...'

'What the hell are you saying? That you picked up Jørn Fucking J. at the book fair, without saying a word to me, and you've been kissing his ass ever since?'

'Hannah, goddammit, relax. It's just lunch and a couple of beers.'

'Lunch and a couple of beers? That's a date! A date at the men's club, where you plan how to get rid of the woman who—'

'Hannah, now you're just going on a feminist rant.'

'Fuck you, Bastian.'

Hannah hangs up and chucks the phone onto the bed. What kind of insane conspiracy is going on here? Is this something they cooked up together and carried out behind her back, all this time? No, reel back the paranoia, this was her own idea. But why the hell is Bastian suddenly socialising with her arch-nemesis? What do they have in common. What...? Oh no. This can only mean one thing: Bastian has lost faith in her project. He's already laying the groundwork to get in with her worst competitor. It all makes sense. Jørn fits in well with Bastian's other 'writers'. He's only kept Hannah on for the prestige she gives to the publishing house, so they have a serious, known writer, but now – as she's digging the grave of her own career – Bastian's on the prowl to lure her arch-rival behind company lines. Fucking capitalist pig. Hannah holds back a scream, sees her phone light up: an incoming text. She angrily scoops it up, and sees it's a message from Bastian:

Don't take it so personally. Relax, I'm still your editor. I'm on your side. And Jørn is nice enough, once you get to know him. He's even offered to give you some pointers for your novel.

'Argh!'

Hannah hurls the phone against the wall and the screen smashes as it hits the floor like a fired projectile. What a goddamn lie! 'Pointers for my novel'? Hannah screams into her pillow, tears at it, kicks the bed.

'For fuck's sake.'

Kicks it again.

Ella suddenly appears in the doorway and Hannah slides down to the floor, sobbing over her bloody toe as the down from the butchered pillow cascades around her, like the final cloud of dust settling on doomsday.

'Absurd. It's all just so absurd.'

Hannah is now sitting on the sofa, both wound up and despondent at the same time, her foot outstretched and resting on a chair, with Ella bandaging it up.

'Ow!' Hannah tries to squirm away.

Ella lightens her grip on the swollen ankle.

Shit. Now she'll be hobbling around for the next few days.

'Disloyal is the worst thing someone can be.'

Ella looks up at her, nods. An expression on her face that suggests that she can't agree more. She gently rests the foot on the chair and gets up. Hannah sends her a grateful smile.

'Thank you. And sorry – for behaving like this. They just really piss me off.'

Ella returns with a piping-hot cup of coffee, passes it to Hannah and sits down opposite her. Writes something on the back of an envelope.

Wat now? You give up on the bok?

'Fuck no! Ach, sorry, I swear too much. But this is all just so shit.'

Hannah blows on the coffee, sits there a moment and stares into space. As does Ella. Hannah is gripped by a sudden and overwhelming sense of embarrassment.

'Sorry. I know none of this is a problem, compared to what you're going through.'

Ella writes.

We all har our problemer. Mine don't make yours any less.

Hannah nods but isn't quite sure she agrees. Now her foot is all bandaged up and there's coffee in her cup, her hurt feelings seem positively trivial in comparison to Ella's murdered nephew and the subsequent attempt on her life. But they can't be allowed to get to her like this. Jørn J. cannot succeed in making her abandon her project, if that's what he's trying to do, and he certainly can't be allowed to interfere with his obnoxious pointers. Her pulse begins to rise again. Her foot starts pounding. Pull it together, Hannah – no more talking to Bastian. Do this whole thing without him, without either of them, and show them all that she can write a crime novel, and a damn good one at that. Without anyone's help. That's it, that's the plan. Hannah is disappointed in Bastian though. And genuinely hurt. It's one thing flirting with Jørn for purely professional – or rather, business-related – reasons, but it's something else entirely to abuse her friendship like this. Hannah has always believed that friendships adhere to the unreasonable-jealousy logic of romantic relationships: if there is a person with whom, for certain well-argued reasons, you do not like your partner or friend associating, then naturally you have the right to expect that they won't. Has Viktor forbidden Margrét from seeing her? Hannah reaches over to her smashed-up phone, which Ella has tried to tape back together, but despite repeated attempts, it won't turn on. Oh well. Margrét doesn't even have her number, and she can't be arsed dealing with Bastian, ergo, she has no use for a phone.

25

Another three pages from Esther's perspective and, by the time Hannah realises she should be getting to bed, she has managed to map out and draft a revenge plot of the most brutal nature. In fact, two more lives have been lost in the space of those three new pages: one stabbed to death, and who in Hannah's mind's eye has Jørn's face; and the other with Bastian's familiar traits. Pure catharsis. All that writing has made her thirsty, but the only bottles left in her suitcase are empty. Hannah glances at the clock. Almost midnight. Too late (and pitiful) to limp into town with her busted-up toe. Ella is already in bed, and it occurs to Hannah that the chances of finding something alcoholic in the house might not actually be zero. She may not have seen any wine around, but she hasn't looked for it. Uplifted by the thought, she hobbles downstairs. Kitchen: nothing. Living room: nothing. Hannah grumbles, irritated, and drops into a chair. She's gone through the back of every cupboard and every other conceivable storage space. Contemplates. Her foot now pounding. What about the woodshed? Could there be anything out there? She can't remember having seen anything when she was in there last, other than firewood and tools. What about a basement, if there is one? No, not that she knows of. And it would probably be too optimistic to hope that this rural, working-class home has a wine cellar. But a home-brewing cellar, perhaps? Okay. Deep breath in, try to be at least sixty-percent less desperate. Hannah sits there, feeling sorry for herself and just as she concludes that she doesn't need any alcohol, another room in the house comes to mind: Ella's study. She's only ever sent a few indifferent glances in there, what with it being two doors down from her own bedroom and generally looking equally boring each time she's seen in: a small desk and chair, a full bookshelf, coated in dust and wrapped in an aura of stagnation that reminds Hannah of a museum. Could there possibly be a small bottle of liquor in there somewhere? Her toe suddenly doesn't hurt all that much, and she practically runs back up the stairs.

To her surprise, the door is locked. Damn. Why is that? Has to be a mistake, surely. Ella doesn't even have a lock on the bathroom door – something that has already resulted in a number of awkward situations. And the front door was always left unlocked, up until the drive-by shooting, anyway. Hannah grabs the letter opener from her room and tries to pry open the lock like a burglar. The lock is uncooperative, to put it mildly, and when the little knife snaps in half, Hannah's craving for a drink doubles. She curses silently, convinced now that there *must* be alcohol hiding behind that door. The thought becomes an obsession, and she hobbles out to the woodshed to find a more resilient screwdriver. After clattering about some more inside the keyhole, she realises the pursuit is hopeless. Instead, she firmly jams the screwdriver in between the door and the doorframe, twists it, leans against the door and, coughing loudly, shoves her entire weight into it, so it breaks open. She stops and listens for a moment, but the house is quiet. Ella doesn't seem to have heard a thing. Hannah enters the study and turns on the light. Examines a built-in cabinet first, but it isn't concealing anything other than old clothes that haven't been worn for decades. The bookshelf is then inspected – a few sagas are dotted here and there between the reference books and paperbacks of the kind you used to get with women's magazines. On the bottom shelf, a series of ring binders that look like ledgers, and a photo album. Hannah pulls out the latter. It must've sat there untouched for at least twenty years, almost mummified in dust. She carefully pries it open, the pages of brown card, the photos hidden behind parchment paper. Almost reverently, she lifts the thin paper to reveal black-and-white photos of small children in front of what Hannah recognises as Ella's house – albeit with an extension (a barn?) that must have since been torn down. A young girl with wild hair poses for the camera with a baby in her lap. Ella, with her new-born sister, Vigdis? She flips through several years of the album, watches as the girls grow up, Ella celebrates her confirmation, and then a few years' worth of photos of just the one girl. Vigdis. And one more image of the two of them, Ella now a young woman. And then just Vigdis, and only Vigdis from that point on, until the black-and-white photos stop, the last image only half-developed, as if the developer ran out of ink. Hannah flips through the empty pages, thinking of the very few photos there are from her own childhood. All documentation of her upbringing stopped in her early teens, and from that point on, Hannah has no visual aids to help trigger her memories, just her lived experiences. And Hannah occasionally doubts her memory of what she actually got up to in the years between the ages of thirteen and twenty. But she's not the type of person to sit and flick through photo albums anyway. Hannah lets out a long sigh at the thought of all the photos that exist of her sister's ugly family, arranged in numerous ghastly photo albums, which she has been forced to trawl through more than once. But why does Ella seem to disappear for what seems like a good few years? Hannah flips back through the album, trying to spot something she didn't pick up on the first time. Why is Ella not around for so many of her teenage years? Camera shy? Boarding school? Did Iceland even have boarding schools back then? Hannah studies the images again. Something seems to change in the young Ella's gaze between the last picture before her disappearance, and that after her return: her eyes look empty. Hannah continues through to the end of the album again, and now sees a pattern she did not see before: Ella smiling in all her childhood photos, and then in those of her adolescence, not a single smile. Hannah shakes her head – she's not one for smiling much in photos either. She must remember to ask Ella a bit more about her life story. It occurs to her that she knows very little about her host. She puts the album back in its place and continues her search.

The desk drawers hide neither flasks nor any other secret vices, and the bottom one is locked. Hannah is overwhelmed with curiosity, and this time, the lock is easier to pick. After a slight twist of the larger half of the letter opener, the drawer slides open. Folders. Hannah rifles through them: insurance documents. As she goes to close the drawer, frustrated about her failed alcohol raid, her hand brushes over a hard object beneath the folders. A small, porcelain sugar bowl. A strange place to store such a thing. She lifts it out and takes off the lid. Inside: a necklace. Hannah gently takes the chain in her hands – it doesn't look particularly valuable, in fact, she doubts that it's made of any precious metal at all. Silver, maybe, but it looks most like a cheap souvenir you'd buy at a market. The coarse chain is broken and holds a pendant, which is easily recognisable: Thor's hammer. Hannah hazards a guess that the special location of this rather cheap piece of jewellery, in its sugar-bowl-in-a-locked-desk-drawer hiding spot, means that it must hold some sentimental value. Why else would Ella keep it hidden away so carefully when she leaves her big gold rings lying around in the bathroom? Hannah puts the necklace back, closes the drawer and even manages to lock it. The study door, however, she cannot put back in the same way; the frame has splintered somewhat where she forced the screwdriver in and the lock out. She picks a few of the rogue pieces of wood from the floor in an attempt to minimise the traces of her vandalism. Hopes that Ella doesn't notice.

Hannah lies in bed for a long time, staring out into the Icelandic darkness, until she eventually falls asleep, and when the dreams do finally infiltrate her subconscious, they plough through it like a freight train full of memories that do not belong to her, but which played out in this very house, over fifty years ago.

26

Morning. Her toe aches. It feels like there's a little troll trapped beneath the bandages, hammering and trying to get out. Hannah forgets for a moment that her phone is broken, and sighs as she tries to turn it on, without success. What time is it? She hops over to the window and pulls the curtain aside. The overcast sky seems to be keeping the start of the day at a distance.

On her way to the bathroom, something makes Hannah jump. The door to the study is open, and standing in the middle of the room is Ella, scowling at her. It is the first time she has felt any anger from her host, and Ella's piercing gaze hits her like a shockwave. Hannah shrinks. Clears her throat. Lies.

'I thought I heard someone in here last night.'

Hannah glances at the doorframe.

'I was worried that they would come back. They, being whoever shot at us. And as I didn't have the key, I broke the door down. To chase them away ... if they were in here.'

Ella's gaze feels like a lie detector. Hannah can hear how obvious the lie is. Christ.

'Sorry, I should have thought it through more. I was desperate for a drink and thought that there might be something in here. Spirits, or something like that. Dumb, I know.'

Ella looks as if she's weighing up whether or not to believe Hannah. A moment passes. It looks as if she reaches the conclusion that the explanation is pathetic enough that it must be true. But no forgiveness follows the truth.

Ella turns off the light and closes the door behind her, locks it demonstratively. Sends Hannah a withering glare.

'I'll pay for the doorframe to be fixed of course. I'm sorry.'

Ella doesn't respond, but as she heads downstairs, Hannah hears her grumbling something in Icelandic. Thinks she is able to decode a few expletives. She remains standing there for a moment.

Embarrassed at being so driven by her own cravings, which were strong enough that she broke down a locked door, but more embarrassed about the fact that she violated her host's trust. Fuck's sake.

A few minutes later, standing in the shower, trying to wash away her sins, Hannah can't help but wonder why Ella couldn't just wave aside her little stunt this time. Obviously it's a pain that one of her doors is now broken, but the Ella that Hannah knows would, on a good day, laugh it off and just get it fixed. But it doesn't seem to be the splintered doorframe that has annoyed Ella. More the fact that Hannah went into her study in the first place. Is she hiding something in there? Hannah turns the knob for the cold water and rinses away the thought with a little scream; she wasn't hiding anything in that room other than a dusty past.

Hannah decides to skip breakfast. She has no interest in feeling Ella's heated disappointment, nor in having to explain herself any further. With a cowardly 'see you later' she slips out of the front door with her laptop and a plan to spend the day writing at the bar. However much she needs to get out of the house, she can't let a day go by without working on the book. Her naïve hope is that she'll manage to double her efficiency by writing in a public space where she may also be able to glean some new information for Thor's murder investigation.

She orders coffee, toast and a soft-boiled egg. As the first of the bar's guests that day, she decides to sit at one of the tables, hoping that the regular customers don't come in until much later. Morning isn't exactly the time she is at her peak productivity, so she orders a little shot of whisky to go with her coffee, just to kick-start the system and get the creativity flowing. Isolating herself from her surroundings with a pair of headphones, which aren't actually playing anything, Hannah gets a few pages written in the space of an hour, and when the first of the retired fishermen start to drift in, she moves over to the bar for a bit of a change of scene. Once there, she orders another whisky with her coffee, and tries to drum up a conversation with the leather vest. She starts with some small talk.

'Not so busy in here in the mornings then?'

The leather vest shrugs, turns the page of his newspaper. 'Gives me plenty of time to read this.'

Hannah can't quite work out if that means he wants to be left in peace. But she's too curious. Remembers that sometimes you have to offer a bit of gossip to get some back.

'I don't know if you heard, but we had a little scare the other day. Or, rather, quite a big scare. Someone attacked the house.'

The leather vest raises an eyebrow from over the top of the newspaper. Okay, so he hasn't heard about the shooting. Hannah straightens up. Bingo. She throws out another titbit.

'Someone shot at the house in the middle of the night. Grim stuff.'

Hannah tries to look shaken up, and it works. The newspaper is folded up and put aside. She has his attention.

'Was anyone hurt?' The bartender's concern appears to be genuine.

Hannah shakes her head.

'Just a shattered window and a few bullet holes in the sofa. Seemed more like an attempt to scare us rather than actually harm us. But still, really unpleasant.'

'And you don't know who did it?' The bartender's eyes examine Hannah, perturbed.

She shakes her head and shrugs, resigned. 'I really can't imagine Ella having any enemies or someone who would want to hurt her.'

'What makes you think that she was the target?'

Hannah shuffles uneasily on the seat. What did he mean by that? Was she the target?

'You don't think whoever it was, was out for me, do you?'

The leather vest shrugs. Then turns to another customer, the woman with the dog. Hannah takes a sip of her coffee and whisky. Is she perhaps getting a little too close to exposing the murderer?

Hannah knows enough about crime and investigations to understand that the detective's life is always at risk when they get close to the truth. But it still seems rather absurd, given she's not at all close to revealing the truth. Thus far, Ægir is her one and only suspect. And the dead ends she's wound up in have been one too many. She drains the cup. What now, if it does turn out to be her and not Ella that someone is trying to intimidate? Is it because she is a sharper detective than Viktor? Hannah chuckles to herself. Okay, she doesn't actually think that highly of her own investigative skills. But why shoot at her? Or could Viktor be involved? A shiver runs down her spine, and she decides that now is probably the right time to stop making up conspiracy theories. She must re-evaluate the case.

The woman with the dog looks neither welcoming nor thankful when Hannah approaches her, balancing two cups of coffee in her hands and a scheming smile on her face, which she hopes looks inviting, but which most likely makes her look like an idiot.

'Hi there. Sorry to bother you, but I noticed that we were both sitting here alone, drinking coffee, and so I thought ... that perhaps we could do so together?'

The woman looks blankly at Hannah, who feels as dumb on the inside as she must look on the outside, two cups of coffee in her hands. She tries the idiot smile again.

'But I now see that you already have plenty of coffee in your cup. That was silly of me...'

Hannah runs out of words and dignity. She is just about to turn and leave, when the dog woman takes one of the cups and points to the barstool beside her. Hannah hesitates, and then sits.

'I've noticed your dog. He's so cute.'

Hannah glances down at the dog and hopes the lie isn't too blatantly obvious. The dog drools. Just so long as she doesn't have to pat it. What breed is it, even? It looks up at her meekly through a load of fluff – maybe some kind of sheepdog? The woman empties the coffee from the cup Hannah gave her into her own and slowly takes a slip. There is a certain calmness about her hands that is almost disconcerting, somehow – a self-assurance that makes Hannah nervous. She observes her new bar friend. Close up, she doesn't look like the alcoholic Hannah first assumed she was.

'I always come here to get my coffee.' The dog woman talks as if she has read Hannah's thoughts.

'Same here.'

Hannah feels ridiculous. A lie in every single sentence so far – a bad start to a new acquaintanceship.

'I'm just visiting, so I don't know many people here in town. I'm Hannah.'

The dog woman looks sideways at her. 'You're staying at Ella's, no?'

'Uh, yes. Do you know her?'

The dog woman nods. Of course.

'I imagine you must've heard about the murder. Tragic.'

The dog woman turns to face Hannah. 'Are they saying it's a murder?'

Oh, no! That's not meant to be public knowledge, the fact that Thor's death is being investigated as a murder. She wants to bite her tongue. Hannah tries to withdraw the statement, but murder is a difficult word to downplay.

'The death, I mean. Thor's death. I don't know whether a crime occurred, of course, but I believe they always look into it, just in case.'

Always look into it? This conversation needs to be nipped in the bud as soon as possible. How does she manage to be so incredibly ungraceful – trying to extract information out of someone, but ending up sitting there, doing all the talking herself, like some inane chatterbox? There must be something she can get out of this otherwise failed attempt at getting some new information. The dog woman's eyes have glazed over, and it looks like the information that there may have been a murder has transported her somewhere else entirely, which is fair enough. Who wouldn't be afraid at the thought of a murderer on the loose in town?

'Did you know Thor?' Hannah tries to lure her conversation partner out of her reverie.

She succeeds. The dog woman looks at her again, this time with an indeterminate expression in her eyes. Fear? She shakes her head.

'Not really. But he seemed like a nice young man. A shame, to die so young.'

Hannah suddenly feels something wet on the back of her leg and looks down to see the dog drying his disgusting, slobbery mouth on her trouser leg. He looks up at her, expectantly, grumbles a bit. She pulls her leg away, the owner notices, realises what the dog is doing and tugs on the lead.

'Rex, no! Sorry about that.'

'It's fine.'

Hannah puts the idiot smile back on her face, convinced she looks like a child molester trying to coax a kid into her van. Unfortunately, the dog woman steps down from the barstool and pulls the dog away.

'Thanks for the coffee. And sorry about the drool.'

'No problem.'

Hannah smiles at the dog, and suddenly thinks of something.

'Actually, there was one little thing … I know this is a bit of a crazy question, but you haven't by any chance seen anyone around town with a head injury, have you? From something like … being hit with a bottle?'

The dog woman stares at Hannah, as if Hannah really is an idiot.

'Why?'

'Oh, it's just … you know what, forget it.'

Hannah admits defeat. But the dog woman takes a step towards her, whispers, 'Do you think that whoever has an injury like that could have had something to do with the murder…?'

Hannah nods cautiously. Reluctant to reveal more about her own suspicions, but unwilling to miss any potential leads.

'The homeless guy. He has a large bump on the back of his head.' The dog woman tells her this with a serious expression.

'Gísli?'

Hannah is taken aback – can it be? The dog woman pauses, then nods. But before Hannah can ask her anything else, both the dog and the woman have disappeared outside. Hannah sits for a while. Only then does she realise that she didn't ask the woman's name.

27

Gísli is not in his shack. Of course. Hannah has downed another whisky and coffee before heading out to try and find him. What if Gísli is the murderer? She finds that hard to believe, which is perhaps the reason why she isn't more concerned for her safety. But Gísli, for some reason, isn't anywhere near her radar of people capable of committing murder. But maybe we are all capable or killing another person, if the circumstances are right. And Hannah can't rule out that they might have been for Gísli that night: perhaps he came across Thor, they ended up in some sort of argument, maybe a tussle. Thor ends up hitting Gísli with the bottle of vodka, and as a countermove, Gísli strikes Thor in the neck with something blunt. Thor falls into the water. Gísli panics and holds his head below the surface until the lifeless body stops jerking. Riddled with guilt, he then heads to Bragginn and drinks himself into a stupor. Returns to the scene of the crime and sees Ægir pulling his son's body out of the water. It all fits together a little too well. Hannah once read somewhere that many murderers actually contact the police themselves after killing their victim. If it is the case that Gísli has a vodka-bottle-inflicted wound, then it is highly likely that he is also the perpetrator. A sadness washes over her at the thought.

Waiting in the shack – Gísli's little kingdom – she watches the waves as they break against the rocks, her legs tucked beneath her. A feeling starts to gnaw away at her, or rather, a longing. A longing for Margrét to be sitting by her side, taking in the view with her.

She is strangely warmed by the thought. Imagines a night spent in the shack, the two of them entwined, to protect each other from the wind…

'I love getting visitors!'

Hannah jumps, embarrassed by her own fantasy, as if it were visible to others. It's Gísli, whose happy head appears in the doorway. It doesn't look like the face of a murderer, but what does she know? Perhaps a murderer would smile like Gísli, perhaps they would also have those friendly wrinkles around their eyes and a mischievous hint of concern around their mouth, as the man now entering the shack does. Hannah notices her pulse begin to rise, and she tries to make herself seem calm and collected.

'I just wanted to see how you were doing, after the other day.'

'Why, thank you. That's very kind.'

Gísli sits down next to her, seems genuinely touched by her consideration. He fumbles around with a carton of beers. Finds two and passes one to Hannah. She shakes her head – isn't enough of an alcoholic to scrounge a can of booze from an almost-homeless man.

'It's been bothering me.' Gísli cracks one of the beers open with his left hand and stares out over the sea.

Hannah watches him closely, her pulse now rising to breakneck speed. She tries to regulate her breathing. Is he about to confess?

'The image of Ægir pulling Thor out of the water. It keeps coming back to me. It makes me feel queasy. And sad.'

Okay, not so much of a confession. Hannah considers Gísli. Does he have a vodka-bottle wound back there somewhere? It's hard to tell, as his hat is pulled far down over his ears. Hannah holds her hands up to cover her own.

'Christ, my ears are freezing.'

Gísli turns to look her.

'That's because you're not wearing a hat. Iceland in November without a hat is … stupid.'

'I know, I just left it at home.'

'Do you want to borrow mine?'

'Ah, no, I don't want you to go without.'

But before Hannah has a chance to say anything else, Gísli has taken off his hat and placed it on Hannah's frozen head. It reeks, and Hannah tries to dispel all thoughts of the bacteria that may have just been transferred from Gísli's head to hers. She can't bring herself to look at him, it was almost too easy swindling him out of his hat – his kindness is all too easy to see through.

'Better?'

Hannah nods, smiles. 'Thank you.'

She slowly turns to face him, starts studying his head. His hair is tangled in a way only scissors could rectify. It clings to his scalp, but Hannah can't immediately see any wounds or bumps. She needs to come up with an excuse to have a look at the other side of his head. She gets up, raising her arm to protect herself from the wind now blowing in from the sea, battering the shack.

'Oh, it's so nice to feel that fresh air.'

'Are you no longer freezing?'

Hannah wraps her arms around her body, a little too buoyant, too restored. As if she has only just discovered the wind and weather.

'We city folk have a strange relationship with nature. We love it and hate it in equal measure. It's like a bad date: we kind of want it, but don't know how to dress for it.'

Gísli smiles. Takes a mouthful of his beer.

Hannah turns back to the shack, and nonchalantly sits down on Gísli's other side. She glances at him again, scans his head for evidence of the crime. Can't see anything. Takes a deep breath, summoning all her courage for her next move, which she hoped she wouldn't have to resort to. She starts to caress his head.

'Your hair is so nice.'

'Really?'

'Really. You can tell that it's nice and thick, it could just do with...'

'A trim?'

Hannah nods. Closes her eyes and gropes around Gísli's scalp, trying to make it seem like a normal, friendly gesture. Her hand moves across the top of his head: nothing but matted hair. No bumps, no – wait ... Something, at the back of his head: a small bulge, and something else that feels like a cut.

She goes to touch it again, lightly, so it hurts, when Gísli firmly grasps her wrist.

'I'm sorry, but I think you might have misunderstood.' The smiling face now replaced by a grimace that Hannah can't quite decode.

'Sorry, I wasn't trying to...'

Gísli removes her hand from his hair but continues to hold on to it.

'I'm not ... While it may be that I haven't been with a woman for a good few years, you're not ... I mean, you're not my type.'

Hannah tries to suppress a grin. Gísli thinks she's making a move on him. And he's rejecting her. Fair enough. Hannah gets to her feet, half relieved, half disturbed at the fact that she ended up finding the evidence she was looking for. She takes off the hat and hands it back to Gísli.

'Thanks. And sorry again.'

Without another word, she hastily departs, and tries to get as far away from Gísli, the sea, the wind, and the myriad of emotions the whole situation has given her, as quickly as she can. She has to pass her recently confirmed suspicions on to Viktor, and she can't waste any more time.

His car isn't on the driveway, which means he's probably not home. The thought stops Hannah in her tracks for a moment. What if Margrét thinks she's come to see her? But she's wrong: it is Viktor, not Margrét, who opens the door. Hannah is overcome with both relief and disappointment, which must result in a rather indeterminate facial expression, as Viktor's own face looks suddenly concerned.

'Everything okay? Has someone shot at the house again...?'

He already has a hand on his jacket. Hannah stops him.

'No, no, everything's fine ... I'm not here to talk about that. But I think I might know who killed Thor.'

Viktor looks surprised. He examines Hannah – she feels there is a hint of disbelief in his gaze, but perhaps that's because there is still a trace of the morning whisky on her breath. Regardless, he invites her into his office. Wordlessly, Viktor offers her a coffee, to which she responds with a nod, then clears her throat, and launches into her explanation.

'I know this will be hard to believe, but you know that bottle I found...'

Hannah can see that Viktor is already about to object, presumably tired of hearing about the bottle, but before he can interject, she continues with her explanation.

'I know it wasn't the murder weapon. But I think ... I believe that Thor hit whoever killed him with it, in self-defence. The blood was fresh. And I've looked into the matter a bit more.'

Viktor raises an eyebrow – this is not what a stressed policeman working on a murder investigation wants to hear. Yet another civilian intervention.

'I thought if I could find the person with a head injury, then I would find the murderer. And now I've found someone with exactly that.'

Dramatic pause.

'Gísli.'

Viktor folds his arms across his chest. Closes his eyes, a deep wrinkle appearing on his forehead.

'And how did you manage to check Gísli's head for that kind of injury, exactly?'

'I felt it.'

'You felt it?'

The forehead wrinkle becomes two. As if Hannah has just admitted to groping an almost-homeless man. Which she has.

'I know that it sounds a bit odd, but ... I did manage to get a feel of the back of his head. And I both saw and felt it. The lump, the wound and dried blood.'

Viktor looks like he would really rather Hannah hadn't told him. As he is probably now obligated to investigate such an accusation. He sighs, and Hannah almost feels sorry for him.

'Gísli has an unfortunate history of getting involved in bar fights. When he's had a lot to drink, and a bad day, he can be quite ... not quite the kind-natured person he usually is when he's only half drunk and half depressed.'

'Half depressed?'

That doesn't sound like the Gísli Hannah knows. But maybe this makes it all the more likely that he could commit such a violent act, one that could cause a death. The thought triggers another.

'But that must be quite easy to prove then, right? I mean ... if the blood from the bottle matches Gísli's DNA?'

Viktor thinks for a moment. And nods.

'I'll follow it up. But this is my last warning: stop doing my job or I'll stop you from doing yours.'

'Doing mine?'

'I'll have you sent away.'

Hannah looks at Viktor sceptically.

'You can have me sent back to Denmark?'

'That's not what I mean. I can have you prosecuted for interfering in police matters.'

Hannah stares at him, speechless. Here she is, bringing him this vital information, and he makes this threat? Without another word, Viktor shows her the door and closes it behind her.

28

A note tells Hannah that Ella isn't home and that she's up at Vigdis's, which makes Hannah both relieved and sad. She decides to make up for the night's wrongdoings by fixing the doorframe, and remembers having seen a few extra planks of wood out in the shed. After spending a while rummaging around, she manages to find something similar to the wood of the doorframe and a handful of nails that look to be about the right size. Again, she can't find a hammer, so again, she fetches the pickaxe from the living room. And she surprises herself by managing to repair the doorframe, so it looks ... maybe not exactly how it was before, but a doorframe, nonetheless. Or rather, the door can close properly now, at least. Hannah hoovers up after herself and takes one last look into the secret room before closing the door and deciding never to break Ella's trust again. She will cook dinner tonight and show Ella her less ugly side. It is dark again when Hannah sits on the front doorstep and lights a cigarette. She suddenly feels a pang of guilt – only a short while ago, she was convinced that Gísli was the murderer, but what does she think of him now? What if the DNA from the bottle doesn't match, but he's willingly provided a sample of his hair to compare with the sample from the bottle, thus making him a prime suspect among the townsfolk, which will probably only increase his sense of isolation from the local community? But then an even worse thought: that the town idiot *is* a murderer. Hannah shudders. If her theory proves correct, could her investigation into Gísli actually put her in danger? Perhaps it would be good to keep a low profile until things are a little clearer. So she doesn't end up in prison, or worse: dead.

Luckily, the kitchen cupboards are always so well stocked with food that Hannah needn't worry about buying in anything for dinner, or for a nuclear disaster. There are enough provisions in this house to ensure Ella's survival even if Iceland were cut off from the world for two to three years. Hannah makes her go-to meal, developed over many years of subpar cooking for herself, and the only dish she can get to taste homemade: pasta with tomato sauce. Stirring the tomatoes and herbs in the pan, she has the rare feeling of being home, strangely safe. She tastes the sauce and scores it above average – sure, it could do with a good splash of red wine, but she's done more than enough snooping around the house in the hopes of finding something like that. In what may almost be a good mood, she starts to lay the table and even lights a candle. It is now pitch-black outside, and the fireplace is also given a little wood and a lit match. Hannah sits down and waits. It can't be long now before Ella returns. At half past eight, the spaghetti starts to resemble what it really is: a cheap and lacklustre meal. And cold. Hannah paces around the table for the twentieth time, glances over at the house phone again, and this time, picks it up. She flips through Ella's little address book, so full of crossings out and scribbles that it takes a few read-throughs to find the number she's looking for. Fortunately, Vigdis herself picks up. Hannah has no idea what she'd have done if it had been her husband. The conversation doesn't take long. Vigdis informs her that Ella left hours ago. Hannah hangs up with a feeling of unease in her body. Hours ago? What in the world could she be doing? It hits her then that she didn't think to call Ella directly – odd given she's seen for herself that Ella has a mobile phone, and quite a modern one at that. But, of course, she doesn't have the number. Hannah leaves the food on the table, grabs her jacket and walks out the door. But she barely reaches the bottom of the steps when the headlights of Ella's car swing onto the driveway. She stays there like a worried mother as she watches her host step out of the car.

'Where've you been?'

Ella doesn't respond, just walks straight past Hannah. There is a look in her eyes, a fury, that wasn't there before. Hannah stares at her. Could she still be that angry about the door? She runs after Ella into the house.

'I've fixed the doorframe, or tried to anyway, of course it's not as it was...'

But before Hannah gets to finish her explanation, Ella starts writing:

I go to bed.

And before Hannah can present to her the apology dinner she has made, Ella disappears into her bedroom. After a moment spent evaluating the situation, Hannah sits and eats the cold pasta alone. The flames in the fireplace begin to die down, and Hannah can't decide whether she should be worried or curious, or concerned that she'll be thrown out of her accommodation. In the end, she thinks it best not to feel anything at all. The truth of the matter won't become evident until the morning anyway.

It is impossible to write anything, so Hannah climbs into bed, light years too early according to her inner clock. But sleep evades her, so she picks up the saga and tries to find where she was up to. She surprises herself, when forty minutes later, she puts the book back down, having finished it. It was actually far more exciting than she had anticipated. Too much drama for her liking, but entertaining nonetheless, thought-provoking even. To keep one's word. To keep making the same mistakes time and time again. Are people really so stupid? Hannah doesn't come up with an answer before she falls asleep.

The chief of police scratched at his beard. He now had three murders to solve, and the two new additions were no easier to untangle than the first. His primary theory was, naturally, that the same murderer was responsible for all three. But the MO for each of them was so markedly different, it was hard to imagine that could really be the case. The first was executed rather subtly: blunt-force trauma to the back of the victim's head, then shoved into the sea. The second and third: savage knife attacks committed in the victims' respective homes. There must be two different murderers. But if there were two murderers on the loose in his small town, how could they ever return to normal?

Hannah clicks her tongue a few times, satisfied. Early to bed and early to the desk isn't an entirely stupid writer's cocktail after all, now that her usual red-wine-and-late-to-bed method is no longer an option. She pauses to listen for a moment. Ella's morning movements sound familiar, and if it weren't for the memory of her furious gaze the night before, Hannah could almost believe that everything is back to normal. Perhaps the events of yesterday have actually been reset. Hannah opens the window, and some rare November sunlight finds its way into the room. She takes a deep breath in. You know what? Yes, the air is a little more fresh up here.

It genuinely is like Ella has forgotten everything there was to forget about the day before. The coffee is poured as Hannah appears at the bottom of the staircase, and freshly baked buns await her on the table. Ella smiles. Hannah wishes her good morning, testing the waters a bit. Seems okay. Ella's mellow mood holds up.

'About last night. Where were you?'

Ella looks quizzically at Hannah. Writes something.

With Vigdis.

'And after that?'

Ella adds to the sentence:

All aften.

Hannah is about to protest, wants to mention the fact she had called Ella's sister to check, but something makes her choose not to. The amicable atmosphere between them may still be fragile, and there is no need to risk ruining it. It is also not out of the question that Hannah could have misunderstood Vigdis, that perhaps Ella left their house ten minutes before she'd called, not hours. They eat the buns in silence. Ella reads the newspaper, Hannah writes a bit in her notebook. She's had an idea for a plot twist: there will be a horse. Like in the saga, the novel will have a horse that no one must ride, but which the prime suspect for the murder steals and rides away on. Away, but where to? Hannah repeatedly clicks the button on the ballpoint pen – an annoying habit that has Ella raise an eyebrow over the top of the newspaper. Hannah notices.

'Sorry, I was just thinking of something. The last few days have been so ... unusual. But it's made me realise ... I haven't actually seen much of the area around here yet. I'd quite like to get out and see a bit of the local landscape. On horseback.'

Ella stares at her like she hasn't quite understood. Or she has, but she's trying to picture Hannah on a horse. The latter seems most likely, as the old woman breaks out in a smile. And nods.

'Farðu þangað. Það er best.'

An address is scribbled down, and Hannah thanks her for it.

'Do you know if this place is open today?'

Ella nods. Hannah thanks her for breakfast, helps clear the table and wash up. Skips the shower. There's no need to freshen up when you're heading to the stables. Realises that she's actually quite looking forward to her spontaneous little excursion – it is with a fair amount of excitement that she starts Ella's old Jeep, which she has been allowed to borrow.

The place is easy to find. In addition to the very precise description of the road provided by Ella, it is pretty much signposted the whole way there. Upon arriving at Guðmunður's ranch, she is met with a shock so great that her mind goes blank and she forgets to hit the brakes. She just stares ahead through the filthy windscreen in disbelief. That can't be right. It can't be him. It *can't* be him.

29

Hannah stays there for a while, sitting in the car, fighting the urge to turn around, back away, sneak off, get far away from this place. But something in her – roused by a mixture of fury and curiosity – forces her to stay put. She takes a deep breath in, unsure as to how the next few minutes are going to play out, and decides to confront the situation. Fuck it, he can't just come here and encroach on her territory.

He smiles when he sees her, as if he has anticipated that she would turn up here at any moment. As if they have a date planned. His offensively bleached white teeth look fake, like they don't belong in his mouth, as he bares them in a large, insincere smile. Hannah could choke on the sight of Jørn Fucking Jensen.

'What the fuck are you doing here?'

'Well thank you for the warm welcome. It's nice to see you too.'

'No, I mean it. What the hell are you doing here?'

She storms towards him like a homeowner protecting her private property. Gives him a critical glare. He's wearing a pair of riding boots, practical outdoor trousers and a waterproof jacket from some expensive Norwegian brand. With a riding helmet tucked under his arm, he looks well and truly dressed for the occasion.

'I felt like riding an Icelandic horse. I haven't ridden one since I was a boy.'

'There are horses in Denmark too.'

'But not of such a beautiful nature. I'm here to do some research for my next book. And I'm already so incredibly inspired, I mean, look around you. It's all so wild here.'

Jackass Jørn throws his arms out wide. Like a poet who's just discovered a truth he wants to share with the mob before him. Hannah feels light-headed.

'You look so fucking stupid in that get up.'

She mentally smacks herself on the forehead. That wasn't what she was supposed to say. What she was meant to say was: *You've only come here to sabotage my project, to stick a spoke in my writing wheel to provoke and deprive me of my motivation.*

'We can't all look as elegant as you do.'

Jørn smiles again. Hannah realises how dumb she must look herself, wearing tatty old clothes borrowed from Ella. She twists her body a little in the slightly too oversized woollen jumper, which rasps against her skin under the jacket spotted with oil stains.

'Where's Bastian?'

Jørn looks surprised.

'I know you two are best friends now, or whatever. Does he know you're here?'

Jørn hesitates. Nods.

'It was his idea, actually. He thought that it would maybe motivate you, if you saw me. Give you the devilish will to win the bet, if you saw my "fucking stupid" face.'

Shit. Why is he being so agreeable – to the extent he's almost self-deprecating? And does Bastian understand her so damn well that he knows exactly what works? The main question, however, is something else entirely: why on earth would Jackass J. agree to stage this elaborate charade when he knows it will help Hannah write her novel? Or maybe he's unaware of what role he plays in all this? As soon as the thought comes to her, Jørn unwittingly demonstrates that she has guessed correctly.

'Bastian felt that you might benefit if I could help you out a bit. With a few tips and whatnot.'

'A few tips?'

'If you were stuck.'

Bastian is close enough to her to know she would rather saw her own arm off with a bread knife than take any writing advice from Jørn. But Jørn's theory tells her two things. One: that he doesn't believe in his wildest dreams that she is actually capable of completing the project. And two: that he has come to witness her defeat himself, to take pleasure in her misery. No, not a chance in hell – he won't be taking pleasure in a damn thing. She hates him more than she ever has as they stand there, in front of the stables, him, with his hundred million kroner in his bank account and an unwavering belief in himself as her literary saviour.

A man – probably the owner – walks over to them, a pony in tow, which looks far too short and podgy to be able to carry an adult human being. Jørn buckles the helmet and climbs onto the small horse, without any help. His feet almost reach the ground. Keep your mouth shut Hannah, he already looks stupid enough.

'If you want, you're welcome to join me? I've booked my own

guide to get out and see some of the landscape, but you can come along for free.'

'Thanks, but I'd rather die than ride around with you.'

'I thought you might say that.'

Jørn raises a hand to the helmet in a salute, a gesture that he probably thinks looks cool and noble, but actually makes him look even more comical. He turns and steers the horse away, trotting lightly, and bouncing up and down on its back, so he resembles one of the Elvis figures Ella has mounted on her car dashboard. Hannah has never seen anything more irritating in her entire life.

After a long talk with the owner of the ranch, Hannah receives a chestnut-coloured, rock-solid, child-sized horse. She pauses a moment, before making an attempt to swing her leg over and onto it. She's never sat on a living animal before, and it feels a bit like committing a minor assault. But then reason wins over self-righteous nonsense: it is in the horse's nature to cart people about. And if Jørn can do it, so can she. Hannah grabs the reins, places one foot in the stirrup and pulls herself up. Surprisingly unproblematic. She can't say the same about the large Swedish family, who she casts a worried glance at, and who appear to be accompanying her on the guided tour. Typical – the first time she actually bumps into any tourists on this trip and it's when she has decided to play the tourist herself. The children have already managed to get their horses worked up into an impossible frenzy, running around and around in circles on the courtyard – their parents' anti-authoritarian strategy seeming to have no effect. Hannah makes the decision to ride at the back of the group. She refuses to be thrown off her horse as a result of the Swedish children's equestrian bloodlust. She carefully tightens the reins and leans down to give the horse a pat on its side – a declaration of confidence, and an attempt to ensure a peaceful ride. But then the herd is set in motion by the Icelandic guide – a man of around fifty with a weather-beaten face and a mane that rivals that of the horses – and Hannah's brown mare rushes to the front. Hannah holds on tight. Her helmet, which is far too big, slides down her forehead, so she can't see anything but the horse. As she passes the guide, she manages to catch his laughing remark:

'You've got the leader of the pack!'

Hannah recalls his opening speech about the horse being a pack animal with an inherent flight instinct, and she immediately regrets her foolish idea to spend the day on horseback. She pictures her own demise: thrown off a horse and trampled to death by every member of the Swedish family, who simply stomp over her body, the hooves mutilating her. But just as the thought reaches its grizzly end, her horse stops in its tracks and stands there, calm and steady, looking out at the vast horizon. Hannah casts a nervous glance back. She's at the front, the smiling horse-mane guide right behind her, and the large family of Swedes behind him. She tries to relax – now, she must be one with nature.

It *is* beautiful. Although the late-autumn chill nips at her cheeks, fingers and feet, Hannah can't help but be captivated by the myriad of yellows, the flecks of green, brown and red that almost invoke the taste of earth in her mouth. There is a bluish tinge to the sky, with its hazy grey clouds, and a touch more snow seems to have settled on the mountain tops. Hannah shuffles a little in the saddle. The chestnut-brown mare calmly and quietly continues forward, but remaining seated in the saddle seems a more laborious task for her middle-aged body. She's glad to have only booked a short trip. Hannah draws the crystal-clear air deep into her lungs, tries to fill up on her surroundings, feel present in the moment. It helps. A bit. The horse sways as it walks, and she tries to follow its movements. She breathes out. Feels a tad lighter. Maybe she just needs to rise above the situation, not let it get to her. The book is progressing, and if she can just maintain her focus on it, not let herself get distracted, then maybe Jørn will give up and go home sooner rather than later. Maybe she'll never have to see him again. The thought calms her down a little. The town isn't that big, so she'll stay indoors for the next few days. Avoid the bar and other public places. Forget the fact that Jørn is even here. Yes, that's what she'll do. She won't allow him to rile her, he will not be allowed to be a big fat spoke in her very nearly smooth-operating crime-writing wheel.

They reach a small stream, and the horse stops instinctively.

Hannah turns toward the human ponytail.

He nods. 'Just carry on.'

'Carry on?'

'Don't worry, you won't get wet. The horse is used to it.'

Hannah takes a sceptical look across the flowing water. It looks freezing. But before she can do anything else, the human ponytail clicks his tongue and the horse makes a start, wading out into the water. Hannah lets out a tiny squeal and clings to the animal, which splashes its way through the stream, soaking her legs. The helmet slides down again, covering her eyes. She can hear the Swedish children laughing behind her. In the middle of the stream, the horse stops. Hannah shoves her helmet back up and looks around nervously – what now? The rest of the herd doesn't move from riverbank, and Hannah turns helplessly towards them.

'Is this the right way?'

'Yep, yes it is, just cross the water.'

Hannah looks ahead. Thinks it looks quite far to the other side. Why aren't the rest of them crossing the water, if this is meant to be the right way? She looks back again, flings out her arms, and the ponytail signals to just continue onward. Hannah gives the horse a gentle kick in its side and tries to encourage it with a few giddy-ups, but the horse simply won't budge. The cold from her soaked-through legs starts to get to her, and she just wants to get out of the stuck-in-the-middle-of-the-stream situation as soon as possible.

'Harder!' the guide shouts from the bank. 'Kick harder.'

It doesn't feel natural to Hannah to kick the horse harder, but regardless, she swings both legs out and digs her heels into either side of its belly. And with that, the horse takes off with such ferocity that Hannah loses her balance and slides back off the saddle, the reins flying through her hands. She hits the water with an almighty splash. Argh! Never in her life has she ever felt cold like this. For a moment, she genuinely believes she might die. Her arms and legs jerking about, she eventually finds her feet on the shallow riverbed. The icy water penetrates her skin. Up on the bank, the Swedish devil children are dying of laughter, while their parents try in vain to shush them. The horse-mane man is already heroically riding over to her. Hannah manages to stand, close to weeping. And then remembers the horse, and looks around for it, only to see that it has now ridden to the other side. But it's not alone. Beside it, an Icelandic guide on his horse, and beside him, another person on a horse. Jørn J. He waves an arm in the air.

'Move! It's important you move your body around, so you don't get hypothermia and die.'

30

Her teeth won't stop chattering. This is her body's betrayal: it won't let go of the shock. Hannah feels her skin – it's red hot, the beads of sweat run down her body. She sits in the sauna at the back of the ranch, a towel wrapped around her. The door opens. The human horse mane holds something up: a bottle of whisky. Hannah has never been so happy to see a man in a much-too-small loincloth with a much-too-long ponytail. She can't bring herself to do anything but nod. He comes in, closes the door behind him. Sits beside her, pulls the cork out with his teeth, and passes her the bottle. She takes it and downs a hearty mouthful. Feels the fiery liquid warming her from within. The guide also takes a good mouthful. Puts the stopper back in.

'Better?'

Hannah nods – with the alcohol now entering her bloodstream, she does feel a bit better.

'That hasn't happened before, to tell you the truth. You'll get a refund, of course.'

Hannah shakes her head, it's not about the money. You can't buy your way out of humiliation. She closes her eyes tight, tries to forget the sight of Jørn on the other side of the stream. Her whole being burns. Her body's chattering starts to ease off. A thought hits her, and she turns to the horse-mane man.

'Did he know I would be here?'

'The other Danish author?'

'He's not an author, he's a franchise.'

Hannah regrets answering so briskly. The horse mane can't have known that.

The heat from the fire draws forth small beads of sweat from the Icelandic guide's skin as he stares ahead, contemplating his answer. Then he nods. Turns to Hannah.

'Is he your lover or something? He seemed very happy to see you.'

Hannah snorts. Lover? She takes another mouthful of whisky. It tastes more bitter than before.

'Enemy?'

The horse mane almost snatches the bottle back out of Hannah's hand as he asks the question. Hannah closes her eyes, lets the whisky scorch her insides.

'I hate everything about him. I hate the way he smiles, I hate the sound of his voice, and I hate everything he stands for. I hate that he calls himself an author, I hate his books, and I hate that people read them and like him. I hate his success.'

Hannah opens her eyes – it is dark in the sauna. She feels a sense of relief at her uncharacteristic honesty. The horse mane stands up, pours water onto the hot rocks, removes the little loin-cloth towel and flicks it at the steam, so a wave of heat flows over them. He sits again, leans back. They take in the warmth.

'I also used to be envious of other people's success. I used to spend a lot of time wallowing in misery over the fact that other, less talented people than me were getting opportunities that I could only dream of.'

Hannah looks at him. 'Doing what?'

'Acting.'

She nods. 'What did you do to stop hating them?'

The horse mane contemplates her question. Stares into the fire. 'Nothing. I still do.'

'But you stopped acting?'

He nods.

The drive home feels long. The Jeep jolts up and down along the gravel road. It's already dark out, even though the day feels like it has only just begun. Hannah turns on the main-beam headlights. She has always been a night person, but the variations in darkness throughout the day here have started to get to her. Hopefully she won't descend into a full winter depression before the book is done. She didn't manage to pick up much horse inspiration either. Is still holding on to her anger at Jørn's sabotage – not only is he interfering with her motivation, but also with her research. But if there's one thing she is sure of, it is the theme of her novel, and that will be revenge. Revenge in every conceivable form. She will probably need to decide who the murderer is soon as well, given there will likely be a few suspects on the cards, and then it will get really exciting. She pushes her foot down on the accelerator a little more firmly. Has to get home, has to find a killer.

A thorough interrogation of all the locals should've cast new light on the case, but it was as if they had some sort of collective memory loss about the night of Tore's murder, and the brutal murder of his mother and father had left the community similarly silent. The chief of police himself was born and raised in the town, knew all the townsfolk, and should therefore be able to figure out who the murderer was just by analysing their behaviour. Had anyone changed, picked up new habits, diverted from their

previous routines? He scratched his beard, contemplated his options - perhaps have a few technical
tests performed on a small sample? Just to see if it
would encourage someone to start talking. But it
would probably trigger a tidal wave of wild rumours
and slander, so he'd have to tread lightly.

Hannah looks up, suddenly struck by the thought that she isn't sure
if reality is actually serving as a blueprint for her novel, or whether
her novel may end up predicting reality. It certainly isn't a bad idea
– to look into whether anyone in town has started acting strangely
recently. Someone who keeps to themselves, or someone who has
suddenly left town, even. Hannah will pursue that lead tomorrow,
but first she must do something she has been putting off all
afternoon. She grabs her new phone – which she bought on the way
home, at the local shop, the staff also helping her set it up with a
prepaid SIM card and everything. After three consecutive missed
calls, she deems it impossible to get hold of Bastian, and gives up.
Fuck him. She stares down at the phone, as if it were a co-
conspirator in his betrayal, and her conviction in her earlier theory
intensifies: Bastian has genuinely taken the opportunity to get rid
of her once and for all. Her last book's critical success was so long
ago, she seems like too much hassle these days. And he's been using
far too much energy on just the one person. So, of course, he
decided to run with her deluded idea of writing a crime novel,
encouraged her to go ahead with it. Not with the aim of actually
publishing the book, but purely to bring an end to her writing
career. He would then be free to concentrate on other, more
promising, authors. But would he really do that to someone he has
known for all these years, the very man she calls her friend? Perhaps
friendship doesn't last forever after all. Perhaps you can have enough
of a person like Hannah. She tries to swallow the lump in her throat.
If she was the type of person who cried, she'd certainly be sobbing
at this point. She tries to rework the idea, test it from new angles,

reject the thought with her rational mind, but nothing helps. It's stuck. Rage slowly begins to replace self-pity. It's fucking bullshit. He can't be allowed to win; can't just cast her aside and then put all his energy into Jackass J. She's going to finish her novel, even if it's the last book she ever writes.

Hannah is still shaking when she grabs her jacket and announces to Ella that she's heading out on an evening walk. Ella, who is sitting in front of the fireplace, scribbling away in a notebook, looks up. Waves Hannah over. Hannah falters, doesn't have time for this right now. But obeys.

'What's going on, is something wrong?'

Ella jots something down in her notebook. Hannah must be tripping. Reads it again. Feels like she has butterflies in her stomach. Reads it one more time.

'Margrét called? For me?'

Ella nods.

'Why?'

Ella shakes her head, returns to whatever it was she was writing. Hannah watches her for a moment, indecisive. Peers over Ella's shoulder.

'What are you writing?'

Ella writes another little note for her, and holds it up to Hannah, who reads, *Speech til Thor's funeral*.

It is freezing outside, when Hannah closes the door behind her and steps out into the evening darkness.

31

She takes a deep breath, once she's standing in front of Viktor and Margrét's house. What could Margrét want with her? The door opens before she has a chance to knock. It's Margrét, looking down at her, as if she's done nothing all afternoon besides wait there for

Hannah. An unusual, hectic energy seems to emanate from her. Hannah smiles, but it is not returned. Wordlessly, Margrét makes room in the doorway for her, so Hannah can step inside. Hannah does so, looks around her nervously.

'Viktor?'

'Out.'

Hannah observes Margrét, who is now busy searching for something in a drawer. She even looks beautiful in just a pair of old jeans and a grubby T-shirt, but it's impossible to read anything from her face. Hannah wants to take Margrét's hand, kiss her, lay her down on the floor, right there in the hallway, tear her clothes off, feel her skin—

'Come.'

Margrét interrupts her fantasy. But it isn't an invitation to eroticism, rather a determined and cold command. An order. Margrét walks through the house with powerful, purposeful footsteps. Hannah is baffled – where are they going? She doesn't dare ask, just follows. Margrét finds a key from the bundle in her hand and unlocks a door. Hannah right on her heels. Margrét turns on the light, and Hannah now recognises that they have entered Viktor's office, or the police station. Is surprised to find that they have access to it from the house itself, but then again, recognises that this wouldn't be the way Viktor tends to bring guests into his office. Having them walk across the courtyard seems more official. Margrét crosses the small office in three steps and unlocks another door. Hannah halts. Behind the door: Jonni, sitting on the bed. He looks up at Hannah. Half human, half ghost.

'You have ten minutes, before Viktor gets back.'

Margrét nods toward Jonni, and Hannah suddenly understands – she has just been given the greatest gift so far in her investigation. An off-the-record interview with the main suspect.

Margrét remains where she is, standing on the threshold, and nods encouragingly to Jonni. She leaves the door open, as if sure that he won't try to escape.

She says something in Icelandic. Jonni nods slowly. Looks down at the ground.

'You can ask him whatever you want.'

Hannah nods, and drags a chair over to face Jonni. Tries to create something between them.

'You were with Thor the night he died, is that correct?'

Jonni nods.

'And you argued?'

Jonni glances up at Margrét, uncertain, but she nods reassuringly. Hannah feels sorry for the young man, who mostly resembles a boy, sat there in his joggers and oversized black T-shirt.

'Yes, we argued. But I didn't kill him.'

'I know that.'

Strictly speaking, Hannah can't possibly know that, but her gut instinct tells her that Jonni is innocent.

'Then why did you turn up at his parents' house with a shotgun?'

Jonni stares at the floor. Looks as if he is trying to hold back tears. He hesitates. Hannah gives him time.

'We ... Thor was my boyfriend.'

Jonni looks up. Hannah meets his gaze. Suddenly sees the world in a whole new light. The pieces fall into place. The leather vest at the bar, who thought Thor was different, not like the other teenagers. Margrét's hesitation in saying how well she knew Thor. Jonni's hatred of Ægir, who doesn't seem like the kind of man who would be comfortable with his only son being homosexual. Hannah wants to kick herself for not seeing it; something she should've guessed ages ago. Despite her own, what she would call fluid, sexuality, she is often blind when it comes to looking at other people as anything other than heterosexual. Perhaps because the world has been set up that way, to make it seem like everyone is. She tries to shake off the annoyance over her own blind spot and redirects her thoughts to Ægir – was he the reason the two boys quarrelled that night? Hannah doesn't even have to ask.

'Ægir wanted Thor to break up with me. He had just found out about us, that evening.'

'And did he? Break up with you?'

Jonni shuffles nervously in his seat. Shakes his head.

'But he was beside himself. Said he didn't know what to do. His father had thrown him out, and he just went into a full-blown panic. Thor was close to his parents, really close.'

Hannah nods. 'An only child. A miracle.'

Jonni is fighting to keep the tears from flowing. Margrét glances at her watch. Hannah's synapses are firing on all cylinders. She has a thousand questions and not enough time to ask them all. Must start with the most important. The night of the murder.

'So what happened after that? After your argument?'

Jonni shrugs.

'We ... I said we should leave, go to Reykjavík together. Study, read, whatever... Just be together, far away from this shithole. But Thor didn't want to ... He wanted to stay. Take over his father's fishing business. So stupid ... Thor, a fisherman? He couldn't even swim.'

Jonni wipes a tear from his cheek. Looks like a person who has lost everything. Hannah wants to put an arm around him, tell him that everything will be okay. But she also finds it difficult picturing a way out of this situation for him.

'He was at home with you, and then he left?'

Jonni nods. 'He was angry, I was angry. I ran after him ... But I also hoped that he'd be hit by a car or something. How messed up is that?'

Jonni looks up. Hannah holds his gaze.

'I loved him and hated him that night. Regardless of what happened, it was my fault. I made him act like that.'

Margrét intervenes. 'It is not your fault.'

Jonni looks at her. Says something in Icelandic. She says something back. Hannah looks at her watch, desperate to get back to the conversation.

'Do you have any idea who killed him? His father?'

Jonni shakes his head. 'I don't think ... I mean, everyone knows how angry Ægir can get. But he loved Thor...'

Margrét takes a step closer to Hannah. 'You have to go now.'

Hannah hesitates, isn't done talking to Jonni. But Margrét insists. 'Viktor could come back at any moment. And he can't find you here – again.'

Hannah feels a little jab, in the way Margrét says it, reminding her of that night. As if what she did was wrong. She nods.

'Thank you, Jonni. I hope you'll be out of here soon.'

To Hannah's great disappointment, Margrét does not invite her back into the house, and instead, ushers her out via Viktor's office door. Hannah stops on the threshold. Wants to say something to Margrét, but doesn't know what.

'Thank you for doing this for me.'

'I didn't do it for you, I did it for him. The more people who know the truth, the better ... Maybe you can do something good with it, now you know. But you really have to leave.'

Hannah looks at Margrét, tries to hide her disappointment. Margrét hasn't once mentioned their affair, and is impossible to read ... Was it a mistake? Has she already repressed the memory, decided to never do it again? Hannah is desperate to kiss her, standing there in the doorway, half in, half out. But Hannah doesn't want to risk losing the access she may have to Jonni. Doesn't want to assume anything either. So she composes herself, goes to step out into the courtyard with all the self-control she can muster. But she isn't even fully out of the doorway before Margrét grabs her, pulls her back in and kisses her. Hard. As if neither of them will ever have the chance to kiss another person again. Hannah is about to implode. But Margrét lets go.

'Maybe you should get a new phone.'

Hannah looks at her quizzically. 'You've been trying to call me...?'

'Just get a new phone. I don't want to have to call Ella next time.'

Hannah nods. Finds it difficult not to smile. Then pulls her notebook out of her pocket. Hurriedly writes down her number on a spare page. Rips it out and hands it to Margrét.

'I've bought one already.'

She sends Margrét one final glance, turns and leaves. And suddenly thinks of something.

'What was it Jonni said to you, in Icelandic?'

Margrét hesitates.

'He told me what he said to Thor. Before he left that night.'

'What was it?'

'I hate you.'

Hannah swallows. Fuck. Your final words to the person you love before they were murdered.

She walks home with a hammering heart, a kiss on her mouth and a feeling that everything is far, far more complicated than she'd originally thought.

32

Officer Axelson scratched at his beard, shocked by the events of the last few days and the four murders he now had to solve. The young Esther was now in custody, like a wild animal in a cage. She had chopped her father-in-law into small pieces, but she was still a minor, so how would he deal with her? He had a load of technicians on their way from Reykjavík, and among them, of course: his annoying rival from his former police college, who had chosen to stay in the capital and qualify as a detective. Pétur had always been an arrogant prick, and the fact that he was now staying in town to help with the investigation was almost unbearable. Axelson was

determined to keep him out of the case by any means
necessary, even if the murders had to remain
unsolved. Rather that than that idiot Pétur getting
yet another feather to put in his ugly detective cap.

Hannah stops, scrolls back a little. It's starting to look like a book.
But is she focused enough? Or is she letting her real-life emotions
guide her to too great an extent? She realises she doesn't have any
idea about how it will all end either – who the murderer is. As it
stands, the story just branches off in various directions – she will
have to pay closer attention to the plot. Must make her work more
structured. With a bit of light knocking about at the bottom of the
pack, she fishes out the last cigarette and lights it, without opening
the window. The wind is far too strong outside for that, and as the
window has threatened to break free from its hinges the last few
times she has opened it, she's afraid of pulling it clean off. She has
never reflected so deeply on her own writing process. From the
outside, you could call it intuitive, or, if she lived in a more romantic
era, governed by divine inspiration, but she doesn't believe in the
artist being a noble genius with a direct spiritual connection to God.
Yet neither does she believe that the art of writing can be learned
by studying theories of fiction or rigorous analyses of plots and
literary devices. So what is it she believes? She has a strong belief in
her own sense of taste, in her understanding of the human psyche,
and her insight into life. But, Christ, she barely has a strong enough
insight into her own life. Maybe that's why she writes. To try and
find meaning. She gets up, restless. Stretches her legs, paces round
the bed – the only route the little bedroom allows. Her eyes meet
the portrait of the Virgin Mary. How can someone look so calm
and Zen when her only son was crucified in the most brutal
manner? And it wasn't even her own son, but the son of God, as ...
Holy shit! It suddenly hits her. Why hasn't she thought of it before?
It might not even be significant, for the investigation anyway, but
may nevertheless be a piece of the puzzle that could shed light on

the whole picture. God's son, Ægir's son. Who finally came along after years of marriage. Just as Vigdis turned forty and hope was starting to wane … But what if Thor is not Ægir's biological son? Hannah's heart beats faster. She can't see how it's important, she can just feel that it is. She must ask Ella. Even if they still aren't on quite the best of terms, after Hannah broke into her study. With her pulse racing, she hurries downstairs, into the living room, hoping that Ella hasn't already gone to bed.

Ella contemplates her with an unreadable gaze, Hannah becoming more uncomfortable by the second. She rubs the palms of her still-cold hands over the fabric-clad armrests of the chair. Sitting right on the edge of the seat, half excited for Ella's answer, half regretting having asked the question. Seconds pass in silence, Hannah's gaze flickers up to the new window, which almost makes the living room look like it has never been subjected to a drive-by shooting. Only the elephants testify to any visible disorder; they are now scattered about the various surfaces of the living room like a random invasion, finding a home wherever there is space. Hannah clears her throat. Maybe Ella didn't understand the question? She considers repeating it, or perhaps it would be in her best interests to pretend she never asked it. But then Ella leans forward, finds a scrap of paper, and writes. Hannah waits, tense.

Ægir is definite father til Thor. It was Vigdis, who could not. It was happy, when she endelig got pregnant, after many years.

Hannah reads, half disappointed, half distrusting of the note. Ousts the desire to correct Ella's English-peppered Danish. Weighs up whether she should dig deeper. How cheeky can she afford to be?

'But isn't it usually the case that the woman says she can't, when in reality, it's actually the quality of the man's sperm making it impossible? And I'd have thought a man like Ægir wouldn't voluntarily book in with a doctor and admit to doubts about his ability to reproduce. Even though he's much older than Vigdis, and—'

A sinewy arm flies out and grabs hold of Hannah's, stopping her flow of speech. Ella looks at Hannah; there is a visible ferocity in her eyes.

'Ægir er pabbi Þórs. Ég er alveg viss. Ég veit ekki hvert þú ætlar en þú verður að stoppa. Spurningar þínar leiða bara til vandræða.'

Hannah stares at Ella, one big question mark. It seems as if Ella has forgotten that Hannah doesn't understand Icelandic. Ella quickly jots something down on a piece of paper. Hannah assumes it is a repetition of what she just said:

Stopp the questions. You'll get yourself in trouble. And me.

Hannah examines the note. Ella's piercing eyes force her to nod. But the warning has only fed her need to find out more. Silently, she rises from her seat and returns to her room.

It's not even light out when Hannah wakes up with a plan that she knows is doomed before she's even set it in motion. But she has to try. She has spent most of the night lying awake in bed, speculating, tossing and turning, restlessly looking up at the moon. She keeps on coming to the same dead end, still has far too many questions, and far too few people to ask. No one, actually. That's why she needs to discuss them all with someone neutral, someone who doesn't usually live here in town, and someone not involved in any of this. Regardless of how much she hates to admit it, she must spar with Jackass J.

She doesn't have to ask anyone where he's staying – she's already passed his giant 4x4 rental car. Twice yesterday alone. And even though she leaves Ella's house later that morning feeling like it is the best and most fruitful way forward, she still ends up having to stop outside the large house and draw the air deep into her lungs. This cannot be seen as a cry for help, it must come across as her extending a friendly, collegial hand. Reconciliation and all that. Hannah walks up to the door and rings the bell.

33

First he's surprised, then sceptical (naturally) and finally a smile breaks out on his well-groomed, healthy, weather-beaten face. Hannah has to force herself not to say anything snide that might give away her intentions. She must be nice. Friendly. Not spit in his face, kick him in the shin and quickly run away.

'There's nothing I'd love more than to brainstorm with you. Come in.'

He opens the door wide, and Hannah – against all her instincts – steps inside like a civilised human being. Reminding herself that she's only here to get something out of him. Use him, without him realising it. She doesn't intend to give even a micron of herself.

'I was just about to indulge in some morning yoga, do you mind if I do a few stretches while we talk?'

There is nothing Hannah would mind more, but she simply nods.

'Of course. I'm the one bothering you, anyway.'

'Super. Then I'll just do a few sun salutations. You should try it – it's really good for flexibility, not just for your body, but for your mind too. Mind and body, as they say.'

Hannah observes Jørn, who appears to be wearing some sort of adult joggers and is standing there like an utter moron, hands stretched high over his head. She must admit, he does look very peaceful. It makes her throw up in her mouth a little. She swallows. Sits on the rather tattered sofa. Flicks away a breadcrumb.

'Who actually lives here?'

'Some family. My agent arranged it all for me, so I don't know much about them.'

'Where are they now?'

Jørn bends down, sticks his arse in the air. Downward-facing dog.

'Uh, I hadn't thought about that.'

Hannah resists the burning temptation to comment on the fact that the family are probably having to stay on some relative's sofa so Jørn can frolic around the house by himself. A few toys catch her eye, and she wonders whether the kids are missing them. Although, to be fair, she has technically invaded Ella's home too.

'How long do you intend to stay?'

Upward-facing dog.

'As long as I want. Like I said, I'm here to do a bit of research for my next book.'

'Will it be set here?'

'I haven't got that far, to tell you the truth. But I think it'll take place somewhere in the rugged wilderness. It'll focus on a man as he battles against the elements, but it'll really be about battling his own problems, himself. Fleeing from his own life. Until he finds the body of a beautiful young woman, who has been raped, killed, and thrown into a creek. And he comes to realise that he has to save the woman to solve the murder.'

'How can he save her when she's already dead?'

She watches Jørn, full of loathing, who is now on the floor in an annoying plank position. He looks ahead, philosophically.

'He saves her in a more symbolic way. He saves her by finding her murderer.'

She considers him – has often fantasised about sinking some sort of sharp object into his stomach. Tear out his insides. And here he is, standing with his arms in the air, eyes closed, body completely exposed. She could actually do it, if she wanted to. She shakes the thought away. Back to the case.

'I'm sure you've heard about what happened? The young man who drowned a few days ago?'

'I have. Such a tragic accident.'

Hannah pauses. Is she doing the right thing? But Jørn sits on the sofa opposite. Pours a glass of water for them both. No going back now.

'It wasn't an accident. Everything points to it being a crime.'

At first, Hannah can't tell whether Jørn has understood or not.

He observes her for a long time. Doesn't he believe her? She feels a small wave of disappointment at the fact that he doesn't seem even the slightest bit shocked.

'Are you using it in your book?' Jørn can't help smiling a little.

Hannah stares at him, irritated, but waves it away. Fuck the you're-such-an-amateur vibes radiating off him. She will have to be honest if she's going to get his help. She still lies just a little, for the sake of her dignity.

'It's not like I'm copying it directly. I've put a lot extra in myself. Twists and turns.'

Jørn nods as if to say, *Yeah right.*

'And now you're stuck, because the book is based on the investigation into the death of that unfortunate young man?'

Okay. No more superiority, Hannah has to steer the conversation back to the essentials. She takes a sip of water. Jørn pulls at his knuckles – it's unbelievably grating.

'It's important to stretch every joint in your body, every day.'

Hannah doesn't say anything.

Crack, crack.

'There are several suspects, but none of them quite fit. It's like something is missing. A vital component.'

Hannah stands. Paces around the room. Jørn follows her with his eyes.

'Murder weapon?'

'Blunt object, not found.'

'Suspect?'

'Father, gay lover, a random sort-of homeless guy who was present when the body was found, and who also has a wound on the back of his head, long story.'

'Witnesses?'

'The homeless guy with the wound.'

'Motive?'

Hannah stops. Damn, he's good. Why hadn't she thought more about that? Jørn answers his own question:

'The lover: jealousy. The father: shame. The homeless guy: homophobia. All strong motives, if you ask me.'

Hannah sits back down.

'But you haven't met them. Jonni is kind, not the jealous type. The father may be full of shame, but he loved his only son, too much, arguably. And the homeless guy is too nice to be a homophobe.'

Jørn shakes his head, again, can't help grinning at her.

'I thought your cynicism and lack of confidence in other human beings would be an advantage for you in such criminal matters. But here you are, soft as butter.'

'Who says I lack confidence in other people?'

'You've said it yourself. In an interview with *Politiken*, a few years ago.'

Hannah can't help but feel strangely flattered. Jørn read an interview with her. But she still wants to punch him. 'Soft as butter.' He speaks like he writes: like a fucking cliché. She defends herself.

'My lack of confidence in others is more on an abstract level. A distrust in humanity.'

Jørn shakes his head. Makes a gross sucking sound with the corner of his mouth.

'Hannah, I would never have thought that I would say this to you, but you are far too naïve to be a crime writer.'

The fantasy of killing Jørn returns, this time with the feeling that it may actually be a genuine option, but Hannah manages to mobilise her entire personal morality and suppresses the urge to whack him over the head with the metal teapot. Wait! Why is she always so violent in her thinking? Why do fantasies of violence come so naturally to her as soon as someone so much as annoys her? A shameful and frightening sensation spreads through her body. If she herself is so primitive, so impulsive in her way of thinking, is she also capable of, or even predisposed to, committing a violent attack, a murder, maybe? And what then separates her from all the other potential murderers out there? Hannah notices one of her hands trembling slightly. She tries to hide it, but Jørn spots it.

'Abstinence?'

Hannah screams internally. Externally, she smiles psycho-pathically.

'I'm not an alcoholic.'

'And I'm not a multimillionaire, with a gorgeous summer house in Hornbæk and a share in a champion racehorse in northern Germany.'

Jørn smiles at Hannah, who can't help smiling herself this time. What the fuck is going on? That was actually quite funny. Could it be that she does actually, maybe, like him just a tiny bit? No! Focus. She's only here to use him, milk his trust for all it's worth, exploit his love of himself and get him to help her solve the case, without him realising it. That's why she came. Not to become friends.

'Going back to what you said about a motive. You're right that all three suspects do have strong motives – on paper, that is. But as I said, you haven't met them. I simply don't think—'

'That any of them are capable of doing it. You've said that. But, of course, you're the expert on the human psyche.'

Is there a hidden compliment in that last remark, or was it another satirical insult? Hannah can't make her mind up, but opts for the latter.

'You may call me naïve, but I consider my reasoning as a form of resistance against cliché. A way to look for options other than the most obvious.'

'Cliché's worst enemy is research.'

Jesus Christ, the truism. Did he really just say that? Hannah stares at Jørn, struggles to hide her loathing.

'I thought the cliché's best friend was you.'

Jørn regards Hannah. She bites her tongue. Bloody hell. Don't go down that route. Not down. That route. She leans forward, trying to make it look like a conciliatory gesture. If she's going to get anything out of having to sit so close to Jørn that she can smell his morning yoga breath, she will have to take a little more care.

'Listen: I haven't come here to act like a fool in front of you. We have our differences when it comes to writing, and life in general, but as I said, I genuinely want your input on this. And it may well be that you're right, that one of the three suspects I mentioned could be responsible, but if we just try to play a game where we exclude them, what direction could we take then?'

Jørn cracks his neck (ew) and discreetly scratches his crotch (double ew). It is clearly a game he wants to play.

'Okay, a good crime novel has three crucial components. One: a spectacular and violent opening, preferably a murder. Two: false leads and false suspects. And three: this is where it gets exciting for you...'

Jørn takes such a long pause that Hannah wonders whether he may come out with the meaning of life.

'Three.'

'I'm listening.'

'Point three is: surprises.'

'Surprises?' Hannah looks at him sceptically. Is that all?

'What would surprise you most? If you think about that – what you would find most surprising – you might just get closer to finding out who killed Thor. Or the murderer in your own novel.'

Hannah thanks him for the help and gets up with a feeling that she hasn't managed to get anything out of Jørn that she couldn't have found herself in a quick, two-minute Google search. Surprises and research. Is that how you end up being able to afford a share in a German racehorse?

Standing at the front door, Jørn makes himself extra wide, a stance suggesting that he thinks himself some sort of king. A crime-fiction yogi-king. He watches Hannah so intensely, she feels that one final, well-meaning piece of advice is imminent. And she's right. Jørn looks at her, a serious expression on his face.

'If I can be perfectly honest, I strongly doubt that you'll be able to use the ongoing investigation for anything. It may take months before it's solved, that's if it is ever solved, and then it'll probably just turn out to be some unfortunate accident. To me, I see it as a total dead end, and you should probably use this time to read some good crime novels, watch a few crime dramas to get some inspiration on how to write a proper crime novel. And then I would talk to a bunch of retired police officers and read a few of their old journals, and there you have it, a super, well-thought-out crime. And, oh yes, remember, the main character shouldn't be likeable. No one likes a likeable protagonist in crime.'

Hannah stares at Jørn a fair while, suddenly seeing him for what he really is: a bad plagiarist. This does not, however, generate any sympathy for the man, but rather a deeper disdain. She shakes her head and starts to walk away, shouts over her shoulder.

'You're wrong. Reality is far more exciting than fiction.'

She should take the road back home, but instead, Hannah crosses a field, as well as an invisible boundary around how far she is willing to go to solve Thor's murder.

34

Hannah needs to see things from a new perspective, so goes to the most terminally boring building in town: Olí's petrol station. Aside from the young girl behind the counter, the shop is completely empty. Hannah scans the room for something alcoholic, but can see only soft drinks, sweets and hot dogs for sale. It suddenly occurs to her that Iceland probably has laws preventing regular shops selling anything stronger than light beer – wine and spirits must only be available in the state-run stores. Shit. Well, at least it'll be a conversation starter. She leans against the counter.

'Do you know where I can buy any alcohol around here?'

Hannah forces herself to smile at the girl standing behind the cash register. She can't be older than sixteen. Is it even legal for a child to staff a petrol station by themselves? The girl looks up – from her phone, Hannah assumes, and for that reason alone she is already annoyed at her. Hannah can't stand apathetic teenagers.

'Yeah, you can go to Vínbúð.'

'Is it far?'

'Nothing's far here.'

The girl's attention is diverted down to her lap again. Hannah is just about to deliver a verbal tirade, when she sees what the petrol-station child is engrossed in: a book. Hannah is instinctively more sympathetic towards the girl.

'What are you reading?'

The girl holds up the book, and Hannah suddenly has the urge to adopt her: *Bonjour Tristesse* by Françoise Sagan. Perhaps there is hope for the world after all.

'"A strange melancholy pervades me to which I hesitate to give the grave and beautiful name of sorrow."'

'You've read it?'

The girl studies her with a new interest. Hannah nods. An unfamiliar sense of companionship comes over her, and she feels that if she prevents herself from pushing the moment away, it may be possible to form a certain confidentiality between them.

'It was my favourite book as a teenager ... In fact, it was...'

Hannah is surprised to find herself on the verge of saying something entirely truthful and revealing about herself. She's already a little embarrassed, but the girl is watching her expectantly, so she has to finish the sentence.

'It was actually reading that, that made me realise I wanted to become an author.'

Now she really has the young girl's attention.

'You're an author? What's your name?'

'Hannah Krause-Bendix.'

The girl's eyes light up. A sign of recognition?

'Wait, seriously? It's you?'

Hannah feels herself blushing. Looks around, a bit unsure of what to do with herself, feeling like a toddler who has just received praise. The familiarity with, or more like the *recognition* of her person, her accomplishments, makes her heart beat a little redder and her body feel a touch weightless. This is what she always swore had no importance for her, but here she is, standing in a grotty old petrol station in some random town in rural Iceland, feeling vanity wrap itself around her like some sticky candyfloss that she wants to savour as it melts on her tongue.

'I've only read one of your books, *My Days Alone*, but I loved it. How the protagonist doesn't talk to anyone for a whole year. It's so ... emo.'

Okay, just the one book. The petrol-station girl may not be the world's most dedicated fan, but still. Hannah feels like she's been given yet another insight into this town, which keeps opening up to her in perplexing and irritating ways, only to close itself off from her again. She feels like the moment is ripe to reap the fruits of this civilised conversation with a fan.

'If you want, I can send you a few of my other books?'

'I don't earn much working here, so...'

'No, no, I'll send them as a gift, of course. I don't think I've ever met such a young reader of mine. It'd be my pleasure.'

Strangely, it doesn't feel odd to Hannah to be this genuinely friendly, and she's surprised at herself for having offered to send the books without a second thought. That thought, however, is creeping up on her now.

'Could I get a twenty pack of King's?'

The girl slides the cigarettes over the counter. Hannah fishes the money out of her pocket. Tries to sound casual as she switches to the most sensitive of subjects.

'Did you know Thor, the young man who died...?'

The girl looks at her, surprised by the sudden change in conversation, but nods. 'He was a little older than me, but we had a lot of mutual friends.'

'So not close friends?'

The girl shakes her head. Boo.

'So you haven't...?'

'Haven't what?'

Hannah falters, thinks. Must formulate her next sentence carefully.

'Haven't heard any rumours about what happened that night? I mean, young people talk, and sometimes ... I don't know. Maybe you've heard something that you didn't want to go the police with...'

The girl shrugs. 'Everyone *is* talking about it, actually. But I don't really listen.'

Hannah nods. As if she thinks it makes sense. 'Sure. But ... what *are* they saying?'

The girl looks up. Is she starting to realise that Hannah is actually here to talk about this subject? The teenaged head tilts slightly to the side, and Hannah feels strangely undressed.

'You know what I really admire about you? That you don't write shitty crime novels like all the others do. I think that it's super cool, the fact you write books that only us weirdos read.'

Hannah smiles. What can you say to that? Now she can't ask her a damn thing, or use her crime-writing project as an excuse. Fuck.

'Thanks for the cigarettes, weirdo. See you around.'

Hannah heads towards the door, but just as she's about to step outside, the girl calls after her.

'Hey. You forgot to get my name and address.'

Hannah looks back at her, quizzically. The girl's gaze wavers, now unsure.

'Unless you didn't mean what you said, about the books?'

Hannah smacks herself in the forehead. Walks back to the girl and pulls out her notebook.

'Of course, I almost forgot. You can write it here.'

Hannah watches the girl as she writes in the notebook.

'Iðunn? What a pretty name.'

The girl named Iðunn hands the notebook back to Hannah.

'I'm sorry I can't tell you more about the rumours around Thor's death. I know you specialise in human psychology, and that you might find inspiration in that kind of thing, on the character level, I mean.'

Hannah nods. 'On the character level, yes ... That's exactly why I asked.'

'There's a party tonight actually, if you wanted to come? Or ... it's not so much a party, more a ... All the teenagers in town are planning to get together to hold our own memorial service for Thor. In our own way. I'm sure you'd hear something or other, if you came by...'

Hannah considers Iðunn, wants to throw her arms around her – what an unexpected lifeline for the investigation.

'Yes, of course, I'd love to come!'

Iðunn breaks out in a wide smile. And Hannah immediately realises why, when the teenager grabs her sleeve to stress her final sentence.

'Great! Just one last thing though ... Could you stop by Vínbúð beforehand and get us some drinks?'

35

Half a day, a fair amount of nervous waiting about, a trip to Vínbúð and a long nap later. Hannah has barely stepped into the room before she wants to turn and leave. Iðunn was right. It certainly looks like all of Húsafjörður's teenage residents have gathered together here, in this little basement, which actually seems like it might be someone's bedroom. She scans the room. An unmade sofa-bed, which looks like it may have never been made, a gaming corner with two computer screens on a much too small, dusty desk, and a huge office chair that looks like one of those you'd find at the helm of a spaceship. The walls are lined with posters, all curling at the edges and featuring bands Hannah has never heard of. On the floor, a haphazard heap of stuff of an undefined nature. In another corner, a rowdy football table. Other than the fact that Hannah feels about a thousand years old, she also feels claustrophobia closing in on her in the cramped room, the memories of her own teenage years spent at boring flat parties suddenly coming alive in her head like an inner tic. Iðunn seems to sense Hannah's urge to back out of the room. Her new young friend from the petrol station takes a firm grip on her arm, as if Hannah is a child about to walk out into the road, and Iðunn is the parent, preventing her from escaping.

'I know it's a little strange, given you could be everyone's grandma, but seriously: you're the coolest person in this room.'

Is Hannah supposed to feel flattered by that? It has the entirely opposite effect, but she allows herself to be pulled further into the cave. Upon reaching the room's epicentre, a little coffee table apparently painted with a layer of dust and food debris, Hannah opens the bag she has discreetly carried in with her. Applause and a few yells of delight fill the room when the youths realise what its contents are: sweet white wine and two bottles of vodka. Hannah hurries to pour herself a glass of the former before it's divided up between the eager teenage hands. She drinks half of it in one go, while analysing the space around her. There are around twenty to twenty-five people aged between fifteen and twenty, and Hannah once again feels as if she's been dragged back into her own youth. Maybe it's something about the way they carry themselves: the slightly hyper conversations mixed with a trembling insecurity their attitudes and overzealous gestures overcompensate for. Behaviour that transcends time, that all teenagers seem to adhere to. She is reminded of her own maturity at this age, which does not help to decrease the degree of social discord she is currently feeling, and instead reminds her that Iðunn may actually be correct: she could be their grandmother, or at least their mother. Some indie rock music blasts out of a single but very large speaker, music Hannah can't quite date. It sounds old, but to an extent that it could also be very modern. Men playing electric guitars never goes out of fashion. As she expected, there is no queue of dedicated fans waiting to speak to her, but she is still a little surprised to find that no one seems interested in her presence. They barely notice that it is her, Hannah, who with great generosity has brought alcohol to the party. Out of the corner of her eye, she can see that Iðunn is already lost in conversation with a group of other girls, and Hannah is left to herself for a while. Which is fine, as it gives her time to identify the individuals who may be most useful to talk to. Despite her best instincts, she decides not to approach one of the gawky guardians of the dark corners, but instead seeks out one of the youths standing in the middle of it all, entertaining the crowd like a stand-up comic in a tiny, amateur club. The boy is broad-shouldered, or perhaps well-built, Hannah can't quite tell the difference, but he could well be one of the young men she saw on the football pitch the night she met Thor. The guy has thick, dark-blond hair, cut short on the sides, and his face is harmonious without being decidedly beautiful. All in all, he comes across as someone you would gravitate towards – to share gossip with or reap appreciative praise from. Hannah waits until he heads out to the toilet.

And then she strikes. Pretending she is also queuing for the toilet, she traps him on his way back to the party.

'Cool shirt.'

She tries to bring her tone down to a level that feels like a reasonable distance between a mother or a female paedophile. The guy scrutinises her, clearly trying to place her in his world. But without success.

'Who are you, exactly?'

Hannah is prepared for the scepticism and, smiling, extends a hand, desperately hoping that he has washed his before leaving the bathroom.

'Hi, I'm Hannah, a friend of Thor's.'

The guy reciprocates with a damp, limp hand, still looking sceptically at her. She refines her lie.

'Or, rather, a friend of Ella's, to be more precise. Thor's mother's sister...'

Once again another, in Hannah's opinion, well-founded, sceptical gaze. She tries one last time, the smallest lie.

'I'm a friend of the family. A distant relative from Denmark.'

The thick hair nods, but not in the way that he thinks it all makes perfect sense.

'And they wanted me to … That is, the whole family are obviously super upset about it all, and they asked me to come and collect nice memories of Thor. For the funeral.'

Hannah feels like smacking some sense into herself, but she does have to offer some sort of excuse.

'And why would you think I'd have anything to say?'

'You knew him, didn't you?'

'That's not what I said.'

The boy is now leaning against the doorframe. Is he flirting with her? In any case, she's got his attention now. So far, so good. Hannah takes a step closer. He seems to like it.

'You don't need to rattle off a load of praise about him, if you don't want to. But if there's anything you wanted to mention…'

'What do I get in return?'

'What?'

The boy has shuffled a little closer to her, staring directly at her breasts, clearly very drunk. Making it difficult for Hannah to play dumb.

'Forget it. I'll find someone who knew him better.'

Hannah turns to head back into the party, but a strong young arm grabs hold of hers.

'Wait! What if I told you that I saw Thor that night – the night he died?'

Hannah's every muscle tenses up. She studies the young man. Has she underestimated him? Is he playing a more advanced game of exchanging-knowledge-for-sexual-favours than she has thought him capable of? She concludes that he's bluffing and yanks her arm out of his grip.

'Good luck with the girls your own age.'

Hannah heads back to the party, but in one, last, desperate teenage attempt for attention, he calls after her. Hannah stiffens – did she hear that right? She turns. The guy nods, no longer with that mischievous gaze. For a moment, he looks sober, sincere.

'I mean it. I saw Thor heading home that night. And then a car stopped and picked him up.'

Hannah stares at him.

'What did you say your name was?'

Hannah can't get out of the teenage party fast enough, but in the short amount of time she spent in the toilet-queue conversation, the alcohol has entered the bloodstream of the rest of the youths, who have managed to turn the small bedroom into a bouncy castle of bare torsos bumping against each other in time to the nineties grunge music blasting out of the speaker, all shouting along to the lyrics. Hannah tries to fight her way through the pulsating arms, legs and sweaty, alcohol breath, and for a brief moment has the desire to never drink again. She's jostled back and forth for a while, and then becomes trapped between a boy and girl who are jumping up against each other as if they've only just discovered dancing. Hannah struggles to catch her breath, wants to lash out. How many teenagers could possibly fit into twenty square metres? She tries to signal to them that she wants to get out, but she's blocked in on every side. Her rescue comes in the form of her buff toilet friend, who has found his way back into the party, and suddenly grabs hold of her and pulls her out of what was developing into an involuntary threesome. He yells over Nirvana:

'I didn't think you were the dancing type.'

He smiles at her, does a few embarrassing dance moves himself, and Hannah makes a face as if she hasn't heard what he's said. Apologising with her arms, she's now far enough away from the purgatory of the dance floor to muscle her way through the last stretch to the exit. But just as she reaches for the handle of the door to freedom and the pursuit of a new lead, Iðunn steps in front of her.

'You can't leave now.'

Hannah is hit with a sense of guilt over not saying goodbye to her new friend. She tries to look like she's coming down with something.

'I'm not feeling great, I just wanted to get out for some fresh air.'

'Perfect. We're almost ready to get started on the ceremony anyway.'

Hannah looks as clueless as she actually is.

'Ceremony?'

'For Thor. Just take this.'

Before Hannah can say another word, Iðunn has piled two cans of lighter fluid into her arms, and Hannah now notices that Iðunn's own arms are full of pieces of light-green cardboard. Behind her: another girl holding a handful of marker pens in one hand and a box of matches in the other.

'Are we setting fire to something?'

Iðunn smiles.

'Precisely.'

36

The party-goers have filtered outside at miraculous speed – within mere minutes – and are now gathered beneath the starry night sky. It's as if an invisible force has pulled them out, or perhaps someone just turned off the music. Hannah shivers and looks around. The adolescent energy that previously radiated from them all is a little more subdued now, beneath their thick winter coats and hats, as if everyone knows what is about to happen, and they wait for a while in reverence. Iðunn seems to be the leader – she removes the cans of lighter fluid from Hannah's arms and empties them liberally over a large pile of various flammable materials: old wood, furniture, branches. A thought occurs to Hannah. As the only actual adult there, should she not be trying to prevent the drunken youths from setting fire to things? But she can't bring herself to say anything – it feels as if she shouldn't be here at all. As if something is about to happen, but she is not a part of, is observing from the outside. Someone strikes a match. A piece of wood immediately catches. Then another, and one more. The fire travels, and the flames soon rise into the air like a winter-time midsummer's pyre. Iðunn stands before it, holding up the cardboard, and projects her voice into the night.

'Eitt á mann.'

Hannah looks around, confused. Tries to keep up with what's going on, and watches as all the youths each receive a piece of cardboard and a pen, and start writing. Some of them talk softly among themselves about the content. Some smile, others are moved. But none are mucking about now. Iðunn approaches Hannah.

'We're all writing a message to Thor, and then we'll throw them onto the fire. We hope he's sitting out there somewhere, and will receive them.'

Hannah nods. Observes them all. A little lump forms in her throat as the first of the cards are thrown into the flames.

'Would you also write one?'

Hannah looks at Iðunn, surprised.

'Me? I didn't even know him.'

'If I were Thor, I would be crazy happy to receive a card from you after I'd died.'

Hannah tries to ignore the bizarre comment, but why not: what harm is there in writing a card? She nods, takes a piece of cardboard and a pen. Thinks for a moment. She has never been good at this kind of writing, these short messages for other people. She stands against everything about the card-writing genre: the platitudes, the indifferent words, the congratulations and the condolences. She received cards from her parents throughout her adulthood: every year on her birthday. They always wrote the same thing. Until the year she stopped receiving the card. She knew well enough that it was her mother who wrote them and that her father couldn't continue the tradition after her death. And in that moment, Hannah realises that she has genuinely missed receiving those stupid cards over the last four years. She chews the end of the marker pen. What do you write to someone who is dead and who you never knew? She puts the pen to cardboard.

*Dear Thor. I'm sorry that your bright life came to an end too soon.
Even though it doesn't mean anything now, you have inspired many
people, especially me.*

Hannah pauses. Then quickly scribbles down one last sentence:
I will find your killer.

She folds the cardboard and chucks it into the flames. Watches
as the fire swallows it up, devouring her promise.

'Are you still here?'

Hannah recognises the voice, turns to see where it came from,
and to her surprise, finds Jonni standing beside her, green card in
hand. What's he doing here? It was only a day ago she visited him
in custody.

'Are you...?'

'I've been released. So I didn't break out, if that's what you were
thinking.'

'But are you still ... a suspect...?'

Jonni shrugs as if he's not even sure himself. Hannah, however,
notes that he looks happy to be out, to be free. In the orange glow
of the fire, he almost looks like a regular teenager. She bites her lip
– there are so many things she wants to ask him, but something
holds her back. He should be allowed to be with his friends tonight,
surrender to the grief that must have been unbearable, sitting alone,
under arrest. The wind changes direction and blows smoke in
Hannah's face, forcing her to take a step back. She shivers in the
crisp night air, lets her gaze follow the ascension of the flames, and
watches the smoke disappear into the stars. An unfamiliar pang of
sentimentality hits Hannah as she wonders whether Thor, in some
sort of metaphysical way, will receive their green words of grief. She
surprises herself. Where's this come from? Just a few days ago she
would have laughed scornfully at this whole mushy, pathos-filled
ceremony, but now it's as if it inspires calm, gives meaning to what
happened. Not just for the youths, but for her too. Hannah allows
herself to wallow in it for a moment. Several people have wrapped
their arms around each other, some crying. She observes Jonni.

Iðunn and the girl with the matches are on either side of him, holding him. Once again, Hannah feels a strange surge of hope for the future, not necessarily for herself, but for the coming generations. It feels like the right time to leave. She slowly backs away from the fire, and when she is far enough away, she turns, and for the first time in days, walks calmly back into town.

Hannah can't bring herself to go straight home. She has to pass on her new-found information to Viktor. Not just because she wants to see his face when she delivers such a vital lead in the investigation, but because she almost feels it her duty as a citizen to inform him about the car. Hannah tries to memorise the details the toilet-queue boy told her – the model, its appearance – while suppressing indulgent thoughts about seeing Margrét again, as she, a few moments later, readies herself to knock on the door of law and order.

'It's after midnight.'

The bags under Viktor's eyes are so dark that they look like they've been painted on. His hair is all over the place, and Hannah realises that this is the first time she's seen the man unshaven. Yet, it is clear that she hasn't actually woken him up. And for once, he's in uniform.

'I have some important information.'

'I told you to keep out of the investigation.'

'I just bumped into Jonni. Is he no longer a suspect?'

'Stay out of it.'

Viktor closes the door, but Hannah just manages to stop it with her foot. Viktor looks at her, exhausted. No longer angry, just tired.

'Did you know that someone saw Thor get into a car the night he was killed?'

Hannah catches a glimpse of surprise in Viktor's face.

'Black or dark blue, a four-wheel drive. It was one of Jonni's friends who saw it. He'd snuck out that night to smoke pot with some friends, which is why he hasn't said anything before now. But he saw Thor that night. And must be the last person to see him alive. Aside from the murderer, of course.'

'Assuming that what your supposed witness says is true. Who was it?'

'Of course it's true.'

'Name?'

'I promised I wouldn't say.'

'Goodnight, go away.'

Viktor slams the door onto Hannah's foot, and she has to muster all her self-control not to scream.

'His name is Stefan. Stefan Haraldsson.'

The door opens a fraction, so that Hannah can squeeze her now howling foot out of the doorframe and step inside behind the creased police shirt.

Hannah finds herself sitting on the brown leather sofa once again, but is offered neither red wine nor sex this time. Viktor pulls over a kitchen chair and sits in front of her, with the appearance of someone struggling to maintain their last sliver of a façade. In vain.

'The results of the DNA test from the bottle came back. The blood was definitely not Jonni's, but the fingerprints were probably Thor's.'

Viktor pauses. Preparing himself for his confession.

'So I think you were right. Thor probably hit his assailant with the bottle. We didn't have enough evidence to keep Jonni in custody, and his lawyer had plenty of good arguments for releasing him, despite the threat against Ægir. The fact he's so young, was blinded by grief, had no previous criminal record, that kind of thing. So now … well, we don't have a single thing. Other than the bottle.'

'And the car.'

Hannah tries to sound encouraging. Can't help feeling a certain delight in the fact that she's managed to force herself into the middle of the investigation again.

'We're looking into Gísli. Testing to see if it is his blood on the bottle.'

'So he's a suspect?'

'We're looking into him.'

Viktor pauses again. Deflates, the last bit of air leaving him.

'Or rather: I'm looking into him. I don't exactly have many colleagues around here to help out. Other than the coroner and lab in Reykjavik, I am utterly alone.'

'Can't they send anyone to help you?'

'There aren't enough resources for that, unless we can be one-hundred-percent certain that it was a murder.'

Hannah looks at him, startled. 'Are we not?'

'Are you aware how many people die around here as a result of the natural world? Drunk people freezing to death, fishermen falling into the sea. And anyway, it's much easier to register the death as an accident.'

'What about the coroner's report?'

'I'm still waiting for the final results. The wound at the back of his head ... There's nothing to suggest he didn't just fall over and hit his head on a rock.'

'But didn't you say that there were marks on his shoulders that would suggest someone held him under the water?'

'Marks that can be interpreted as the result of some natural cause as well, apparently. We still lack conclusive proof.'

'The results you're still waiting on, then – what are they for?'

Viktor pauses. He's already told her far too much, but he clearly doesn't have anyone else he can share his thoughts with. Hannah doesn't need to say anything more to convince him to talk – her silence and patience are enough.

'To see if there was anything in his blood.'

'Alcohol, drugs, that kind of thing?'

Viktor nods. 'I'm aware that both he and Jonni were drunk. But Thor wasn't the kind of kid to take drugs. So if anything does show up ... then it could be. Murder, that is.'

Hannah mulls it over. It seems all they have is desperate hopes branching off in very different directions: the not-homeless homeless guy, who is most definitely a penniless alcoholic, seems to be the only reasonable suspect in a case in which the victim may, or may not, have consumed some sort of substance before meeting his cruel fate. Other than that, they know the young man got a lift in an expensive car, which certainly could not have belonged to the homeless guy, and that he most likely hit his murderer over the head with a bottle. But was he intoxicated or not? Hannah is aware that buff Stefan could potentially have been lying, but despite everything, he did seem trustworthy, and perhaps a little too stupid to make up a lie like that on the spot. But the information doesn't seem to have helped Viktor in the slightest – quite the opposite, in fact.

'I know it's not exactly a great consolation, but if you want someone to discuss the case with, to use as a sounding board ... I really mean it. And not to hassle you or anything, but you know, there may be a reason why I've been able to find some things out that you couldn't.'

Viktor stares at her.

'The bottle. The car. For some reason, people open up to me in a different way. Maybe because I'm not from around here. Or maybe because they think I'm too stupid to put all the pieces together.'

Viktor smiles. Looks at Hannah as if analysing her. As if he can see through her.

'Or maybe because you're more friendly and trusting than you like to admit?'

Hannah shuffles on the sofa a bit, uncomfortably moved. Stands up, to get the conversation back on track.

'I mean it. If you think it could be of use to involve me in all this, then I do really want to help. Without getting in the way or breaking the law.'

'And without sneaking around in my backyard?'

Hannah freezes. Had happily forgotten her embarrassing garden quest, but it's not the reminder of it that gives her goosebumps. It's the thought of what Viktor actually meant when he said 'sneaking around'.

37

Hannah leaves Viktor's with the satisfaction of having been given an unofficial role as investigative assistant, but with the added feeling that she must be more vigilant. When she slides under the cold duvet half an hour later, her thoughts race around her head in a way she only ever experiences when she's particularly drunk. The thoughts start to stumble over one another, and her brain can't make the connections stretch far enough to create any meaning. Her phone suddenly beeps and lights up, and she feels a twist in her stomach – could it be Margrét? She snatches her phone off the night stand and couldn't be more disappointed: Jørn. Wanting to thank her for the good chat they had earlier and remind her that she can always come to him, if she ever needs any help. Maybe they could go on a few trips around the local area together, do a bit of research for their respective books? His four-wheel drive can take them anywhere. Jørn's message ends with an irritating car emoji. Hannah doesn't respond, puts the phone on silent, closes her eyes and tries to forget all about him. She quickly falls into a deep sleep, and to her surprise, wakes up at exactly seven o'clock the next morning, feeling alert and refreshed, which she has not once felt in her entire adult life. Ella isn't up when Hannah heads downstairs, puts the coffee on and some bread in the toaster. All humdrum acts, but they give her a sense of achievement. Control. She sits at the dining table and takes a crunchy bite of her jam-coated breakfast, washes it down with hot coffee and tries to focus on her novel.

The alarm hadn't been raised when Esther escaped from prison. It was several hours later that Officer Axelson finally realised she wasn't there. Hours in which she could've done harm to herself, or worse: to others. As he drove around, searching for her, he tried to figure out how all the pieces fit together. She had killed her boyfriend's father, but had she also killed her boyfriend? It didn't make sense, they were in love. Axelson scratched his long beard. Hold on! A thought suddenly hit him: there was more than one murderer. He got goosebumps at the thought; there wasn't just one dangerous young woman on the run, but an accomplice too. Perhaps this was the person Esther was going to meet? Perhaps they were planning more murders together? He had hardly had the thought before he was struck with another: everything made far more sense with two murderers in the picture. It explained Edith's alibi, explained the mysterious messages on her phone, and above all, it explained how she could escape from her cell - and particularly how the lock had been broken from the outside. Boom! A loud, ear-splitting sound bored into Axelson's skull, and everything turned black. He hadn't even had time to register the car before it had driven straight into the left-hand side of his.

Hannah pushes her reading glasses onto the top of her head, satisfied. Now there's a car crash in the mix as well, which can only be a good thing, if the book were to be adapted for TV. And it most likely will, it is crime. Beep. Hannah has to do a double-take after glancing at her phone, just to make sure she hasn't read that wrong. No. It's an invitation from Margrét to meet her at that part of the Icelandic wilderness Hannah fears most: the foot of the glacier. Perhaps it's even worse – maybe she'll suggest they trek up it. She contemplates her answer, while knowing full well what she'll say. She doesn't quite have a chance to write *yes* before Ella appears in the kitchen, interrupting her with her morning hunger and scrutinising gaze.

'Coffee?'

Ella nods and sits down, Hannah pours her a cup. Smiles.

'Relax, I'm not losing it. I just had a good night's sleep is all. Maybe I'm on the path to being a fully functioning human being.'

Ella nods, but there's no trace of a smile. Hannah remembers that the funeral is tomorrow. It must be a tremendous weight on her shoulders. She feels a pang of shame for having forgotten about it, for only thinking about her own sleep. The new and improved Hannah turns to her host with genuine compassion.

'Is everything ready for tomorrow?'

Ella nods. Finds a scrap of paper. Writes.

I go to se Vigdis today, hjelp with the last few ting.

'Shall I go with you?'

Ella shakes her head.

'I mean it, I want to help. If there's anything I can do, just say.'

It's not a lie either, Hannah genuinely means it. Even if it means she can't go on her little glacier trip with Margrét. Ella writes quickly and resolutely.

Thanks, but I want to go myself.

Hannah offers the basket of toast to Ella, who holds her hand up, almost as if it were an undue amount of stress to take one. Hannah looks at Ella's arms, which look like two pieces of gnarled but fragile bark. She seems to have aged in the last few days. Her cheeks look more hollowed, her hair thinner. Thor's death has hit her hard, and Hannah suddenly remembers stories of people who've become sick and died immediately after the death of a loved one. Probably more the case with a partner, or children though – Hannah has never heard of it happening following the death of a nephew. But if Ella isn't to lose her will to live as a result of Thor's death, who else's could have so great an effect on her? Hannah butters a piece of toast for Ella, before disappearing upstairs to take a bath. When she comes downstairs half an hour later, Ella still hasn't touched the food, and her cup of coffee is still full. And is probably as cold as Ella's eyes, staring into space.

38

The energy pumps around Hannah's body as she stomps towards the glacier. She has tried to make herself look as attractive as possible while sporting wool-on-wool. Freshly washed hair and a touch of mascara was all she had to work with.

It's a few miles uphill to the foot of the enormous ice sheet, and on her way there, Hannah manages to raise her hopes as to how her date with Margrét might play out. There surely has to be a reason why she wants to meet here specifically, and not somewhere in town. Hannah smiles. 'In town' is basically just a collection of cabins on a field by the sea. She draws the air deep into her lungs. Almost there now. But she can't see Margrét. Hannah's thoughts circle around all the reasons why Margrét may have invited her here. She can only come up with one, and it generates a warm sensation beneath all her layers of wool. So when she does finally catch a glimpse of Margrét a few steps later, her shoulders automatically drop as she deflates with disappointment. She's not alone – Margrét has brought the children. For a split second, Hannah considers turning around, but it's too late. One of the small, snowsuit-clad menaces is now pointing at her. Hannah waves and smiles, trudges over to them. The children – four of them, about three to four years old, she would guess – are jumping around from rock to rock, all of which look just as smooth as the glacier, sticking its huge tongue out behind them. Hannah stares up at the mass of ice, which seems even more terrifying and stained with black than she thought it would be. But she must admit, it does make for a good playground. A little under-equipped, but the kids seem to be enjoying themselves, haring around like little trolls, collecting stones. As long as none of them fall and end up seriously injured. Hannah can't imagine herself having to assist in sorting out a child's broken foot.

'Good of you to come.'

Margrét, who somehow manages to look quite stylish in her

warm, practical attire, is sitting on a rock, smoking a cigarette. Hannah walks up to her, but doesn't sit herself.

'Well, it's not like I had a million other things to do. Other than writing a book.'

'And solving a murder.'

'And solving a murder.'

Hannah wonders whether Margrét is aware that Viktor has loosened his grip a bit and is now letting her participate more in the investigation. Maybe that's why Margrét wants to talk to her? Hannah puts out a feeler.

'I know this is all a bit complicated, with my trying to get involved in the investigation. And Viktor, now ... uh, I don't know whether he's said anything to you about it, but we've agreed that I can go ahead and try to sniff out a few things in town. To share with him. And then he'll share what he knows with me. Unofficially, of course.'

'We are married. Do you think we don't talk?'

Margrét's gaze drills into Hannah, as if the glacier were reflected in her eyes. Is there a bit of a flirtatious look in her expression, or is that just wishful thinking?

'I don't know ... how much the two of you talk, exactly. About work, and ... other things.'

Margrét smiles. 'I've not told him about us, if that's what you're getting at.'

A wave of relief spreads through Hannah. Not just because their affair is still a secret, but because this is the first time she has heard Margrét verbalise – confirm – that there is, actually, something between them. It feels meaningful.

'That's what I wanted to talk to you about.'

The meaningful feeling drains from her body. Of course that's why. She's hauled Hannah up here, into the wilderness, to end their affair before it can really begin; in front of her frolicking children, so it all seems as harmless and innocent and every-day as they are, nullifying it like a snowflake on hot asphalt. Hannah nods. Would like to avoid the humiliation of being rejected.

'No need to say any more. I understand – all the complications and what not. And it's only been a distraction for me as well. A silly distraction. I hope I haven't messed anything up.'

Margrét nods.

'For me, distraction isn't necessarily a bad thing. And it's not the first time that I've ... sought something more, if you get me. It's just not often that that kind of distraction, uh, presents itself around here.'

Hannah stares at her. Remembers what she wanted to ask her.

'Did Thor confide in you, about his relationship with Jonni? I ask because you were so ambiguous about how well you knew him...'

Margrét nods. And when she meets Hannah's eye, looks a little annoyed.

'For the love of God, are you going to sit down or what? You'll freeze your ass off standing there. Come, I've got a blanket here.'

Hannah has forgot that she is still standing there, like a salt pillar in the wind. Margrét shuffles aside, making room for her on the rock, and Hannah sits beside her.

'Do you have some sort of agreement then? You and Viktor?'

Margrét snorts.

'An agreement relating to the fact that my desires lie elsewhere and not with him, even though he's sweet and kind and fun to be with, and that life – in general – isn't all that bad, as long as I can occasionally take a few liberties for myself, so I can endure such a life? Is that what you mean by an agreement?'

Hannah has never heard anything so reactionary in her entire life, and has to restrain herself from launching into a long monologue about living life true to one's nature. How can Margrét be content in living half a life? Hannah studies the woman beside her.

'But why? You could move to Reykjavík, be with someone whose back you don't have to sneak around behind. You could have everything you have here, but without having to live a lie.'

Hannah can hear how sanctimonious she sounds, but when it comes down to it, she's just stating facts. Margrét, however, doesn't seem all that affected by Hannah's sermon. She's probably had the exact same thoughts hundreds of times herself. Margrét watches the kids, still tearing around.

'This. A good, safe life. We have everything we need. Materially, spiritually. Nature, community. You're part of something, here. I'm part of something. I'm the policeman's wife, a stay-at-home mother, a child minder, who people can count on. My children breathe fresh air, they go to bed full, safe and happy every night. And when I get old, there will be someone to look after me, and when I die, someone to miss me.'

Hannah stares at Margrét. Does she mean that?

'When you die? Is that what you think about? The fact you'll have a nice funeral, and the whole town will come and pay their respects, because you were a good, decent citizen? Someone who always contributed to the status quo, someone who made sure that everything was quiet and calm and good?'

'Something like that.'

'But disasters happen anyway. Take Thor for an example.'

'You misunderstand. It's not some catastrophe I'm scared of. It's the long, arduous life that can become unbearably lonely if you stray too far off the beaten track.'

'But you're not risking anything in your life here.'

'And what do you risk?'

Margrét looks at her with a gaze that makes Hannah feel stupid.

'And, anyway, if that were true, and I don't risk anything, then what am I doing here with you?'

Now that's an argument Hannah can't contradict, but it's still hard to accept that Margrét is genuinely, truly happy living this life. But, then again, perhaps it is *because* Hannah has never compromised on anything in her life that she now lives with a permanent feeling of loneliness. She shakes off the thought. Rather be lonely than trapped. Hannah wants to dig deeper, ask more, challenge Margrét's worldview, extract details from her about Viktor and their life, and find out what Margrét dreamed of as a child. Instead, she asks what the children's names are, whether they come up here, to the glacier, often, and how Margrét can bring herself to spend the entire day in the company of creatures who can't speak properly or go to the toilet by themselves. One key nugget of information she does find out is that Margrét has lived in Húsafjörður her entire life – all of her friends and family are here. There's probably some value in that too.

Hannah suddenly feels a cold tingling on her neck. Which quickly travels down her spine in one bizarre, icy sensation. It takes her a second to realise that the children have snuck up behind her and have dropped a clump of snow from the glacier down the back of her top. She jumps up, hyperventilating as she hops and dances about, trying to shake the snow out from beneath her many, many layers.

'Argh, God, it's so cold. I'm dying!'

The children are laughing so hard that their little flight suits look ready to fly off. Hannah succeeds in dislodging the chunk of ice from under her numerous tops, but the cold water clings to her back. She wants to chase the laughing snowsuits far away, but she realises that Margrét is also laughing, and suddenly sees herself from the outside: in that moment she really is just a stuffy, farcical killjoy. Behaviour as predictable as rain falling from an overcast sky. She decides to surprise herself, Margrét and the little vermin, and she runs up to the glacier, scoops up a handful of snow, and starts running after the children.

'Aha. Now you're going to pay!'

The children don't understand her, but that doesn't matter – they squeal with joy and scatter in every direction, so Hannah doesn't have to pretend that she's bad at playing tag to avoid having to actually catch them. She eventually gives up and throws the snow at them, and they happily evade her attempt at revenge. Hannah just about manages to take a proper breath in and out, before a large snowball hits her square in the forehead. A few metres away: Margrét, waving mischievously, while the children shriek with laughter. Hannah hears her own laughter, realises how fast her heart is beating and that her cheeks are aflame. And it hits her that she can't remember the last time she genuinely laughed like this. What will happen between them from this point on remains unsaid, but on the way back into town, Margrét unexpectantly takes Hannah's hand and gives it a little squeeze. Not much, but enough for Hannah to know that whatever this is, it isn't over.

39

Hannah feels restless. She walks with Margrét and the children the last hundred metres down to their home-cum-police-station, which is actually a detour for her, but she doesn't have any other plans. The excursion is nearly over, and she doesn't know when she'll next get to see Margrét. With or without the children. She watches the small snowsuits use up the last of their strength after the gruelling trip to run towards the house. She walks a few steps behind Margrét, trying to think of a plausible excuse to stay a little while longer. But as they approach the house, Hannah gets the nagging feeling that things aren't quite as they should be. Viktor's car is parked diagonally across the driveway, a bit too far from the house, as if it's come to an abrupt stop. A few steps closer, they see that both the driver's and passenger's doors are open.

'What's all this?'

Margrét stops, having seen the same as Hannah. The children are now only a few steps from the front door, which is also wide open. Simultaneously sensing something's wrong, both women sprint towards the children to prevent them wandering inside. On the threshold, Hannah catches a handful of one of the kid's snowsuits and drags them back – as she does noticing something splattered across the floor of the entrance hall. Blood.

'Bíddu!'

Margrét stands beside her, two of the children in her arms, her face completely white. The children laugh a little, perhaps thinking that this is another fun game. They squirm to try and get free. Hannah and Margrét lock eyes, the latter's radiating undiluted fear, looking like someone who could shatter like a particularly frail ice sculpture. Something Hannah would do anything to prevent from happening.

'Stay here with the kids. I'll go in.'

Without another word, Hannah manages to manoeuvre all of the children into Margrét's protective embrace, and notices out of the corner of her eye that she's backing the flock away from the house, murmuring soothing words, which may work on them, but clearly isn't doing anything to convince herself.

'Be careful!'

Hannah just manages to catch the warning as she steps through the door, which also appears to be covered in blood. Her heart hammering, she tiptoes slowly into the living room. Has seen enough action films to know that now is when she should be pulling out a weapon, or waiting for reinforcements. But she has neither a weapon to draw nor anyone to call. And she realises that she isn't actually afraid, just extremely tense about what sight awaits her. She sneaks towards the living-room door, expecting the worst, and hops inside in one quick movement, so she ends up standing in the middle of the room, where everything is completely silent and normal. Apart from the glass of water that's been knocked over on the coffee table, the contents silently dripping onto the carpet. It feels like Hannah stares at the pool of water for several seconds, until she hears movement coming from the kitchen. It sends a shiver down her spine. Now she feels afraid. But there's no turning back. She must search the rest of the house, must ensure it is safe for the children waiting outside, cold and tired. She edges towards the kitchen, frantically looking around her for any kind of weapon, and ends up grabbing a brass candlestick from a chest of drawers, raising it high above her head. Intending to appear both dangerous and fearless, and with a genuine willingness to bring the heavy, sharp-edged object down onto the intruder's head, she darts into the kitchen with a yell, surprising herself. Surprising, too, the figure who is leaning over the kitchen sink, and is visibly frightened when they spin round with a start to face Hannah's raised, makeshift weapon. The figure shields their face with a resounding scream. Mere milli-seconds before the adrenaline drives Hannah's arms downward into a well-placed blow, she realises that she is looking into a pair of eyes she recognises: Viktor's.

Hannah lowers her arms, her pulse about to burst out of her veins, and looks confusedly at Viktor who, pale and blood-soaked, was clearly trying to bandage his right arm, which has already bled all over a tea towel on the counter beside him. The sweat drips from his forehead, cascading down his arm and over the blood from a wound that looks both deep and long. Hannah looks around.

'Is someone else in here? Who did that to you?'

Viktor strains to shake his head, looks like a man about to collapse. Hannah pulls over a chair and eases him into it. Takes over the bandaging-his-arm project, forces her eyes to blink intensely so as to not faint herself. Blood has never been her strong suit – she gets dizzy just watching a gory film at the cinema, and even small cuts cause her body to shut down. It must be the adrenaline keeping her conscious as she hurriedly wraps the dressing around Viktor's arm. She can see that the wound is a long cut, most likely caused by a kitchen knife. Her eyes search for the knife, but it's nowhere to be seen, and she is once again hit by a wave of fear – the person who presumably stabbed Viktor with it in his own home may still be somewhere in the house, knife in hand. She pours a glass of water and holds it in front of Viktor. He seems confused, and Hannah can't tell if it's from the pain or the loss of blood. She holds the glass up to his mouth, and he drinks greedily.

'Are you absolutely sure that there's no one else here?'

Viktor nods. 'Absolutely. He left. Ran. He'll be long gone now.'

'Who?'

Hannah could die of curiosity.

'Gísli. It was Gísli.'

The surprise washes over Hannah, and she stares, mouth agape, at Viktor.

'Gísli? Are you sure?'

'Of course. I drove him here myself.'

The children who do not live at the police station house have been picked up, and Margrét has placed her own children in front of the TV – with a cartoon and sweets to distract them – away from the serious conversation now taking place in the kitchen. Hannah managed to quickly wipe up the blood so the children could enter the house without being traumatised for the rest of their lives. And it doesn't seem that any of them have picked up on the gravity of the atmosphere permeating their home. A bit more colour has returned to Viktor's cheeks, as he starts explaining what happened to him.

'I received the results from the bottle. It did turn out to be Gísli's blood, so I think you were right. It was him – he was the one who Thor hit that night.'

'And he was the one who killed Thor?'

Viktor shrugs. Or rather, the shoulder not in a homemade sling shrugs.

'You said yourself that you didn't think he was capable of violence. But when he realised that was my theory, that it was the reason I was questioning him, well … he lost it.'

'But what about the car? Did he try to drive away in it or what?'

Viktor shakes his head.

'No. I found him out in his shack, asked him to come back with me, just for a chat. He was very reluctant, asked questions the whole way here, seemed extremely nervous. But I wanted to talk to him properly, not in the car – with a cup of coffee and a table between us. Wanted to see his face when he answered my questions.'

'But you never got that far?'

Hannah is impatient, wants to know everything immediately, but also knows deep down that Viktor won't be able to offer her a satisfactory explanation. The fact that Gísli could be the murderer ... Everything points to that, of course, but it feels almost too straightforward. Or too sad. Hannah can't describe why, but this doesn't feel like the right development in the case.

'He was so insistent, I ended up telling him about the bottle and the blood samples there in the car. I didn't even have to explain the theory that the blood on the bottle probably belonged to the murderer – he just instinctively felt that he was being accused. And that's when he started to attack. Hit me, while I was driving. I managed to get the car home, pull him out and get him inside. It was never my intention to arrest him or use handcuffs, but with that level of resistance, I ended up having to. Or rather, I would've, but I never got that far.'

'Before he got his hands on a kitchen knife?'

Viktor nods. 'I didn't even realise what was happening, just suddenly felt it slice my arm, and then he ran off. I would've run after him if I wasn't bleeding so much.'

Hannah and Margrét look at each other. Concern. Margrét speaks first.

'It was good that you didn't go after him. It sounds like he would've done anything to get away.'

'We have to find him.'

'I've called for back-up from Reykjavik. I can't deal with him alone. And certainly not like this.' Viktor nods at his arm.

The doctor is also on the way, and Hannah predicts several stitches.

'When will they be here? The back-up.'

'As soon as they can. Which will be a few hours yet, realistically.'

Hannah shakes her head. 'We can't wait that long. If Gísli is that out of control, he might end up seriously hurting himself, or someone else. The sooner we find him, the better.'

'*We* aren't doing anything. You are a civilian, and you certainly won't be going out there looking for a murderer with a kitchen knife.'

'But he isn't—'

'Stop!' Viktor raises his voice – but sounds as if he has used his last remaining strength to reclaim some control over the situation. 'You are not going out to look for Gísli, do you hear me?'

Hannah stares at Viktor – the pain doesn't seem to have worn off yet, despite the cocktail of over-the-counter medicines Margrét has given him. Hannah has no choice but to nod. Which is followed by a knock on the door. Margrét leaves the room to open the front door for the doctor, and Hannah follows her, so as to not be any more in the way than she already feels she is.

Hannah plods home, slowly. Her whole body is buzzing – she can't possibly just go back to the house and wait around, restless but idle. She has to do something. But she's also fully aware of the danger of confronting Gísli and facing the same kitchen knife. She gets goosebumps at the thought of the sharp blade penetrating her flesh. No, she can't. For a brief moment, she considers turning round and asking Jørn if he wants to join her. There's much to be said about the man, but he is still a big, strong bloke who would surely be able to handle a trembling, nervous alcoholic. Then again, Viktor couldn't. And what if Hannah has underestimated Gísli? What if it does turn out he was a cold-blooded murderer all along, one who is not afraid to have the murder of yet another human being weighing on his conscience? When she thinks about it, he may be even more dangerous, given he has nothing to lose. No job, no family, nothing other than his freedom to drink and gaze at the ocean. But perhaps that is worth defending until the bitter end. Hannah shivers, feels something touch her forehead. Something light and cool. She looks up and realises that it has started to snow. Large snowflakes float down from the sky, coming to a rest in her hair, turning her jacket white. No, she should keep Jørn out of all this. She should just go home and await updates on the situation, of course. Not provoke any more crimes or play the heroine. She will go home to Ella, drink a cup of coffee and discuss tomorrow's funeral, offer her help. Sit in the warm living room and let the police do their job. She is convinced that Viktor will at least keep her informed of whatever happens, and she can use the events of the next few days in her book. These sensible ideas get her thinking, but something makes her suddenly stop in her tracks. In front of her: a figure. Just standing there, as if they have emerged from the dense snowfall like a spirit of the fog. Hannah swallows and tries to calm her rapidly growing panic at the realisation that the figure before her is Gísli.

40

They stand like that for a while, facing each other. Hannah and Gísli, waiting like two cowboys in a showdown. Hannah searches him with her eyes, looking for the knife, but can't locate it. He stares back at her with a wounded look, or perhaps his eyes are just glazed over from the alcohol? Hannah takes a deep breath, tries to stay calm. Reminds herself that Gísli doesn't necessarily know she's aware of what he's done. Maybe she can talk to him as if everything is quite normal, lull him into believing he has nothing to fear, and then perhaps she can get past him and go home, without the situation becoming dangerous. She can't run back. The risk of him catching her is too great. But she can't walk past him without saying anything. She tries with a banal, run-of-the-mill remark.

'The snow's come out of nowhere, hasn't it?'

Gísli doesn't respond. Just stares at her. There's a good ten metres between them. Too far for Hannah to interpret his expression properly, and too close for her to ignore his presence.

'What do you do, actually, when it snows? I mean, you can't stay out in your shack when it's this cold, right?'

Silence. The snow is falling faster now, thicker. Hannah thinks it might be getting a little harder to see Gísli.

'I have my apartment.'

Oh, sweet relief … Hannah had forgotten about his apartment, but at least she's succeeded in getting him to talk about something other than the matter at hand. It seems like the 'lull him into the belief that everything is normal' strategy is working. Maybe. She delivers a response, joining in on the act they may, or may not, both be performing.

'I'd forgotten about your apartment. Is it far?'

'I can't go back there.'

Gísli sounds genuinely frustrated. Hannah sticks to her role.

'Why not?'

'I just can't.'

There's something defiant in his voice. Hannah knows exactly why he can't elaborate, and refrains from pushing that button again. She makes the decision to walk around him, when he says something so startling that it launches her into a panic.

'Maybe I can go home with you?'

Hannah gapes at him. Did she hear that correctly? Is he testing her? The snowflakes are like tufts of cotton wool, acting like a dimmer on the world, the half-light making the situation all the more surreal. It occurs to Hannah that if it continues to snow this intensely, it may be difficult to get home. This thought then snowballs into another, where Gísli has rammed the knife into her, and the fresh, snowy landscape is stained with blood splatter like a macabre Danish flag. She can no longer see his face. She needs some sort of assurance that he does not intend to slaughter her and Ella, but also knows that whatever reason he gives for wanting to go back home with her, she won't be able to shake off her distrust. Which is why she ends up doing something totally and completely irrational. She invites him home.

'Come on, let's get out of this unbelievably cold weather.'

They walk in silence. All Hannah can think about is whether she's walking towards her own death, with her executioner two steps behind, and how she can call for help as soon as she gets to the house. She doesn't dare pull out her phone and call someone – she is too exposed, too close to Gísli, who has his eyes fixed on her back. A more practical thought interrupts her concern over her potentially imminent death: what will Ella say? And what should she say to Ella?

By the time they reach the house she still hasn't come up with anything suitable. Hannah sees, to her relief, that Ella's car is parked out front, and the lights within shine through the windows. It is surely more difficult to kill two than one.

'And we're here.'

Hannah forces a strained smile as she asks Gísli to take his boots off beneath the little porch canopy. An intrusive thought comes to her in the form of a new title for her book: *The Barefoot Killer*. He is not, however, entirely barefoot, and she has difficulty tearing her eyes away from his dirty, ragged socks as they walk over the threshold and are met by the warm scent of the fire and Ella, standing there in the entrance hall with a concerned, motherly expression on her face.

'I've brought a guest with me – I hope that's okay? I don't know if you know Gísli?'

Hannah tries to seem calm, nonchalant. Wonders whether the two of them can hear her voice quiver. Ella nods, as if she was expecting Hannah to bring a kind-of homeless man in threadbare socks home. She says something in Icelandic, perhaps something about the sudden snowfall and coffee. Gísli follows her into the kitchen, where Ella starts fumbling around with the coffee machine. Hannah keeps her distance. Is very aware of the phone in her pocket, and waits for the right moment to go outside and call Viktor. But can she leave Gísli alone with Ella? What if he attacks her or takes her as his hostage? On the other hand, if she doesn't do anything, he may suddenly pull out the kitchen knife and stab them both. It might just be a question of time before he realises that

Hannah knows more than she has let on. She has to call for help.
She excuses herself.

'I just need to go to the toilet.'

Gísli stares at her – in a disconcerting way? Fighting all her
instincts, and with her pulse rising, Hannah's feet move swiftly out
of the room and into the bathroom. Shit, fuck! The panic implodes
the moment she shuts the door behind her and remembers the fact
that there's no lock on the door. She instinctively turns on the tap,
as if the sound of it can drown out everything. Three taps on her
phone, and a tedious dialling tone on the other end of the line.
Come on! Hannah glances nervously towards the door.

Seconds pass by. And finally:

'Húsafjörður Police, Viktor speaking.'

'It's me, Hannah. He's here. At Ella's.'

'Who's there?'

Viktor sounds like the most bone-headed cop. Hannah feels
desperate now – he should by in his car by this point, on the way
here. She almost shouts:

'Gísli is here!'

And as the words leave her mouth, she catches sight of her
reflection in the dark window before her, and someone else's. Gísli
– standing in the open doorway, watching her.

Hannah sits down softly on the couch, her heart in her throat. Not
daring to look up. She can feel Gísli's eyes on her, glances at her
phone in his pocket. She retracted her statement to Viktor, told him
she was just messing about. An extended hand was enough for
Hannah to give Gísli the phone, and a nod of the head was enough
for her to walk back into the living room, calmly and normally.
Coffee and cake has been laid out on the table. Ella sits facing
Hannah, dropping down into the snug armchair, blissfully unaware
of the fact that this may be the last cup of coffee she will ever drink,
the last slice of cake she will ever eat. The sofa lowers two degrees
as Gísli sits down next to Hannah. She can smell him, the bitter

stench of a wild man. She can feel his presence, almost hear his pulse, as if it were a part of her. Or she a part of him. This must be what a real, genuine fear of another person feels like. Hannah gulps, glances at the unnecessarily large cake knife Ella has brought out to divide the shop-bought cake with. She holds her breath as Gísli picks up the knife. He hesitates for a moment, and then starts to slice the cake. Looks Hannah in the eye as he does? He sounds friendly, with his Stanford English.

'Would you like a slice?'

Hannah doesn't dare do anything but nod. Ella babbles away, something in Icelandic, Gísli answers, and it seems as if they are already acquainted and enjoy each other's company. Maybe that is all this is, Hannah thinks. Maybe he did just need to see a friendly face, have a conversation, some warmth, out of the blizzard. Maybe he doesn't care that she's called Viktor – he'll eat his cake, drink his coffee, and be off. Maybe he's not as dangerous as—

'If you say anything to Ella, I'll slice you open with this cake knife.'

Gísli is smiling at her, and it suddenly occurs to Hannah that he just spoke in English. He must know that Ella doesn't speak it. He can say anything to Hannah without alarming Ella.

Hannah also realises that this may be her only opportunity to talk some sense into him, without sending Ella into a panic about the precarious situation. So Hannah puts great effort into sounding like she's talking about something quite normal.

'You should turn yourself into the police. I know what you did to Viktor, and they'll find you sooner or later.'

'They?'

'The reinforcements, coming from Reykjavík. I know you didn't mean to harm him, that you were desperate—'

'You don't know anything,' Gísli interrupts her.

Hannah glances at Ella, but it doesn't look like she has any suspicions about what they are talking about. Her attention is now directed at a crossword puzzle.

'I was the one who found the bottle with your blood on it. But I don't think you're the one who killed Thor.'

Ella looks up at them. Probably because she heard Thor's name mentioned. Hannah switches to Danish to explain.

'Gísli was expressing his condolences for what happened to Thor. I was just telling him that the police are doing everything they can to find out what happened that night.'

Ella nods, takes a sip of coffee. Stares into the fire for a moment then returns to her crossword. As if they were just three, lonely people, sitting there, enjoying each other's company. Hannah tries again, turns to face Gísli.

'You should turn yourself in, for your own sake. Say that you stabbed Viktor because you were under stress. Everyone will understand that – you'll receive a mild sentence. But the longer you wait, the more reckless you'll get and ... well, it'll accumulate. You'll just be making things worse for yourself.'

Gísli looks inquiringly at her. 'What do you know about crime and punishment?'

Hannah suppresses the urge to start talking about Dostoevsky and instead turns her palms out. Changes tack.

'You're right. Nothing. But allow me at least to beg you not to do anything to us. Not to me, not to Ella. It's not our fault that you've ended up in this unfortunate situation. But I want to help you. I can drive you to the station. I could take you home first, if there's anything you want to get?'

Gísli continues to stare at her, his eyes hiding somewhere beneath all that hair. He is still wearing his coat. Is he considering her suggestion? Hannah is dubious – it looks more like he's somewhere else entirely. Then he looks at her again, and this time his gaze is more imploring than commanding.

'Alcohol – do you have any?'

Damn! Hannah knows full well that there isn't a single drop of alcohol in the house, but she'll do anything to keep him satisfied right now, or rather, to prevent him from becoming agitated and violent. She remembers the empty wine bottles hidden in her suitcase, and opts to lie, buy some time.

'I have a few bottles of wine upstairs in my room. Shall I go and get one?'

Gísli nods. 'I'll come with you.'

The trip upstairs only takes a few seconds, but it feels like years. Hannah regrets this undertaking. This is the tamest diversion tactic in the history of womankind. In two minutes, Gísli will realise that she has duped him, and there will be nothing to quell his alcoholic and violent nerves. Her thoughts race as she tries to think up a new plan. Why isn't Viktor here yet? He must've heard her desperation over the phone, should be doing everything in his power to get here before blood is once again shed in his little district. As they step into her bedroom, Hannah glances at the window, which she must have forgotten to close. In any case, it is still ajar, and snow has settled on the windowsill. To her great disappointment, she can't see the flicker of car lights approaching the house through the hazy, chalk-white night. Gísli remains in the doorway, while Hannah walks over to her suitcase and kneels down in front of it. She pretends to rummage around. If only she could get him to come in, maybe she could lock him in her bedroom, shove the heavy chest of drawers in front of the door, escape to the Jeep and drive her and Ella to safety.

'White or red?'

Hannah holds up the two wine bottles, grasping them from the top in the hope he won't notice that they have long since been liberated from their corks and contents. She deliberately didn't turn on the bedroom light to prevent the empty bottles from revealing their secret. Only the light from the little hallway at the top of the stairs streams softly in through the doorway.

'Bring both.'

Hannah nods, swallows, stands up, and prepares herself for the great revelation, the truth of her hoax. Gísli has not moved from his position in the doorway, but if her plan is to succeed, she needs him to take a few steps inside.

'Do you mind if I just close the window? So I don't die of frostbite later.'

Hannah feels like bashing herself over the head with both the empty wine bottles for talking about death and the near future in front of her potential murderer. Amateur victim. Gísli nods, and she clambers onto the desk to close the window. And, pretending it's stuck, rattles it about a bit. She turns imploringly to him.

'Could you help...?'

Gísli hesitates a moment, then walks over to her. She lets him lean over to the window, grab the handle with his left hand, and tug it, as if there hasn't even been a problem. And then Hannah brings one of the bottles down so hard on the back of his head that she loses her balance. She steadies herself on the edge of the desk, losing a few crucial seconds, as Gísli tries to figure out what just happened. She just manages to catch a glimpse of his bared teeth and hear his scream as he grabs her back with both hands and pushes her with all the force he can muster, out of the window. Hannah tries to grab hold of the window ledge, but watches her own hands lose their grasp, and just has time to think to herself that this is the worst possible outcome of her unbelievably daft plan, and that this is one scenario she could never have imagined: fighting with a man twice as strong as her in front of an open window. In the milliseconds it takes her to fall, Hannah feels her body topple backward alongside the falling snow, then the painful thump as she lands on her back on the frozen ground. She also manages to catch sight of Gísli's murderous face poking out of the window, before the snow covers her eyes, and everything turns black. Completely black.

41

Hannah is dead. She is wrapped in a cloud, in cotton wool, she is one big ball of fluff, lying there, waiting for someone to pour water on her, so all her fibres can transform into another structure, so she can come alive again. Her eyes are wool. Everything is foggy, woollen and white, shadows move like ripples in a dream – this must be what heaven looks like. Her mouth is also wool, she tries to open it, say something, but the dead have no voice. She tries to move, lift her left hand, but her arms weigh a thousand kilos, and she can't feel her fingers. Does she have feet? With that thought, she moves her legs, but doesn't actually move anywhere.

'Is she awake?'

Hannah's ears are full of cotton, but a female voice penetrates the wool, drilling into her nervous system. Is that God talking? She tries to sharpen her sight, force her eyes to focus through the milky fog. Light, sharp light piercing her eyes, the darkness, and she closes them. The light is gone when she opens them again. And then the contours of a woman dressed in white appears, looking down at her as if she is trying to probe her soul. God?

'She's coming round.'

Hannah is confused, coming where? She blinks again, slowly, and it's as if someone removes a thin layer of cotton from her eyes. She can see now that the woman is middle-aged, has grey hair and that the white clothes are a uniform. There is a name tag on her uniform. Surely God doesn't need a name tag? Hannah tries to read what it says. Dr Something.

An Icelandic name. Two thoughts: she isn't dead, and she's in a hospital. Slowly, she remembers the fall from the window, Gísli's face protruding out of it, the snowflakes floating down, covering her face as she lay there, staring up at the sky. How she got to the hospital, however, and how long she has been there, she has no idea.

'How long will it take until she's fully conscious?'

Hannah picks up another voice, a man's. She recognises it but cannot place it. A kind of understanding of the world starts to form in her head: She is in hospital, surrounded by doctors and perhaps other people, all concerned about her well-being; she is alive, but has only just awoken from an unconscious state. Another realisation hits her: Ella! She hasn't heard her voice, she is not in the room, and after Hannah's fall, she was left alone in the house with a murderer. Hannah's voice vibrates as it travels through her woollen throat.

'Ella...'

'Sorry, we can't hear you...?'

The feeling of a person, leaning in close to her.

'Ella?'

'She's asking after Ella.'

The man's voice again. It's Viktor. She also realises that his hand is on her arm. A soothing hand.

'Ella is at the funeral.'

Hannah misunderstands at first – Ella's funeral? But then it hits her – Viktor means Thor's funeral. She therefore can't have been away for more than half a day. She tries to talk, but her throat feels like sandpaper.

'Water...'

Someone understands her rusty request, a straw is inserted between her lips, and she sucks on it greedily. It's like the water washes all the cotton wool out of her body, almost like a heavy duvet being lifted away. She can see fairly clearly now too: the female doctor, Viktor, whose upper arm has been properly bandaged, and a nurse. Hannah tries again to get her body to obey, to move. But it won't respond. The panic wells up.

'Am I paralysed?'

Hannah desperately seeks out the doctor's face, and is met with a smile.

'You were lucky. You could have broken your spine in that fall, you only broke your right forearm. We still had to operate, however, so your body is likely a little numb from the anaesthesia.'

Hannah looks down at her body now, and discovers that she is dressed in a white hospital gown, and that her arm is in a cast.

'The anaesthetic will wear off fully in the next few hours, and I think you'll probably feel quite sore at that point – not just your arm, but your whole body. Judging from all the bruises, moving in the next few weeks isn't going to be fun.'

'But I can move?'

'As I said, you were very lucky. As soon as you feel able, you can go home. But you'll have to take it easy for the next few days. I'll prescribe some painkillers, and if you need anything else, just ask the nurse here.'

The doctor writes a few notes on a piece of paper, and a smiling nurse in the background nods at her.

'I'll get you some food, and if you need anything in the meantime, just pull the string there.'

The doctor and nurse leave. Hannah looks at Viktor, who is watching her with an expression of concern.

'How are you feeling?'

'Like I fell out of a window and I've been drugged.'

Viktor smiles. 'The fall hasn't taken away your sense of humour then.'

She looks at him. At the thick dressing on his arm.

'And you?'

'A hell of a lot of stitches, but the wound wasn't as deep as it looked, fortunately. A good dressing and some painkillers, and it'll be healed soon enough.'

Hannah tries to push herself up, but feels a stab of pain shoot through her body.

'Wait...' Viktor picks up a control unit attached to Hannah's bed, presses a button, and the bed moves, automatically raising her.

When she is eventually in a sitting position, her body starts complaining – it's uncomfortable, but the feeling of having a body she can actually feel brings at least some relief.

'Gísli. It was Gísli who pushed me out of the window and after ... What happened then? Did he ... do anything to Ella? Himself?'

The desperation in her voice is palpable, but Viktor calmly returns her gaze.

'He ran off, haven't been able to locate him. But he was kind enough to leave this.' Viktor pulls out Hannah's phone and rests it on the duvet. 'Probably so we couldn't track it.'

Hannah looks at the phone, and then at Viktor.

'And Ella?'

'It was Ella who found you. If she hadn't responded so quickly, things could've been much worse. She dragged you into the house and cared for you until the ambulance arrived.'

Hannah stares at him, doubtfully.

'Ella dragged me inside? Ella? She weighs, what, forty-eight kilos?'

'Well, if she hadn't, you'd have died of hypothermia. It took the ambulance almost an hour to get to you, because of the snow.'

It occurs to Hannah that Húsafjörður doesn't have its own hospital.

'And where am I now, exactly?'

'The hospital in Østfjordene.'

'How far is that from Húsafjörður?'

'A forty-five-minute drive. Depending on how well they've managed to clear the roads, that is.'

Hannah looks around the room, desperation rising within her.

'What time is it?'

Viktor glances at his wristwatch.

'Just after ten.'

'The funeral is at half-ten!'

Hannah swings her legs out of the bed and wants to scream from the pain exploding through her body.

'What are you doing?' Viktor stops her with a steady hand.

'We have to go to Thor's funeral.'

'We can't do that.'

'Didn't you say it'd take forty-five minutes?'

'Yes, but with the snow and your condition, the earliest we can get there will be in an hour and a half.'

Hannah summons all her strength to muster a smile that masks the pain coursing through her.

'But you can put the lights and siren on, and we can get there a little faster, right?'

Viktor sighs, helps her out of bed and into her own clothes, shoes and jacket.

A startled nurse looks up five minutes later to the sight of a middle-aged Danish author who, supported by a police officer, shuffles her aching body past her, down the hallway and out of the hospital.

Hannah is silent for the first leg of the drive back to Húsafjörður. She can only bring herself to point weakly with her left arm, to ask Viktor for water and her painkillers. Her right arm is strapped into a sling across her chest – it feels like a foreign limb, one that doesn't belong to her. She looks down at the thick, heavy cast.

'How long do I need to have this on?'

'Four weeks.'

Hannah is momentarily overwhelmed by the depressing prospect: four weeks. Now there's no chance she'll be able to finish writing her book. She must have expelled a little, frustrated grunt, as Viktor looks over at her, concerned.

'Everything okay? I'm trying to drive as gently as possible, with all the snow ... But it's hard.'

'I won't be able to write for the next four weeks. Nothing matters now.'

Hannah stares out at the snow, lying thick and heavy across the Icelandic tundra. Half a metre must've settled since she's been gone, and it has changed the landscape to such an extent, it now looks as if they are on a completely different planet; a mythical realm located between dreams and reality, a place that intensifies Hannah's wrapped-in-wool feeling, strengthens the sense she's being restrained, as if she were battling against a strong wind, or running in a dream without actually going anywhere.

'Could you drive a little faster?'

'Sorry, but with these conditions ... I'd rather we get there alive.'

Hannah can't argue with that and refrains from pushing him any further. The road has turned white in the thick snow, and even though Viktor has a competent grip on the steering wheel, it feels as if they're driving on an ice rink. They sit in silence for a while. An oncoming car passes by. Hannah turns up the dial for the heated seat, tries to find some Zen in the situation.

'You and Margrét have become good friends then?'

Hannah stiffens at the question. Tries to sound relaxed, cool.

'Yes, I suppose ... or ... friends? I'm not sure that's what I'd call it.'

'What would you call it?' Viktor looks sideways at her. For more than one reason, it makes her uneasy.

'Look where you're driving.'

Viktor turns his gaze back to the ice-rink road.

'It's good for her.'

'Good?'

'To talk to other adults. Spending all her time with small children, day in, day out, she's far too clever for that. She should have other people around her, people who think as deeply as she does.'

'It seems to me that she is happy with the children though. And good with them.'

'Yes, true. But it was only meant to be temporary. While our own are so young. But now I don't know ... I'm afraid she'll never do anything else.'

'What else would she do?'

'She qualified as a librarian. You must have talked about it, given how often you've been over?'

Hannah shuffles uncomfortably. As if the heated seat is burning her. She turns it off. What does Viktor actually know?

'This is a little embarrassing to admit, but to be honest, I've probably mostly just talked about myself. I've not really asked her all that much...'

Viktor smiles.

'Typical Margrét. Always listens to everyone else's crap. I mean, sorry ... I'm guilty of that myself. Unloading everything onto her and forgetting to ask how she's doing. I often think she's too good for me.'

Hannah looks out over the snow again. Pure white. What should she say?

'I think she seems very happy.'

'Do you mean it?'

Hannah thinks back to Margrét's speech about security, about her joy of being something for someone. It makes her nod, convincingly.

'That's what she said to me, anyway. That her life here ... She is fulfilled, can't picture another life, somewhere else.'

Viktor nods himself, as if the information makes him truly happy. But then his expression changes.

'I know you've been having sex with my wife, but that stops now.'

Hannah stares at Viktor. Did he just say what she thinks he just said?

He points at her arm. 'Four weeks with that cast – everything will be a lot more difficult for you from now on.'

Hannah turns back to stare out of the window. Outside, the snow is falling again. Thick and fast.

42

Hannah can't get out of the car fast enough when they finally park in front of the small church in Húsafjörður, which – judging by the number of cars outside – is filled to capacity. She doesn't wait for Viktor, just hurries inside to catch the last few minutes of Thor's funeral. She enters in the middle of a hymn. Trying to be discreet, she manages to squeeze into an already full pew at the very back, nodding excuse-me's and thank-you's, to what looks like an entire family. Whether they knew Thor personally, or have just come to pay their respects, she has no idea. Hannah tries not to think about the conversation she had with Viktor on the way here, or about her body, which really could do with a couple more painkillers. She tries to remember how much the doctor told her to take each day, while staring up at the crucified Jesus, feeling like she relates to him, in a way. She stretches her neck and finds Ella sitting on the very front pew, beside Vigdis and Ægir. She can only see their backs, can only imagine how crumpled their faces must be with Thor's white coffin in front of them. The hymn comes to an end, and the last notes from the organ die away. A priest takes his position at the altar, ready to deliver the sermon, and with a deep voice, embarks on a solemn speech. Hannah tries to decode the Icelandic, catches Thor's name every now and then, but eventually gives up trying to understand any of what is being said. Instead, she observes the other guests. Extra chairs have been placed in the aisle, and it looks like the entire town is present. She recognises a few of the teenagers from the party, including Jonni and Iðunn, as well as the leather-vest barman, sitting a bit further away, the woman with the dog, and a handful of other Bragginn regulars. Viktor has also crept inside and found a place in the centre of the church, next to Margrét. She also notices Jonni's parents, and a number of other faces Hannah believes she has seen around town. But her gaze suddenly stops on the back of a neck, the sight of which gives her goosebumps. The neck turns, and on the other side is a face, now smiling at her. Jørn.

The ceremony ends a quarter of an hour later as Thor's coffin is carried out of the church and into a hearse, which drives away through the falling snow, seemingly silencing the sobs of the bereaved congregation. Hannah forgets all her attempts to be discreet, and instead of offering her condolences directly to Vigdis and Ægir – or even more importantly, going to comfort Ella – she storms over to Jørn and smacks him in the back with all the strength she can muster in her left, somewhat healthy, arm. It can't have been that hard, however, as he smiles when he turns to face her. A concerned smile, though.

'Hi, Hannah. How are you doing?'

'What are you doing here?'

'Showing my respect.'

'You didn't know him.'

'I've heard so much that I feel like I do.'

Hannah suspects an ulterior motive. Has Jørn come here to use her life as inspiration for his own work? The thought releases a wave of anger. No fucking way he's going to steal her story! It belongs to her.

'You're not coming to the wake.'

'I heard what happened. I'm so glad it wasn't worse.'

'Sure you are. But as I said: go home and stay there. You're not welcome here.'

'Am I mistaken, or have you come over a little territorial?'

Hannah glances at Ella, who has spotted them. She really should go over to her. Help her get through the day.

'This is a very difficult day for everyone. The last thing they need is a stranger intruding on their privacy while they try to grieve.'

'Funny, coming from you. You barely know the family.'

'I'm not a stranger. I live with Thor's aunt, and I've been here since all this began.'

Jørn hesitates. Looks over at Vigdis and Ægir, who are surrounded by consoling funeral guests. Nods.

'Fine, fine, you can have this to yourself. But remember, the murderer often turns up at the funeral.'

Jørn looks at Hannah, a serious expression on his face, and she can't help smiling at his stupidity.

'If Gísli is dumb enough to turn up, he'll be arrested on the spot.'

Jørn lets out a laugh.

'Classic!'

Hannah squints at him, confused.

'What do you mean?'

'Classic, that you think the most obvious person is the murderer. That is never the case.'

Hannah stares at Jørn in disbelief. Is he so wrapped up in his crime-fiction world that he believes it genuinely dictates reality? That his plot rules apply outside of his books?

'Sorry, but I have to go, you are simply annoying me too much.' Hannah turns on her heel.

'Just say the word, if you want any help writing the book, what with your arm like that. I write fast – you can dictate, and I'll write.'

With her left hand behind her back, Hannah manages to send Jørn a discreet fuck-you middle finger as she walks away, over to Ella, who she wraps her arms around with all the care her exhausted body and mind can muster.

It feels like déjà vu, being at the wake in Thor's house, and aside from the fact that the person in question is not lying on show in the middle of the room, it is an exact copy of how it all looked a week ago. The same people, the same heavy atmosphere. Hannah stands by a small table of drinks, trying not to burn herself with the piping-hot coffee as she awkwardly tries to pour herself a cup with her left hand. She spills some on the table and hurriedly wipes it up with her cast. Is hit by another pang of frustration when she remembers how long it will have to be on for. She glances over at Margrét, who is standing on the other side of the room, talking to Jonni. She wants to go over, but what is there to say? Hannah flips some biscuits onto a plate and successfully manages to balance it on her sling while picking up the coffee with her other hand, and to walk over to Ella.

'Here you go.'

Ella simply nods, despondent, takes the plate from her, but does not touch the biscuits. They were only able to speak briefly about what happened, during the drive from the church. Hannah thanked Ella for her heroic efforts, but Ella didn't think it was worth mentioning. Overall, she seems rather mute. Hannah wonders whether that is because of the funeral, or whether she is traumatised by Hannah's fall from the window. Hannah follows Ella's gaze and realises it is fastened on Ægir, who is just a short distance away, surrounded by funeral guests, clutching a piece of paper.

'Is he going to say something, do you think?'

Ella looks at her.

'A speech?'

Ella shrugs, stands up and walks away. '*Salerni.*'

One of the few words Hannah has learned: toilet. She stands alone for a moment, acutely aware of her discomfort, a result of the thick sorrow currently filling the room with sniffling, quiet chatter and respectful self-control. She looks around, thinking back on Jørn's words – was the murderer at the funeral? Are they here now? She shakes off the thought. No. Gísli did it, the evidence is there, clear as day: the bottle and his assaults on both Viktor and Hannah. It won't be long until he is caught and they can draw a line under all of this. At this point, she could probably go home and finish the book, if it weren't for this damn arm. She'll have to find some sort of practical solution – perhaps dictating it to someone isn't all that bad an idea. Just not to Jørn. There is still the issue that the murderer lacks a motive, though. She can only guess at Gísli's reason for killing Thor, and she doesn't feel any great desire to ask him why directly. She'll come up with something. There has to be a reason – it can't be that it was all just an accident. If it was, it would be like any other story. There must be a greater, moral dilemma at play if the crime is to feel justifiable – you can't write an entire book based on an unfortunate, unintended death ... Or can you? Hannah ponders whether she could surprise readers with her novel, do something different, challenge the genre's very DNA and wrap the whole thing up in a coincidence that actually highlights the true futility of searching for someone or something on which to place the blame – an authorial responsibility that may not actually exist – thus providing a deconstruction of the human need for a moral compass...

'Nice arm.'

Hannah was so engrossed in her own thoughts that she hasn't noticed that Margrét has walked over to her. She is suddenly, un-comfortably aware of how haggard she must look. She tries to joke it off:

'What people will do to avoid writing a book, am I right?'

Margrét just stares at her. Doesn't smile.

'I've been worried about you. I wanted to go with Viktor to the hospital, but with the kids ... Someone had to stay with them.'

Margrét's genuine concern for her well-being fills Hannah with a sudden and surprising desire to let herself be lowered into bed, to sleep, be pampered, to rest her body and not have to think about anything other than getting better again. It's as if the weight of her body, not just of her useless blasted arm, overwhelms her – her entire being wants to let go and let itself be wrapped up in someone else's care and in the freedom from any obligation. Maybe she should've stayed at the hospital.

'It was kind of Viktor to come and pick me up. Especially with his arm as it is.'

'Ach, sure, kind ... He had his own stitches and bandaging done at the same time, and was able to bring in the witness who last saw the perpetrator ... It all worked out very well – purely practical.'

Hannah considers Margrét, somewhat taken aback. Is there a trace of jealousy in her voice? Or perhaps a slight annoyance at the fact that Viktor seems, through his work, to have a reason to have constant access to Hannah? She glances over at him, standing nearby, talking to some of the teenagers. Has a feeling that he is keeping an eye on her, even with his back turned to them.

'Not to complain or anything, but I kind of hoped there'd be some sort of alcohol here. I could really do with a little treat right now.'

Margrét looks at her, shakes her head. 'I think the last thing your body needs is that poison.'

Margrét lays a hand on Hannah's functioning arm. The inconsequential, completely normal gesture feels daring. Margrét looks intensely at Hannah.

'Come with me. Two minutes?' She raises an eyebrow. Hannah thinks she understands the signal.

Margrét walks out, Hannah fiddles about with some biscuits,

does a quick round of the room, offers a few platitudes to a few indifferent guests, then follows Margrét. She finds her in the kitchen, alone. Hannah closes the door behind them. They look at each other. As if it were enough to just be alone together, without anyone else. Margrét steps forward and kisses Hannah. The determination in her movement takes Hannah off guard. Margrét pulls back and looks at her. Entwines her hand resolutely into Hannah's plaster-free one.

'I mean it. I was really worried about you. When Viktor got the call that Gísli had pushed you out the window ... I thought you were dead.'

Again, Margrét's concern warms Hannah in a way that touches her deeper than she herself truly understands. For the first time in many, many years, she feels tears threatening to break free. Cannot explain why. Maybe it's because she has only just now come to terms with how close she has been to dying. Was it Gísli's intention to kill her when he shoved her out of the window? Hannah suppresses the instinctive urge to regain her self-control, to push the emotions far, far away. She drops her shoulders slightly, allows a tear to roll down her cheek. To run all the way down to her chin, before wiping it away. Shakes her head at herself.

'Look at me ... at a funeral, crying about myself.'

'Isn't that what people usually do at a funeral? It just gives us the excuse.'

Hannah stares at Margrét. Imagines what it would be like to have someone like her by her side every day, the kind of person who always supports you when you don't have it in you to do it yourself. She reaches out to her, wants to feel her close, against her, even if it is much, much too risky and inappropriate here, in the middle of Thor's funeral. But Hannah doesn't care, she just wants – selfishly, and with her entire being – to be held. Margrét gently caresses her cheek, when they suddenly hear a cry for help. They freeze, stare at each other.

'What was that?'

'It sounded like Ella.'

Both of them dart out into the small hallway, frantically look around for the source of the sound, and hear a man's voice yelling a brisk command. Margrét throws open a door, and they simultaneously stop in their tracks: in the middle of what looks like an ironing room, Ægir stands hunched over Ella, his large hands clasped around her neck. Her top half is lying across the ironing board, atop the creased shirts, and judging by the look of desperation on her face, Ægir is choking her with every ounce of his being.

43

The murderer often turns up at the funeral. Jørn's irritating words echo in Hannah's head, but this probably isn't what he meant: that the deceased's father would commit another murder at the funeral. Hannah feels completely and utterly helpless as she watches Margrét run towards them and throw herself onto Ægir with a cascade of Icelandic words, presumably along the lines of 'Stop, let go, leave her alone'. But her efforts are futile. A one-sided struggle – it's as if Ægir intends to force the life out of Ella in front of witnesses. He remains steadfast in his crime, almost possessed. Hannah is nearly bowled over as Viktor and a few other townsmen hurtle through the door and come to Margrét's aid. Together, they manage to pull the iron hands away from Ella's neck and behind Ægir's own back in what ends up being a rather clumsy attempt to restrain him. Hannah sees Ella collapse onto the sofa, and is beside her almost instantly, supporting her with her working arm, checking for her heartbeat. It takes her far too long a moment, fumbling around, to feel Ella's neck, which is inflamed from Ægir's grip. *Dudum. Dudum. Dudum.* Hannah is relieved to find her alive, even though Ella is now unconscious. Several funeral guests stand behind Hannah, wearing a mixture of shocked and worried expressions as they look from Ella to Hannah, as if she is a doctor who can inform them of Ella's condition. Hannah has no medical knowledge, but some common sense at least.

'She's fainted. Grab her legs and lift them up. And can someone get something cold for her forehead?'

As if they are a tight-knit military unit, the bystanders manage to coax Ella out of her unconscious state within a few minutes. She is groggy and frightened. Whispers something in Icelandic, her eyes wide. As if she can see everyone and no one. She carefully moves her hands up to her neck, groans. Hannah takes Ella's hand in her own.

'Don't worry. It's over.'

Only now does Ella seem to actually see Hannah, who tries to smile soothingly at her. Ella's gaze passes over the onlookers, who are all staring down at her, as if she has just been resurrected from the dead. Which she has, in a way. Hannah sensed the commotion behind her, but it is only now, when she turns to check, that she sees that Ægir, Viktor, Margrét and the quick-witted rescuers have disappeared from the room. She turns back to Ella.

'How are you feeling?'

Ella nods. As if to say she's okay. Someone comes in with a glass of water, and she drinks. Slowly, as if her oesophagus has been squeezed shut. Now that everyone has ensured that no lives are in danger, an evaluation of the incident commences in an excessively high-pitched manner – some crying, others just frozen with expressions of pure shock on their faces. In the doorway, Hannah spots a figure who looks more like a ghost than a human being. Vigdis.

Ægir's attack concludes the wake, with the guests slowly trickling out of the house, following a short – and, to Hannah, baffling – speech by Viktor about how Ægir and Vigdis need some peace and quiet. A core group of guests remain. Were it not for Ella's insistence on staying to help clean up her own assailant's home, Hannah would have made her escape long ago. In addition to Hannah and Ella, Viktor, Margrét and the leather vest also stay behind. And, of course, Ægir and Vigdis, who Viktor, probably out of some feeling for small-town sensitivities, allowed to disappear into the sanctity of their bedroom as the house emptied. Once Viktor has made sure that the last of the guests have left, he turns to Hannah and Margrét, who are standing on either side of a table, clearing up the cups of coffee.

'Do you mind giving me a minute to talk to Ella alone?'

Viktor looks inquiringly at them. They both nod, and Hannah has the strange feeling that Viktor's gaze is on her back as she heads into the kitchen. Margrét closes the door behind them, and it's as if half a century has passed – rather than half an hour – since they last stood here together.

'What the hell was all that?'

Hannah looks at Margrét, who has opened the window to smoke out of. She lights the cigarette, inhales, exhales.

'Ella and Ægir have never got on. But hating her that much ... that, I wasn't aware of.'

'Maybe he has some sort of grief psychosis?'

'Is that a thing?'

Hannah shrugs. 'People do crazy things when they're grieving.'

Hannah studies Margrét, who is now staring out of the window. As if she wants to climb out of it and run off. Hannah wants to go over to her, but it feels wrong now, somehow. Maybe because of the vibe Margrét is giving off, or the way she's standing, turned away from her, her arms crossed over her chest. Hannah changes the focus.

'The way he had his hands on her neck ... it was like he was completely prepared to kill her. As if killing her didn't mean anything to him.'

Margrét turns to Hannah, an analytical look on her face that makes her nervous. 'What do you mean by that?'

'I just mean, maybe ... maybe that wasn't the first time Ægir has tried to kill someone. If he was capable of doing that back there, I ... Maybe he was capable of killing his own son.'

Margrét takes a deep drag on the cigarette. Holds the smoke in her body for a moment before allowing it to escape out into the fresh air.

'Or he believes that Ella has something to do with Thor's death.'

Hannah looks at Margrét, appalled. 'Do you think Ella could've killed Thor?'

Margrét shrugs. 'How well do you know her, really?'

Hannah feels a prickling sensation begin to spread throughout her body. A burgeoning anger. That's the second time today that someone has suggested that she doesn't really know Ella or the family that well.

'Ella could never cause someone harm, and especially not Thor. She adored him!'

'I'm not saying she intentionally killed her own nephew. But accidents happen. And sometimes people cover them up. It wouldn't be the first time it's happened to Ella.'

Margrét takes one last drag of the cigarette, flicks the butt out of the window, and without closing it behind her or providing Hannah with any further explanation, leaves the kitchen. Hannah is left with an indeterminate, uneasy feeling. The wind blows in from outside, passing directly through her clothes, skin and her whole body.

The interrogation didn't take long. According to Viktor, neither Ella nor Ægir will explain what provoked the violent attack, and Ella has refused to report Ægir, so Viktor has to drop the matter. What else can he do? It is with significant anxiety that Hannah watches Ella drive the Jeep home with a focus that Hannah must admit is impressive for someone who has just been subjected to an attempted murder. A stab of pain shoots through her arm beneath the plaster cast every time they hit a little bump in the road, and a feeling of resentment grows in Hannah at the thought of Ella turning down the leather vest's offer to drive them home. Even though Hannah can't drive at the moment, she still thinks she could steer the car a little more smoothly than Ella right now. The snow continues to fall relentlessly, and the car jolts with every bump.

Hannah bites the bullet.

'Why wouldn't you tell Viktor what happened?'

She looks at Ella, who just shrugs.

Tries again. 'You just don't do something like that. It was extremely violent. If we hadn't come in when we did, he could have choked you to death.'

Ella remains silent. Her gaze fixed to the road. Hannah gives up. Thinks about what Margrét said: what has Ella covered up in the past? Does Margrét genuinely suspect Ella of causing Thor's death? It is such an absurd thought that Hannah can't even entertain the idea it's true; she shakes it out of her head. But Margrét knows something about Ella that she refuses to disclose. Contributing further to Hannah's current sense of unease. They pull up outside the house, and Ella is forced to park on the road, as the knee-high snow on the drive is far too much to drive through, even for the Jeep. Hannah trudges up to the house right behind Ella, trying to walk in her deep footsteps. Each step feels like a balancing act, with the infernal plaster cast weighing her down. Under the little porch canopy, Ella turns to face Hannah. She looks as if she wants to say something, but changes her mind. She opens the door. Once they have both taken off their snow-laden shoes in the hallway, Ella disappears into the kitchen. Returns with a little notepad. Writes.

Stopp snooping around, it is dangerous. Let it go. Write your bok.

Hannah reads the note and can't help but smile.

'You don't need to worry about me. I'll manage. I managed to do this, didn't I?'

Hannah lifts her arm. But Ella doesn't smile. Just looks Hannah dead in the eye and writes again.

Stopp asking about Thor's death or you will have to move out of mitt house.

Hannah's smile fades. What is going on? Without saying another thing, Ella turns and walks into her bedroom. And Hannah is left standing there, feeling like a child who has been scolded and has no idea why. She pulls her phone out of her pocket and calls Margrét. Has to call twice before Margrét's voice finally answers.

'You shouldn't call me.'

'Sorry, it's just, what you said about Ella earlier, I need to know what you meant, and—'

'Listen,' Margrét interjects.

A long pause. Hannah momentarily wonders whether the connection cut off, until she hears Margrét's voice again. She sounds tired.

'Viktor and I just had a long talk. About you and me.'

'Okay...?'

Hannah's heart is pounding. And breaking, a little. She knew this would eventually come.

'We can't see each other for a while, and you can't call me.'

'I thought that you two had some sort of agreement, an understanding?'

'Not about you. Sorry, but ... Please, just don't call me. It's making my life really quite miserable right now.'

'Sure ... Of course.'

'Thank you. Thank you for understanding.'

Margrét hangs up, and Hannah understands absolutely nothing. How has she just lost her two closest confidants in town in the space of a few minutes? She feels completely and utterly alone, a feeling that – for the first time in her life – actually frightens her. She never really needs anyone, has never been the kind of person who has called and burdened a family member or a friend with her problems and loneliness. On the contrary, she has always prided herself on not depending on anyone else, always preferring her own company, if she has the choice. But now, it sends a cold shiver down her spine to realise that she does in fact have an overwhelming urge to be with another human being. Even if the only other person she can think of right now is Jørn.

'Hi.'

His voice always sounds so obnoxiously happy and cheerful, as if he has been sitting there, just waiting for a pleasant phone call. And while Hannah finds it difficult to admit to herself, that is the exact kind of prize idiocy she requires right now. She works hard to make herself sound neither too aggressive nor too pathetic:

'I could do with a drink. I can't drive with my arm like this, and there's so much snow I don't dare walk into town – I might end up breaking the other one as well. So ... I was wondering ... would you mind picking me up and driving me to Bragginn and, uh, if you want to, I guess you could also have a drink, while you're there.'

Hannah swears she can hear Jørn smiling on the other end of the phone.

'Are you asking me to have a drink with you?'

Hannah takes a deep breath.

'Just say yes or no.'

'Sure. I'll hop in the car right this minute.'

Hannah hangs up, furious with herself for her being so weak. But also a touch relieved.

44

'I told you so.'

They have only been sat at the Bragginn bar for a few seconds before Hannah feels an uncontrollable urge to hit Jørn. He really doesn't make it easy for her to resist, being *that* annoying. At the same time, though, she is genuinely grateful for the speed with which he got her out of Ella's house. Hannah hadn't even had time to take her jacket off, before the monster four-wheel drive had pulled up on the road outside, and he'd honked the horn to let her know he was there.

'Yeah, yeah. The murderer often turns up at the funeral. But we don't know that Ægir is definitely the murderer.'

Hannah abstains from telling Jørn about her new-found suspicions about Ella. For now, it is enough to introduce Jørn to the circumstances around the strangulation attempt. She also keeps to herself any of the details involving Margrét. She downs half a glass of red wine, clumsily, but it was overdue. Washes down a few painkillers too.

'How's it going?' Jørn nods at her arm.

Hannah shakes her head, as if to say it isn't going at all. Which, in a way, it isn't – it's a pain, having to drink with your left hand.

'You're stuck.'

Hannah looks inquiringly at Jørn. 'What do you mean?'

'You have no idea what's going on around you or who you can trust. You're doubting whether you'll ever find out the truth about Thor's murder. And because of that, you don't know how you'll finish your novel.'

The arrow on Hannah's provocation gauge is pointing well above boiling point now, and she wants to get up, leave the bar, walk out into the snow and keep going, so she never has to hear a single word from Jørn ever again. He is, however, correct. Unfortunately. She looks for a way to phrase her response so she doesn't actually have to admit defeat. But gives up. Surrenders to Jørn.

'You look as annoying when you're right as when you're wrong.'

'Sorry, that's just my face. What can I do to help?'

Hannah analyses him. There's not even a hint of schadenfreude in his voice, only pure, genuine interest.

'To be completely honest with you, I genuinely don't know what to believe or think. I've been able to get people in town to talk to me, and up to now, I've had the impression that an answer was right around the corner. But now I don't seem to know anything. And I just want to ... give up.'

Hannah has always maintained that she would rather die than ever say those words. Especially not to Jørn. But, in that moment, saying them triggers an unfamiliar sense of relief. As if admitting defeat is the greatest freedom she has ever felt. She suddenly feels the gravity of the last few days' events weighing heavily on her body: Viktor's attack, the confrontation with Gísli, the fall from the window, the funeral, the broken arm, Viktor unveiling his knowledge of everything between her and Margrét. Margrét's rejection, Ella's threat.

'I'm not an investigator. I'm barely even a crime-fiction writer.'

Hannah stares into the dregs of red wine in her glass but does not feel like drinking them. She can feel Jørn's gaze on her.

'You are impressive.'

Hannah looks at him. Thinks he could have waited a minute or two before taking a jab at her ego while she's down. But there appears to be no trace of sarcastic, gloating pleasure on his face. Just something that may actually be admiration.

'I mean it. I've always had great respect for you. The way you write. Your belief that literature can do more than entertain. The way you insist on always striving for excellence. It's impressive.'

Hannah is perplexed. Is Jørn ... praising her?

'Do you mean ... Have you read my books?'

Jørn nods. 'All of them.'

An odd sense of pride, combined with a hint of shame, collide deep inside Hannah. Has she underestimated Jørn this significantly? Never in her wildest dreams has she imagined that he would be able to stay awake long enough to get through even one chapter of her books, let alone the entire collection ... A smile finds its way onto her face, but soon disappears when it occurs to her that this is most likely just lip service. To smooth-talk her, dig deeper into her soft spots, before striking.

'I must say, I'm surprised. The fact that you've read all of my books ... I didn't think...'

'Didn't think that I read?'

'That you read the kind of books I write.'

Hannah scrutinises him. He wears the mask well.

'What did you think of *Summer Nights We Lost*?'

Jørn smiles at her, as if he's figured out that she's testing him. He looks like he's ready for battle.

'To be completely honest, I was disappointed with the ending. I felt like it was unnecessary for the dog to die, and that it was lacking when it came to what would happen when they did eventually reach the North Sea. But I loved your depiction of the women in the knitting club. All of the layers hidden beneath their mundane chats ... It was well written.'

Now it's Hannah who is impressed. Everything he just mentioned were all thoughts Hannah had herself, but neither her reviewers nor her readers have ever pointed out. So these must be his original ideas.

'That's a sharp analysis.'

'My analytical skills aren't so bad after all.'

'But why...'

Hannah stops herself. Jørn, however, already knows what she was going to ask.

'Why don't I write in a way that, in your eyes, is better?'

Hannah hesitates, wishes she could praise Jørn's work in return, but aside from acknowledging his vast readership, she doesn't really have any genuine praise to give. Again, it's as if Jørn understands.

'I write what I am able to write. If I could write how you write, my books would, of course, be different. It's not a result of my not making the effort, but I'm also not going to try and be something that I'm not. I would rather be a really good Jørn Jensen than a shit Shakespeare.'

Hannah can't help but smile. So dumb and so wise at the same time. She is amazed at the self-awareness and truth of his statement. Why has she never thought about that? That he writes the kind of books he writes because that's what he's good at? And is there anything wrong with that? Many people read his books with great appetite, and they're probably much better than all the other shite those people could choose to entertain themselves with. Crap films and TV programmes. Perhaps through his books, Jørn is actually opening up a world of different genres to his readers, so maybe they'll occasionally choose to pick up another type of book, while they wait for his next release ... maybe even one of *her* books? Hannah feels a little emboldened at the thought, but is also embarrassed that she is still only deeming Jørn's writing as valuable if it were to lead to her own success. Maybe it is absolutely fine for readers to be happy and satisfied with reading only Jørn Jensen.

'I'd like to apologise.'

It is surprisingly easy for Hannah to say those words.

'I admit that I have never had particularly high opinions of your writing, and even though I would really like to reciprocate the kind words that you have said to me ... the reality is that I will never truly appreciate the way you write. But I actually have – and I mean it when I say this – a deep respect for the fact you are able to reach so many people. That you can get them to queue up for your books. That time and time again, you deliver something that brings people joy, and that you have never disappointed your fan base. That, I feel, requires that you dedicate a huge amount of care and attention to your work, and I have been blind to the fact that that is exactly what you do. And...'

Hannah hesitates a moment, the last thing is a little harder to say.

'Maybe I envy you a little, how you're able to move so many people.'

She forces herself to be woman enough to look him in the eye as she says it, so he understands that she truly, genuinely means it. Jørn doesn't smile – in fact, he almost looks sad. But Hannah understands then that he's touched. He puts a hand on his heart in a bit of an aggravating, neo-Buddhist way, but it is nevertheless a gesture that tells Hannah that he genuinely and deeply appreciates what she has said. And will likely live on those words for a long time.

'Thank you.'

His words hang in the air between them, sealing the moment. Jørn opens his mouth to say something else, when the door to the bar suddenly flies open. The woman with the dog: standing there with a wild panic in her eyes. The snow blows in around her, and she flings her arm back out into the blizzard, screaming something in Icelandic.

'Gísli er dáinn. Hann liggur við fótboltavöllinn!'

A long pause follows her statement, as if people are waiting to understand the message, and then suddenly the room is full of the sound of chairs scraping back, hitting the floor, the sight of coats flying through the air as people hurry to put them on, pints of beer being downed in one gulp. Hannah and Jørn are caught up in the commotion that is at first incomprehensible, then unbelievable when someone eventually translates the woman's announcement into English. They join the chaos as it pulls them out into the ice-cold winter night to see if it really is true that Gísli is dead.

45

He has killed himself with a knife. There is a quick consensus on this, as the little congregation from the bar crowds around Gísli's body. Thin, frozen rivers of blood run from the wrist of his left arm. Unlike Thor, there is nothing peaceful about his dead body; on the contrary, his eyes are open, an eerie death stare, testifying to the pain and agony of his final moments. Hannah looks away. The thought of lying down behind an unsightly football pitch and slicing your own veins open. She shivers, and feels exposed beneath the tall stadium spotlight, which lights a small circle of terrain in the middle of the otherwise all-encompassing darkness.

'Það var Hrafn sem fann hann.'

The woman points at the dog, as if to make it clear that it found the corpse; she has to pull violently on its lead, to prevent it going over and licking Gísli's dead body. The leather vest once again appears to take on the role of town leader and turns to the group with his arms raised, as if to protect Gísli's corpse, which lies behind him. He raises his voice and says something incomprehensible, but with great authority. Hannah interprets it as something to do with staying away from the body. To show respect. In any case, everyone takes a few steps back, and some even turn around and walk away. Now they've seen it for themselves, it'll be something to talk about over their next beer. Hannah's feet feel like icicles in her only semi-lined leather boots, and she can't fully close her jacket over the plaster cast, which is far too chunky to fit into the sleeve. She marches on the spot, the snow crunching beneath her feet. The leather vest turns to face her and Jørn.

'Drive to Viktor's and get him down here now!'

'Why us?'

The last thing Hannah wants to do is drive to Viktor's house and deliver yet more bad news while he's enjoying the comforts of home.

'Because you're the most sober ones here.'

Jørn nods, glad to be entrusted with the task. 'We'll get there as quickly as we can.'

Jørn is already jogging back to the car. Hannah quickly considers her options, but comes to the decision that it is better to join Jørn in his warm car than stand here in the dark and freeze, or sit alone in Bragginn with her lukewarm red wine and far too many thoughts.

They arrive at Viktor and Margrét's house in less than five minutes. Jørn hammers on the door, as if their own lives were in danger.

'There's been another death. An older gentleman seems to have taken his own life in one of the fields.'

Hannah is frustrated that Jørn managed to get the first word in, pretty much the moment Viktor opened the door. And why is he being so bloody grandiose? Of the two of them, he's the one who knows the least. Hannah corrects him.

'It's Gísli. He's been found at the back of the football pitch.'

'You can hop in my car with us, it's a four-wheel drive with seat warmers.'

Jørn clearly loves being given the opportunity to play the hero, and Hannah can't bring herself to be irritated by it. She watches Viktor, who stands there for a moment with a sombre, silent expression and then hurriedly shoves on a pair of boots and grabs his coat. He shouts something into the house, and Hannah briefly catches a glimpse of Margrét before the door closes and the three strange musketeers rush towards Jørn's preheated monstrosity of a car. As Hannah climbs in, she suddenly feels drained, like she can't handle anything else today. The thought of returning to stand and stare at Gísli's frozen body, or even worse, debrief with Jørn back at Bragginn, triggers an acute headache, and she feels her body start to tremble.

'Are you okay?'

Jørn glances at her, worried, while he navigates the car back towards the crime scene – quickly, but with a calm sense of control. Where does he get all his energy from?

'You look very pale.'

Hannah gives in. Fragments of thoughts about the inappropriateness of entrusting Jørn with the role of civilian co-investigator flicker before her, but they don't really stick, and she feels a growing indifference towards the case, the book – and him. All she wants is to get home, go to bed and sleep. Her voice is unusually weak as she turns to Jørn, with an almost imploring look in her eye.

'When you've dropped Viktor off, can you drive me home?'

The house is silent when Hannah eventually steps inside, deciding not to turn on the light, so as to not attract Ella's attention and end up in a big conversation about life and death. She grimaces as she walks into her little attic bedroom, which she hasn't entered since Gísli pushed her out of the window. There are no signs of their struggle, everything is tidy, the floor hoovered, the window closed and the bed made. Something Hannah has not done even once since getting here, so Ella must've done it for her. It fills Hannah with a warm gratitude, and the tidy room makes her almost feel safe. For the sake of further safety, however, she turns the key in the lock. With great difficulty, she brushes her teeth with her left hand, and with even greater difficulty, manages to peel the clothes from her body. When she finally falls into bed, having guzzled a handful of painkillers, she feels a thousand years old. How did everything go so wrong so quickly? And then it hits her, and she feels the weight of Gísli's death. Despite him attacking her, Viktor, and probably Thor, she is overwhelmed by a sadness that pins her to the mattress and prompts rare, glossy eyes. What a sad fate. To be such a gifted human being, with a family and a career, and lose it all, to spend the last few years of one's life as an almost-homeless alcoholic – only to kill a young man, resulting in further attacks and, eventually, his own suicide. A price he must have thought he had to pay. In the grand scheme of things, these events have no significance, and it is this that hits Hannah the hardest. Everything seems to have happened under such tragic circumstances, each incident feeding into the next and causing a downward spiral of misery that has sucked in the whole town, and which could have been avoided, had Thor not come across Gísli that night down by the water. Hannah falls asleep with the final, consoling thought that if the main suspect is dead, then the case is now closed. Regardless, the night's dreams are filled with Thor, Gísli, Margrét, Ella, Viktor and the other townsfolk, all of whom take it in turns to come to her with their assortment of troubles.

Hannah awakens in the middle of the night with a pounding pain in her plaster-cast arm. Even though she made sure to lie on her back, with her arm raised on a cushion, as prescribed, it feels like it's been crushed in a printing press. She turns on the bedside lamp and looks down at it: it's still there. Her shoulder aches too, and with a fair amount of struggling, she manages to fight her way out of bed to track down more painkillers. Suddenly remembers that she left them in the bathroom. Half asleep, she shuffles out into the hallway, and a few steps later, stops. Light is streaming from Ella's study. Was the light on in there when she got home last night? Hannah is almost certain that the door was closed. And she now hears the faint sound of someone talking. Or rather whispering with a hint of suppressed anger. She stands stock still, listening intently. Can only identify one voice: Ella's. It stops occasionally, indicating that she must be talking to someone on the phone. Hannah stands there for a long moment. If she continues, she will inevitably draw attention to herself, and some sort of conversation with Ella will be unavoidable. But Hannah cannot bear the alternative – the thought of going back to bed without her painkillers. She pulls herself together and quickly scurries past the half-open study door, into the bathroom, grabs the pills (which did turn out to be on the sink, where she'd left them) and hastens back to her door, with the victorious feeling of having accomplished her mission without a confrontation with Ella. But, as she is about to set foot in her bedroom again, Ella steps out into the dark hallway. With the light of the study behind her, it's hard for Hannah to see Ella's face, which is cloaked in shadow. Has she noticed her? They stand there for a moment, like two ghosts haunting the same house.

'Hi. I just woke up, needed to grab these.'

The night chat has become a reality. Hannah waves the white strip of pills in the air for Ella to see.

'For my arm, it's killing me.'

Ella remains standing there in the hallway, silent, prompting a wave of unease to come over Hannah. With her healthy arm, she fumbles about on the wall to turn the main light on, blindly sliding her hand across the surface in an attempt to locate the switch. Ella is right next to her. Hannah instinctively takes a step back, but Ella simply flicks the switch. It was behind Hannah. She blinks a few times, feels like she's in a nightclub when the lights suddenly come on and you discover the horror of what everyone actually looks like. And you realise that that harsh reality applies to you too. Ella looks old, tired. Almost as if she, too, has shrunk – or maybe her pyjamas are just too big for her? In any case, she looks like a fragile old woman – grey and vulnerable. An immediate and very unfamiliar urge to hug Ella wells up in Hannah. The feeling of wanting to take care of another person is so strange to her that she can do nothing but obey. Hannah wraps her functioning arm around Ella and pulls her in, and it's as if Ella has been waiting for someone to do exactly that. Hannah feels Ella's body relaxing, as if she is a child, finally receiving some reassurance. They stand like that for a minute, which feels so long that it could easily be five, and Hannah alternates between feeling a tenderness for Ella, and a growing unease about where she stands with her host. She does, however, have a clear sense that she should not ask Ella who she was whispering to on the phone in the middle of the night.

46

Sedated on a self-prescribed combination of painkillers, Hannah sinks into a deep, dreamless sleep that provides a temporary break from all her pain and worry. When she does eventually open her eyes – in slow, gradual stages – it's to a haze of grogginess, somewhere between consciousness and unconsciousness. She allows herself to lie there, eyes open, for a few minutes, before fumbling about for her phone on the night stand, only to find that she has slept through the entire morning. Half-twelve. Is that right? Hannah thinks the light coming through the window has some tones of twilight, which it may well be, given the dark will soon extinguish the hours of daylight. She struggles to get out of bed, cursing her broken arm as she does so, and pulls the curtain aside. Outside: snow, snow and more snow. It has enveloped the world, as if the clouds are resting just above the rooftops, pumping heavy, white fluff onto the town below. It fills Hannah with a momentary feeling of claustrophobia. She recalls yesterday's dramatic events: the funeral, Gísli's suicide, Ella's threat, her rare longing for comfort. Margrét's rejection. Hannah sits back down on the edge of the bed, grabs her phone with her left hand, scrolls through her contacts, and taps the name of the only person she feels relatively comfortable talking to today: Bastian. He answers immediately.

'Hi there. I almost thought you'd forgotten about me.'

'Funny, I was going to say the same to you. In fact, I'm surprised you even picked up.'

It wasn't Hannah's intention to sound so resentful, but she suddenly realises how alone she feels – personally, but also in terms of writing this infernal book. It was Bastian, of course, who sent her on this damned mission, so why hasn't he been in touch more? She feels an angry bubble rise within her from a very vulnerable and bitter place, and this only adds to her frustrations, as the point of the call was to talk to a reasonable, consoling person, without having to worry about being overly negative or whether they have any kind of agenda themselves. Fuck. She forces herself to suppress the urge to scold Bastian.

'Sorry, I've not called to bitch at you.'

'That's new.'

Hannah smiles wearily to herself. She's missed Bastian. He clears his throat somewhere back in Denmark. His voice takes on a slightly softer tone. More caring.

'I've actually been feeling bad about not calling you more. But I've been thinking of you a lot. How are you doing?'

Hannah tries to not sound too dramatic. 'To be honest, I've been having a pretty rough time.'

'Writer's block, homesick?'

'Well, someone attempted to murder me, that someone being the suspect in the murder investigation, but he has now committed suicide, and that's on top of the fact that everyone I've met here has now lost trust in me, and then ... oh yes, Christ, there's Jørn, who's sneaking around with God knows what strategy to try and sabotage my crime-writing project. But he's the least of my problems. In fact, he's actually been ... helpful.'

Silence on the other end of the line. Hannah can't even hear the sound of breathing.

'Hello, are you there?'

Silence. A little cough. An incredulous voice.

'Uh, yes, it's just ... an attempted murder? Do you mean that as in...?'

'An attempted murder? Yes.'

'But how...?'

'I was pushed out of a first-floor window, lost consciousness and now my arm's wrapped up in this bloody cast. I got off easy, but still. It's my right arm, annoyingly. So it's not been particularly fun, these last few days.'

'And who did you say pushed you?'

'Probably the same person who killed Ella's nephew. But he cut his own wrist over on the football pitch, so he is no longer a threat.'

Hannah feels a certain energy taking hold as she tells him of these events, and it feels like, with some distance, it is starting to take the form of ... yes, a good story. A story that might make it easier to recover from the impact the events have had on her. It also occurs to her that, sometime in the not-too-distant future, once she's back home, she can use everything that has happened to her here as a tragic yet phenomenal anecdote to regale people with, and – now she's really fired up at the thought – to write her book. Yes, at home she can get some qualified help to finish writing it, maybe Bastian could even assist her with typing it up, or else find her an ambitious literature student who would kill to take on the assignment. Maybe this godforsaken crime novel can still be completed in the proclaimed month-long period after all. Hannah then remembers the real reason she called Bastian: to get her home as soon as possible.

'You can get all the details when I'm home, but I was mainly calling to ask for some help booking a ticket back. I'd do it myself, but with just the one functioning arm and all that, typing everything in while holding a credit card and finding the passport number, well, it'd be great if you could help me sort that out, hopefully for a flight tonight?'

'I mean, I'd love to do that for you but...'

'But what?' Hannah senses an unease on the other end of the line.

'Air traffic in and out of Iceland has been shut down. Haven't you seen the news? There's a cold front on its way across Northern Europe. It's everywhere. They're calling it a mini ice age.'

Hannah feels winded. 'But what ... why?'

'They're describing it as the worst snowstorm to hit Iceland in years. You must've heard about it?'

Hannah deflates. Realises that she hasn't seen or read any news since arriving in Iceland.

'But ... for how long?'

'Indefinitely.'

Hannah hangs up without saying another word. Stares out at the snow, which she notices hasn't stopped falling. In fact it flies at the windowpane, leaving just a tiny view of the off-white world, from which Hannah has no idea when she can escape.

The living room is warm with its flickering orange glow, the roaring fireplace and aroma of freshly brewed coffee. Ella smiles when Hannah steps inside. From her blanket-wrapped seat on the sofa, she nods at Hannah to come join her, and it almost feels as cosy and carefree as the first night Hannah spent here. She can do nothing but surrender herself to the situation: she sits and pours herself a cup of coffee. It's hot, strong.

'Did you hear about Gísli?'

Hannah looks inquiringly at Ella. Despite their awkward night-time embrace in the hallway, Hannah couldn't bring herself to inform Ella of the news of the tragic death right then. Ella nods. Jots something down in a little notebook.

Message fra Vigdis. Viktor call last night and told dem.

Hannah nods. Drinks some coffee. Feels no need to reveal to Ella that she was there when they found Gísli's body.

'It's tragic. To end your life that way ... completely alone.'

Ella shakes her head, writes. Quickly and passionately.

He deserves it. Punishment for killing Thor. And for that he did to you.

Ella draws a little angry face, which almost makes Hannah smile. She can't blame Ella for lacking sympathy for her nephew's murderer, even though both deaths seem utterly meaningless and tragic. And the fact that Ella also recognises Gísli's death as a kind of retribution for his wrongdoing towards Hannah is an odd display of affection that Hannah, bizarrely, appreciates. She drops the subject and moves on to different – maybe even more dangerous – territory.

'What you said yesterday, about leaving the case alone or I should move out ... I understand why you said that. Everything it must have brought up for you ... I'm sorry if my focus on the investigation has upset you at all. If it's hurt you.'

Ella nods, accepting the apology with a dismissive wave of her hand.

While it may make no difference, as Hannah will be out of Ella's home and life once flights resume, it still feels good to be reconciled. Hannah nods towards the snowy windows.

'That weather. How long will it last?'

Ella holds a finger up, says something in Icelandic.

'A day?'

Ella shakes her head. Hannah's shoulders slump with the unbearable realisation.

'A week?'

Ella nods.

'But...'

Hannah stops herself. Almost can't bear the thought. As cosy as it is in the living room right now, the thought of staying with Ella for another week is intolerable. And she won't be able to finish the book either. She formulates a new plan. She must get to Reykjavík as soon as possible. Check in to a hotel, find a Danish-speaking assistant who can help type up the last few chapters. Yes, that's what she'll do. Hannah can't bring herself to ask Ella for help in executing the plan, however, which is why she excuses herself and hurries over to the kitchen, finds Jørn's number, and calls him. He doesn't pick up. Damn. She considers her other options. Hesitates, and then taps on Viktor's number. After a few rings, he answers. Fatigued.

'What do you want now?'

'A lift to Reykjavík.'

A deep sigh. 'Do you think I'm a taxi service?'

'No, but you must know someone around here who can help me. I don't want to ask Ella to drive me – not in this weather, and not with everything that's happened.'

'That's thoughtful of you, but unfortunately, I can't help either.'

Hannah refuses to give up.

'Think about how nice it will be when I'm gone.'

'Believe me, if I could, I'd drive you as far away from this town as possible, but have you looked outside? All the roads are closed. We're advising against any travel.'

Fuck. How dumb can she be? Hannah had thought there would be some sort of snow-clearing operation at least, and with a good four-wheel drive, she could get to Reykjavík in no time. She walks towards the front door, opens it. The flurry of snow batters her face, and she feels like she's been knocked out.

'Hello?'

Viktor is still on the other end of the phone. Hannah closes the door, turns her back to it, leans against it and slides down, until she can't go any further. She just sits there on the floor, staring at her shoes and jacket, which probably won't get to serve their purpose just yet. Her gloves have fallen on the floor, the leather ones, which she'd placed on the cabinet. With an awkward crawl, the phone nestled between her ear and shoulder, she manages to shuffle over and pick them up. Places them apathetically on her cast, ready to get up, and tries to come to terms with her current reality.

'How long do you think it'll be before the roads are open again? A week, along with the weather?'

'Difficult to say, it probably won't be that long. But we've never had so much snow at this time of year before.'

Hannah nods, as if Viktor can hear her doing it. She's not sure why she hasn't hung up yet. Or why he hasn't. Especially after everything that has happened with Margrét and the investigation.

'Forgive me for butting in again, but I hope it all went well, moving Gísli. And that you ... that you can relax a bit now. Now that this is all over.'

Hannah hopes that he picks up on her implied promise, meaning all that happened between her and Margrét is over too. Viktor answers solemnly, but isn't hostile.

'He's in the morgue now, and I wouldn't say that I can relax exactly ... There's still so much to do. Paperwork, closing the case.'

'I assume you're not getting any help from Reykjavík?'

'They've postponed sending any assistance, what with the weather.'

'Ah, yes. Of course.'

It occurs to Hannah how incredibly lonely Viktor must feel. In every respect. Maybe that's why neither of them has hung up yet. Hannah can't think of anything else to ask though, so she starts thinking of ways to wrap up the call, when another thought hits her. She stares at the leather gloves, picks one up – the left one. And the imbalance she felt upon seeing Gísli's body suddenly makes disconcerting sense. Her voice trembles slightly, as she whispers into the phone.

'Viktor, I'm sorry to bring this up, but I just ... I don't think Gísli took his own life.'

'What do you mean?'

'It was the wrist on his left arm that had been cut, right?'

'Yes...'

'But I've seen Gísli open beers and close the window with his left hand. That's not something you do if you're right-handed, believe me.'

'So you're saying he was left-handed?'

'Yes. It makes no sense whatsoever to suddenly use his right hand to do something like that.'

'But you saw it yourself: The knife was in his right hand.'

'It must have been placed there.'

A moment of silence.

'That would confirm my own suspicion.'

'Which is?'

Hannah already knows what his answer will be. But to hear Viktor say it himself still gives her goosebumps.

'That Gísli was murdered.'

47

The flames hop and dance as Hannah stares into the fire, hypnotised. What else can she do? The conversation with Viktor has left her feeling powerless. An open road to Reykjavík seems a few days away at least, and it would appear that there is still a killer loose in town. One cold-blooded enough to stage Gísli's suicide to cover up their first murder – Thor's murder. Hannah shuffles uncomfortably on the sofa. Her arm is throbbing, and there is an itch beneath the cast that she cannot reach. Luckily, Ella leaves her to her thoughts, but it may only be a matter of time before Hannah is invited to take part in some sort of joint activity such as baking or conversation. Ella has already laid out a few recipes on the kitchen table for what look like traditional Icelandic cakes and confectionaries. Hannah could try hammering out a few lines of the book with her left hand, spend her time doing something sensible, now they're snowed in. A few sparks shoot out of the fireplace, and Hannah relinquishes any thoughts of getting some work done. What she really wants to do is lie down on the sofa and sleep, dream about getting home quickly and safely. She swings her legs up, lets her head rest on the armrest, closes her eyes and tries to drift off, when she is hit by a fresh wave of anxiety: if the murderer was prepared to kill Gísli to cover up their own tracks, could they come after her too? Hannah pushes herself up resolutely. She can't just sit here, waiting to be the next victim. And how easy it would be to become just that. Injured and isolated in a remote house with an old woman. No, she must take action, must make one final effort to help solve the case. She has to take advantage of the current situation: if the murderer feels like they've got off scot-free by framing Gísli, then they won't be on the alert. So now would be the best time to start snooping around again. And Hannah knows exactly where to start: a lead she hasn't thoroughly explored yet. Someone she must question again, someone she let off too easily last time they spoke.

Wrapped up like a piece of fragile porcelain in a suitcase, Hannah waddles out into the blizzard – half woman, half samurai. Ella protested of course, using her words, arms and legs, but Hannah managed to insist stubbornly that the situation calls for a pack of cigarettes, and she had to get down to the petrol station immediately. Even if that meant risking her life in the snowstorm. Which feels like a genuine possibility as she leaves the house, walking with heavy and purposeful steps through the snow. She doesn't particularly care about the cigarettes, but she does sincerely hope that Iðunn is working today. She stomps through the snow and catches sight of the lights from the petrol station ahead – to her great relief, the road doesn't appear to be entirely snowed under, as there is a hint of it remaining, like a subtle clue as to which direction the town lies in. They must have tried to clear it at least once or twice, before the snow plough gave up, as Hannah manages to trudge through a twenty-to-thirty-centimetre deep layer of snow, all the way up to the green neon sign indicating that the building is open. It is with even greater relief that she sees Iðunn sitting behind the counter. The young girl gives a little start of surprise when Hannah steps inside, looking like a worthy competitor for the abominable snowman. She shakes off the snow, removes her hat and smiles at Iðunn.

'Boy, am I happy to see you here.'

'I've got an air mattress and a sleeping bag in the back. Planning to sleep here until tomorrow, when they can come and clear some of the snow off the roads.'

Hannah nods, impressed at Iðunn's resilience. She walks up to the counter.

'Have you had any other customers today?'

'A few this morning, but we've just had the one since lunch, when they called off the road clearing – someone on skis. But my boss insists that we stay open in case anyone does pass by.'

'Lucky me.'

Hannah smiles and frees herself from her coat, which is a painstaking and inelegant task with her broken arm. Iðunn studies her.

'Not to flatter myself, but it almost sounds like you've come all the way down here just to talk to me?'

Hannah finally manages to pull off Ella's impossible waterproof trousers. She looks at Iðunn.

'You're entirely wrong. I actually need your help, and it'd be ideal if no one else turns up in the next hour.'

It takes Hannah several minutes to explain the assignment to Iðunn, who moments later is in full swing, responding to her request for help. Hannah watches her work with tense concentration behind the large, desktop computer in the back room, seemingly happy to have been liberated from her petrol-station boredom. And by such an exciting task!

'How far back do you want me to go?' Iðunn turns to look at Hannah.

'Maybe a few days before Thor's death, and a few days after too?'

'Can do...'

Iðunn faces the screen again, starts typing away. Hannah could smack herself – why hadn't she thought of this days ago? That young man, Stefan Haraldsson – who she met in the queue for the toilet at the teen party – is, of course, their best witness, and if they can help him remember exactly which car he saw Thor get into the night he was murdered, then they'll have found the murderer. And cars need petrol. So if the culprit stopped by the petrol station, then not just the car, but the man himself, would have been caught on camera. All they need to do now is trawl through enough of the surveillance footage to find all the four-wheel drives and show them to Stefan, so he can point out the right car, and therefore the murderer. Hannah watches impatiently as Iðunn loads the CCTV footage, rewinds back to the right day, stops, and takes screenshots of all the cars that park up at the pump.

'Do you want me to do all of the cars or just the 4x4s?'

'Do them all, to be safe.'

'Okay, but it'll take a while.'

Hannah nods, trying to be understanding, but feels restless. Suddenly has a burning desire for one of the cigarettes she pretended to come for.

'I'm just going out for a smoke. Call me if you find anything.'

'Of course.'

Iðunn doesn't even look up, she's so engrossed in her task, and Hannah heads back into the shop, grabs a pack of cigarettes with the least gruesome bogeyman photo on, reminding herself to pay for them later and to invest in a healthier lifestyle when she gets back to Denmark. Under the eaves of the building, she lights a cigarette, and turns away from the *No Smoking* sign, convincing herself that the snow would help prevent a fire, should a spark break free. She enjoys the silence, the occasional sound of the snow whistling along the petrol-station wall, watching it settle like a large duvet on the landscape. Then she hears the sound of an engine approaching, not like that of a car, however, more like a motorbike. What moron would be out riding a bike in this weather? But then she catches sight of the vehicle, and it hits her that it's obviously not a motorbike, but a snowmobile. Travelling at full speed right at her. It soars over a mound of snow, and lands softly, reducing its speed and coming to a stop a few metres away from Hannah, who is watching the rider – their face is hidden beneath the large motorcycle helmet – in fear. Has the murderer finally come to do away with her? A second later though, the helmet is removed, revealing Jørn's merry, childlike face, beaming up at her.

'How cool is this? I'd hoped that we'd get a big snowfall so I could give my new friend here a whirl.' He pats the scooter as if it were a horse.

'How is it that you always know where I am? It's like you've installed a GPS in my neck or something.'

Jørn smiles cheekily.

'Who knows ... Maybe I have. Haha, I'm only kidding. To be honest, I really just wanted to get outside and race around on this gal here.'

Pats the scooter again. Hannah rolls her eyes. Jørn doesn't notice.

'So, I don't really have any reason to be here. What about you?'

'Same, same. Just needed to get out a bit.'

Jørn nods. Hannah really does not want to involve Jørn in her new investigation and hopes he'll soon drive off again.

'Well, should we grab a cup of coffee then, while we're both here? Maybe debrief about what happened with Gísli yesterday.'

That is the last thing Hannah wants to do, but with their new-found sort-of friendship – or rather, their tolerance of each other – it would look suspicious if she turned down his offer. So she heads back into the shop, leading the way to the automatic machine, where they each get themselves a cup of coffee. Iðunn doesn't appear – she must be too wrapped up in solving the mystery of the car to realise that someone else has come in. Jørn looks around.

'Is there no one working here today?'

'Believe it or not, I'm actually keeping an eye on the shop at the moment, while the young girl who works here has stepped out to call someone. Relationship troubles, I think. I don't know. Something about an argument...'

Jørn doesn't seem to question her little lie, even though it must seem highly unlikely that Hannah has randomly become the petrol-station warden. Nevertheless, they each take a seat on one of the high stools facing the window, which makes this – in more ways than one – one of the most peculiar café visits Hannah has experienced.

'Did you go back to help Viktor after dropping me off?'

Hannah takes a sip of her coffee and tries not to sound overly interested. Jørn nods heroically.

'I helped to set up the cordon, but it was difficult getting people to move away. In some ways, it's a good thing that it was suicide, otherwise it would've been next to impossible to secure any evidence from the crime scene, with all those people trampling around it.'

Hannah nods, thinking that now there's even more pressure to find the footage of the car. If there's nothing from Gísli's crime scene to go off, then it may be their only clue.

'He's a good man, that Viktor. He asked me in for a beer afterwards.'

Hannah feels a sudden pang of jealousy. Are Viktor and Jørn friends now? And what about Margrét – has Jørn ingratiated himself with her too? It takes a great deal of effort to remove any trace of bitterness from her voice.

'Did you have a good time?'

'Oh, I said no. I was much, much too tired. But I said I'd owe him one. Maybe we can go up together sometime, when the snow has melted away a bit? You two have become good friends, haven't you?'

Hannah wonders how much Jørn has managed to find out about her relationship with Viktor and Margrét. Could Viktor have said anything? She thinks it unlikely, but she also gets the feeling that Jørn knows more than he's letting on. About everything.

'I think you'll have to go without me, unfortunately. As soon as the road to Reykjavík is open, I'll be leaving. So I can take the first and fastest flight back to Denmark.'

Jørn nods, probably isn't that surprised that Hannah wants to get home sooner rather than later.

'And the book? I assume that means you've dropped it?'

Is there a little glimmer of hopeful malice in Jørn's eyes? Or perhaps it is just genuine sympathy. Hannah is unsure.

'Until the deadline has actually passed, I won't be submitting any notices of surrender.'

Jørn smiles. Raises his thin latte in a toast.

'Good. I'd expect nothing less.'

'Cheers to that.'

Hannah knocks her paper cup against Jørn's, spilling a bit of coffee on the table.

'I'm relying on getting some sort of transcribing assistance in Copenhagen, so I can finish it.'

'You know what'll happen, then?'

'Yes. I've got it all up here in my head. It just needs to be written down.'

Hannah takes a sip to conceal the lie.

'If you want, I could—'

'No thank you.' Hannah intercepts his offer. Certainly won't be having any writing help from Jørn. And then Iðunn steps triumphantly from the back room, holding a USB stick up in the air.

'Got the photos! All we need to do now is show them to Stefan.'

Hannah is so annoyed at Jørn's puzzled face after hearing this message, she wants to tip her cup of coffee over his head. Now she'll have to tell him about her plan. Shit, shit, shit.

48

'Hold me tighter!'

Hannah closes her eyes, suppresses all of her instincts and pulls herself closer to Jørn's back as he gives the snowmobile full throttle. It feels like an absurd metaphor, her sitting there on the back seat, helplessly clinging on to him as he races across the landscape, the hero. With just the one arm she can barely even hold on. Hannah feels amputated, in every way – yet she has to admit that Jørn's offer to drive her up to Stefan's house, so he can look at the images and hopefully point out the murderer, was a most-welcome suggestion – one that outweighed her pride. They could have just sent the pictures to him, of course, but Hannah wants to see Stefan's reaction with her own eyes. Have the opportunity to question him, to try and push his memory for the details. Hannah's cheek is now buried in Jørn's expensive outdoor jacket, which probably has the proper high-tech Gore-Tex lining. The blizzard's ice-cold wind whips through her own coat, making her wish that she was as practical as Jørn in terms of clothing. It seems like he has an outfit for every occasion. But he can afford it. Hannah pulls herself together: no, she is better than that. She doesn't need to be envious of Jørn's fortune. In this moment, she is just grateful that his resources can help her out of yet another dead end.

'I'll give it some more gas!'

Before Hannah can say that she thinks that they're already going more than fast enough, Jørn opens up the throttle, and she has to fight to stay in the seat. A little, terrified scream breaches her defences, and all she can do is concentrate on surviving.

After about ten minutes of Jørn's death drive through the snow, they approach Stefan's home and he finally hits the brakes.

Hannah's heart is pounding like mad, the adrenaline making her body tremble.

'How fun was that?'

Jørn has a huge grin on his face. Hannah looks at him, grumpily.

'Oh yeah. About as much fun as being strapped to a car driving 200 kilometres an hour down the motorway.'

It is Stefan's mother who opens the door, and it takes her several minutes to understand who Hannah and Jørn are and why they want to talk to her son. When they are finally let into the house, the mother – a small, sprightly woman with a double-barrelled name that Hannah has already forgotten – flits into the kitchen to make coffee and tidy up a bit, as if she were hosting a royal visit. Hannah finds it unbelievably uncomfortable having to wait in the family's warm living room, where a little girl sits in front of a large TV, watching a cartoon that, to Hannah, looks both violent and stupid. But maybe that's what children enjoy – the little girl is laughing along and hasn't seemed to notice their presence. Perhaps she is used to random foreigners traipsing into her house in the middle of a blizzard, or maybe she just doesn't care. It takes an eternity for Stefan to answer his mum's calls to come downstairs. Hannah, meanwhile, notices with great irritation that Jørn is whole-heartedly distracted by the cartoon, chuckling as one of the characters trips over its tail. The little girl laughs as well and smiles broadly at him – looks happy to have someone to share the cartoon experience with. The sprightly woman finally comes in with some coffee and a giant tub of the type of caramel chocolates people buy at the airport but never actually finish. On her way through, she, thankfully, calls for Stefan again, and a few moments later, the CrossFit bear enters the living room, a little confused in the way that teenagers always seem to be, and with no sign that he recognises Hannah. How can it take a seventeen-year-old boy ten whole minutes to leave his bloody bedroom? Hannah forces herself to smile.

'Hi Stefan, I don't know if you remember me, but we met at the party...?'

Stefan's face instantly lights up. 'Oh yeah. You were the old woman Iðunn invited.'

Hannah: strained smile then straight to the point.

'Do you remember telling me about how, on the night Thor disappeared, you had seen him get into a car?'

Stefan's mother develops a nervous twitch. 'What is this about?'

Hannah turns towards the mother with all the kindness she can muster, suddenly aware of the fact that Stefan is, of course, still a minor.

'We've brought some photos of a few cars that we would like

Stefan to have a look at. We believe that one of them may be the car Thor got into the night he died, and if Stefan can point it out to us, then, well...'

'Then we can find the murderer.' Jørn looks around at them all with a serious, paternalistic expression, and Hannah resists the urge to elbow him hard in the nose for his stupid input.

Stefan's mother looks at them both, confused. 'I thought it was that alcoholic who ... I mean, who did that to Thor. Does ... does this mean the killer is still out there?'

The little girl has lost interest in the cartoon now. Whether that's because she understands the word 'killer' or simply because she can sense the sombre atmosphere in the room, Hannah can't be sure. In any case, this has all become unnecessarily complicated, getting Stefan to just take a glance at a few damn photos. Hannah tries to look as calm and harmless as possible.

'We simply want to map out everything that happened that night. As I said, I'm living with Thor's aunt at the moment, Ella, and naturally, she has been hit hard by all this. When I mentioned what Stefan had told me, well, she couldn't let it go, hence why I promised her that I would get to the bottom of all this with the car, so she can sleep at night. There's nothing to it at all, just a kind of soul-soothing exercise. I'm sure you understand.'

The mother looks at them sceptically. They all sit in complete silence. Until Jørn plunges his hand into the caramel chocolate tub and pulls out a colourful caramel, which he slowly and annoyingly opens and pops in his mouth.

'So you're not with the police?'

Hannah smiles reassuringly, sends an irritated look at Jørn, who is now chewing loudly, trying to pry some of the caramel out of his teeth with his little finger.

'No. We're just friends of the family, trying to make an old woman feel safer.'

They somehow get permission to go into Stefan's room without his mother and little sister, both of whom have already heard more than enough. Stefan sits on his unmade bed and invites them to take a seat too. Jørn gladly plonks himself down, but Hannah would rather be burned alive than spend any time on the same bed as Jørn. Even if it is only to sit and look at the images. She passes Stefan the plastic wallet with the printed-out screenshots from the CCTV cameras.

'Take your time.'

Stefan nods, taking the guidance seriously as he thoroughly studies the first image for a very, very long time. Hannah glances impatiently at her watch. If he's going to take this long looking at each image, they'll be here until Christmas. The room is stuffy, as if it hasn't been cleaned or aired out in a long time, or ever. Hannah looks at Jørn, and suddenly feels like she can't breathe. She steadies herself on the back of a nearby chair, which is piled high with clothes.

'I just ... need to go to the toilet. I'll be back in a moment.'

Hannah dashes out, finds the bathroom, locks herself in and throws open the window, exposing herself to the blizzard, and almost getting sucked outside. She stands there for a second, trying to regain a feeling of balance. Takes one last, long breath in and, struggling, closes the window with her non-plaster-cast arm. She stops for a moment to look at herself in the mirror. She looks pale and run down. Her hair is all tangled, presumably from the death ride over here, and she has huge black bags under her eyes. She finds it difficult to understand why Stefan's mother let them in in the first place. Maybe it was Jørn's charm.

Knock, knock!

Hannah jumps. Another two hard knocks on the door, and she opens it. Standing there: Jørn, whose face seems to have lost all its colour.

'Stefan has identified the car. And you won't believe who it belongs to...'

Hannah stares in disbelief at the photo of the car, which Stefan is now holding up in front of her, insisting that it *is* the car he saw Thor get into the night he was murdered. But that just cannot be.

'Are you sure? Lots of people in town own that kind of car.'

Stefan shakes his head. 'Not like this one. It's old, which is why I recognised it. And I remember seeing it around town before, but it was only when I saw this photo that I remembered ... look, the tail-light, there. It's smashed.'

'There must be plenty of cars in town with a broken tail-light. If that's what you're basing this on, then it's a little shaky...'

'But it's not just that. This is it, I swear!'

Stefan's eyes are almost glistening, in the same way a child's does when they're frustrated and powerless, being scolded for something they haven't done when the adults won't believe the truth.

'He does seem convinced. I believe him.'

Jørn looks at Hannah, a serious expression on his face again, and she realises then that she may just have to trust Stefan on this. Or at least take responsibility for the consequences. She stares again at the images from the surveillance camera, at the car he insists is the one he saw Thor get into that night. There is no doubt that the car belongs to Ella.

'So what now?'

Hannah and Jørn stand beneath the tiny awning in front of Stefan's front door, a kind of emergency consultation that they felt they couldn't have in a random stranger's home, nor on the snowmobile in the middle of a raging blizzard. Hannah's brain is stuck on the image of Ella's car, cannot fathom what their next move could even be, or come up with a plan, and least of all a sensible analysis of the situation. Instead, at a loss, she just stares at Jørn, who, judging from his question, seems to believe that she *does* know what they should do next. Hannah tries to organise her thoughts.

'I can't go home to Ella.'

'That much is clear. We have to inform Viktor, so he can arrest her. But with his arm out of action ... Maybe it would be better if I performed a citizen's arrest.'

Hannah stares at Jørn, incredulous.

'And what then? Bind Ella's hands, fling her over the back of the snowmobile and drive up to the police station?'

Jørn mulls it over, absentmindedly rubbing at his stubble.

'It may be too dangerous to bind her hands, but otherwise, yes, something like that.'

Hannah shakes her head.

'You've been reading far too many of your own books. If Thor did actually get into Ella's car that night, it doesn't necessarily mean that she was the one who killed him. She could've just driven him somewhere, where he then met his murderer.'

'But why hasn't Ella mentioned it? If she's not the murderer, why wouldn't she have said anything about seeing Thor that night?'

It's an annoyingly good question, and Hannah has to think it through, trying to find an explanation that preserves her host's innocence. And then it hits her: Ella hasn't lied at all, she's just not brought it up.

'She hasn't been asked!'

'What?'

'Ella hasn't lied because no one has thought to ask her what she was doing that night, and whether she saw Thor. Naturally, Ella should have made that information known, so it is still a mystery why she hasn't. But that's exactly what I'm going to get to the bottom of. Come on.'

The plan is suddenly crystal clear. Hannah hurries back to the snowmobile as quickly as the perilous surface allows. She uses her non-broken arm to clear the layer of snow continuing to settle on the seat. Jørn, however, is still standing beneath the shelter of the porch canopy, blinking at her.

'Where are we going?'

'To Ella. I have to see her. Ask her, face to face, why she picked up Thor that night.'

49

Hannah feels a little nervous, stepping back into Ella's home. Jørn has insisted on staying on the lookout, parked up a little way away, so he can come to the rescue if the situation should escalate out of her control. Hannah, however, finds that hard to imagine. How could Ella, all forty-eight kilograms of her, be able to overpower Hannah with a force she couldn't resist? On the other hand, Hannah isn't exactly fighting fit at the moment, with her right arm in a cast, and if Ella really did kill Thor, then ... Hannah shudders, shakes off the thought, which she still can't make any sense of. She raises her voice, making it as light and friendly as possible, as she calls into the living room.

'Ella? What a wild storm it is, out there. I thought I might never find my way back.'

Hannah battles with her jacket until it suddenly slides off her, almost by itself. She turns to find Ella standing right behind her, the jacket in her hands. Hannah didn't even hear her host's footsteps, nor did she feel her take hold of her jacket. Ella smiles warmly at her. Says something in Icelandic, which sounds friendly but frightens Hannah.

As always, they sit opposite each other in what has now almost become a ritual of coffee-drinking in front of the fireplace. Hannah sips cautiously.

'Thank you. Nice to feel the warmth again. The cold really got to me.'

Ella reaches for another blanket and holds it out to Hannah, who declines the offer – she already has one draped across her legs and doesn't need to be any more wrapped up for the conversation she is about to embark on. She takes a deep breath. And to get to her point as fast as possible, she lies a little.

'There's something I wanted to ask you about ... I met this guy down at the petrol station just now, called Stefan. I don't know if you know him?'

Ella shakes her head. It doesn't really matter. Hannah just wanted to make sure she has Ella's attention.

'We ended up talking about how I was staying here with you, and so Stefan said ... Well, I know how strange this sounds, but he said that he saw Thor get in your car the night he was killed.'

Hannah starts to rub one hand over the other, wants to dig inside the plaster and scratch. She said the last sentence very quickly, wanted to make sure she didn't regret it halfway through, but as she watches Ella now, she grows uncertain. Has she understood the accusation concealed within the apparently innocent anecdote? Ella returns Hannah's gaze, scrutinising her – she must have understood. She writes something on a scrap of paper. Hands it to Hannah, whose pulse rises as she takes it and reads:

Do you think I killed Thor?

The sentence winds Hannah, seeing the accusation in writing, an accusation she hasn't been able to fully comprehend until now. But, seeing it written there, black on white, suddenly makes it a genuine possibility. Hannah backtracks.

'Of course not. But hearing something like that ... I just wanted to make sure I got your side of the story, is all. Was he mistaken, or did Thor actually get into your car that night? And if so, what for? And why haven't you said anything? You might have been the last person to have seen him alive. You could be a vital witness, you know? That's the kind of thing you're supposed to mention!'

Hannah has managed to work herself up to such a level that her fear that Ella may in fact be guilty is now palpable. The anxiety seeps out of her like a poisonous gas, ready to stifle them both. Ella continues to stare at her – a look in her eye that Hannah can't read. She then leans forward and demonstratively pulls the piece of paper back to her side of the coffee table. Writes. Slides it over to Hannah.

Of course I not drive Thor anywhere that night. I would have said. It hurts me you believe it.

Before Hannah has a chance to answer, Ella is on her feet.

Eschewing her usual routine, she doesn't put the coffee and biscuits on a tray to take with her, nor does she blow out the candle. Instead, she mumbles an Icelandic goodnight and leaves Hannah to wallow in her own shame, a feeling of having ruined the rapport between them. Perhaps irrevocably.

'The way she denied it so vehemently makes me uncomfortable. Maybe I'm over-analysing the situation, but I think there was a sense of guilt in her resentment. I mean, if it really was such an absurd accusation, wouldn't she have just laughed it off, dismissed it as a bad joke?'

'Come sleep at mine.'

'What?'

Hannah frowns at Jørn, crouching down, all wind- and weather-beaten, behind the woodshed, where Hannah has summoned him for a rendezvous after her talk with Ella.

'You can't stay here tonight, it's too risky. What if she murders you in your sleep?'

Hannah wants to laugh at Jørn's dramatic ways, but there's the smallest grain of possibility that what he says might actually be true, so she holds herself back. But the last thing she wants to do is leave now and spend the night at his place.

'It'd look too weird. If I sneak off now, she'll know that I know, and then who's to say what she'll do? Innocent or guilty, I don't want to risk Ella having a nervous breakdown or doing something reckless. She has to feel like I still believe her.'

'But do you?'

Hannah stands in silence for a moment.

'The correct thing to do is to stay. I'll sleep with one eye open, then you can bring Viktor tomorrow, when the storm has settled down a bit. And we can all get to the bottom of this.'

'You saw yourself how steadfast Stefan was. There's something your gal pal in there isn't telling us.'

Hannah ignores the grating way Jørn describes Ella as her 'gal pal', as if they were schoolgirls and Hannah an accomplice in her shenanigans.

'There's no reason to stir the pot. I'll stay here tonight, and I'm sure we'll find out how it all fits together tomorrow.'

She sends him into the dark blizzard, back to the snowmobile, with the assurance that she'll lock her door and sleep with a kitchen knife on the night stand. Tired and somewhat scared, Hannah finally gets into bed half an hour later, and even though she knows that she shouldn't give in, shouldn't expose herself to the unconsciousness of sleep, she nonetheless slides quickly and without resistance into it.

She awakes in the middle of the night to the sound of a conversation out in the hallway. Instinctively, she grabs the kitchen knife and holds her breath, straining to listen more intently, but can only hear Ella's whispering. Is she sleepwalking and talking to herself? With difficulty, Hannah scrambles over to the door and puts her ear against it. She can still hear only Ella's voice, and she sounds agitated, but in a controlled way that suggests she can't be asleep. Maybe she's talking on the phone again? But then Hannah hears another person answer her – indistinct, impossible to tell whether the voice comes from a man or a woman. Although her instincts are screaming at her not to, Hannah can't resist but open the door and creep out into the hallway to see who has paid Ella this night-time visit. She waits a moment, until the voices sound like they have moved further away, along with the bodies they belong to, and gently turns the key in the lock then pushes the door open a fraction, her heart pounding in her chest and cursing the creaky hinges that force her to stop mid-movement. Pause. Listen. The low hum of their voices sounds like it's coming from the floor below. Hannah takes a deep breath and opens the door just wide enough for her to squeeze into the hallway. The light is off, and she has to blink a few times to get used to the darkness. She sneaks towards the staircase, reaches the top step and grabs the handrail, stopping dead in one breathless moment: the voices have vanished. Have they left the house? Hannah didn't hear any doors closing, nor did she notice the lights or sound of a car outside. She strains to heighten her senses. Has it stopped snowing? She thinks through her options. She can either stay here, or walk straight into the living room. She can't go back to bed. She counts to ten, listens again, but can only hear the sound of her pounding pulse. Takes the first, tremulous step down the stairs, hugging her brick of a broken arm tight into her body, a nervous hand clutching the banister. Halfway down, she sees the light on in the living room and the silhouettes of two people in close conversation. They are whispering, Ella standing over the other, whose face Hannah cannot see. She watches them. Is there something threatening about Ella's stance? Hannah has to get closer, must find out who it is sitting on the sofa, hidden by Ella's slight, shaking body. She feels like a disobedient child, sneaking downstairs to spy on the adults when it's well past her bedtime, hoping to catch a glimpse of the exciting and unknown world of the night. But even though Hannah does feel a certain excitement in her venture, it is anxiety driving her now. Anxiety that desperately wants to know whoever it is that might clear Ella of guilt by showing themselves as the true murderer. Hannah just needs to get a little bit closer. But then ... A loud shout suddenly erupts from Ella – the person on the sofa gets up, pushes past her and tears toward the front door, all before Hannah can move fast enough to get back upstairs and hide – or rather, lurk somewhere out of the way but where she can still see the person's face. Shit! She has to catch a glimpse of them before it's too late. In one swift, unwise and self-exposing dash out into the hall, Hannah reaches the bottom of the stairs and the hallway, from which the night-time guest has just disappeared. Hannah stands there, her heart in her throat, dressed in her pyjamas and an expression of disbelief, looking out into the night, with a clear view now of the fleeing person. The snowflakes swoop inside and hit her square in the face. Her senses failed her. It hasn't stopped snowing. The fleeing person is Margrét.

'Ég hélt að þú værir sofandi.'

Hannah spins round and sees Ella standing behind her, watching her with a frightening hostility. Hannah throws a glance back over her shoulder, at the open door, at the darkness and the snow, and for a moment considers running out there, but she is barefoot and in her pyjamas, and certainly would not survive the trip into town. Hannah's eyes dart towards the bowl atop the little cabinet next to the door, where Ella keeps her car keys, but the Jeep is so snowed under that even with two functional arms, it would take a hell of a long time to dig the wheels free of snow, and Hannah doubts she could do it all with just her left arm and a shovel. And even if she were able to free the car, the roads are so snowy, she wouldn't even make it a few metres from the house. All she can do is stay where she is.

'What was Margrét doing here?'

Hannah looks directly into Ella's glass-green eyes. What is her host keeping from her? Ella takes a step closer. Hannah instinctively takes a step back, but Ella simply walks past her and closes the door on the dark and the snow. Then holds Hannah's gaze. A long time. As if she is considering what to do about her. If feels like an eternity, then Ella takes a small notebook from the cabinet and pulls it towards her. Writes with great care.

You must back to Danmark tomorrow.

Ella holds the note up for Hannah, as if to make sure that she definitely understands. Her eyebrows rise in search of a confirmatory nod. But she doesn't receive one. Instead, Hannah musters up all her strength and puts a reassuring hand on Ella's shoulder.

'Something is going on here that I don't understand, but I know you're wrapped up in it, and it's clearly plaguing you. Whatever it is, I can't leave right in the middle of it. I'm not saying that to intrude, I'm saying it because I have come to truly care about you over these last two weeks, and because I have witnessed what you've been through. I can't just leave now, with all this uncertainty and concern. You don't need to tell me what's going on, but you can't send me away until it's over. I want to stay here and help you, whatever it is.'

Hannah is almost out of breath by the end of her speech, and to her own, somewhat mild, surprise, realises that she genuinely means it. She is truly and wholeheartedly concerned about Ella and what might happen to her. Hannah no longer cares about solving Thor's murder, no longer cares about whether it was Ella who did it. All she wants is make sure that everything is settled and no one else gets hurt. Ella's eyes flicker a little – is there an apathy in them now? It is as if Hannah's words have trapped her in a kind of limbo, between the desire to collapse and break down, and the desire to maintain control. Hannah, still with her hand on Ella's shoulder, gives it an encouraging squeeze. Surrender now. But Ella waves her hand away, picks up the paper again, and points at it.

You must back to Danmark tomorrow.

She presses the paper into Hannah's chest and walks resolutely upstairs to sleep, and to think who knows what. And Hannah is left standing there, the note in her hand and a feeling of being at a complete and utter loss. The plan to send Viktor after Ella seems up in the air now, given that Margrét seems to play some sort of role in it all. Perhaps it would, after all, be best not to get any more involved in all of this and simply go home? But the more she thinks about it, the harder it is to accept such a lack of resolution. Hannah therefore sneaks back upstairs herself, silently pulls on an extra-thick jumper and a pair of thermal leggings. She stops outside Ella's bedroom for a moment and listens, but there isn't so much as the sound of a creaking bed or the heavy breathing of sleep. When Hannah closes the door behind her and sets out into the Icelandic night snow, it is with a hammering heart and a hope that she may potentially find an answer, some meaning to all of this, now, before it's too late.

50

It is completely unhinged, to be fair. She is well aware of that. Turning up at someone else's home at three o'clock in the morning, expecting to have a reasonable conversation. But Hannah has no choice. She can either confront Margrét about her mysterious night-time visit with Ella, before night becomes day and Viktor wakes, or wait and let others control the course of events, with who knows what results. But Hannah receives yet another surprise, when, after a careful round of knocking and calling outside Margrét and Viktor's front door, she suddenly finds herself looking into Viktor's open eyes. Standing in the doorway, looking down at her, as if he has been waiting there for this very purpose.

There is, however, also a hint of disappointment in his gaze as he says, 'Where's Margrét?'

Ah. Viktor has been sitting up, waiting for his wife, so not only has Hannah's plan to be discreet failed, she has also traipsed over here in vain. Margrét isn't home.

'I thought she was here. That's why I came.'

'In the middle of the night?'

Viktor looks questioningly at Hannah, who doesn't even bother to come up with another lame excuse.

'Margrét came to visit Ella a short while ago, and they had some sort of argument. It all seemed very ... suspicious. Margrét stormed out, and Ella wouldn't tell me what they were arguing about, so I thought...'

Hannah hesitates. Knows she has nothing sensible to say from this point.

'So you thought you'd leave the house in the middle of a blizzard to walk over here and question Margrét?'

Hannah nods. Shivers. The intensity of the snowfall has subsided, but it's still too bitterly cold to be standing on the doorstep in the middle of the night, and in such a dilemma.

'Can I come in?'

Viktor paces back and forth, digesting Hannah's explanation of the night's events, having made Hannah recount them to him numerous times – every single detail, even though there aren't that many to give. Didn't Hannah understand anything that was said? How long does she think Margrét spent at Ella's house? Did she look more angry or worried? Which way did she walk and at what speed? It irritates Hannah, this question after question, and the fact he's even asking them confirms that he has no idea what's going on either.

Viktor glances at his watch. 'You said you left not long after Margrét?'

Hannah nods. Again. 'As I said, I'd like to go out and look for her.'

'The kids are sleeping. I can't just abandon them.'

Viktor looks at Hannah, and she thinks for a moment, to her horror, that he may be considering asking her to babysit.

'Sorry, I can't ... If they wake up, I wouldn't know what to do.'

'The last thing I want to do is expose my children to the trauma of waking up in the middle of the night to find that the only person here for them is you.'

Hannah nods. Relieved and insulted at the same time.

'But ... that might be necessary. We'll give her ten more minutes. If she's not back by then, I'll go out and look for her.'

Hannah wants to protest, but, even though they are both injured, each with their own wounded arm, it'd probably make more sense for Viktor to be the one to venture out into the snow. It is his wife who has disappeared, after all. And him who knows the town best. Double whammy. Ten minutes is a long time when you're worried and waiting in silence with someone you have wronged.

'That ... with me and Margrét. It was just ... I mean, short-lived. It didn't mean anything. And anyway, it's over now.'

Hannah feels that some kind of apology is called for, even if she doesn't mean it. At least not the part about it not meaning anything. She shuffles in her seat, trying not to reveal how sincerely worried she is about Margrét. How scared she is that something may have happened to her and that she may never get to see her again. But it's not Hannah's place to be the worried partner – it is, of course, Viktor's wife, the mother of his children, who has disappeared. Viktor observes Hannah, scrutinising her.

'When we first met at Bragginn ... there was something about you that I really liked. Even though you've shown yourself to be particularly annoying in a variety of ways.'

Hannah looks at him, unsettled – where's he going with this?

'But ignoring all the ways you've been a pain in the neck, my first impression of you remains: there is something about you that I find likeable. I'm glad, in a way, that it was you this time. And not just because you'll be leaving soon.'

Touché. Hannah has to respect the elegant way in which Viktor has managed to compliment her and yet reduce her to a simple, meaningless bump in the road of Margrét's life. 'This time'. Just one in a series, nothing more. Most likely already forgotten about. That doesn't, however, make Hannah any less worried about Margrét. She glances at the clock. Five minutes.

'Should we go?'

Viktor shakes his head. 'Five more minutes.'

A man of principle. Hannah rises from the hard dining chair, wanting to pace away the remaining minutes. She purposefully walks towards the wall. To a photo of Margrét, Viktor and their children. They look happy. Hannah suddenly cannot bear the thought of something having happened to Margrét. She continues walking around the room, trying to overcome her nervousness. It is odd that Margrét hasn't come home – there's nowhere else for her to go in town at this hour. Unless, of course, she has another lover elsewhere. Is that why Viktor is taking this relatively calmly? Hannah doesn't know which scenario is more unbearable. She comes to a halt in front of a chest of drawers, and her eyes fall on an object. It is not the object itself that makes her stop in her tracks, but the way it has been left there. In a plastic evidence bag. Hannah picks up the bag, and holds it in the air, looking at Viktor.

'Evidence?'

Viktor leaps out of his chair. 'Put that down!'

Hannah is taken aback by his sudden aggression and flings the bag back down ... Stares at it, and its contents. Suddenly understands what it is.

'Is this the murder weapon?'

She points to the bag, in which lies a hammer. With a smattering of blood on its head. Viktor nods, almost regretfully.

'It shouldn't be just left on the side there, but I'm waiting to send it for tests in Reykjavik. It was discovered yesterday, in one of the fields about five hundred metres from where Thor was found. Looks like someone had tried getting rid of it by throwing it into the sea but didn't throw it far enough. Anyway, it seems to have gotten stuck in the ice ... until someone found it.'

'Who?'

'A man, out walking his dog. Or rather, the dog actually found it.'

Hannah nods, but her thoughts are elsewhere entirely. She stares down at the hammer, a vague feeling she has previously felt now developing into a sense of conviction.

'That hammer ... it belongs to Ella.'

Hannah tells him about Ella's strange tool collection on the wall of her living room, and how this exact hammer has been missing the whole time. Viktor looks at her doubtfully.

'If the hammer has been missing this whole time, then how do you know what it looks like?'

'It's the same type of antique tool as the rest of them.'

Viktor still looks unconvinced.

'Right, so you can recognise the hammer just by looking at the other tools?'

Hannah grabs hold of the evidence bag, turns it over, and searches for something through the plastic. Looks up at Viktor, triumphantly.

'There! TJ. That's engraved on all of her other tools as well.'

'TJ is the name of the carpenter who built most of the town. He's been dead for years, but the shop is still there. And they still mark all their tools with his initials. Everyone in town has one of these.'

'But an antique one?'

'I'd imagine that most of the older generation have kept hold of their old tools, yes. They're good quality.'

Hannah looks at the hammer again, disappointed. Hesitates, not wanting to be the one to accuse Ella, but she feels like she no longer has a choice.

'I spoke with Stefan – he saw Thor get into a car the night he was murdered. And ... he confirmed that it was Ella's car. I showed him a few photos...'

Viktor jumps up again, as if the chair has given him an electric shock.

'Why didn't you tell me this before? When did you talk to him?'

'Earlier today. Or, technically, yesterday. I would've said something but, I mean ... he could've been wrong. But now with everything else – the hammer, Margrét...'

Hannah isn't given a chance to say another word: Viktor is already on his way out the door. Hannah throws a quick glance behind her. Does he want her to stay here with the children? And then makes the decision. They've slept through up to now, they may as well be left alone a little longer.

51

Under normal circumstances, it's only a brisk, fifteen-minute walk from Viktor's police-station home to Ella's house, but through the thick snow drifts, the trip takes a little over twice as long. Sun, rain, snow – Hannah is getting tired of the route. Once they do finally arrive, they pause outside the front door, a moment of hesitation that indicates their mutual, unspoken fear of what may be awaiting them. They sneak inside. The house is dark, quiet. Hannah points wordlessly to Ella's bedroom and rests her non-plaster-cast hand against her cheek, in an attempt to show that Ella is probably asleep. Silently, they move towards the room, and Viktor gets into position to kick the door down. Hannah hisses at him:

'You'll give her a heart attack!'

'Maybe. But I'm not risking being hit on the head with one of her other tools.'

Before Hannah can protest again, Viktor kicks the door in, and there is a little scream. And Hannah realises that it came from her own mouth. The bedroom is pitch-black. From the hallway, Hannah can see Viktor's silhouette, furiously searching the wall for a light switch – she comes to his rescue, reaches around the doorframe and flicks the switch. They look around, surprised: it's empty. No Ella in her bed, nor anywhere else. Like a crap detective film, they both instinctively start to search the room, opening the wardrobe doors, looking behind the door, under the bed. But no trace of Ella.

'Did you see anything in the living room?' Viktor looks at Hannah.

She shakes her head. They investigate the rest of the house, but Ella is not there. In the entrance hall, Hannah notices that Ella's coat is gone, but her car is still parked outside.

'Where the hell could she have got to?' Viktor asks the question Hannah is thinking.

Although the blizzard has started to ease off, it is still deadly cold out, and quite the challenge to get anywhere, especially in the dark and on foot ... Who could she possibly be visiting, in these conditions, in the middle of the night? Hannah can think of only one answer. She turns to Viktor.

'My guess is that she's gone to Vigdis. If Ella is upset or maybe even afraid or in trouble, then her sister is definitely the person she would turn to.'

Viktor nods, has already pulled out his phone and is searching for Vigdis's number. He calls it. Hannah watches him tensely, but the seconds pass, then she can hear the familiar sound of an automatic answering machine on the other end. Viktor looks at Hannah, exasperated.

'I only have their home phone number. Do you know if Vigdis has a mobile?'

Hannah thinks for a moment, and nods. Curses inwardly. She actually did have her mobile number, but that was before she destroyed her phone. And then she remembers: Ella's phonebook. She frantically starts searching for it. Asks Viktor to help.

'A small, black book ... She keeps addresses, phone numbers, that kind of thing in it.'

In ten minutes they search through the entrance hall, the living room, kitchen and Ella's bedroom, with no luck. In the meantime, Viktor tries calling Margrét again, and is, again, disappointed when she doesn't pick up.

'This is a waste of time. We have to go straight to Vigdis and ask her outright.'

Viktor moves swiftly towards the front door, but Hannah insists on checking one last place: Ella's locked study.

'Vigdis and Ægir's house is at the other end of town, practically in the mountains, it'll take us at least half an hour to get there in these conditions, and if it turns out that Ella isn't even there, then we'll have wasted a whole hour that we could've spent looking for Margrét. And an hour is a long time, if she...'

Hannah stops herself. There's no reason to say out loud what they're both thinking: that Margrét could be lying out there somewhere, in a mound of snow, freezing to death. It takes Viktor a matter of seconds to break down the door to Ella's study, and almost as little time for Hannah to locate the little notebook in one of the drawers. She goes to close the drawer again, when Viktor stops her.

'Wait. What's that in there?'

Viktor carefully plucks out a necklace, the one with Thor's

hammer pendant that Hannah had previously found and placed back in the sugar bowl. It has since been removed from the bowl and is just lying there, visible at the front of the drawer. She watches Viktor as he studies the chain, as if it were the most expensive piece of jewellery he has ever seen.

'Is there something special about it?'

Viktor looks at her. Gravely. Holds the pendant up so she can see.

'This is Thor's. He was wearing it the night he was killed.'

Hannah looks at him sceptically.

'How can you know that he was wearing that specific necklace?'

Viktor turns the pendant over in his hand, examines the little hammer.

'The inscription there, the little "t". Jonni had it engraved and gave it to Thor. He was the one who said that Thor was wearing it that night.'

Hannah's head explodes: why the hell is it lying here in Ella's drawer then, if she isn't guilty? Everything suddenly makes sense: Ella's violent reaction to Hannah breaking into her office, her annoyance at Hannah's involvement in the case, the attack on Ella's house ... Someone must have known what she had done and sought revenge. Ægir, perhaps? But why hasn't he killed her already, then? If Ella has, in fact, gone to Vigdis for comfort, Hannah thinks, then it wouldn't be exactly the safest place for her to stay. And if Ægir manages to get to Ella before they do, then they may never find out what her conversation with Margrét was about, or where Margrét could've gone. Or why Ella killed Thor ... Hannah has already flicked through the book, found Vigdis's mobile number and typed it into her phone, when Viktor stops her.

'Shit ... Look at this.'

Viktor passes Hannah something else from the drawer: a piece of paper, and on it, a short, hand-written letter. Hannah's eyes glide over the writing – it is in Icelandic.

'Ella's hand-writing?' Viktor looks questioningly at Hannah, who nods – after all the notes she's written to her, there is no doubt in her mind. The letter has not been signed, however, and it looks unfinished. There are crossings out and edits throughout – a draft. Hannah looks at Viktor.

'What does it say?'

'It looks like a confession.' He translates for her: '"I am sorry for all the accidents, I just want to make everything right again. If I could give Thor his life back by giving my own, I would."'

They look at each other. And then suddenly hear a voice, Vigdis's, coming from Hannah's phone. She must have pressed the call button by accident.

'*Hæ þetta er Vigdís. Ég kemst ekki í símann svo skildu eftir skilaboð og ég hringi í þig eins fljótt og ég get.*'

Viktor looks at her.

'Voicemail. Come on, we can't waste any more time!'

Viktor has one foot out into the hallway, when Hannah grabs him. She shakes her head.

'We need back-up, and I know just who to call.'

As if it couldn't get more humiliating than sitting on the back of Jørn's snowmobile, Hannah is now fighting for dear life, holding on to her last vestige of dignity as she is flung around in the passenger sled attached to the back of the snowmobile, on which the other two are sitting. Through the snow being launched into her eyes by the small rubber tracks, which churn up the white surface below them and hurl it into the air, she can just make out Viktor clinging on to Jørn's leather-clad back. Hannah feels like a child, sitting in the little cart at the back. She closes her eyes and both hates and loves Jørn in equal measure. You could almost believe he had been circling Ella's house all night, the alacrity with which he arrived on his snowmobile, complete with his smiling, helper face. At the speed they are travelling, Hannah guesses the ride up to Vigdis and Ægir's house will now take less than ten minutes. Vital minutes saved. On top of which, they now have Jørn: a large man who isn't hampered by a broken arm or a stab wound. Who can hopefully help apprehend Ella. The house looks disconcertingly dark as they approach, and Jørn turns off the engine. The three unlikely musketeers stand there for a moment, pausing to think in the late-night silence. It has stopped snowing altogether now, and Hannah catches sight of the moon above – it has emerged from between the receding clouds, casting a placid light down around them. She doesn't know what she was expecting. Screams, fighting, blood on the doorstep? Perhaps one light on inside, at least. But the house lies in complete darkness and total silence beneath the moonlight. Viktor knocks on the door with a commanding hand, calling out to the residents of the house with great authority.

Hannah and Jørn glance at each other.

'They're probably asleep.'

Hannah rolls her eyes at Jørn's obvious analysis, but finds the thought that he's right – and the consequences of him being so – intolerable. Because then they'd have absolutely no idea of where to look for Ella and Margrét. Viktor gives the residents of the house another minute to wake up from their potentially deep sleep, then grabs an empty flower pot and smashes it through the small window of the front door, shattering the glass with a loud ringing sound. Both Hannah and Jørn give a little start.

'I thought the police had equipment to open locked doors?'

Hannah looks at Viktor, who shakes his head.

'Nothing as effective as this.'

He sticks his arm through the window, locates the lock, twists, and opens the door. Cautiously enters with the flower pot raised above his head. Hannah suddenly remembers that Icelandic police don't carry weapons. A good practice, sure, but it seems utterly insane in this moment that the long arm of the law should be bearing only a flower pot. Hannah and Jørn creep behind him like asymmetric reinforcements. They only get a few metres into the house before a light comes on, and Hannah feels something cold and hard pressed against her temple.

She carefully turns her head and finds herself looking straight down the barrel of a rifle.

'*Hvað í andskotanum eru þið að gera?*'

'*Slappaðu af. Niður með byssuna.*'

Hannah looks, horrified, from Ægir, who is pointing the gun at her head, to Viktor, holding the flower pot threateningly at the stone man. This could all go very, very wrong. Viktor says something else in Icelandic, a kind of de-escalation tactic that doesn't seem to work. In any case, Ægir continues to aim the gun at her with undiminished ferocity, and from the corner of her eye Hannah can just make out his finger resting on the trigger. Fuck, fuck, fuck!

Bang! Hannah's eyes are closed. Is she dead? No. She opens them, only to see Ægir lying on the floor, unconscious, and next to him, Jørn, with a police baton in his hand. He smiles heroically at Viktor.

'I also have pepper spray, but I thought the baton would be best in this instance.'

Neither Hannah nor Viktor comment on Jørn's weaponry, or his, no doubt semi-illegal, possession of them, but together, they haul Ægir out of the hallway, into the kitchen and onto a chair. Jørn splashes some water on the great stone man's face, and he has come round by the time Vigdis enters the kitchen in her nightdress, a horrified expression on her face. The entire scene has played out in the space of mere minutes. Viktor nods at Vigdis, who stands there, frozen.

'*Eru aðrir í húsinu?*'

She weakly shakes her head. Walks over and sits beside her husband, who is bleeding from the top of his head and seems groggy.

'Stay here while I search the house.'

Viktor disappears through the kitchen door. Hannah bends down to talk to Vigdis, her tone friendly.

'Has Ella been here?'

'What, no ... when?'

'Just now. Tonight.'

'No ... Why would she? Why have you come here and ... and attacked us in our own home? What did Ægir do?'

Hannah rubs her forehead, she lacks the proper questioning techniques. Looks dismayed at Jørn, who happily steps in.

'You can relax. I'm sorry for hitting him with the baton, but it was a tense situation, and my old military brain kicked in to remove the danger. "Safety first" – that's my motto.'

Hannah stares at him, speechless. How is that meant to help? They have to find out where Ella and Margrét are, now. She turns to Vigdis again.

'Has Ella called you at all in the last few hours? Are you sure that she hasn't come here? Could she have come over without you knowing it?'

'Nú er komið nóg!'

Hannah jumps at Ægir's sudden outburst. She can see that all his muscles are strained and that his fists are balled into two massive boulders, which would be the last thing you'd want hitting you in the temple. Vigdis starts to cry.

'Please ... We don't know anything. We were just in bed, sleeping. Has something happened to Ella?'

Hannah's fears are confirmed: they've gone down a dead end. Which is reinforced by Viktor, who appears in the doorway and shakes his head.

'She's not here.'

Hannah contemplates how much she can tell Thor's parents, who have already been through so much. Is this the right time to tell them that they suspect that Ella may have been the one who killed their son? Would it help them find her? Probably not. Hannah decides to keep the information private.

'We have reason to believe that it was Ella who killed Thor, and that she may have taken her own life.'

ARGH! Hannah has never wanted to strangle Jørn quite as much as she does in that moment. He, however, continues to look at Vigdis and Ægir, as if he's just told them the weather forecast or passed on a recipe for a good Saturday night dinner. Hannah sends him a murderous look, which he clearly doesn't pick up on. Vigdis looks ready to fall apart at the seams.

'What did you just say?'

'Apologies for my colleague, Jørn, his English isn't great. What he means is, we believe that Ella has important information on what happened that night with Thor, and that it's vital that we find her before, well ... Yes, before any more accidents happen.'

Viktor nods at Hannah: good way to de-escalate the situation. Hannah, however, would be amazed if she's done as she intended and managed to confuse Vigdis and Ægir enough to prevent them realising what's really going on and falling into a pit of despair. She quickly tries to avoid any further questions from them by posing one herself.

'Do you know of anywhere that Ella might have gone? Somewhere in town, or out in the countryside, where she often likes to goes?'

'Where she often likes to goes? In this weather? In the middle of the night?'

The stone man, Ægir – who has thus far sat there, silently tense – looks at Hannah as if she is the dumbest human being he has ever seen. The contempt radiates from him. It provokes her.

'We're actually trying to help and hopefully save Ella's life, so don't look at me like I'm an idiot. Right now, it's actually you who's the idiot.'

'Out!'

Ægir rises and grabs hold of Hannah, a tight grasp on her jacket collar, so it bunches up at her neck, his face right up against hers. She can see the hatred in his eyes, the anger and the froth at the corners of his mouth, and hopes he possesses even the slightest ounce of self-control. The strength and aggression with which he's holding her triggers a fear in her so alien to her, yet universal for all women: The way a man can completely obliterate a woman's will and person in one single, powerful, muscular grip must feel the same, no matter where the assault takes place in time and space. Hannah feels powerless for a short moment, and is saved only by a steady hand on Ægir's shoulder: Jørn's rational man hand, which seems to exert reason and mutual respect. Not between Hannah and Ægir of course, but between Ægir and Jørn himself.

'I understand your anger, but you have to let go. Let's talk about this instead.'

To Hannah's great surprise, Jørn's manoeuvre works. Slowly, Ægir loosens his grip and she takes a step back, towards Viktor. Jørn nods at them.

'Can you two wait outside? I'll just have a chat with Ægir. Man to man.'

Outside, Hannah seethes with rage, kicking at a mound of snow, which only seems to launch it into the air above her, falling and sticking to her clothes, making her look as ridiculous as she feels. She and Viktor then wait under the shelter of the little porch canopy.

'What the hell has he got himself into? Believing he can just save the situation by talking to Ægir "man to man"? And why did Ægir just let him do it? We should go back in and insist that it's fucking us who have the right to question him, and that Ægir should just spit it out, all he knows.'

Viktor shakes his head. 'Men like Ægir only respect men who remind them of themselves. He feels they understand him and have earned his respect.'

'Jørn hasn't earned anything!'

'No, but if he can get something out of him...'

Hannah grabs the door handle. 'I should talk to Vigdis in the meantime.'

'And what? Comfort her "woman to woman"?'

Hannah stops. Viktor's right. She has no idea how to summon up enough sisterly solidarity to pry into Vigdis's life and get anything useful out of her. Or at least not while she is so frustrated she wants to set the house alight. It's all a waste of time, and yet Hannah still accepts the cigarette Viktor offers her. He lights it and she inhales, closes her eyes. Where is Margrét? And where is Ella? Hannah has a feeling that if they don't find them before the night is over, then they won't find them alive.

'Ta-da!'

Jørn steps out of the front door, clearly pleased with himself.

'I know where they are...'

Hannah looks at him dubiously. Jørn downgrades their expectations a notch.

'Or rather, I know where they might be. Apparently Ella has a little cabin outside of town where she goes when she wants to be alone.

This makes absolutely no sense to Hannah, given that Ella is alone all the time, living in that massive house by herself. She turns to Viktor.

'Did you know that?'

'Nope. But we can't waste any more time. Where is it?'

52

Once again, Hannah is relegated to third class, travelling in the little cart dragged along behind the snowmobile, but this time, she doesn't have the privilege of being irked by Jørn's dangerous driving. Now, she can't think of anything other than what awaits them at Ella's secret cabin. It takes fifteen minutes to ride over there, the moon accompanying them the entire way. Hannah is impressed by Viktor's sense of direction as he guides them across the fields, past frozen lakes, distant mountains, and out into the vast nothingness. And, suddenly, a cabin appears, as if it has been waiting for them all this time. Jørn turns off the engine, and the three of them glance at each other. There is no doubt that someone is in there. There's a car parked outside, and a faint light illuminates the cabin from within.

'So, how are we doing this?'

It's Jørn who calls for a plan, implying that he doesn't have one himself. Perhaps the severity of the matter has finally dawned on him. Hannah and Jørn look expectantly at Viktor, who, despite his police authority, must be as unprepared for this kind of situation as they are. He nods at them, a serious expression on his face, and lowers his voice.

'We need to proceed with caution, we don't know what's in store for us in there. And there have been far, far too many accidents already for us to go in there now and cause another one. Jørn, you come with me. Hannah, you wait out here. If we're not out in five minutes, I want you to call this number. It's the officer on duty in the next town over.'

Viktor hands her his phone, on which an emergency number has already been dialled. All she has to do is call it.

'Why don't we just call them now?' Jørn looks inquiringly at Viktor.

'Because it'll take them over an hour to get here in this weather.'

'So it won't matter if Hannah calls them in five minutes or ten minutes?'

'It does matter.'

'How?'

'It'll help her get out of this alive and avoid having to see whatever happened to us, if we don't come back out in five minutes.'

Jørn is white as a sheet. 'What do you think might happen in there?'

Hannah puts the hand of her non-broken arm on Jørn's shoulder. 'You stay here, I'll go in.'

'No!' Viktor shakes his head. 'I'll need someone with me who has at least two fully functioning arms. You stay here.'

Hannah knows he's right – if Viktor ends up in a dangerous situation, she wouldn't be able to do much to help him. While Jørn, on the other hand, has already proved that he can be useful. She nods. Watches him compose himself and straighten his back, a movement that almost completely conceals his fear. But only almost. Hannah feels a pang of sympathy for him, and for his courageous approach.

'Hannah – remember, if we don't come out: call for help. Do *not* go in there yourself!'

Her heart beating like anxiety's xylophone, Hannah couldn't be more tense than if she were about to walk through that door instead of Viktor and Jørn. She checks the time on the screen and sets a countdown for five minutes.

After forty seconds, she hears a loud noise, then silence. After a minute and a half, she hears voices. Then silence. After three minutes, her thumb is itching to tap the number on the screen, but she waits out the remaining one and a half minutes. In silence. Until the sound of two gunshots, which paralyse her for several seconds. When she finally tunes in to the sound of her own breathing again, it is the only thing that punctures the silence. She waits a moment longer to see if anyone comes out of the door, but in vain. Against all her instincts, but driven by an urge to act, Hannah gently pushes down the handle of the artfully carved wooden door and walks in, her heart twisted in fear. She seems to have walked directly into the kitchen, but the room is in darkness, so it may also be some kind of living room. From the outside, the cabin seemed relatively large, so Hannah estimates that there must be at least a couple more rooms on the ground floor, and perhaps one upstairs? But she can't see a staircase. Wants to turn on the light as she can't even tell if there is anyone in the room with her, but decides it's too risky: she doesn't want to alert the shooter to her presence. Slowly, and with shaky hands, she fumbles about along the cold furniture, her thoughts racing: who fired the shots, and who was hit? Who was here when Jørn and Viktor came in, and who is here now? Can anyone sense that she's here, and what are they planning to do? Hannah knows she should've stuck to the plan instead of going in. Now regrets having not at least called for help before entering. How dumb can you be? But it's too late now, she can't call anyone while inside the cabin, and she can't go back outside again. She suddenly catches sight of a staircase, but it leads downstairs, not up. Hannah hesitates, then walks towards it and takes a deep breath. Down into a fucking basement. What a cliché. The stairs are steep – with no handrail and a broken arm, Hannah struggles to keep her balance. On the last two steps, she loses her footing and slides down, a scream escaping her. She stumbles as she tries to push herself up from the dirty, cold stone floor. Finally gets to her feet, disorientated but ready to fight, ignoring the throbbing pain in her ankle.

Bang, bang.

'Help!'

Hannah spins round, looking for the source of the pounding and cries for help, and spots a little electric lantern. She grabs it, turns it on, and the yellow glow illuminates the basement. It is clearly used as some sort of storage depot, where boxes containing the world's supply of all things pickled and cured have been neatly piled up on the shelves.

Banging, and another yell. Hannah now sees a small door, made for someone the size of a dwarf, by the looks of it, and hurries over. It's padlocked.

'Jørn?'

'Yes, it's me. Hurry up and open the door, I'm injured, and Viktor...'

'What about Viktor?'

'Just open it.'

With the fear surging through her body, Hannah searches for anything she can use to smash open the padlock, can't see a single thing that might help until her eyes finally land on a long screwdriver. She jams it into the back of the padlock with all her might in an effort to break the hinge free.

'Hurry!'

The desperation in Jørn's voice only makes Hannah more stressed, and a layer of sweat begins to form on her forehead. She curses at the fact she can only use her left arm and can't get a proper grip.

'The lock is too strong.'

'Keep going. You have to open it before they come back!'

Hannah wants to ask who 'they' are, when a little screw falls out and loosens the hinge just enough for her to remove the padlock entirely with one final, powerful ram of the screwdriver into the gap between the hinge and the door. The little door flies open, outward, almost smacking her in the forehead.

Jørn throws himself out.

'Argh! I can't breathe...'

Hannah steps back, staring at Jørn in horror as he gasps for air, clutching hold of his thigh, which is soaking wet. Blood.

'Shit! Have you been shot?'

Hannah nods at the wound, which Jørn has managed to wrap a tight piece of cloth around. He sounds out of breath, exhausted.

'Yes, but I think the bullet went straight through ... And I've put pressure on it, so I think the bleeding has stopped. Viktor's is worse...'

'Where is he?'

Hannah stares at Jørn in fear. He points into the little black hole that he's just launched out of.

'In there.'

Hannah takes the deepest breath of her life, bends down, and turning on her phone's flashlight, crawls inside.

53

Ice cold and lifeless. The tears obscuring her vision, Hannah grabs Viktor's arm, which falls back to the cold, concrete floor, limp. She moves the bright light of the phone torch across his bloodied body, which someone – presumably Jørn – has tried to bind to the best of his ability. Jørn's shirt, now drenched in blood, has been tied around one of Viktor's shoulders, where he was shot, and it appears to have stopped most of the bleeding. Hannah feels a small glimmer of hope that there may still be a trace of life inside Viktor's body. She firmly smacks his cheek.

'Viktor. Hey, wake up!'

She puts her ear close to his mouth, holds two fingers against his neck in a desperate attempt to find a pulse – her own working overtime – while her brain frantically searches through its memory for any useful knowledge on resuscitation.

'Come on, come on!'

Why the hell has she never taken a first-aid course? Why does all her knowledge of chest compressions and mouth-to-mouth procedures come from terrible American medical dramas? And all that blood! She closes her eyes. The sight of the red liquid only increases the amount of sweat now dripping from her forehead, giving her the instinctive desire to black out. Of all the people a serious wound could want to be found by, Hannah would probably be the last. She looks back over her shoulder, out into the basement. Can't Jørn do something? With his military background, he must surely be an expert in first aid. Her voice breaks as she desperately shouts out for him through the hatch.

'Jørn, come back. You have to help me. We have to start CPR.'

No response. Hannah peers out of the door but can't see him anywhere. Where is he? She is just about to call out for him again, when she suddenly feels something. A weak, very weak, pulse. In a moment of euphoria, Hannah grabs hold of Viktor's arm, shakes it, and hits his cheek a few more times.

'Viktor, wake up. You're alive!'

And then a hand reaches through the door, a hand belonging to Jørn, holding a glass of water.

'Here. Give him this, he'll be dehydrated.'

Hannah looks at the water. How is this going to help a gunshot victim? Regardless, she gently lifts Viktor's head and brings the glass to his lips.

'Here, drink this.'

His eyes are still closed, but his mouth opens a fraction and accepts a few drops of water as Hannah slowly pours. A warmth spreads through Hannah. Viktor isn't dead. Together, she and Jørn manage to pull him out of the hole and back up the steep, basement staircase. With Hannah's broken arm and Jørn's injured leg, it is quite the feat, and Hannah can't remember any other time in her life that she has ever worked in that way with another person. They manage to get him onto a sofa and cover him with a blanket. It takes all of Hannah's strength to look at the wound, but it actually seems less gruesome and life-threatening than she initially thought. Hannah finds some hard liquor in the kitchen and gently cleans the wound, accompanied by the sounds of Viktor's howling. She finds something that looks like a clean kitchen towel and watches in admiration as Jørn bandages him up. Hannah suddenly becomes aware of her own breathing, as if she has held her breath since first entering the cabin. The adrenaline has kept her hyper-focused on Viktor, but now a shiver of fresh fear runs down her back. She grabs Jørn's arm.

'Are we sure there isn't anyone else in the house?'

Jørn turns to her, nods calmly.

'They left, after they locked us in.'

'Left, where? I was standing outside the whole time.'

'Out the back door, they escaped on skis.'

Hannah stares at him, thoughtfully.

'How do you know that if you were locked downstairs?'

'There were skis outside when we got here, and now they're gone. And the house isn't any bigger than what you can see, and they aren't in here.'

'What about upstairs?'

Jørn looks at her reassuringly. 'I've checked – no one's here. I also called the police when I came up to get the water. Now we just have to wait for help to come.'

Hannah shakes her head. Just sitting here and waiting about is the last thing she can do.

'You said "they" shot you. Who are they?'

'Ella and another woman.'

'Margrét?'

Jørn shakes his head. 'Another woman. Can't remember whether I've seen her before.'

Hannah starts to feel dizzy, has to sit down. Another woman whom Jørn has never seen before? It can't be Vigdis, then.

She looks at Jørn. 'Young? Old?'

Jørn shrugs. 'Sort of middle-aged.'

That doesn't help. Hannah gets up. Viktor, who has thus far been lying in a daze, listening to them silently, speaks:

'I recognised her.'

Hannah looks down at him, surprised.

'I don't know her name – I think she may have moved to town recently. But it's her, the one who's always at Bragginn. Always scowling. The woman with the dog.'

Fuck! It took precious minutes to convince Jørn to pursue the two fleeing women on the snowmobile, and as Hannah, unfortunately, can't drive it with just the one arm, she is forced to sit behind Jørn again, clinging on to his Gore-Tex back. It's not the chase Jørn opposed, but leaving someone with a serious injury alone on a sofa in such a remote cabin. Luckily, Viktor himself argued that they should chase after the women too, probably strongly motivated by the thought that Margrét's life could still be in danger. Maybe Hannah should've offered to go with him to the hospital, but it seemed pointless sending Jørn out alone, with his injured leg and little knowledge of Ella and the woman with the dog. The woman with the dog – who is she? And what is her relationship to Ella? Does she have anything to do with Thor and Gísli's murders? Hannah notices a trail of blood dripping from Jørn's leg, flying off into what feels like an eternal night, painting dots in the snow like a morbid *Hansel and Gretel*. She shivers. The cold cuts through her body, and somewhere behind her nervous, beating heart the fatigue lies in wait, desperate to take over. Fortunately for them, it is easy to follow the two cross-country ski tracks back into town. And a quarter of an hour later, they reach the end of the tracks, and the outskirts of town. The harbour opens out in front of them, cold and illuminated by the fishing boats and a line of small, closed workshops. Jørn turns off the engine. The harbour itself is clear of snow, and the cross-country ski tracks are quickly dissolving on the hard surface below. Hannah looks around. Where could they have gone? She turns to Jørn.

'What the hell could they be doing at the harbour in the middle of the night?'

'Maybe it's just a way to lead us astray? From here, they could've headed off in any direction.'

Jørn throws his arms out to emphasise the endless, untraceable options, as if to say they could have escaped by land, water or air. Despite the small airport only being a few kilometres away, that route is rather unlikely, and the thought of them making a run for it on the main road in this weather seems like it would've been excessively reckless. On the other hand, they are pursuing two people who shot both Jørn and Viktor, and may very well be responsible for a few other murders too. To Hannah, there are only two real options left: either they are hiding somewhere in town, or they are on their way out to sea. She jumps off the snowmobile.

'Damn it, if only we had the address for the woman with the dog.'

'Well, unfortunately, I don't think that'd be of much use to us anyway. I mean, if you had just shot two people, one of whom was the local officer, would you head back home, put your feet up and wait for the police? No, home is probably the last place we can expect to find either of them. Something all my years of research have taught me.'

Hannah reminds herself that they are allies now so she has to suppress the urge to poke her finger hard into the gaping wound on Jørn's leg, which she can see is causing him pain. She applauds him for being so consistent – even in an emergency, he manages to be as annoying as ever. But, to her great irritation, he's right. Hannah wants to lash out at the hopelessness of their impasse.

'So, what brilliant idea do you have for us now?'

'We can search the harbour. I mean, there's good reason to suspect that this is where they've come. There are plenty of sheds to hide in, for example.'

'Yeah, or boats.'

Hannah stares at the harbour, exasperated. It is crammed full of both large and small fishing boats, which look like they've all been brought back to shore to protect them from the bad weather. It'd take them hours to search the whole area. She looks at Jørn, who, in a great deal of pain, swings his injured leg over the snowmobile, the sight of which forces her to correct herself: in their pitiful state, it would take them days to inspect every snow-laden boat, not to mention how impractical it would be for the two of them, climbing aboard and somehow managing to make their way into each wheelhouse. That won't work.

'If only there were more of us.'

Jørn seems to have said it as a throw away comment, but Hannah latches on to the idea. That's it. If they can gather together enough of the townspeople, then they'd be able to search the area in no time. Not to mention that they will also be able to implement a town-wide emergency response, should anyone see the two women trying to leave.

'Great idea!' Hannah claps Jørn's shoulder. 'Go into town and wake up Leather Vest. He can get hold of a good group of people, and then we can start searching from one side of the harbour to the other. It won't take long if there's about fifteen to twenty of us.'

Jørn looks at her, sceptical. 'First of all: who is "Leather Vest"? Second of all: are you insane? We can't send a load of civilians out to play hide-and-seek with two armed murderers.'

'Tell people to bring their rifles and carving knives with them. And Leather Vest is the owner of Bragginn, he lives above the bar. Tell him I sent you.'

Jørn shakes his head. 'And what will you do in the meantime?'

'I'll start searching the smaller boats. We can't waste any more time.'

Hannah allows herself a moment to watch Jørn as he disappears into town on his snowmobile, before she turns back to face the fishing boats. She has to work systematically, and therefore chooses to start with a cutter in the middle of the harbour. From there, she'll work her way around. It is not without fear that she climbs on board the first boat, which rocks from side to side, making it difficult to hold on with just the one useful arm. The deck is coated with snow, and Hannah has to cling to the railing so as to not slide around even more than she already is. She wobbles toward the wheelhouse, while keeping an eye out for any footprints. She can't see anyone inside, but for safety's sake, she leans in through the window and peers down into the unlocked cargo room. Nothing. With difficulty, she struggles back to the dock. This is all too slow: if she stumbles about every boat like this, she'll never find a thing. She looks at the various craft, tries to spot signs of movement or at least a particular boat that someone might want to hide on. If there is even such a boat. It's a shot in the dark, she knows that, and maybe the whole thing is just a bit of a non-plan. Maybe she should just wait for Jørn to come back with their reinforcements. And what could she even do if she did find Ella and the woman with the dog? Persuade them to surrender? It hits her, with force, that the mission is, in fact, hopeless, but then she hears something. A woman's voice. She turns in its direction and thinks she can see a figure on a boat, docked in a poorly lit part of the harbour. She girds herself and moves toward it.

54

Hannah stops in front of the fishing boat where she believes she saw the small figure lurking. Was it definitely here? And what now? What if she actually finds what she's looking for? She shakes off the fear and climbs onto the boat. The wind pushes her back, and she has to hold the railing to keep her balance, gives herself a moment to re-orient herself. 'Fishing boat' is perhaps an understatement. It looks more like a modern trawler, albeit a small one, but nevertheless big enough to haul enormous quantities of fish ashore. And big enough to hide in. She looks towards the wheelhouse, which doesn't seem to contain anything suspicious, until she catches a glimpse of footprints in the snow. Or rather, tow tracks. As if someone has dragged a heavy sack along behind them – or a person. The tracks are covered with a light, fresh layer of snow, which is why Hannah didn't see them at first. Which also indicates that the tracks must be at least a few hours old, from before the snow stopped falling, anyway. She doubts for a moment whether this is the boat she saw movement on, but then sees fresh footprints too, careful steps along the very edge of the boat. Seemingly belonging to two people. Hannah slowly follows the prints, which – like the tow tracks – lead into the wheelhouse. She clutches the railing, hoping that all this will soon be over.

There is no time now for hesitation or deep breaths. Hannah violently flings open the door to the wheelhouse. Expects to be met with the worst, entering with all the courage she can muster, back straight, chest out. If she is going to die now, she can at least meet her fate with open eyes. But no, nothing. She looks around – it's empty and cold. Other than a mass of equipment, making the small command room look more like a cluttered cockpit, and two padded chairs bolted to the floor, the room is unoccupied. Hannah is surprised at how high-tech and comfortable it all looks, which contradicts her slightly romantic picture of a fishing boat with a little wooden oar. She is about to turn around when she hears a sound. A human sound. She strains her ears and turns towards one of the tall-backed chairs, which is facing away from her. Did it come from there? Cautiously, she approaches it, hears the sound again. There is no doubt in her mind that there is someone sitting there, waiting there for her. Keeping a safe distance, Hannah steps around the chair and to her surprise and relief, she is met with the sight of

Margrét – bound to the chair, but alive. Waking up from a period of unconsciousness.

Hannah bends down.

'Margrét! What happened to you?'

Hannah shakes her a little, checking her over for any injuries, but besides the blue marks on her skin from her bonds, she doesn't seem to be injured. With desperate eagerness, Hannah begins to loosen the rope binding Margrét's arms to the chair's armrests. It's all starting to feel like a surreal jumble of Hannah's most-hated clichés. As if she were in a really bad James Bond film, or even worse: one of Jørn's books. It proves harder than it looks to free Margrét, but all Hannah's yanking and pulling on the rope seems to bring the captive back to consciousness. Hannah looks into her eyes as she battles with the last knot.

'Who did this to you? Was it the woman with the dog? Or Ella?'

'It was Sigrun.'

Hannah frowns at Margrét, confused – was she hit on the head or something?

'Sigrun?'

'That's her name. The woman with the dog.'

Hannah nods as if she suddenly understands, but she doesn't. Although she has now identified the suspected murderer, and thus has a reasonable overview of everyone involved, she still has more questions than answers. Who is Sigrun? What was her motive for setting this chain of unfortunate events into action, why has she tied Margrét to a chair on a random boat, and most importantly: where is Ella, and what is her role in all of this?

'Where's Ella?'

Margrét turns to Hannah, a puzzled look on her face as if she, Hannah, should know that, and as if it was the exact question she, Margrét, was about to ask.

'I thought she was with you,' Hannah continues. 'That's why we've been searching all over town for you both, and why Viktor was shot and...'

Hannah stops herself. Notices Margrét turn as white as a ghost, and wants to smack herself for the crude way she's let slip that information.

'Viktor's okay, or, rather, he's alive. He will be okay.'

'Where is he?'

'At Ella's cabin, just outside of town ... I thought you knew...'

Stop. Again. Margrét looks groggy. And Hannah realises that Margrét doesn't know anything about any of this either.

'How long have you been tied up here?'

'I don't know ... A few hours maybe? But ... if Viktor is alone and injured up at some cabin, who's with the children?'

Hannah looks guiltily at Margrét, having forgotten all about the children.

'They're at home, asleep.'

'Alone?'

Hannah doesn't have to say another word. Margrét is already up and dashing towards the door, desperately pulls down on the handle, then turns in horror to Hannah.

'It's locked. Did you lock it?'

Hannah shakes her head, walks over and tries the door herself. It really is locked – could it be jammed? But as she looks up, through the little window, she sees someone on the other side: the woman with the dog, gazing at them with a disconcertingly cold smile. Hannah is so startled that she lets out a little scream.

'Sigrun! Let us out!'

Hannah hammers her fist on the glass, but Sigrun just watches her, pleasantly surprised, as if Hannah is unexpected prey that has managed to stray right into her trap – a trap set up for something else entirely. The indifference in her gaze terrifies Hannah, who again pounds her fist on the door, appealing to her to let them out. But then she catches sight of something that makes her gasp, and falls silent. In Sigrun's hand: a pistol. Hannah's clenched fist stops in mid-air, and with limp fingers her hand slides down to her side. Sigrun doesn't seem to have noticed Hannah's panic, or doesn't seem to care. She seeks out Margrét's eyes and says something in Icelandic. Hannah turns to Margrét.

'What did she say?'

'That you have to smash your phone.'

Hannah hesitates. Fuck. She looks at Sigrun again, who waves the gun in the air, encouragingly. Hannah fishes out her phone. Puts it on the table. Glances over at Sigrun, who shakes her head. Hannah pauses again – if she destroys her phone, she destroys their lifeline. Sigrun knocks on the glass with the mouth of the pistol. Margrét looks despondent at Hannah.

'I think ... unfortunately, you'll just have to do it.'

Hannah waits a few moments. And then brings the phone down hard on the edge of the steel table, over and over again until both the screen and its insides are dangling from the frame, now just small, unusable scraps of metal and plastic. She looks back at Sigrun.

'Happy?'

Sigrun says something in Icelandic through the window. Margrét looks around, searching for something.

'She said something about cable ties, that she wants us to tie our hands together with.'

They find the pack of simple plastic strips at the same time, and look at each other, at a loss for words. Margrét takes the ties, goes over to the window, and gets as close to Sigrun as she can. Holds the cable ties up and submits a question in Icelandic. Sigrun nods, responds. Margrét turns to Hannah.

'Come here, turn around.'

Hannah wavers – what is going on here?

'We have to, or she won't open the door.'

'Sorry, but have you seen this brick on my arm? I can't just force it round my back.'

Hannah holds her plaster cast demonstratively in the air. Margrét sighs, clearly having forgotten about it entirely. She grabs Hannah's hands and brings them together in front of her. Hannah has never felt as powerless as she does when allowing Margrét to tie the plastic strips around her wrists.

'Ow, Christ!' Hannah twists away. 'Do you have to tighten them that much?'

'Sorry, I can't do anything about it now.'

Hannah's broken arm is bent into an unnatural position, like some contorted Barbie doll. Her wrists are burning already, and she doubts that any blood is actually making it to her hands.

'Now you do me.'

Margrét turns her back to Hannah, already holding her hands behind her, making it easier for Hannah to get the job done. An absurd picture pops into Hannah's head, an inappropriate vision of an entirely different situation in which this act could be happening between them. Sigrun knocks on the window, again using the gun, and the seriousness of the situation removes the intrusive thought immediately.

'Step back.'

A moment later, Sigrun has opened the door and ushered them out of the wheelhouse. Beside her, of course, the drooling dog, which now looks even more ferocious than Hannah remembers. Is it even the same dog? With the pistol aimed at their backs, they are ordered across the deck, and Hannah is hit with a fresh surge of fear as she looks down into the sloshing, icy water surrounding the boat. Is Sigrun going to make them walk the plank? A montage suddenly starts playing in Hannah's head: images of her desperate attempts to survive in the arctic water, splashing around, trying to stay afloat. She was a bad enough swimmer with two functioning arms. If she does end up in there, it'll be certain death. Sigrun does not direct them over to the edge of the dark, wet, icy depths, however. She instead leads them down to the cargo hold. Hannah stops. This is almost worse: locked into a dark, freezing fish tank only equates to a slightly slower, smellier, cold death. She tries to resist by demonstrably digging her feet into the snow, but the sensation of the pistol against her temple activates her survival instincts.

'Niður.'

Hannah understands the command. They don't have a choice. She stares down into the dark tank. The smell of fish makes her nauseous. How far down is it? Two metres, seven? Regardless, and no matter how you look at it, if she jumps down, the risk of either breaking both her legs, or dying upon landing, is quite high.

'No, I'm not doing that, it's far too ... Argh!'

Hannah isn't allowed to finish her sentence before Sigrun, with a resolute shove in her back, pushes her over the edge. It feels like an eternity passes before Hannah lands at the bottom, performing a kind of drop and roll. She's able to protect her head by holding her hands up in front of her, but it costs her a painful blow to the already hard-done-by plaster-cast arm. Hannah barely lets out a pained groan, before she looks up into the weak light above to see another figure flying down towards her. Margrét. Hannah throws herself away from the landing area and just manages to catch sight of Margrét reaching the bottom, landing perfectly on two, standing legs. How the hell has she managed that with both hands tied behind her back? Before the hatch door is fully closed, and the already minimal light disappears entirely, Hannah has enough time to estimate the distance between the top of Margrét's head and the roof – judging from her height, and the space above her, the room must be about two metres high. The hatch shuts, and it becomes completely, utterly dark.

55

Light. From a torch. Hannah shields her face from the unexpected and violently bright beam that feels as if it is shining right through her head.

'Ella!'

It is Margrét who first realises who is sitting there with the little handheld torch, shaking in the corner of the room, which Hannah now sees has a thin layer of viscous slime on the walls, but luckily, doesn't appear to contain a single fish. They both rush towards Ella, who looks cold and confused.

'How long have you been down here?'

Hannah feels dumb asking, as she already knows the answer: Ella fled the cabin with Sigrun, so she can't have been down here for more than the twenty to thirty minutes Hannah spent dawdling about on the harbour. But it seems as if she is suffering from hypothermia already. She looks up at them.

'*Ég reyndi að stoppa hana en gat ekki.*'

Hannah turns desperately to Margrét.

'What did she say?'

'Ella is not the villain in all this.'

Hannah sees the genuine concern in Margrét's gaze as she looks at Ella. Ella looks ready to give up entirely, after a long life of turmoil. What is it that Margrét seems to know, but Hannah doesn't? Before she can ask, Margrét says something in Icelandic and turns her back, and thus her bound hands, to Ella. She wants her to help free them. Hannah becomes aware of the pain in her own arms and hands, which she can hardly feel now as a result of the pressure from the cable ties. Ella looks apologetically at them – she clearly doesn't have any tools she can use to help break them free. Margrét says something else to Ella, which Hannah interprets as a request for her to use the light to look around, as that is exactly what Ella does. The beam searches the cargo hold as Margrét keenly follows it with her eye.

'There!'

Hannah doesn't get a chance to see what Margrét has pointed to, but she still follows her and the light source into a corner, where she finds a nail sticking out from the wall.

'We can file them down here. You first.'

Hannah has no desire to rub her arteries up and down against a sharp nail, but she knows it's the only option. She carefully tries to catch the nail in a grinding motion over the strip of plastic, very aware that one wrong move could slice open her wrist. With beads of sweat running from her forehead, she prays to some unknown, higher power that that doesn't happen, that this won't cost her her life. Pop! The cable tie springs apart, and Hannah's hands are finally free. She barely has time to acknowledge just how much they ache, before Margrét turns her back in an appeal for Hannah to do the same for her. It is even worse knowing that you're risking another person's life than it is your own, and it is with her heart in her mouth that Hannah does her best to free Margrét's hands without accidentally killing her. Luckily, it is easier with two operational hands, and after a half a minute's nervous grinding, Margrét is also freed from the restrictive plastic strips. So far, so good. They return to Ella, who has helpfully held the flashlight up for them as they worked. Now, they need an explanation for all this. But, before they can say anything, they hear the loud, grinding sound of the engine, close by, in the adjoining room, and the side of the boat now scraping against the harbour, as it moves away from land in a violent rocking motion, out towards the open sea.

'No. We have to get out!'

Hannah jumps desperately up towards the hatch. Throughout all of this, she has had it in the back of her mind that Jørn will be on the way soon with reinforcements from town, but if they sail out to sea, then there's no one to help them. Hannah screams, jumps up and down, hammering on the hatch, but it's locked from above – impossible to open. The hopelessness of the situation hits her like a lead bullet to the temple. She only just manages to sit down to stop herself from fainting. She is dizzy, overwhelmed with powerlessness and despair. Is this how her life is going to end? Is this all it comes to? A few half-decent books, a failed crime-writing project and a lonely death in a fishing vessel, somewhere out in the North Atlantic? Hannah feels ready to let go, drown in self-pity, when she looks up to see two worried faces looking at her in the weak glow of the flashlight.

'Don't worry. It'll be okay.'

A hand brushes over her forehead.

'Here, take this.'

A coat is wrapped around her.

'Deep breaths.'

They pull the air deep into their lungs, to encourage her to do the same. Hannah slowly inhales the cold, fishy air, closes her eyes, and breathes in time with the two women in front of her. A calm settles over her, and she feels two, soothing hands on her shoulders. Hannah opens her eyes and disappears into Margrét's caring gaze. On the other side of her: Ella, equally concerned. Slowly, a new thought starts to form in Hannah's mind. She isn't alone. She isn't lonely. Her life is not indifferent to that of other people. She is something, she is someone. Not because of her books, but because of this – all that she has been involved in since coming here, to Iceland. She has been a friend and a love interest. She has gone out of her way to help someone else. She has been genuinely worried about them, and here she is now. Her own life on the line to try and save other people's. Just before all this boils over into sentimental self-importance, Hannah composes herself. She has read enough of Jørn's ghastly books to know that it is in precisely this kind of situation that you mustn't just give up. It's all a matter of having a plan. She looks at Ella and Margrét, resolute. Straightens her back.

'At some point, she will have to open the hatch, and we have to be ready.'

It is a surprise, even to Hannah herself, that she's strategic enough to plot a counter-attack against Sigrun. Nevertheless, it is crystal clear to her what they must do when their captor opens the hatch. She shares her plan with Margrét and Ella, and they nod and agree without objection. Enlivened by the fact that there is something they can do, and fired up at the prospect of launching their offensive as soon as Sigrun comes back, the three woman get into position and wait for their chance. But it doesn't come immediately. Or for a while either. In fact, the minutes pass by – so many of them that they lose track. But all they can do is sit there, rocking from side to side and becoming more and more seasick. Margrét turns to face Hannah.

'What if she never opens it? What if she just intends to sail into the middle of nowhere, shoot herself and let us drive around until we die?'

'Then we'll at least be found by a coastguard.'

'But that could take a really long time. And it might be tomorrow before anyone even realises a boat is missing. And by that time we could've been driven to who knows where ... Or into a tanker or a whale ... Or suffocate.'

'Or freeze to death.'

Margrét stares at Hannah.

'We can't just sit here forever and die of hypothermia. Maybe we should huddle together a bit?'

Hannah nods, and Margrét moves from her hiding spot to settle down between Ella and Hannah. Hannah immediately feels the warmth from her body, and it soothes her in more than one way. If she is going to die in this fish tank with Margrét, it may not be the worst fate she could have imagined for herself. One thing is certain, however: she can't die without knowing why Sigrun has done what she's done, and how Ella is involved. If it is all going to end here, then she has to ask. Hannah is aware that she could be heading into a dangerous situation, but she needs answers.

'Why did Sigrun kill Thor, and what was your role in it?'

Hannah leans forward slightly, over Margrét, to talk to Ella, in an effort to make sure that Ella hears and understands the question. Ella looks directly at her but doesn't respond. Hannah tries again.

'Who is Sigrun?'

A few seconds more, but still nothing. Hannah is impatient, raises her voice.

'I know you understand what I'm saying, and to be frank, I think you owe me an explanation. I've been subjected to a drive-by-shooting, assault and a murder attempt as a result of my living with you, and I've stayed throughout it all, so I refuse to die without knowing how and why this chaos came about.'

Hannah has warmed up a little purely as a result of her agitation. She sees a tear roll down Ella's cheek, but still hears no words. A hand gently pushes Hannah back. Margrét's.

'Sigrun is Ella's daughter. And ... Ægir is the father.'

Hannah stares at Ella. What?

'But how...?'

Margrét turns to Ella, as if to ask if she has permission to tell her story. Ella remains silent. Margrét clearly interprets the silence as a yes. She turns back to Hannah.

'All of this goes back to the time when...'

Kniiiirk! Margrét stops talking. It's the hatch opening. The three women all look at each other: now! They silently crawl to their own corners of the fish tank. Huddled into hers, Hannah waits, her pulse rushing through her ears as she waits for Sigrun to fall into their trap. Jump down to them, so they can overpower her. But she doesn't come down. The hatch is open, but no Sigrun. Hannah had believed that if they hid away in the corners, Sigrun – thinking she had the advantage and believing Hannah and Margrét still had their hands bound – would have the confidence to come down, to see where they are. But the minutes pass, the hatch remains open, and absolutely nothing happens. Hannah suddenly feels a hand on her arm. She jumps with fright, but it's only Margrét, who whispers, almost inaudibly.

'Shall we climb up?'

Hannah shakes her head. It must be a trap. They wait a few minutes more, their eyes firmly fixed on their freedom, the square of light from the harbour, streaming down through the opening above, until Sigrun suddenly pokes her head over the edge and says something in Icelandic. Hannah feels Margrét's grip on her arm tighten in fear.

Hannah turns to her, whispers: 'What did she say?'

Margrét's fingers dig into Hannah's healthy arm. Hannah wants to yell out, but doesn't.

'That we can either go up there, or die down here. She is planning on sinking the ship, and said we can either die on deck, or in this tank.'

Before Hannah is able to fully digest the information, Ella has appeared beneath the hatch, signalling for one of them to give her a hand getting up. As Hannah can't lift anyone up with her plaster-cast arm, it is Margrét who steps out, and before Hannah can protest, lifts Ella to her death on deck.

'What are you doing? It's a trap!'

'We don't know that. And anyway, I'd rather take the chance than die in a freezing, dark fish container. Shall I help you up?'

Hannah hesitates, but she really has no other choice. Once Margrét disappears up through the hatch, she can't do anything. She positions herself below the light.

'This is insane.'

Margrét doesn't respond, just lifts Hannah high enough off the floor for her to clamber out of the hole. Hannah turns back and reaches down with her functioning arm to help Margrét up, but Sigrun suddenly slams the hatch door down on her nose.

'She can stay down there. It's you I need.'

56

Never has Hannah felt such a bitingly cold wind. She stands on the deck of the trawler as the black waves pummel its sides, moving up and down in the ice-cold nothingness; if she wasn't standing face to face with death, she'd have passed out from sea sickness. The pistol, now pointing directly at her, means her survival instinct overpowers all her other senses: physical and emotional. Hannah looks around. Where is Ella ... Has Sigrun already thrown her overboard?

'Ella?'

Sigrun just stares at her. 'You tell my story. And then I might let you live.'

'I tell your story?'

'The world needs to know what people have done to me. What happens when you hurt someone. When I saw you, I knew the time had come. You are the outside voice I have been waiting for – who can tell people about the atrocities that have been committed here. That's why I had to kill Thor.'

Hannah stiffens. Breaks out in a cold sweat. Kill Thor? Is she the reason he's dead? Again, she casts a glance around, looking for Ella. Where is she? Alone, with a broken arm and no weapon, Hannah can't do anything other than indulge Sigrun. But curiosity doesn't drive her questions now. Hannah no longer wants to hear anything else. Just wants to survive, go home. So she has to force herself to assume her most friendly and welcoming tone.

'Why don't you start from the beginning? What story do you want me to tell?'

Sigrun seems relieved at Hannah's willingness. She gestures with the gun, pointing towards the wheelhouse. Hannah cautiously steps inside, doubts screaming at her as she does so. Is this a good idea? To allow herself to be lured into a small room with an armed murderer? Either way, that's what she does, and to her great concern, finds that Ella isn't waiting for them in there either. Has she been pushed into the waves, to her death?

'Have a seat.' Sigrun casually waves the gun towards one of the stools as she sits down in the other. 'Do you want to write this down?'

Hannah smiles nervously at the absurdity of the question. As if she were a journalist interviewing Sigrun for some women's magazine. To buy some time, Hannah picks up the notepad and pen lying on the table – probably placed there by Sigrun for this very purpose. She has clearly planned all this out. Hannah plays along.

'Go on.'

It's like Sigrun's shoulders deflate, as if 'go on' were the magic words that take the burden away.

'It all started when Ella was thirteen years old, and Ægir raped her. And she became pregnant with me.'

Hannah gulps, gapes at the woman in front of her.

'I'm sorry, what?'

With her untrained left hand, Hannah struggles to scribble down the childlike letters that she tries to make look like some sort of legible text, but it's mainly just pro-forma note-taking. She doesn't need to write this down to remember it.

'So Ella is your mother and Ægir your father?'

Sigrun nods.

'And Thor was my brother. Ægir and Vigdis got engaged a few years after, but Vigdis didn't know anything, she just thought Ella had gone away for a year to study somewhere, and that she treated Ægir so badly because she was envious of them.'

A thousand questions start popping into Hannah's head. Fratricide was the last thing she had expected – but why?

'Why did you kill Thor?'

Sigrun shakes her head. 'No, from the beginning, like we agreed.'

Hannah nods. As long as Sigrun continues to talk, no one dies.

'Ella was sent away to live with some relatives in a small town up north. Things were bad enough for her here, but they were even worse up there: aside from having to live with the trauma of being raped and having to carry a life-threatening pregnancy to term, one her body was not at all prepared for, not to mention the fact that the birth itself almost killed her, she was also humiliated and degraded by everyone; the adults and the other children at school. It has been intolerable for her.'

'How do you know all this – you weren't even born?'

'The way she has been spoken about my entire life. A horny little child, good for nothing. Likely so I wouldn't try and reach out to her. But as an adult, of course, I came to realise that none of it was Ella's fault.'

'But you're sure that it was rape. That Ella didn't...?'

'Want it...?'

A perilous wrath clouds Sigrun's face. Hannah's mild scepticism is obviously just fuel on an already blazing fire.

'It was a brutal rape. I can tell you about it in detail, but I'd honestly rather not have to repeat it. In fact, it was against my will that Ella informed me of the precise circumstances, when I did eventually track her down. But it turned out that she needed to talk about it, when someone finally asked. It was the first time she had ever spoken about it.'

Sigrun sighs. Reliving Ella's confession, Hannah imagines. Sigrun looks at her.

'I believed the story about her for years. That it was her own fault, that she'd brought me into this world through guilt and shame, and that was why it was right to treat me as they did. For years, I loathed her.'

'Who raised you?'

'My foster parents. Distant relatives who already had five children of their own. I was the one they could beat and kick, because I was the child of a whore, of course. And when I became a teenager, all the young men in the town thought I'd be just like my mother...'

Sigrun stares out into the dark ocean waves, and it occurs to Hannah that no one is steering the boat. Is it anchored? She can't feel the difference. Hannah should probably be pursuing the path Sigrun is taking her down, but somehow, she already knows where it ends. And yet she craves more knowledge of Ella.

'If you were so concerned about Ella, why did you kill the person she loves most in the world? And use her own hammer to do it?'

Sigrun looks at her bitterly.

'I was the one who should have had the love she gave to Thor. The hammer was symbolic.'

'So you killed him out of jealousy?'

Sigrun shakes her head.

'I didn't do it to hurt Ella, but to get revenge on Ægir. He is responsible for both my and Ella's misfortune, and yet he is the only one to never face the consequences of what he did. On the contrary, he has a good life: managed to snatch up all the fishing quotas, built the town's biggest house, positioned himself as a man whom everyone looks up to. People like him do not get punished in this world. This world punishes his victims.'

Hannah tries to stick to reason, because even though there may be a certain rationale to Sigrun's story, it does not justify her actions.

'But if you wanted the truth to come out, you could have just said something, or Ella could have come forward about it. This needn't have cost lives.'

'I've been trying both options for years. The former is more difficult – Ella didn't want to relive it all by going through it in public, and without Ella to back me up, I'm just some crazy woman trying to disturb the peace. No one wins if they listen to me. And that's why I was so happy when you came into the picture. I saw the chance to finally tell my story.'

Hannah stares at her.

'Through ... me?'

Sigrun nods.

'It was you who shot at the house ... to try and get my attention?'

Sigrun smiles, but only with her mouth. Her eyes look dead.

'You're smart.'

'But why didn't you just come and share your story with me in the first place?'

'I've been trying to do that my entire life, and so this time, I wanted to do something that couldn't be ignored.'

'Murder?'

'Murder.'

Sigrun smiles in a way that sends chills down Hannah's spine.

'Nobody wants to listen to a victim, but murderers get plenty of airtime. And these days, you really have to kick up a fuss to get through to anyone. So this is my way of getting my voice heard. Not just in Iceland or Denmark, but around the world.'

'But...' Hannah looks at her quizzically. 'If you wanted to attract all that attention, as a killer of not one but two people, why did you stage Gísli's death to make it look like suicide?'

Sigrun sends her a cold smile.

'Plot twist. And anyway, he was causing too much confusion with the way he was behaving. He was overshadowing me.'

'So you hit Gísli with the bottle that night you killed Thor?'

Sigrun shrugs.

'He came down to the beach, drunk out of his mind, and I was worried he would get in the way of my plan.'

'So you beat him unconscious, and he woke up just in time to see Ægir pulling Thor out of the water?'

Sigrun smiles. 'Very sharp.'

Hannah looks at her, fearful. If she had any doubts before, she has no doubt now that Sigrun is willing to do anything to get her message out. And it'll take more than Thor and Gísli's deaths to achieve that – it requires an even greater tragedy. One that involves numerous murders. For example, four women on a boat. She clings on to reason still.

'If I die then your story will never be told.'

Sigrun smiles again.

'That's why you'll be the only one on this boat to survive the night.'

57

Never in her life has Hannah been in a greater dilemma: should she indulge Sigrun and save her own life, resulting in the death of Ella and Margrét, or should she risk her own life to stop Sigrun? She glances at the gun balancing on Sigrun's lap, the trigger hand resting eerily calm on top. The odds are against her: no weapon, a broken arm, and in inherent fear of making a decision that could mean someone else's life or death. Sigrun, on the other hand, has already demonstrated that she won't hesitate to take someone's life, and although she needs Hannah to tell her story, Hannah still isn't convinced that she will actually spare her if a critical situation were to arise. That's it. Hannah must avert a critical situation. As long as she can maintain control, no one dies. And maybe someone will come to their rescue in the meantime. Maybe there's already a helicopter on the way...

'I want to help you.'

Hannah leans towards Sigrun slightly, not threateningly, but to create some intimacy.

She can't tell if it works, but Sigrun does look at her with a certain interest.

'You'll tell my story then?'

Hannah nods.

'What Ægir did is unforgivable. It's one thing to have raped Ella, the pregnancy, the denial ... everything that led to your and Ella's troubles. But it's what he hasn't done ... He hasn't helped either you or Ella. He could have stood by his actions, taken responsibility for the shame and your suffering. And I agree with you: he must face the consequences of what he has done to you. But you know, if you think about it, you have technically already got your revenge. Thor is dead, and I'll tell the world about what happened here. There needn't be any more tragedy coming out of all this – this is no reason to take the lives of two other innocent people, and you don't have to kill yourself either.'

A small smile glides over Sigrun's lips, and then disappears, like a cloud drifting across the sky.

'No one will cry for me.'

'Ella will. And now I know your story, I will.'

'Ella's life will also end here. I know I've caused her pain, so it's better if I just put an end to her suffering.'

'That is not your choice to make. Who says she won't have several good years left to live, to enjoy?'

Sigrun sits there, staring at the pistol. She looks resolute, like a woman who has made her decision. Hannah feels a bead of sweat slide from her forehead to her ear – how long does she have until the bloodbath begins? She wishes she'd watched a few more crime dramas, or maybe read a few more of Jørn's books, so she would know how to talk a murderer down from the edge, from killing again. She is used to observing people and imagining what it is they are hiding, what their secrets are, what they desire, but she is less experienced in actually talking to people about them. And she already knows what Sigrun's secrets and desires are. The way of reason seems impossible, but Hannah gives it one last shot.

'Margrét. There's no reason to take her down with you. She hasn't done anything.'

'Exactly.'

Sigrun's eyes darken.

'Margrét has known about Ella's story for years, and yet she's kept it secret just like all the others.'

'Maybe Ella didn't want it to get out. If you ask me, it seems that despite everything that happened to her, all the injustice, Ella has managed to make a good life for herself. Maybe that was her way of surviving?'

Hannah reflects on the lively, positive Ella she has come to know. The Ella who picked her up at the airport in her spluttering Jeep, eager to invite a stranger into her life, and feels an awful wave of guilt wash over her, at the thought of having not been more gracious to her host from the start. Ella had decided to make a good life for herself, despite all the evil that had happened to her, and if she could move on from that then, she can certainly do the same now, after all that's happened here. Ella's life – and Margrét's; and her own for that matter – cannot end here. Again, Hannah listens to the whistling of the wind, but there is no helicopter on the way, no lights from other approaching boats. The chance that Jørn and the rest of the town have any idea that they are currently on a boat, miles out in the ocean, is practically zero. If the four woman are going to survive, it's up to her.

'I understand. You feel like your life is meaningless. You probably think you don't have anything to live for, and recent events have dragged you even further into that black hole in which you were born and which you have never been able to climb out of. But that is not the case. You are always capable of change, you can always find new hope in your life. I know that from my own life.'

Sigrun looks at her.

'Have you ever had to pull yourself out of a life spent in lonely misery, and find a way to move on from having murdered and assaulted several people?'

Touché. It feels embarrassing to compare her poor book sales, omnivorous envy and self-imposed bitterness with Sigrun's miserable situation. Yet, there is something in this self-realisation that fills her with the genuine belief that Sigrun's life is worth fighting for.

'I'll admit it, you won't be able to avoid prison time. And you'll have Thor and Gísli's lives forever on your conscience. But that doesn't mean that it all has to end here. Think about it: if you live, you can tell your own story. I'd help you with that, but wouldn't it be more satisfying to be able to control the narrative? Think of all the murderers who have become superstars. You'll serve your sentence, maybe write a book in prison, it'll do well, then you'll sell the film rights, get out for good behaviour after a few years, spend a bit longer under house arrest, receive fan mail from all over the world, from people who sympathise with your story. Politicians will change the law on rape, a nice, sweet man will write to you—'

'Bullshit,' Sigrun interrupts. And Hannah realises that she's right. She is romanticising Sigrun's future life as a convicted murderess. What the hell is she doing?

'Okay, I let myself get carried away a bit, but think it through: is death really the best way out?'

Sigrun looks out into the night again, seems to sincerely contemplate Hannah's question. But then she turns back and picks up the gun, a renewed hopelessness in her eyes.

'Revenge is inescapable. Maybe it won't come in the form you think it will. Maybe not from the direction you're expecting. But if you do others wrong, if you destroy their lives, then there's a price to pay. For Ægir, it was losing his son, just like I lost my mother. I know what you're trying to do, but I've made my decision. And now, this ends.'

Sigrun loads the gun, stands up and walks toward the open wheelhouse door and to the final moments of her own, Ella's and Margrét's lives. Hannah jumps up, grabs hold of her.

'Stop! Don't do it, I'm begging you, please.'

Sigrun looks directly into her eyes. A dark, dark gaze.

'Promise me you'll tell my story or I'll kill you too.'

'If you kill anyone, including yourself, I won't tell anyone so much as a single word about you and your life! Then all your secrets will die with you, Ella and Margrét.'

Sigrun hesitates. Hannah feels a rush of relief; this is the key to stopping her. But then Sigrun smiles that dead smile at her.

'The police will reveal the general gist of what's happened anyway. And the rest I don't think you'll be able to keep to yourself, when Ægir starts defending himself. Then you'll make sure that the truth of his crimes, and their consequences, comes out.'

'You don't think I'll be able to keep it to myself?'

Sigrun shakes her head.

'No. Because then your colleague, that moron, Jørn or whatever he's called, will end up copyrighting the story, and I don't think you'd want to give him that.'

Hannah feels completely and utterly at a loss. Perhaps it's the fact that Jørn was mentioned, or the frustration of being manipulated and so seen, or it's the fear of dying, or perhaps it's the combination of all three. Regardless, an unknown force erupts inside Hannah – she feels the blood and adrenaline coursing through her body, raising her to new levels of bravery. With a roar, she throws herself at Sigrun and the loaded gun – This ends now! *Bang*. Hannah topples over, feels her back, her functioning arm, and then her head slam against the floor. Something warm drips down from the top of her head, she raises her hand to feel it and looks at her fingers: blood. The wound from the handle of the gun, which Sigrun has used to hit her, seems superficial, and although Hannah feels groggy, she is quickly back on her feet. But Sigrun has gone, the door bangs shut behind her. Fuck, she must be set on executing the others now. Hannah crashes after her, as quickly as her bruised body and poor balance allow. The deck is black, smooth and slippery from the rain that has replaced the snow. She can't see a thing – has Sigrun gone to slaughter Margrét or Ella first? Given that Hannah has no idea where on the boat Ella even is, if she is still on the boat, Hannah rushes towards the hatch, opens it and jumps down.

Margrét shines the flashlight on her.

'Hannah!'

Hannah desperately looks around.

'She's not here?'

'No, but I heard someone running towards the stern a few seconds ago.'

'Quick. She's going to shoot Ella, and then you.'

Hannah doesn't know how Margrét succeeds in getting them both up on the deck, but seconds later they are standing there in the rain, and half run, half slide towards the back of the boat, where the fishing net and work equipment decrease their visibility and increase the number of potential hiding spots. Hannah and Margrét look at each other, mirroring the other's desperation. Hannah doesn't dare shout for Ella for fear of revealing their whereabouts. She waves for Margrét to come closer – this is something they have to do together. Slowly, they examine the rocking boat's stern. Knowing full well that they are living targets, they start to move. They don't even think about trying to hide themselves now – they just walk forward, backs straight, hearts first. Until suddenly – they hear a shot, and a scream. Without so much as looking at each other, they scramble in the direction of the sound. Before them: Ella, her back against the railing, and Sigrun, aiming the gun directly at her. It looks like the first shot missed. Probably because of the rocking waves below. Or maybe because it's harder to shoot her own mother than Sigrun thought. Ella sees them and releases a little scream that makes Sigrun turn and point the gun at them instead. Hannah wants to walk towards her but is paralysed by a hitherto unprecedented level of fear, which cements her feet to the wet, swaying deck. She closes her eyes. It's over. Even in that decisive moment, she can't make her body comply, not even to move out of the path of a deadly bullet. But then ... Hannah senses a sudden tumult, opens her eyes, and sees that Margrét has hurled herself at Sigrun; both of them are now lying on the deck in a determined battle for the pistol. Ella throws herself into the tussle too, and the glue sticking the soles of Hannah's feet to the surface finally gives way and, reconnecting with her body, she throws herself, with a yell and the hard plaster cast, into the fight. It wasn't her intention to use the cast as a kind of bat, but in a bizarre turn of events, Hannah manages to knock Sigrun out as she falls, resulting in an unsightly and cluttered scuffle on the wet deck of the fish trawler. Margrét tugs the gun out of the murderous hands, while Ella holds down Sigrun's legs. With a powerful, shot-put throw over the railings, Margrét hurls the pistol into the greedy sea, which devours the danger and the proof of how close the night was to ending all four of their lives. Hannah looks at Margrét, then at Ella, and finally at Sigrun, who is on her back, dazed and helpless beneath them. And then, tears of relief escape Hannah's eyes. They survived. It's finally over.

58

Hannah watches in awe as Ella steers the trawler back towards land. If only she could drive a car as well as she pilots a boat. They found a couple of old blankets tucked away in a box, which they have wrapped around themselves to protect their already cold, wet bodies from getting any colder. Ella looks at Margrét, who is sitting next to Hannah, both of them sitting behind her at the helm. Ella then casts a glance back towards the corner of the little wheelhouse, where Sigrun is curled up under a blanket, with her hands bound behind her back, which seems almost pointless now, given how apathetic she looks, staring into space, far from any hint of rebellion. Hannah watches Ella.

'There's one last thing I can't quite get my head around.'

Ella looks at her, but not with an expression that invites questions. Hannah asks anyway.

'That night ... when you picked up Thor in your car ... you had his necklace in your drawer. Why?'

Ella moves her gaze to the sea, to the lights of the approaching harbour. Doesn't look like someone who is planning on answering. After a few moments of silence, Hannah tries again – she looks from Ella, then back to Sigrun. Trying to find any resemblance between the two women, but she can't see it. Are they really mother and daughter?

'You bumped into him randomly, and offered him a lift home?'

Ella still doesn't respond. Hannah knows she should leave it be, stop asking, let the authorities tie together the last few loose threads, place the blame, if Sigrun doesn't end up having it all put on her. But Hannah can't cope with the idea of never knowing exactly what happened that night, and certainly not if it turns out that Ella was actually involved in any way.

'I have to know if you had something to do with Thor's death.'

Ella looks directly into Hannah's eyes, piercing them with her icy gaze. Says something in Icelandic – not to her, but to Margrét. Margrét nods sombrely. Turns to Hannah.

'Ella knew what Sigrun was planning. Or she suspected it, anyway. Not long before you arrived, Sigrun had gone to visit Ella, told her the time for revenge had come. And that it would happen where it was least expected, where it would hurt the most. Ella had a feeling that maybe it was Thor who was in danger. Which is why she kept an extra-close eye on him. And it wasn't entirely by chance that she picked him up that night. He had called her, was beside himself. Wouldn't say why, but Ella rushed down there to drive him home. The necklace had broken during the argument with Jonni, and Thor forgot to take it with him when he got out of the car, and then he died ... So, she saved it, kept it to herself.'

Some of it makes sense, but Hannah still can't quite piece it all together.

'If Ella drove Thor home that night, how did he end up down at the beach?'

Ella and Margrét exchange a look, as if Margrét is asking for permission to disclose the rest of the story. Ella nods, and Margrét continues.

'That's what has been troubling Ella so much. If only she had taken him home that night, he might still be alive. But he insisted on getting out halfway, said he'd walk the last bit home. Said he was upset and needed some time alone. She was reluctant, but Ella did as he asked. She called Vigdis and Ægir and let them know he was coming back, which is why Ægir then went out looking for him. But she feels like she led Thor to...'

Margrét looks over at Sigrun, who seems to be showing no trace of remorse.

Hannah finishes Margrét's sentence. 'To his murder.'

Margrét nods.

'Sigrun even stole the hammer from Ella, so the murder weapon would be meaningful, symbolic.'

Hannah notices that tears are now streaming down Ella's cheeks. She decides not to dig any deeper, suddenly understands Ella's guilt. But why didn't she just report Sigrun if she knew that she was the murderer? She directs the question at Margrét, who apparently knows all the details.

'She didn't know for sure until a few days ago. She came to the house to try and tell Viktor, but having disclosed it all to me first, she got cold feet. I tried to persuade her to tell him everything too, which is how I got involved.'

Hannah watches Margrét, who also seems to be burdened with guilt, but neither she nor Ella are responsible for what happened. That responsibility lies with Sigrun, and, maybe more indirectly, someone else almost completely removed from all this, who has never been held responsible for anything: Ægir. Hannah raises her gaze to watch as they glide through the channel into the harbour, and hears shouting, can see the townsfolk waving their arms, surrounded by flashing blue lights and two people in uniform – presumably the reinforcements from the next town over. Hannah rests a hand on Margrét, who now looks even more subdued than the murderer sitting behind them. Her gaze is also directed towards the two uniformed officers.

'Viktor will be okay, I'm sure he will.'

Margrét nods, pulls her hand away. A little lurch indicates that they have reached land, and Hannah watches as several of the town's astute fishermen jump onboard to ensure the boat is moored properly. She helps Sigrun to her feet and exchanges one last look with Ella.

'Well done.'

Ella nods, and all four of them walk onto the deck, out into the lights of the harbour and the town's curious expressions. Suddenly, someone starts to clap. Hannah realises that it's coming from Jørn, who is standing right at the front. Just as the inclination to be annoyed at him begins to rise, the rest of the crowd gathered down on the shore begin to clap too. The four women stop dead, looking out over them all – all the people who have come here to help them, in the snow – as they clap, seeming both happy and relieved at the fact they have returned alive. Hannah swallows the lump in her throat. She will not cry again, but the hairs on her arms stand on end. They two uniformed officers leap onboard, exchange a few words with Margrét, who points at Sigrun. The officers grab the now-exposed criminal, but she has long since abandoned any attempt at making an escape. Ella and Margrét are then helped from the boat. Awaiting her turn, Hannah catches sight of Ægir and Vigdis in the crowd. She shakes her head at the well-meaning man wanting to help her off the boat, and instead takes a few steps forward, so that everyone can see her. She looks over at Sigrun, who is being escorted through the crowd towards a police car, the townspeople shooting daggers at the back of her head. Hannah raises her voice, ensuring she has everyone's attention:

'Tonight, we stopped the murderer who has made your town unsafe, who has brought so much sorrow. But when you look at her, and you judge her, you should remember that none of this started with Thor's murder. It started long before that. With a tragedy you all turned your back on, a tragedy you didn't think was important enough to punish anyone for. Maybe not all of you standing here tonight, but your parents, your relatives, they all turned a blind eye to the man among you now who raped a thirteen-year-old girl and faced absolutely no consequences. You've let him deprive you of your livelihoods, build his kingdom by taking whatever he wants from you, never having to deal with the fall-out. But no more.'

Hannah points to Ægir.

'Ægir: if you had taken responsibility for raping Ella when she was just a little girl, then maybe we wouldn't all be standing here today. We can't change the past, but we can make sure that the truth comes out now.'

Hannah looks down at the police car, at Sigrun, who is now being lowered inside. Their eyes meet. Hannah nods to her. She pauses. She nods her approval, lowers her shoulders a little, and lets the officers guide her into the back seat. Hannah looks out over the crowd one last time. They whisper and stare at Ægir, who glares at her. He yells something in Icelandic. Hannah gathers the gist, but she doesn't care. She climbs down from the boat with the support of a few helping hands, and is guided through the crowd, who silently scrutinise her with their eyes: what exactly did she just say? A raging man suddenly appears in her field of vision – Ægir, charging towards her as he shouts curses and expletives in a mixture of English and Icelandic. Hannah recognises various variations of 'bitch', but doesn't want to deal with a confrontation just now, and it is with considerable gratitude that she sees Jørn step out in front of her, shielding her from the frothing powerhouse of a man. It's as if the sound of everything around her blends into one, and Hannah doesn't even catch what Jørn says to Ægir, but along with a few of the other sizeable men in town, they manage to push Ægir far enough away that Hannah can walk freely. She watches as Margrét is led towards a paramedic's car, parked a little way away from the commotion.

'They're taking her straight to the hospital. Viktor's there already. He's stable.'

Hannah turns to Jørn, now standing beside her. The congregation begins to disperse, and all Hannah wants to do now is get away. It's as if Jørn can sense it, as he points toward his hulk of a rental car, where the leather vest is already waiting, ready to help Ella climb in.

'There are more police on the way, but it'll be a while before they get here. I've said I can drive you home and they can question you there. It's nearly over.'

Hannah stares at him, feeling again a certain glossiness to her eyes.

'Thor is dead because of me. If I'd never come here in the first place, Sigrun would have never killed him.'

Jørn shakes his head, puts an unfamiliar arm around her.

'This is not your fault. There's another police unit in Sigrun's house. They've found records and plans that would indicate she's been planning this for months, just waiting for her chance. Thor would have died regardless. If it wasn't for you, we may never have found out the truth. And stopped her.'

'Stopped her?'

'Thor was only the first person she was planning to kill. Then Vigdis, Ella, and Ægir ... but because you got involved, they all survived. And of course, Viktor and me ... Thank you.'

Hannah turns to face him again, his words lifting the weight of the guilt a little, but she certainly doesn't feel like a hero. Far from it. She stares at Jørn a moment longer.

'Thank you. Without you, I wouldn't have been able to solve any of it.'

Jørn smiles. 'We're a good team, you and me.'

Hannah doesn't answer, but nods wearily anyway, frees herself
from Jørn's arm and looks around for Ella, who is standing in a tight
embrace with a weeping Vigdis. Is she possibly the only person in
town who never knew anything of her husband's and sister's past?
Hannah lets them stand for a moment, before walking over to Ella
and wrapping an arm around her.

'Come on, let's go home.'

59

One month it took Hannah to write the first draft of the novel,
thus proving her original statement. A fact Bastian has made sure
to spread far and wide in the press, but it gives Hannah little
pleasure: it only means that there is now quite a buzz around the
publication of her book, which she is convinced won't live up to
the hype. Even though the worst of the plot holes and issues have
been removed, it's still a half-arsed crime novel, and it is therefore
with considerable nervousness that she listens as the room next
door gradually begins to fill with journalists, fans and other curious
book types. Judging by the amount of noise and the constant
scraping of chairs, the room is packed out – something, she must
admit, that has never been the case with any of her other pub-
lications. And they've even booked out Nimb Bar for the night –
a location so grand and fancy, Hannah would never have thought
she'd be hosting a launch party there. She takes a sip of water, looks
at herself in the mirror. Has, for this occasion, replaced her
signature all-black ensemble with a green blouse. The door opens,
and an excited Bastian steps in.

'Congratulations!'

Hannah looks at him dubiously. 'For what?'

'It's heaving out there – we've had to turn loads of people away,
and they're now watching from the street. You've become what you
might call "popular". And let me remind you that this applies to all

of your other books as well – they've been ordered by booksellers across the country.'

Hannah holds back her enthusiasm. 'Yes, you've said that. But with the bad reviews already coming in, there's not much to congratulate me for.'

'Three stars here and there isn't bad.'

'It's below average.'

'Well, maybe you can just forget about that for the afternoon. And if they do confront you about it out there, and you feel like talking shit about your own book, then just remind yourself of all the money you're raking in.'

Hannah nods, simply wants to get through the book launch so she can get started on her next project. She looks at Bastian.

'Anything from Iceland?'

'Ella sends her love, there's a card from Viktor, and that guy from Bragginn has sent you a bottle of Icelandic vodka. Iðunn's thanked you for all the books, and Sigrun posted an update on social media from prison, where she takes credit for having inspired your book. I wonder if she'll be given the leading role in the true-crime series they'll inevitably make?'

Hannah nods.

'...Anything from Margrét?'

Bastian pauses. 'Unfortunately not.'

Hannah nods again. Of course. The messages she's sent to Margrét sporadically over the nearly four months since she returned to Denmark have all landed in a desolate no-man's land. Margrét hasn't answered a single one of them.

'Right. It's time.'

Bastian holds the door open wide for her. Hannah takes a deep breath and walks out into the buzzing room of people about to see her make her first appearance as a crime-fiction writer.

Other than the mandatory wine drinking, book signing and talking to journalists, Bastian has also arranged a twenty-minute session in which Hannah is interviewed by Natasja Sommer, with pre-planned questions, so people get the impression that Hannah is cool and collected. Hannah takes her place on the small, improvised set, opposite Natasja, who is sitting there with a wide smile, skilfully managing to look genuinely excited.

Bastian grabs the microphone, welcomes the audience, says a few words about the impressive fact that Hannah managed to write a crime novel in a month, and about the tragic events that occurred during her time in Iceland, and then hands the microphone over to Natasja Sommer, who initiates a round of thundering applause. In the front row: Jørn, a huge grin on his face, who gives her a lame thumbs-up. Hannah wants to roll her eyes all the way into the back of her head, but instead, she smiles.

'Congratulations on your book and, I mean ... wow!'

Natasja's little, well-rehearsed pause makes the audience laugh with an ease that indicates that everyone in the room knows the story behind the experiment and the events it triggered.

'It really is quite the turn of events your ambitious project ended up taking ... Could you put into words how it feels to be sitting here now, with your published book?'

Natasja nods to the stack of books on the little coffee table between them. Hannah would prefer to not put anything she is feeling into words, but she reminds herself of her promise to Bastian. And herself. She smiles at Natasja Sommer.

'*The Island of Death* was not an easy book to write. To tell you the truth, I really struggled with the plot. That was my main problem – it was actually much, much harder to figure out than I had thought it would be.'

Light laughter from the audience.

'So it was harder to write a crime novel than you'd anticipated?'

'Yes, I would actually go as far as to say that I've gained a little more respect for those who do it daily.'

Jørn smiles at her, and she sends an authentic smile back.

'So, in addition to the difficult nature of the genre, how was it actually writing the first draft in the space of a month, not to mention the tragic events that happened in Iceland while you were working on it?'

'It goes without saying that it was not at all easy writing it in such a short amount of time, and without talking down on my own book, the result can be seen for itself. It's probably the worst book I've ever written, but I would insist that it is the most important.'

'The most important? How so?'

Hannah can see that Natasja is a little uncomfortable, and also a little excited, about the fact that they have strayed from their agreed-upon answers. Hannah hesitates.

'Important because it changed me.'

'Changed you how?'

'The effort it took to write this, and the circumstances surrounding it, enabled me to write my next book, or rather, to return to a book I was writing before all this began. That book was starting to become really rather shit. But since going through this, I've found that I'm able to write it in such a way that it's a little ... less shit.'

A smattering of laughter throughout the audience – polite, amused laughter. Hannah looks over at them all: her readers, those she has never bothered to meet, but they look at her with light in their eyes. The thought that they are here to listen to her, and that they support her, even after writing such a work of garbage.

A gratefulness stirs within her.

'And what is your new book about?'

Natasja looks at her eagerly, and Hannah opens her mouth to answer, when she notices a figure entering at the back of the room, then stopping and watching. She blinks. Can it be? Yes. It is. Hannah's heart bursts out of her chest. The figure is Margrét. Looking directly at Hannah, who smiles nervously – Margrét reciprocates, smiles back. Hannah answers Natasja without taking her eyes off Margrét.

'It is about something as trite as love.'